Recipe for Disaster

Miriam Morrison used to live in Cumbria, where she was a journalist, teacher and hotelier, though not all at the same time. She now lives in London with her daughter, Emily (a genius in the kitchen) and a cat, Poppy (a genius at getting her own way) and is currently working on her next novel.

miriam morrison

recipe for disaster

arrow books

Published in the United Kingdom by Arrow Books in 2008

1 3 5 7 9 10 8 6 4 2

First published in the United Kingdom in 2008 by Arrow Books

Arrow Books
The Random House Group Limited
20 Vauxhall Bridge Road, London, SW1V 2SA

Addresses for companies within The Random House Group Limited can be found at: www.randomhouse.co.uk/offices.htm

The Random House Group Limited Reg. No. 954009

www.rbooks.co.uk

A CIP catalogue record for this book is available from the British Library

ISBN 9780099517474

Typeset by SX Composing DTP, Rayleigh, Essex
Printed and bound in Australia by Griffin Press

For Emily

Chapter One

'Ready to order?'

Somewhere, buried under the avalanche of newspapers on the floor, was the menu. Kate could distinctly recall giving it the briefest of glances before plunging happily into her favourite column in the *Guardian*. She smiled apologetically at the hovering waitress, and quickly ducked under the table to retrieve it.

Kate was a tall girl and the table was small. Wedged beneath it, she glanced over and saw that the elderly couple at the next table were furtively holding hands. Very sweet. Celebrating their diamond anniversary? New lovers? A secret affair? Kate smiled as she rooted around the newspapers strewn over the floor. There was a time and place for indulging journalistic curiosity (or 'incorrigible nosiness', as her brother put it) but underneath a table probably wasn't it. Her very bright blue eyes were just inches away from Jonathan's expensive grey socks and immaculately polished shoes. You could tell at a glance that they belonged to an ambitious man who wouldn't dream of holding hands under tables, she decided.

'Jonathan, move over.' She could just see a corner of the errant menu, underneath *The Times* and Jonathan's foot.

'Um, what?' he said absently, his rather sharp nose deep in a story on page four of the *Mail*. Kate sighed. His intense interest in anything newsprint-related was one of the reasons she had fallen for him, but it was rather hot under here and she was getting a crick in her neck. Kate tugged, finally pulled the menu out and straightened up rather too quickly, banging her head on the table in the process. She rubbed it with one hand, using the menu as a fan to cool her red face with the other.

The waitress shifted her not inconsiderable weight from one leg to the other and gazed glumly into the middle distance as if she was waiting for a bus she just knew was going to be late. 'So?' she said again, sighing.

'Er, I think we are both going to have the lamb, aren't we?' Kate said.

'Are we? Yeah, OK.' Jonathan rustled the paper in agreement without even looking up, clearly expecting her to make this dull but necessary decision, and to do it quickly if possible.

The waitress frowned. This was an expensive hotel restaurant and it simply wasn't the done thing to be so casual about choosing one's food. She whipped out her pad and wrote busily.

'Two lamb cutlets. Would that be the *côtolettes des Ardennes* with a reduction of cauliflower jus or the Herdwick spring ewe poached in a mint sauce?'

Kate wanted to giggle. She was reminded suddenly of a maths class – a question to do with logarithms and her absolute certainty that whichever answer she gave would be wrong. But the waitress's pen was tapping in an intimidating way.

'Oh, well, one of each, please.' Then at least they could swap.

'With the green salad of locally grown lettuce or a medley of winter vegetables, sautéed in olive oil, parmesan and fresh rosemary?'

'What a feast we have in store,' said Kate, rather faintly. 'Um, both, I think.'

The waitress said nothing but her eyebrows rose just slightly, as if she was making a mental note of the sarcasm. Kate bristled – after all, they were paying, weren't they? But then she remembered that Jonathan didn't like scenes so she rearranged her mouth back into a smile.

'Do you want the lamb medium or well done?'

'Oh, for goodness' sake!' Jonathan's face popped over the paper. 'I just want lunch, not a game of twenty questions!' He produced that harrumphing noise that Kate hated because it made him sound a lot older than he was.

The waitress's face managed to convey that she couldn't care less what they ate, that serving them was beneath her anyway, but if waiting was what she was paid a pittance to do then she would have to suffer the consequences.

Kate took charge. 'We'll have one rare, the other well done and' – she glanced at her watch – 'as quickly as possible please. Oh, and two more beers.'

The waitress took off at a clip, watched anxiously by Kate. A word in the chef's ear and poaching cutlets would become a very long process. And how many times could someone sneeze in the salad before it reached them? Oh, well, too late to worry about that now.

'So, which of this lot do you think covered that story best?' she asked, peering curiously round Jonathan's arm to look at his tabloid.

'The *Mail* was too short, the *Telegraph* was too long and the *Guardian* missed the point completely,' he said promptly, and she had to laugh, her good humour restored. As features editor of the *Easedale Gazette* Jonathan never thought anyone could write a news story as well as he and, annoyingly, he was mostly right. Kate had been in the business for a few years, and at the *Easedale Gazette* for the last two, but when Jonathan talked shop it was always worth making mental notes.

He glanced up at her now with that intense, fiery, slightly haughty look that used to make her stomach flip. She smiled back automatically, but her stomach somehow refused to perform any kind of acrobatics. Disconcerted, she grabbed her beer bottle and took a heartening swig from it just as the waitress returned with fresh supplies. She made a point of pouring both into glasses, and Kate scowled at her retreating back, glad of a diversion.

'Honestly, anyone would think this was the Ritz,' she said crossly. 'I wouldn't mind drinking out of the glass if it was clean. They should sack the person who wrote the menu and employ another washer-upper.'

'Why? What's wrong with the menu?' Jonathan reluctantly looked up from the *Mail*'s sports section.

'Well, for example – listen to this – pan-fried trout with peanut butter sauce. How can you fry anything other than in a pan?' she grumbled. Kate had become a journalist because she was obsessed with words. If asked, she would have picked her love affair with writing over one with a man any day. Even Jonathan.

He put down his paper, his attention caught. 'Is it actually possible to combine fish and peanuts in the same dish?' he asked doubtfully.

'You can, but I really don't think you should,' she said, twisting one red curl round her finger as she read on. Kate was a complete stranger to straighteners, and her hair, on most days, gave new meaning to the phrase 'standing on end'.

'Oh, yeah, here it is – fillet of ostrich steak served with wild mushrooms and organic chocolate. I think I would rather go hungry. Mind you, judging by the look in our waitress's eye, I probably will.'

'And they are illiterate as well – they've spelled "trifle" with two fs,' Jonathan tutted, having scanned the whole menu. He looked round the dining room. 'I don't know what's happened to this place – they used to serve real food, decent, simple stuff like sausage and mash, and then the new management decided that if they put something on the menu that no one even knew was edible they could charge an extra tenner for it. Every Tom, Dick and Harry thinks they're blooming Jamie Oliver now, or that one who shouts a lot.'

'Gordon Ramsay?'

'That's the one – used to be a footballer – how did he become a chef?'

'Quite easily, apparently – he's got three Michelin stars,'

said Kate, who secretly thought Mr Ramsay was as sexy as hell. He could tell her off any day.

Jonathan was warming to his subject. He even put down his newspaper and brandished the menu. 'This seems all the rage now, complicated concoctions of flavours with huge price tags attached. No wonder some chefs are rich enough to drive around in Porsches.' Jonathan secretly coveted a Porsche.

Kate's motoring needs were fully met as long as her car actually worked. She looked about. 'It's so quiet in here our cook can probably only afford to come to work on a bicycle.'

'He's certainly not driven by any sense of urgency,' grumbled Jonathan, glancing at his watch.

'Shall I complain?'

'We should, but he will be rather better equipped with knives than we are.'

'I could take him,' she bragged. 'Don't forget I cut my working teeth in a newsroom populated by tough, hard-bitten, cynical hacks – and that was just the women.'

When he laughed, she was secretly pleased. She loved it when they chatted and argued and generally got on.

When their food arrived, finally, Kate looked down at her plate in trepidation. Surely 'raw' and 'rare' weren't interchangeable, even in today's gastronomic climate?

'Well, I can ask Chef to put them back under the grill,' said the waitress doubtfully, when she saw Kate's look of horror.

'If that's not too much bother,' said Kate desperately. The waitress trudged off, dragging her feet in an attitude of long-suffering acceptance.

'How difficult is it to grill a couple of chops?' Kate said, scowling at the artfully arranged salad on Jonathan's plate. 'I bet the chef's not even doing the cooking himself. He'll have some minion doing all the dirty work, while he prowls around sharpening the odd knife and checking his reflection in the mirror.'

But Jonathan had already moved on from the possible culinary crisis in Britain and was back in the newspapers, grinning at a cartoon in the *Mirror*.

The waitress returned with Kate's plate and set it down defiantly. Kate smiled briefly and pulled it towards her, then yelped with shock and quickly shoved her scorched fingers into her beer to cool them down. 'Ow! Can you believe it? They've just shoved the whole plate back under the grill. My julienne of vegetables has been completely cremated.'

Jonathan flicked open his napkin, hissing impatiently, 'For God's sake, Kate, do take your finger out of the glass.'

'Who cares?' She glanced up. Jonathan clearly did, even though no one was watching them. His sense of self-worth would always outweigh his sense of humour. She dried her finger on her jeans, sneaking a thoughtful glance at his face. They'd been together for only three months and theirs was one of those office romances that was probably fairly ill-fated anyway, especially given that he was separated but still married, but it was becoming more and more apparent that they weren't really destined to last. Outside work and their fervent interest in journalism, what did they really have to talk about? She prodded her lamb, which was now so hard it would make a better missile than a meal.

'Eat up – I'm due back for that meeting soon,' he reminded her briskly.

'Yes, and I really want to return to the dig for another couple of hours.' Kate was nearly at the end of a long piece about an archaeological find on the fells outside Easedale. 'I'm almost done with the Roman settlement. I need to get my teeth into another good story.'

'I think I've left some of mine in that bloody chop,' grumbled Jonathan. He took out his wallet and threw some notes on the table. 'Come on, let's get out of here.'

With relief Kate put her knife and fork down on her almost untouched meal. Following him outside, she heard her stomach rumbling loudly. 'I'm still hungry, dammit!'

Chapter Two

Several streets away, in front of a dilapidated building, Jake Goldman stood with his nose twitching. It was barely noticeable, but he was definitely getting a whiff of ancient cooking fat. Jake wished he had been blessed with a less keen sense of smell. Or that he was rich. Unfortunately he wasn't, so was stuck with making the best of things, which meant this place. It was hard now to conjure up the excitement he had felt when he first saw the advert in *Hotel and Caterer*. The writer had taken much care to describe the enormous potential. With judicious juggling of tables, there would be enough room for about sixty covers – easily big enough for a young chef running his first restaurant. There was a flat upstairs and even a little courtyard out the back where he could plant herbs, maybe even grow tomatoes. The night before, he'd hardly slept, his brain too busy planning menus, organising his kitchen, hiring staff . . .

But then, when he arrived for the viewing, the estate agent looked nervous, which was always worrying.

'Now, it has suffered a certain amount of neglect over the years, but as you can see, it's in a prime position.' He waved his arm away from the peeling paint, hoping Jake would take in the rolling green fells peering over the rooftops of

Easedale like nosy neighbours, instead of looking too closely at the roof. But Jake wasn't having any of it.

'The person who wrote the advert obviously suffers from an excess of imagination,' he said severely.

The agent, who was called Eric, was new to his job. He still suffered from an excess of enthusiasm. 'I think this is a place with possibilities,' he began bravely.

'Oh, shut up,' snapped Jake, who never took any nonsense.

Eric clamped his mouth shut and they both gazed at the building in silence.

A faded sign announced that this had once been Joe's Eatery, except that some bright spark with a pen had renamed it Joe's Artery. Fittingly, Joe himself had popped his chef's clogs a year ago, no doubt due entirely to the consequences of eating his own food.

Eric opened the door gingerly. A waft of stale air greeted them. The dingy interior was painted mustard brown, to which at least ten years of grease had stuck. Ditto the floor. Jake's shoes made an obscene sucking noise every time he lifted his feet, as if the yellow lino could spot a mug when it saw one and was determined not to let him go.

Also stuck to the floor was an ancient menu, speckled with blobs of brown sauce, like liver spots. The choice was wide – but everything was fried, even the puddings.

Eric cleared his throat, prepared to throw some more, admittedly puny, muscle behind the sell.

'Don't even start,' Jake warned him. 'Even if you had Wordsworth's power with poetry you could not make this place look any better than it really is. Are you a poet?'

Eric shook his head, his Adam's apple bobbing nervously.

'OK then. Just take me to the kitchen,' said Jake.

For a chef, a kitchen is home – a place to cook, obviously, but also a melting pot of hopes, dreams and ambitions. Jake knew his kitchen would witness all he had to offer, from agony to ecstasy. Oh God. He couldn't work here, surely? The walls continued the mustard theme, but only because no one had bothered to clean them for years. In one corner was a dangerous-looking contraption that might well have been the first microwave ever made. Welded to the opposite wall was a deep-fat fryer – a fryer so nasty it must have been chucked straight out of hell. Jake peered in and shuddered. It was still full of something – possibly engine oil, from the colour. The cooker next to it was so old, it looked like it needed a bus pass and was obviously a complete stranger to Flash, and the few kitchen cupboards were each precariously clinging onto the wall by one nail. There was a scurrying of tiny feet on lino when Jake opened the door to the dry goods larder. On the floor was a giant sack of powdered soup mix. Jake hissed in horror. He was almost more disgusted by this than by the mice.

'And upstairs we have the owner's accommodation – very handy.' Might as well get it over with, thought Eric.

'Go on then. It couldn't possibly get any worse.'

Oh, smashing – more brown walls – and a hideously stained carpet, which might possibly once have been beige.

Artery Joe had thoughtfully left behind his collection of art. This consisted of three posters of Jordan, put up with Blu-Tack and now peeling off the wall so that both men were in serious danger of being engulfed by pairs of enormous paper breasts.

The bathroom was painted the sort of yellow that would make you feel as if you were taking a bath in a bile duct. Neither of them wanted to look down the loo, but both were drawn to it, inexorably. It looked like a test tube for biological warfare.

All chefs are gifted with a vivid imagination. They have to be. Even the very best have been asked at some stage of their career to make a five-star meal out of a piece of bilious-looking stewing steak. This was about as bilious as it got.

'It's perfect – I'll take it,' said Jake.

Eric leaned against a wall to get over the shock. He tried to be quiet, but he couldn't help himself. 'For the love of God, why are you doing this?'

Jake tried to lean nonchalantly against the wall too, but his legs were suddenly shaking too much to hold him up. He slid down and came to rest gently on the carpet, where, despite its griminess, he decided to stay for a while, just until things had calmed down.

'You see a crumbling wreck – I see my future, and it is glittering.'

'Well, actually, structurally it's perfectly sound,' began Eric, then he stopped and peered closer. 'That's it – I thought you looked familiar! I've seen you before. You were in one of the Sunday mags a few months ago – the big piece about new and upcoming chefs. My girlfriend was drool – looking at it. You're famous!'

'Don't be silly,' said Jake irritably. 'It was just an article and I won't be doing any more of those any time soon.'

'Why ever not? Are you mad? Didn't you get loads of cash for it?'

Jake's eyes gleamed with the fervour of a man who has seen brighter visions. 'I've got more important things to do than waste time trying to get rich!'

'So is it a difficult job then? How did you get started? How many A levels do you need?' Butter up the clients, fake an interest in their lives, his boss had told him.

'None. It's got to be all in here.' Jake patted his chest. 'Good cooking comes first from the heart.' He grinned. 'It's a good thing too – I didn't last long at school.'

'Why not?'

'I was chucked out for assaulting another kid,' said Jake, drawing his brows together in what he hoped was a fierce look. It wasn't strictly true, but it wouldn't do any harm to give Eric the impression that Jake was a man who couldn't be pushed around. Then he sighed. He'd had a long journey to get here and it didn't make for a glorious story.

He'd actually had an uneventful time at school, successfully avoiding the bullies, but not getting much out of lessons, apart from cookery. He was sixteen and learning for the first time how to make a marinade when the only other boy in the class – who was only there because no other teacher would have him – had spat his chewing gum into Jake's mixing bowl and called him a retard for actually showing interest.

Jake couldn't have cared less about the insult, but: 'Take that out, you idiot! If you do it again your head will follow,' he said, shoving Wayne's hand in the bowl. The marinade was full of red-hot chillies and Wayne came out in a horrible rash.

Jake refused to apologise. 'Why should I? I'm not at all

sorry. The school has benefited since Wayne's been off sick because we've all been able to get on with our work in peace. I should be given an award for services to education, not punished. If you don't back me up, I'm leaving.'

They didn't, so he did. It didn't take him long to get his first job in London, mainly because no one else wanted it. There was a tradition in catering that anyone who worked as a kitchen porter was either mad or a smack head – who else would choose to wash hundreds of dishes in a hideously overheated kitchen when they could be somewhere else, having a life?

The head chef, Denis, was a six-foot bruiser from Birmingham who had a bottle-of-whisky-a-day habit. He would roar round the kitchen like a mad bull, tossing insults and saucepans over his head like confetti. His attitude was simple – he hated everyone. When it got too much for him, he would sack someone.

His second in command was an anally retentive beanpole who only had one love – his sauté pan. He would never let Jake or anyone else near it. He would wash it up himself, tenderly, as if he was bathing a baby. He had furtive eyes because he spent all day thinking of new places to hide it.

True to form, the chef sacked Jake about a dozen times, but he just kept turning up for work anyway. He did nothing but wash up and chop enormous buckets of vegetables until his hands were bleeding. Sick of this behaviour, Denis promoted him.

Jake resigned and got a job at a French restaurant. This was a serious establishment. Everyone carried knives, lots of them. It was wise to get along with these people. It wasn't the sort of place where you could have opinions about things. Only once Jake had forgotten this and offered a tentative view on the chef's choice of herbs for a sauce. He still shuddered when he remembered how chef Bill Mackie had turned on him.

'Listen, tosser, I want your blood, sweat and tears, not your opinions. You don't move a muscle unless I tell you to – you don't even go for a piss without permission – and the only words I ever want to hear from your fucking gob are "Yes, Chef". Is that clear?' Jake had replied that, yes, it absolutely was. Off duty, he fantasised about throttling Bill, but always forgot this at work, because he was learning so much.

Bill showed him how to set up a proper *mise en place*. This was the Houston control centre of a commis's life, his work station, and all hell could break out if it wasn't in order. If Jake didn't have an immaculately laid out line of salts, peppers, oil, wine, cream and herbs set up at the start of his shift, at some point during service he would turn into a gibbering wreck, unable to cook even an egg. Bill could spot stray crumbs from miles away, it seemed, and he always knew when Jake was slicing the cucumber too thickly, without having to turn round. Jake guarded his station like a tiger with cubs and knew he was becoming a pro when he too took to hiding his favourite knife.

One day Bill came in and said: 'On your knees, sonny, and kiss the toes of my rotting clogs.'

'Yes, Chef,' said Jake, kneeling down. He knew everyone was laughing. It was always fun when someone else got humiliated.

'Right, sonny. You've turned into a real pain in the arse. You're always breathing down my neck, getting in my way and I wish I'd never said you could ask questions. Of course, there's nowt you could ask me that I don't know, but I can't be bothered, and anyway, you make my head ache. I'm sick of it and think you should fuck off to catering college. Luckily, a few people owe me favours. Of course you're an idiot, so you're bound to fuck up the interview. It's tomorrow – if you can find the way.'

The interview was for a place at the most prestigious catering college in the country. It took a few seconds to dawn on Jake that Bill was giving him the chance of a lifetime. Someone actually believed in him. Jake grinned and kissed Bill's smelly, stained clogs, not caring that everyone was roaring with laughter and someone was taking a picture.

The magazine Eric had mentioned described Jake's career as a meteoric rise through the ranks. Jake had smiled wryly when he read this. It had actually taken years to learn a craft that was as old as the history of man. He had lost weight, gained an enormous overdraft and burned and cut himself so often, all the staff at A & E knew him by name.

'It's been a hard road and a few bad things happened to me on the way,' was all he now said.

Eric glanced down at a particularly disgusting-looking stain on the carpet. It seemed to him that bad things were still happening to Jake. 'I still don't understand,' he said plaintively. 'If you were successful and famous in London, what the hell made you decide to come here, to the back of nowhere?'

Jake was just about to answer, when they heard a voice.

'Jake, are you up there?' called a woman from outside, in a tone that suggested that if he was, he really shouldn't be.

Jake pulled up the sash window gingerly, and stuck his head out of the peeling frame. 'Georgia! I'm here!'

Eric leaned over and hit his jaw painfully on the windowledge when he saw a staggeringly beautiful blonde was getting out of a taxi and looking round.

'Oh. My. God,' she said, loud enough for the men to hear her.

'That's my girlfriend. Funnily enough, I think she feels the same about this hole as you do,' said Jake cheerfully. 'Wait there, darling, and I'll come down. You are not going to believe this place.'

'You've got that right,' muttered Eric, hurrying after him, clearly desperate for a closer look at the girl. Surely he was hallucinating – her legs couldn't be that long?

'Hello!' said Jake, giving her a peck on the cheek in a casual 'I can do this any time I want' way that made Eric frown. Georgia was a stunner. Today, dressed in something by Stella McCartney that she'd pinched from a recent photo shoot, she was turning so many heads there would be a collision at the traffic lights soon.

Her flawless face screwed into a scowl, Georgia pushed Jake away and drummed a tattoo on the pavement with one Manolo Blahnik. 'You. Cannot. Be. Serious.'

'Oh, come on – we'll be here all day if you are going to talk like that. Look, you're right. It's a dump. But it's definitely a dump with promise. I'll show you.'

He led her inside, talking quickly.

'OK, imagine this room empty and clean. Now, we'll have the bar in this corner, tables along here –'

Georgia jumped. 'Ohmigod, is that a spider? You know about my phobia, Jake,' she wailed.

'Look – here – I've put it out of the window – relax. Now, I'm thinking –'

'The doors and the windows are completely in the wrong place! I'm getting terrible vibes and you know how sensitive I am to that sort of thing. It needs to be feng shuied from top to bottom! And fumigated.'

Like I can afford that, thought Jake, but she was already making for the stairs.

Anxiously he watched her look round the dingy sitting room, clearly struggling with the best way to convey her utter contempt of this hovel. As far as Georgia was concerned, this wasn't about Jake's dreams for the future – it was about what she was expected to put up with. And she considered herself far too sensitive to put up with very much. 'You're mad!' She turned round and began beating her fists on his chest emphatically, but taking care not to ruin her manicure. 'How dare you even dream that I would live here with you in this unsanitary hellhole! It's disgusting! Oh, no! I feel one of my panic attacks coming on . . .'

'Well, stop shrieking then and start breathing. Here, sit down on this chair – look I've covered it with my jacket. The place won't look anything like this after I've given it a lick of paint. Anyway, you are away so often working, you'll probably only spend two days a week here. And there's a bonus!' Jake took a deep breath, glad the window was still open. 'Think how good all this fresh air will be for your complexion!'

Georgia fixed him with an accusing eye. 'Exactly what is wrong with my complexion at the moment?' she asked icily.

Bugger. He said, 'You know perfectly well I didn't mean it like that!'

'I'm going back to my hotel. I can feel a migraine coming on.' She stood up. 'Well, are you coming?'

'Er, I was just going to wait for the next train back to London. You know, save money and all that.'

'Fine. Absolutely fine. I make a huge effort to meet you here to help you sort out your job. I take the trouble to book us into a nice hotel, but of course that's not right. I've got one of my heads, which of course is going to get worse if I have to sit on the train for six hours and anyway, I thought a hotel would do you good – you look awful, Jake.'

He winced, but she was right. Hours at work followed by hours hunched over a calculator working out his too meagre finances had left him looking considerably less than shiny. He dredged up what he hoped was a winning smile and gently stroked the back of her neck. She was like a cat – she couldn't resist it. Eric was watching with interest and making mental notes, when a tapping noise suddenly came from downstairs. They all trudged back down to the restaurant, Georgia theatrically holding her forehead.

'Are you open?' An old man in a flat cap and a tweed jacket was trying to peer in through the grimy window and knocking on the pane rather too firmly for Jake's taste.

'No. See – there is the closed sign,' explained Jake patiently.

The old man turned round to his wife and bellowed: 'They're not open, Mabel!'

'They're what?'

'THEY'RE NOT OPEN!'

'But they could do us supper, couldn't they?'

'I say, could you do us –'

Jake was now beyond tired and his self-control was evaporating like early morning mist on the fells. 'What part of "this place is closed" do you not understand?' he hissed.

'There's no need for that tone, sonny. We were just hoping for a nice fish supper.'

Jake took a deep breath. He might cook like a god, but it would be pointless if he upset the locals before he'd even started. 'When we are open, I will cook you a wonderful supper with a free bottle of wine to thank you for your patience.'

As soon as they had gone, Georgia turned on him. 'You're not going to do fish suppers, are you?'

'No, of course not. I will call this place Cuisine, because that is what it will be all about – stupendously tasty but simple and sensible.'

Eric was bubbling over with excitement. It sounded like this fool – oops – client was going to buy. 'Maybe you should have cooked them something now to show them what you are made of!'

'If you think I'm waiting here while you –' began Georgia in outrage.

'Oh don't be so silly the pair of you!' said Jake in exasperation. 'I am a chef, not a bloody magician. I can't produce a fabulous meal out of thin air, like a bloody rabbit out of a hat! The actual meal is really only the tip of the iceberg. Underneath that . . .' No, he could see he had lost them both. Lay people didn't have an inkling of the huge amount of effort it took to present a perfectly prepared meal. 'Look at it this way, darling, you wouldn't set off down the catwalk before they'd finished making your dress, would you? You wouldn't go down naked?'

'Well . . . I would have to take laxatives for at least a week beforehand and book a top-class exfoliation and then a spray tan with Amy – she's the only one at the salon that knows how to do it – and of course the lighting would all have to be angled towards the right because of that awful, unsightly dimple in my left thigh – I really will have to think again about surgery – but, yeah, I don't have any real hang-ups about my body.'

Jake looked at her in disbelief, then turned to Eric, who was leaning against the wall with a faraway look on his face, quite obviously picturing Georgia on the catwalk. 'So, how much are they asking for this place?' he said, though he knew perfectly well.

Eric hastily stood to attention and named the price.

'Tell the vendor I'll give them five thousand pounds less. This will be my only offer so they needn't waste their time trying to squeeze any more out of me. As you can see, I have a very expensive girlfriend.'

'Yeah, but I bet she's worth every penny,' said Eric with a wink. As he turned to go, Jake could see that some more of the window paintwork had peeled off and stuck to his jacket.

*

Their hotel room had a view over the lake, which was a pointless extra expense, because it was now dark. Peering out of the window, Jake could see nothing but a few stars. Georgia was prowling round the room, taking stock of all the mirrors. 'I don't see the point of having a lovely complexion like mine if there's no one there to take a picture of it,' she complained. She secretly kept a tally of how many times she was featured in the press each week.

'Come to bed,' said Jake, patting the duvet invitingly. 'We might as well get our money's worth out of it.'

'I still don't know why you want to stop being head chef at Brie. It's one of the best restaurants in London – everybody says so – and loads of famous people go there.'

'I worked there because my boss is a genius, pure and simple, but now it's time to spread my wings. I want my own place. It's the only way I can put my mark on the cooking world.'

'Yes, but why here, in the middle of nowhere?'

'It's beautiful up here. And it's cheap, at least compared to London.'

'Oh, don't talk to me about money! That's all it ever is with you. By the way, do you know you look like a tramp in those jeans?'

Jake shrugged. He wasn't a conceited man – he couldn't afford to be. 'Basically, I can either dress well or buy my own business, but I can't do both. If I want to make it in this game, I have to give up shopping, sleeping, having any sort of hobby –'

'You mean you have to give up having a life! I wish you had told me that before I fell in love with you!' Georgia glared, albeit in such a way that would have had any photographer salivating for a camera. But then she always looked hot.

Her lover, however, was a mess. Georgia sighed. The trouble was, Jake was an irresistible mess. He was tall, with dark eyes, and a lean and hungry look because he often was, always tasting food but never having time to sit down to a decent meal. He had trendily ruffled dark hair, though less by design than because he was always running his fingers through it in desperation at the stupidity of commis chefs. Even his hands were sexy, despite looking like they had done ten years' hard labour in Siberia. They were covered with the scars of burning encounters with hot stoves and were living proof that knives were sharp and saucepans heavy. When they first became a couple, Georgia would kiss each wounded finger tenderly, before guiding them inside her with a moan of pleasure.

They had met at a party Jake had been pushed to attend. Prowling crossly round the room, clutching a beer, he found things began to look up when he laid eyes on Georgia.

Georgia was extraordinarily, incandescently beautiful. She glowed – even at four thirty in the morning, rushing round without a shred of make-up on her luminous skin, clad only in one of Jake's hideously over-washed T-shirts and complaining bitterly that only models had to get up for work this early in the morning. Properly dressed and made up, men would look at her and forget how to speak. Of course, Jake had fallen instantly in lust with her at the party. But it was her apparent vulnerability and fragility that had made him fall in love.

'Ordinary people don't really understand the dark side of my glamorous lifestyle,' Georgia explained earnestly when they finally gravitated towards each other. She looked up at him from under her lashes. 'I so, totally, get why Princess Di had to run away from the paparazzi. They don't know what it's like to be hounded every time you go out for a packet of Tampax. I have nightmares about millions of popping flash-bulbs and then I wake up and relive the nasty things other models have said behind my back,' she explained tragically.

Jake nodded eagerly. He too had been the target of a campaign of malice. He glanced briefly at the surging tide of people swilling around them. He hadn't wanted to go to this party, but now he knew why he was here – to meet this creature.

'Don't you just hate these sort of dos?' Georgia was thinking that champagne was so last year – people were only drinking vodka now – and as for the food . . . 'Do they really think it's cool serving those mini burgers in mini buns?' At a hundred and fifty calories a shot, no wonder no one was eating them.

'Pretentious rubbish,' agreed Jake, who loathed food fads, and blinked as Georgia gave him one of her mega-watt sexy smiles.

How cool he was – complaining about things being pretentious was so in at the moment. 'That suit's not new, is it?' she asked.

Jake grinned; it was his best charity shop bargain. 'Yes, I –'

'How clever you are. That retro look makes everyone else here seem so drab.'

'Well, it's –'

'It's so nice finding someone I can really talk to. Everyone else is here just to talk about themselves. Do you know, I was about to run away but fate stepped in so I could meet you.'

Jake had just come off an eighteen-hour shift, the fourth that week. He was befuddled with exhaustion, blinded by the lights, nearly deafened by the roar from the people around them and in no condition to sift sense from silliness. Georgia, however, was an oasis of calm and stillness. Her ability to stand utterly still and become the focus of attention was one of the things that had made her a great model. But in reality, she was chronically insecure, despite her success, because she lived in constant fear of the competition from other models. All the adulation she got was like a meal without calories: however much she gobbled up she was always hungry for more.

At first, Jake's love was like a breath of fresh air blowing through the hothouse world of competition and spite she moved in. Attention from Jake was freely given and honest and straight, and so she clung to him like a vine. It took Jake a while to realise that vines can be choking.

When Georgia confided to him that she was an avid reader, he was delighted – he was so busy that his girlfriends had to have their own interests. But she didn't make clear at first that the only things she read were glossy magazines and pseudo-psychological self-help books. She had nearly as many of these as he had cookery books. There were books about women who loved too much; women who didn't; women who loved the wrong man, and women who loved cats more than men. They had titles like *Change Is Not a Four-Letter Word* (well, of course it bloody well wasn't), *A Guide Dog for the Spiritually Blind*, *Life Shouldn't Be a Trivial Pursuit* and *Co-dependency – Break the Chain!*. During a night of insomnia, Jake had picked this last one up. After two hours he still couldn't figure out what exactly the hell co-dependency was, except that if you had it you were in big trouble. Eventually he had filled in the questionnaire at the back. Not only was he co-dependent but so was everyone else he knew. In fact, according to this, it was impossible not to be co-dependent. Enraged, Jake had thrown the paperback into a corner and turned to the comforting and sane thoughts of Elizabeth David in France.

Jake wasn't lying when he told Eric that food was his passion. His passion and his life and there wasn't much room for anything else, even something as delectable and irresistible as Georgia. His grandmother was responsible for this. When he was small she told him endless stories about her own grandmother, who had lived in a small village in Poland. Life there revolved around the kitchen – the children sometimes even slept on top of the oven because there wasn't room for them in the one bed. The door was never locked and there was a continual coming and going of people – talking, arguing, crying, laughing – all of which was accompanied by a constant stream of food. What did they eat? asked Jake, who was fascinated by this picture of a very different world. So she cooked for him the comforting and tasty food that was part of her culture: chopped liver, potato latkes and goulash soup. When she was only a baby, the family had moved to Germany in the hope that life would be more prosperous there. And at first they thrived. She was the prettiest girl in her class and the most popular – until the morning her best friend had given her a Nazi salute and her boyfriend dumped her so he could join the Hitler Youth. Then came the lean and terrible years of persecution and flight and hunger. As an old woman, she hoarded food obsessively. When she died, Jake was dry-eyed at the funeral. He had done his crying the night before, when he'd found all the tins and packets of outdated food stacked neatly under her bed.

He sometimes wondered if he cooked to make up for those years of starvation and terror under the Nazis, but when he tried to explain this to Georgia, she had stared at him, uncomprehending. Food was Georgia's enemy, not her friend. She waged a continual, single-minded battle with it, starving herself for days on end and then bingeing. But the first time Jake overheard her throwing up in the bathroom, he was so furious she made sure he was out when she did it again.

'It's a disgusting thing to do to your body! It is wrong and unhealthy, and anyway, if you carry on like that all your teeth will fall out.'

He tried to tempt her with low-calorie but delicious dishes, seeing it as a challenge to his cooking skills, but she wasn't having any of it. When Georgia did eat, she wanted KitKats, Dairylea Dunkers and microwave chips. It was quite a blow to Jake, because surely kindred spirits shouldn't have His and Hers compartments in the fridge?

Now, lying exhaustedly on the expensive hotel bed, he

absent-mindedly admired Georgia's perfect bottom as she bent down to peer into the mini bar.

'I don't see how even you can make a restaurant out of that horrible little chip shop,' she grumbled.

Jake sighed. He wished he could describe the vision in his head, but all his creative powers were in his hands.

'Look, I know I'm no good at explaining things, but try and imagine what it will look like after a makeover. A cheap one,' he added hastily.

'No one will want to eat there – you'll lose all your money.' Then, when Jake shuddered: 'Oh, don't be so silly. I was only joking!'

'Yeah, well, I think I must have left my sense of humour in London,' he tried to joke back, but he was so tired and stressed that he could barely think straight. He wondered guiltily if he would be able to stay awake long enough to make love to her and then felt even worse because he didn't want to make love – he wanted to do his sums again to make absolutely sure he'd got them right and this was all affordable, just, and then draw up another plan for how the restaurant itself should be set out. Maybe there was just room for another six covers. It would be cramped but it could make a big difference to his takings. What were the statistics? One in two restaurants failed within a year of opening. 'I've got to be one of the winners!' he said aloud, thumping the pillow.

'It's funny you should say that. The very nice man who bought me lunch on the train up here was talking about being a winner,' said Georgia, taking off her clothes and leaving them all over the floor.

Men were always trying to buy her meals and then get into her knickers. She really wasn't safe out on her own.

She ran her hands appreciatively down her body, remembering how the very nice man had looked at her. 'He was so charming. Now, what was his name?'

'How should I know – I wasn't there. Now hurry up and come to bed before I fall – I mean, get overcome by lust.'

'But the thing was, he said he knew you. Harold, I think.'

'Never heard of him. Couldn't care less.'

'No! Silly me! It was Harry! He said you were at college together. He said you had worked together afterwards, at that restaurant you don't like to talk about.' She looked up at the strangled noise coming from the bed. 'What on earth is the matter? You look like you've just seen a ghost!'

Jake had jumped bolt upright 'Harry? Are you sure?' he asked hopefully, then when she nodded: 'I wish to God he was a ghost.'

'Oh, he's very much flesh and blood,' giggled Georgia, thinking what very attractive flesh it had been, just the right shape and size.

Jake shivered. He felt shaky and weak suddenly, as if he'd suddenly come down with some dreadful virus.

'I think I would rather come across the plague than Mr Harry Hunter again,' he said, more to himself than anything else.

'What? Oh, don't be silly. He seemed like a perfectly pleasant man,' said Georgia, who was oblivious to nuances, unless they were her own.

'You don't understand,' said Jake through gritted teeth, but she had wandered into the bathroom.

Harry Hunter was Jake's own personal demon, though he still didn't know what he'd done to deserve one. The last time he'd locked swords with this man, Jake had come off very much the worse. In fact, if it hadn't been for an irascible French chef called Louis, Jake would probably now be a hollow-eyed empty shell working in a burger bar. Oh, don't be ridiculous, he said to himself. Pull yourself together, man. What does it matter now, anyway? Lightning doesn't strike twice, does it? But what the hell was Harry Hunter doing in Easedale then?

Chapter Three

'The editor really liked your piece. Actually what he said was, "Only our Kate could make a pile of old bones interesting, but where the hell is her next story?"'

'They weren't bones, Jonathan, they were bricks. And I wish I knew.'

'Well, this has been out for a few days now, so don't leave it too long.' He was always fairly curt in the newsroom, but even more so today.

Kate waited until he was out of earshot and sighed loudly. Neither her personal nor her private life was going well. The previous night at a restaurant, Jonathan had described in rather too much detail a sudden and unexpected reconciliation with his wife. Being Jonathan, he had told the story well and made it both moving and funny. The restaurant had closed and shooed them out before he could come to the subject of what this meant to them, 'them' being him and Kate, but in the end spelling it out wasn't really necessary as far as Kate was concerned. Of course it was over. When she tentatively probed her heart early this morning, she discovered that if it wasn't exactly shattered to pieces, it was quite sore. And even three coffees and a big bacon sandwich later, she still felt a bit frail. She got up resolutely and wandered over to her desk. More than anything, she needed a story now, something to take her mind off things. But flipping through her notebook, nothing shouted out at her.

'Maybe my nose isn't working any more,' she wondered aloud. Kate was famous for her nose.

'Well, use a bloody pen like everyone else!' Seeing her dagger look, Joe, the photographer, pretended to be busy shuffling papers on his desk.

'Your jokes could really do with a makeover,' she said icily.

'Yeah, that's pretty much what the wife says.' Kate winced and he hurried on. 'Oops, sorry – not your favourite word at the moment.'

'Don't worry. Anyway, how does everyone already know about this?'

'Er, because only a fool couldn't read your body language when you both came in this morning. Actually, I think you are both being really professional and civilised about it. You're not really hurting, are you?' he added anxiously.

'No, I'm not. It's just . . . well, three months with me and now he wants to go back to his wife!'

'Well done! You've saved a marriage, not wrecked it!'

Kate gave a wry grin. You had to be tough to take the jokes in a newsroom, but they were mostly kindly meant.

She sighed, wishing she was back on the fells with the archaeologists. Life was simpler there. They spent all day on a bleak bit of hillside, grubbing around in the earth with their trowels, then they sloped off to the nearest pub to get outrageously pissed – and they were perfectly content to spend weeks doing this.

She had been happy there too. Her remit as reporter for the *Easedale Gazette* was simple. All she had to do was sift through the personalities and Roman artefacts for a double-page spread on what it was like to be a real-life Indiana Jones. And all the components for a brilliant story were already there. The guys were a bunch of Americans with a desperate deadline of their own. They were down to the last couple of days of funding before having to return home empty-handed, when it finally emerged under their trowels from the dark soil: a Roman settlement that the rest of the academic world was convinced didn't exist.

And if that wasn't enough for her, she was then given the unexpected bonus of a really fantastic rumpus with the local archaeology department, who hated the Yanks simply because of who they were (there was a lot of stuff about 'yank' rhyming with 'wank', which Kate unfortunately couldn't put in a family paper). The locals claimed the settlement was theirs; the Americans pointed out that they could hardly say it belonged to them and that it didn't exist, both at the same time, and there followed a bit of a stand-off on site, with trowels being waved threateningly. The Americans all had perfectly white and sparkling smiles as well, of course, so the pictures were good. Kate was thrilled.

And then there was Jim, the expedition leader, who looked a bit like a young Harrison Ford, inhaled whisky as if it was oxygen and knew more about the Romans than Julius Caesar ever had. There was something very sexy about a man who was passionate about his work, Kate decided. And of course that was part of the reason she had fallen in love with bloody Jonathan.

That was what she wanted – another good story. Then at least if she didn't have a love life she could count on her career. But her nose for news wasn't working and there wasn't even anything in the newsroom diary. She had scanned it obsessively, trying to convince herself that a weaving collective in south Lakeland was promising. But really, it wasn't. The weavers were a fearsome bunch of women who were waging war against big business. Kate agreed they had a point, but they were very tedious about it and she didn't do boring.

'Our new chief constable could at least have had the decency to keep quiet about the fact that he once smoked dope as a student,' she said to Joe disconsolately, absent-mindedly tidying his desk for him. He winced when he saw the emerging tabletop. Kate was streamlined and minimal in her work space, while Joe could only function in his own brand of organised clutter. She randomly handed him piles of assorted photos and clippings. 'Doesn't he realise that skeletons in the closet are our living?'

'I agree. He's being outrageously honest,' said Joe placatingly, surreptitiously putting the photos back in the same place when she wasn't looking.

She bit her lip abstractedly, and then jumped as the phone rang.

It was her pet constable at the local police station, who often tipped her off with juicy bits of news.

'Kate? Yeah, hi. Do you remember those walkers who

never came off the fells last weekend? Well, they've found them.'

'Dead or alive?' Kate wasn't trying to be heartless. It was part of her job to ask.

'Oh, very much alive. Listen, I can't say any more – got to go – but you might want to nip up there and check it out.'

Hmm. There was more to this than met the eye or he wouldn't have rung her up. Five minutes later she and Joe were speeding off to Brownstone Fell.

'Joe, when did you last clean up this car?' Kate gingerly put her feet down on the floor.

'Oh, dunno. Actually I don't think I ever have.'

'That's my point.' She waved a chocolate bar wrapper at him threateningly. 'I think this has been here ever since I first met you.'

'Probably. Who cares?'

'Well, I do, if I have to sit on it. You are an offence to health and safety.'

'Listen, a few germs never hurt you.'

'Actually, some of them do – and probably most of the ones you are incubating in this car.'

At the bottom of the fell she could see a group of people wrapped in blankets and drinking tea. They looked alive but sheepish.

Kate got out and put on her best empathic face. Sympathy always broke down barriers and loosened tongues. 'I always say, one bit of fell looks so much like another, it's a wonder everyone doesn't get lost!'

'We weren't lost. We knew exactly where we were!' piped up one of them indignantly.

'I believe the weather can turn very quickly,' said Kate.

'Especially if you are stark naked at the time,' said one of the policemen grinning.

'We had to be – we call ourselves the Followers of the Goddess Ceres,' explained one of the men.

'Well, I'd call you a pack of plonkers,' muttered the policeman, as Joe started firing off pictures.

'Stop that! Our religion does not permit the taking of images!' said one.

'Yes, leave them alone!' said Kate loudly, after Joe had given her the signal that he'd got enough. She turned to the leader. 'I'm sorry about that. My colleague doesn't understand these things, but I've always been interested in alternative ways of life and religion. Is this a specially sacred spot?' She hoped she sounded warm and sympathetic.

One of the women nodded eagerly. Kate noticed she had very hairy legs – she would get on well with the weavers. 'It's the Brown Stone, at the top. We believe it has been used in rituals for thousands of years. It is a very significant stone. Ignored for years by you locals, of course.'

'So, er, what did you have to do there?'

'Oh, I don't think you would be able to understand it. It's a very complex ritual,' she said importantly, eyeing Kate's notepad.

Kate generally didn't have any trouble understanding anything, but she gritted her teeth. 'Try me – but make it simple.'

'We were ushering in the spring by using a series of ancient and significant rites.'

'They took all their clothes off and ran round the stone,

only they started a downpour and all their stuff got soaked, including their mobile phones so they couldn't ring for help,' put in the policeman, who obviously couldn't wait until he was off duty and at the pub to regale everyone with this tale.

'The rain will fertilise the barren land!'

'It's been doing that all bleeding winter! Couldn't you have ordered some sunshine instead?' said the constable in disgust.

The woman sighed in an irritating manner, which was a bit rich, Kate thought, considering they had just availed themselves of the considerable help of the fell rescue service, which they didn't have to pay for.

'So, you didn't complete the ritual successfully then?'

The woman nodded, grudgingly. 'Only because we were interrupted at a crucial point. The goddess is angered. There will be many storms to come.' She looked accusingly at Kate, as if she thought it was her fault.

Kate waited to return to the car before laughing. 'God, I love this job!' Then she sobered up. This would make an amusing little piece but it was hardly a ground-breaking feature. In this business you were only as good as your last story.

Kate had wanted to be a journalist ever since she was ten, when she came top of her class for writing an entirely fictitious essay on what she had done during her school holidays. When her teacher had found out and threatened to take the prize away, Kate pointed out that no one had actually said it should be truthful, so she hadn't broken the rules.

Kate loved writing. She saw words as almost magical and certainly precious things. Finding the right word was like getting the steps of a dance correct. No one was surprised when she was made editor of the school newspaper, though she tended to hog all the best stories for herself. As soon as she could she had left school, with an impressive clutch of qualifications, and walked straight into the nearest newspaper office, where she spent a few months making tea and writing reports of Women's Institute meetings. She covered her first major news story because she took the phone call and failed to inform the chief reporter, who would have given it to someone with more experience. Of course he'd bollocked her for it afterwards, but it was already on the front page. Now the years working her way up had softened her a bit, but she was still following stories in the same single-minded way.

They took their time going back into town, because although still early in the year, the narrow roads were already clogged with tourists. While Joe waited at the traffic lights, Kate fidgeted in her seat. Her evening at the restaurant with Jonathan was still replaying in her head and now, topped by this dissatisfying interview, she could feel herself getting edgy again. She glanced idly outside at a café sign that proudly proclaimed it served ice cream homemade made on the premises.

'Funny, I would swear that's a van delivering ice cream round the back!'

Joe tapped the wheel impatiently. 'Eh? What the hell are you on about?'

'That café. Pretty cheeky, don't you think?' When he looked blank she pointed at the ice-cream van just passing underneath the sign. 'It's false advertising really. I've got a food thing at the moment. What we get are too many fancy and pretentious promises. Who knows what restaurants get up to in the back, out of the sight of us customers?' she said sharply, her red hair almost vibrating with an angry life of its own.

'Well, you're in England – the north of England, to be precise – what do you expect?' said Joe tolerantly.

Kate opened her mouth to reply, then she bit her lip. 'Sorry, you're right. I seem to have turned into a complete bitch today.'

He laughed. 'Don't be silly. You're just . . . well, you've got a bit of a sharp edge at the moment.'

She winced. 'I know, I know, it's just that I've been a total idiot. I should never have started an affair with a married man, even if he did swear he was separated at the time,' she said wryly. 'And the whole office knows about it. Every time I walk into a room I feel like everyone has just stopped talking about me!'

'Well, they probably have. But they'll get over it.'

'Actually, I just need to get over myself. What I really need is a cracking story, the sort that will take me out of the office for a couple of weeks until it's all died down.'

Joe nodded. This was only the ninth or tenth time she'd said this today. 'You and me both,' he yawned. 'Since having the twins I don't really have any ideas at all any more, well, apart from how to try and snatch more sleep. I just point my camera, press, go home and try to remember what disgusting shade a healthy nappy should look like. Mary's quite keen on that sort of thing,' he added apologetically.

'The woman was a saint to marry you in the first place, let alone consent to have your sprogs,' Kate retorted, but absently. She was thinking.

She sat in silence all the way home, mulling over story ideas and a short but very funny piece on the lost worshippers to tide her over. Even when she'd waved goodbye to Joe, let herself into her apartment and made a cup of tea, she couldn't stop thinking about ideas – and one in particular. She pulled down books at random, making notes, and was so absorbed in what she was doing that she took a slug of tea without realising it had gone stone cold. 'Ugh,' she said, swallowing it in disgust, and was getting up to make some fresh when the doorbell rang.

Jonathan took a step towards her, but Kate wasn't having any of it. 'I've already written a conclusion to the unfinished business between us last night,' she said firmly. 'It's over and it has been ever since you decided, quite rightly, that you needed to give your marriage another try. I never tried to persuade you otherwise. But we are so not going to have a last screw for old times' sake, or anything else.'

'But I need to make absolutely certain I've made the right decision, and how can I be sure unless –'

'Trust me. From now on you will have to live in your memories,' Kate retorted. She held her breath for a moment – he was still her boss, after all – but then he grinned.

'Oh, well, it was worth a try. Do you know that a new book has come out which absolutely proves that while women are mulling over all the emotional complexities of a situation, men are just thinking about sex?'

'Women have known that for years. We certainly don't need a bloody book to tell us!' God, she was really going to miss this banter. Then she had a thought. 'Look, I know this may sound odd, but I really need to pick your brains. It's about a potential story.'

His ears perked up. 'OK, stick the kettle on and shoot.'

She waved him inside, grinning to herself in relief. Jonathan drank tea by the gallon at work, claiming it helped him think. Now it was a sign that he had become her respected colleague again and she welcomed it.

'Do you remember that awful meal we had – the one with the burned lamb?' she began, when they were sitting on the sofa, mugs in hand. 'Well, it got me thinking. There seems to be a massive gap between what we punters get to see and what really happens out of our sight, in the back of a restaurant.'

'You're right there. If the paper hadn't picked up the tab for that meal, I certainly wouldn't have.'

'Exactly! And that's only the tip of the iceberg! Half the restaurants in this town seem to serve up food that's not even their own. It's been cooked and frozen by someone else. I mean, anyone with half a brain could shove something in the microwave and chuck it on a plate. Yet they pretend it's some kind of elevated cuisine, almost like an exclusive club that we ordinary humans don't have access to – partly because they insist on talking in another language. Do you know that to "mortify" something makes it more tender?' She bent down and rummaged through some papers. 'Oh, yes, and a *fleuron*, which I could swear was one of the aliens attacking Dr Who on the telly last week, is actually a lozenge or crescent made with puff pastry. I mean, pretentious twaddle or what?'

'And chefs are so precious about their reputations. You can't pick up a paper these days without having to wade through one of the celebrity chefs claiming to be the best cook since the invention of the knife and fork,' mused Jonathan. 'I totally agree – all that crap is a waste of good newsprint.'

'So . . .' Kate took a deep breath. 'Chefs – real cooking or just a cover up?'

'Hmm. Could be good. Colourful personalities, scandalous practices and plenty of bullshit for you to expose in your inimitable way. I assume you'd be thinking of going undercover somehow to get the proof?'

'Oh, yes. It's got to be well researched – not worth doing otherwise.'

'I agree. But you are not going to get work as a chef. You've got guts, Kate, but not even you could pull that off.'

'No, but I wouldn't have to. I could become a waitress instead. All they do is swan around and look snooty. An idiot could do it!'

'I'm looking forward to those pictures.' He grinned at her and she quickly looked away, trying not to get caught up in his eyes. Now was not the time to be reminded how sexy a sharp, rugged, carelessly ruffled professional man like Jonathan was. This was now over.

Jonathan was the first to look away. 'I've got to go. I promised . . .' he hesitated.

'You promised your wife you would be home hours ago,' she finished off for him. 'Well, you are late, but at least you've got a clean conscience.'

'Sorry. Sorry about everything, really.'

'I know.' She gave him an awkward grin and propelled him out of the door, patting him kindly on the back. Hopefully, the next time they met, they could just move on. Affairs at work were never a good idea, she thought, prowling restlessly about the room after he'd gone. Glancing around, she realised he might never have been there. He had left nothing that might announce his presence in her life. It had been a bit like having an affair with a ghost.

The next time – and I don't care how long I have to wait – the next time I start a relationship, it will be completely open and above board, with someone who is single and legitimately mine for the taking. There will be no secrets, no lies and definitely no guilt, she thought.

She wandered aimlessly through her flat, checking her messages – there was one from her mum – and riffling through the post: a belated birthday card from her best mate at school cheered her up momentarily. Then she went into the bathroom and disconsolately ran herself a bath, throwing in a generous handful of expensive bath salts. When she got out she would be clean, refreshed and a single woman, ready to start again.

Chapter Four

When Harry Hunter was born, his glorious blue eyes made even the hardened battleaxe of a midwife smile and coo with pleasure. Later on that night, however, he tried to bite her. She was glad she was leaving before he developed teeth.

His grandmother might have loved him just as much as Jake's did. But if that was the case, she never said so.

No one ever said anything like that in Harry's family.

Far back in time, his ancestor Harolde Hunter had performed some vital but unsavoury tasks for that canny old skinflint Henry VII. Henry was grateful, but sick of the sight of Harolde, who displayed, even in those rough times, rather too much eagerness to get his hands dirty. So he gave him a parcel of land up north, where, with a bit of luck, he would get eaten by wolves, or the locals, who were rumoured to be wild.

But Harolde prospered and, among other things, bequeathed to his heirs an unshakeable belief that whatever Hunters wanted, they got.

So, through the ages, Hunters made their mark on the world through skulduggery, cheating, betrayal and all-round nastiness. There might have been nice Hunters, but they never lasted long. They probably just faded away, like a flower does without water.

When he wasn't at work, Harry's father enjoyed living up to his name, and if the Government thought they were going to stop him, well, Hunter Hall was a long way from Westminster, too far to hear horns and the baying of hounds. Harry's mother enjoyed gin and bridge, in that order, and was always having things done to her face in the vain hope people might think she was still thirty-five.

Harry, on the other hand, was a pin-up. He was so vain, the only photo he kept in his wallet was one of himself. Tall and broad-shouldered, he romped through his private schools, winning sporting and academic prizes without even having to cheat. Early on, he mastered the art of looking down his Roman nose at everyone he considered beneath him.

School had its drawbacks, one of which was the sexual habits of some of the masters. No one buggered about with Harry, though, unless he wanted them to, which, on the whole, he didn't, having discovered the fun that could be had at the girls' school half a mile away. He could charm anyone he liked, but then he always despised them afterwards for being so gullible.

Holidays were spent in Aspen or the Caribbean, and there he discovered a love of good food. But, being Harry, he suddenly realised that he could cook it better himself. He started practising at home, when no one was looking, because some people still thought cooking was just for girls.

On leaving school he was at a bit of a loss. Plenty of universities would have had him, but he was bored with academic life. What he really wanted to do was cook. All that chopping and slashing and heat and blood – in a kitchen he was as at home as a shark in the ocean. Other people might wilt under the intense pressure, but Harry just thrived. The white chef's jacket really brought out the blue of his eyes, and everyone knew uniforms were terribly popular with the girls.

For Harry, there was only one way to do things – properly – so once his mind was made up, he had to go to the best catering college there was. Obviously he never doubted for a minute that he would get in.

The Richmond College of Catering was the cooking world's equivalent of Oxford or Cambridge. Some bright sparks, like Harry, went straight from school. He lacked experience but he radiated energy and enthusiasm. Others, like Jake, had actually toiled at the coal face of a real kitchen. The interviewing panel were very impressed by how much he had already picked up. They also noted his steely determination.

The college was looking for raw talent that could be chucked into a furnace of intensive teaching, work experience and fierce criticism. If you survived with your ambition and self-confidence intact, the world was your lobster thermidor.

On the first day of term the entrance hall was crammed with eager young cooks, polished like newly minted coins in their pristine white chef's jackets, the sunshine glinting off a positive arsenal of sharp knives. On the walls were pictures of the college's alumni, some of them now familiar faces on television. There was even an enticing aroma of frying onions and garlic wafting across the room from one of the classes already in progress.

Jake had had to sell his laptop and half his CD collection to buy the set of knives the college insisted they use. He had bought his chef's clobber from a commis who was leaving catering to go into the army – he said he needed a rest. Jake had used up a whole bottle of Vanish getting out the bloodstains. Glancing idly round the room he reflected that at least his gear had been in a real kitchen. Judging by the look of the stuff some of the others were wearing, their whites had only just come out of their plastic wrappers. He grinned to himself at the thought of what some of these kids would look like after the real world of a kitchen had met their snowy aprons. One or two of them weren't even going to last the first week, he reckoned.

Eavesdropping shamelessly, he was able to pick out the kitchen virgins. Listening to them talk it was clear they had picked up vast amounts of theory. They just hadn't done it yet.

One of the advantages of growing up in south London was that you developed a finely honed instinct for possible trouble. There was always one boy in the playground who called you mate, but then stole your dinner money. Jake saw Harry and instantly recognised the type. He was standing in the midst of a group of people as if he owned it. He was perfectly balanced, legs slightly apart, unlike everyone else, who was shuffling nervously from one foot to the other. It was obvious Harry didn't do nervous. He was telling a joke about some TV chef that made it sound as if he knew him.

Harry laughed, throwing his head back and exposing an immaculate set of teeth. He glanced round the room to make sure everyone was joining in and for a brief second his eyes met Jake's. Under the laughter they were cold and calculating before he looked away. No one else seemed to notice. Jake shrugged. He wasn't a schoolboy now; he could take care of himself.

Of that year's intake of budding Marco Pierre Whites, there were a number of casualties. One guy discovered he just couldn't bear the sight of blood. He was nearly sick when asked to cook something rare, and as for steak tartare . . . A few were just too lazy to put in the graft, and one girl was told to leave because, even after a year, she couldn't tell the difference between basil and parsley.

Of the ones that were left, Jake and Harry rose to the top, like the cream in a pint of milk. This incensed Harry, who had been top of everything when he was at school and was not prepared to share.

But charm was one of Harry's strongest weapons. He quickly learned to temper his public-school drawl with Cumbrian idioms from home. He called his mates his 'marras', a term they had never heard before and which made them laugh. He was always generous about lending things from his state-of-the-art chef's tool box, and he went through the pretty girls like a knife through butter. The combination of his good looks, charisma and invitations to weekends at home in the Lake District was irresistible.

Every girl thought she was the one, until she was dumped. Jake became so used to having hysterical females sobbing on his shoulder that it was a bit like living through

Groundhog Day. He became skilled at dispensing cookery and comfort at the same time. Typically his advice always went: 'Yes, Pamela/Anne/Lyndsay, I agree it's awful. Here, take this tissue and try not to drip into my jus/coulis/soup.' Or, 'Yeah, he is a shit, but you refused to listen when I told you this.' Or, 'Now, don't be silly. You don't really want to kill yourself/him, so please put my knife/rolling pin/sharpener back in my box.'

After they had got over the trauma, the girls would then kick themselves for failing to notice earlier that Jake was sexy too, with his heavy-lidded dark eyes and the smile that could be tough or tender, depending on the occasion.

So another thing he had to become good at was explaining (tactfully, of course) that there was no way on God's earth he was ever going to go out with that bastard's cast-offs. There was such a thing as pride, thank you very much. Which made him a man of principle, but rather lonely at night.

But most of the time he was busy doing the important stuff: cooking, and soaking up the theory. He listened, studied, copied and experimented until sometimes he felt like a chicken someone had overstuffed and which had exploded in the oven. But the more he learned, the more he realised there was to learn. After work-experience sessions at places like Le Gavroche and the Ritz, he took to repeating every day, like a mantra, 'A chef is only as good as his last meal.' By the end of the course, he was itching to get back out there.

On their last day, there was a party and the college's own version of a prize-giving ceremony. Klutz of the year went to a guy named John, who had broken more plates than anyone else and even managed to smash a silver salver. Jake's mate Barney got Pudding of the Year. He had put on three and half stones since he started and had got the job of his dreams as a pastry chef on a cruise liner. 'If you go on like this, they will have to reinforce the boat,' said the principal. Barney just grinned and asked Jake if he was going to finish that pudding.

'Joking aside, you have been a brilliant group this year. Well, by and large. Anyone remember that girl who ran off in tears during the first week, when she was asked to try some tripe?'

'Dozy bitch,' muttered Harry, but too quietly for anyone to hear.

'Well, someone spotted her the other day working in a fast-food joint at Oxford Circus.'

There was a shocked and pitying silence.

'Now, I am sure none of you will be surprised that the award for outstanding student has effectively been a two-chef race. During their time here, Jake Goldman and Harry Hunter have proved themselves to be dedicated and talented. I can assure you that the debate over this award has been worse than a meeting of the UN. We argued like fury among ourselves, but eventually, probably because we finally ran out of booze – no, seriously – it was decided – because we feel he had the ability to run a happy and focused kitchen, as well as cook like one of the gods – to present this award to Jake.'

Everyone cheered and threw their bread rolls at him. Jake was astounded. He had never won anything in his life and was always too busy trying to become a better cook to get big-headed about his talent. The award took the form of a little silver chef's hat. Guiltily, he wondered if he could sell it. It would be the only way he could afford new chef's gear.

When he got back to the table, Harry made sure he was the first one to stand up and shake Jake's hand. Anyone watching them would assume they were the best of friends. But when Jake looked into Harry's eyes, he shivered.

The principal banged a spoon on the table to get their attention. 'Listen up, you lot. I said shut up! God, I am really looking forward to seeing those cocky smiles wiped off your faces on your first day at work. Anyway, this brings me to my final announcement.

'It is my great pleasure to tell you all that really, both Jake and Harry have come up winners tonight. The Capital, that famous spot that none of us can afford to eat at, has – and this has never happened before – offered both these guys jobs. Well done, you two. That's a really remarkable achievement!'

Jake could feel a large smile spread over his face. He felt as though he was about to burst. This was the chance of a lifetime. Harry grinned at the crowd, nodding regally, but inside he was seething, and shocked at his very unfamiliar feeling of humiliation. Being top – winning prizes – well, that was his natural place in the world. But no one else belonged there. And certainly Jake didn't.

Harry carried on smiling and talking, while his brain feverishly started producing ideas for teaching Jake a lesson. There were so many things he could do. All he needed was an opportunity. He could wait. In the meantime . . .

'Let me shake your hand again, mate. I think we are going to work very well together.'

'What a gent!' someone shouted, but Jake's delighted smile quickly turned sour. His hand was hurting so much he wouldn't have been surprised if Harry hadn't broken a bone or two.

Chapter Five

The Capital was so trendy it was rumoured that even Gwyneth Paltrow was unable to get a table one night. Members of cool and edgy rock bands ate there, and television presenters who wanted to be seen as cool. It was so expensive that Jake would have had to take out a mortgage to afford dinner.

The chef who had created its reputation was currently off work, enjoying a protracted nervous breakdown. In his place was his brother, who couldn't cook quite as well but was sleeping with the owner's wife.

Jake got the distinct impression that, despite appearances to the contrary, the restaurant was on its way down. It happened. Restaurants come and go – actually, most of them go. Coming down with a bump after the happy glow induced by the principal's praise, he saw in reality that the atmosphere in the kitchen was often so bad (think sinking ship and rats) that he didn't really want to stay, if there hadn't been the urgent matter of an overdraft to pay off first. He had spent a brilliant but pricey week in Italy, learning how to make pasta from a master, and now was seriously in debt. But it had been worth it. The chef's wife had taken him to her heart – literally. Every morning he would be enveloped in a squishy, garlic-and-herb-fragranced embrace, fed huge amounts of food and told that he looked too peaky. He had worked hard, but the food, the glorious red wine and the sun had left him feeling as fit as a butcher's dog.

Harry was furious that Jake hadn't died in a plane crash on the way, or at the least chopped his fingers off in a pasta machine, but they were both lowly commis chefs at the moment so Harry's plan of action called for discretion and cunning.

Harry had plenty of spare energy for this, because on his days off he could kip at his cousin's flat in Hampstead, lulled to sleep on Egyptian cotton sheets and cocooned from the traffic behind triple-glazed windows. When he felt peckish there was always some fillet steak or smoked salmon in the fridge.

Jake, on the other hand, had found the cheapest bedsit in the whole of London. It was above an Indian supermarket, and opposite the sort of pub whose clientele consider it a poor do if there isn't at least one fight at night. Jake would lie in bed, under a woefully inadequate duvet, shivering and listening to the sound of glass bottles breaking over people's heads.

His diet would have been just soup, made from vegetables picked up from a local market, because that was all he could afford. But he had made friends with Mr Patel downstairs, who had left Bombay twenty-five years ago but was still dreadfully homesick, and was thrilled by Jake's genuine interest in Indian cuisine. He took to leaving a portion of the family's curry on Jake's doorstep most nights.

Jake was usually so tired he would eat it cold, standing up, before falling into a fitful doze on a bed so uncomfortable he was tempted to lift the mattress up to see if there were nails underneath.

When he came into work hollow-eyed, Harry would look over in mock concern and say: 'You look rough. Been burning the candle at both ends again?'

Although Jake's work was always impeccable, Harry's words gave the impression that Jake was a bit of a party animal, which made their boss, who was seriously stressed to start with, look at him with some suspicion.

Kitchens are busy places and people often bump into each other, but Jake always seemed to get jostled when he was using a sharp knife or stirring a hot sauce. Scalded or cut, he would swear profusely, and Harry would shrug and grin an apology. It gained Jake an entirely undeserved reputation for being humourless and grouchy.

Also, if they all went out for a drink after work, Harry always bought several rounds while Jake (mindful of his bank manager, who was making increasingly threatening noises) tried to nurse half a shandy through the evening. No one actually said he was mean, but the unspoken words hung in the air alongside the cigarette smoke.

He was often too tired to make much conversation, but he watched. Did the others not realise they were being befriended by a shark? Harry had predatory eyes, clear, focused and hungry. The others might think him a good sort but Jake was determined not to land between those expensive, gleaming white teeth.

The one bright spot was Jill, one of the restaurant's

ever-shifting population of waiting staff. She was freckled and funny, and a truly terrible waitress, but at least she always turned up for work, though this wasn't due to professionalism, but because she couldn't bear to be parted from Jake.

They had been going out for only a week before she said: 'I know this is so totally the wrong thing to say, but I have fallen in love with you. Do you want to kick me out?'

'I haven't finished counting the freckles on your nose yet, let alone the rest of you. I'll let you know when I've finished,' he teased. 'Anyway, the feeling is mutual because you are practically perfect, you know. You're gorgeous, you make me laugh and, most importantly, you don't seem to mind that this bed is as hard as a rock and so short our feet dangle over the edge.'

She was always chronically short of cash as well. If they were off on the same day they would walk to the nearest free exhibition, or lie in bed eating cold curry and making love.

He was enjoying himself so much he didn't want to spoil it by taking her home to meet his family yet. This was because they were mad. Mrs Goldman never believed in using one word if you could slot in at least another fifty, even if they contradicted each other. She was always on the lookout for a molehill to turn into a mountain. Jake was convinced his father had taken up bird-watching just to get out of the house, but as he hardly uttered a word when he was in it, it was difficult to tell the difference.

Four of the kitchen staff had left or been sacked within hours of each other that month, so no one had been able to have much time off. Jake was knackered, but it was his and Jill's first afternoon off together for three weeks and he had it planned down to the last minute. He was going to take her on the bus (cheap) to an exhibition (free), which would leave him flush enough for pasta for two at an Italian restaurant round the corner. He was just outlining this plan to her when his mother rang.

'There is an enormous bird flapping around in the attic. I can hear it!' Jake's mother had a phobia about birds.

'Well, where's Dad?'

'Out.'

'Are you sure?'

'Of course I'm sure. It's always the same. I don't know why he bothers to call this place his home and does he take his phone with him? No! It is right here in front of me on the sideboard. I told him to shut the window in the attic but he must have forgotten, and heaven knows what it is dropping onto the boxes up there. Imagine the smell! Oh my God! Maybe it is laying eggs; before we know it there will be a whole flock of them. There is that box belonging to your oma up there – it is all we have left of her!'

'I'll come right over, Mum,' said Jake, putting the phone down. It was easier to say it now and cut out another twenty minutes of kvetch.

He sighed. 'It's going to take ages to get across London and she won't let me out of her clutches until I've had at least two cups of tea and an update on everything our neighbours have been up to, even though she knows I don't know who half of them are.' He smiled at Jill ruefully. 'Then there will be an intensive interrogation of every aspect of my life for the last six months, followed by analysis, criticism and entirely unsolicited advice.' He didn't want to do any of this, but he was a good Jewish son. In his head he saw his precious time off vanish like smoke. He might as well have been working.

'Don't worry,' said Jill gamely. 'To be honest, I could do with spending the afternoon asleep, anyway.' She kissed him, but although she tried not to show her disappointment, she knew it would be ages before they got more time off together.

'Thank God you are such a nice person,' said Jake, and rushed off.

Jill mooched round the restaurant kitchen in an aimless way. She was tired, but the sun was shining and she wasn't rostered for an afternoon off for at least another ten days. It was all a real bummer.

Harry was apparently absorbed in sharpening his knives but his hearing was acute when it was something that could be turned to his advantage.

'I've been stood up as well. My girlfriend is off sick with a migraine,' he lied. He didn't have a girlfriend at the moment, but he wanted to appear casual and unthreatening. 'It's such a nice day, isn't it? There's supposed to be a good jazz band on in Hyde Park later this afternoon. Hey, do you fancy going? I'll buy you one those mocha coffee caramel things you're always going on about. They sound really revolting, but if you like them . . .' He grinned at her disarmingly.

Jill thought about this. She knew Jake didn't like Harry but she didn't really understand why. He seemed perfectly nice to her so she couldn't see any harm in his suggestion. He just wanted some company for the afternoon, in a brotherly sort of way. She wouldn't even have to tell Jake.

Chapter Six

The following week it was Friday the thirteenth. But Jake wasn't superstitious so he strolled into work whistling cheerfully. It was payday and he planned to cook Jill a fabulous meal that night. He had already been out and bought a bunch of roses on tick from the flower shop on the corner, and a bottle of Mr Patel's best wine, which wasn't actually that good but none of the other off-licences operated a buy now, pay later scheme. Jill had seemed a bit down recently, which wasn't like her at all, but when he asked her what the matter was she had just shrugged and said she must be coming down with a cold or something. Jake wasn't surprised. His room was distinctly damp as well as chilly, but tonight it was full of Mr Patel's entire stock of candles. It would be so warm they might have to eat supper in the nude, which could be fun.

She was already at work when he arrived, polishing wine glasses. He crept up behind her and kissed the back of her neck.

'Hello, beautiful.'

Jill jumped about two feet in the air and dropped a wine glass.

'Oh, shit.'

'Hey, don't worry – it was my fault anyway. You're a bit jumpy this morning.' He tried to kiss her again but she moved her head so that his lips landed on her chin and he sensed it wasn't a good moment to try again.

'Are you all right?'

'Of course,' she snapped, and then gave him a weak smile.

'Sorry, Jake. I've just got such a bad headache.'

'Oh, poor you. Try and survive till tonight and then I will cosset you and comfort you. Leave the glass – I'll clear it up.' He went out and so didn't see the look on her face, which was of intense guilt, mixed with irritation.

Why was he always so bloody nice, she thought, conveniently forgetting that this was why she had fallen in love with him in the first place.

Later that evening Jake looked round his room with satisfaction. OK, most of the candles were the sort you would only use in a power cut and the ones that were scented were giving off a slightly curried fragrance, but the flickering lights hid the damp patch in the corner rather well.

Jill gave a rather wan smile when she saw the roses, before sitting down at the table and putting her face in her hands.

'Jake, we need to talk.'

He went very still. It was not going to be good news. This loaded little phrase never meant anything of the sort. In his experience, 'we need to talk' never involved anything remotely resembling a two-way conversation. No, what it meant was 'I have an overpowering need to tell you lots of things you would rather not hear and, frankly, anything you might have to contribute isn't going to make any difference.' Oh crap.

'I'll just put the steaks back in the fridge then. I don't suppose we're going to want them,' he said coldly.

'Oh, please, just leave them and sit down.'

'Certainly not. Whatever you might have to say will not be a good enough excuse for treating food badly.' He busied himself in the kitchen for a few minutes, putting off the horrible moment. It also gave him a small amount of satisfaction to make her wait.

She was sitting at the table, shredding a napkin into tiny pieces.

'Things haven't been right between us for a while now.'

'Haven't they?' This was news to him.

Jill swallowed and wished he would open that bottle of wine, but he just sat there, very still, waiting.

'I've been seeing someone else.' When he didn't respond, but just looked at her blankly, she burst out: 'Oh, please don't make this more difficult than it already is!'

'For whom, exactly? You or me? Because it's bad enough for me as it is. But let me help you out. By "seeing" someone, I take it you mean you've been sleeping with him. You're terribly sorry; you never meant this to happen and you certainly didn't mean to hurt anyone.'

This was exactly what Jill was going to say, but it didn't sound quite the same coming out of Jake's mouth.

'So, who is it?

'You don't want to know.'

'That means you are too scared to tell me.'

She took a deep breath. Jake wasn't the violent sort, but you never knew, and this might be the one thing that would tip him over the edge.

'It's Harry.'

Jake continued to sit very still and concentrated on keeping his face under control. He was damned if he was going to let her see how shocked and upset he was.

'That's a very stupid thing you are doing.' That was good. He sound quite calm, almost casual, but he knew it had hit home because she flinched.

'I knew you would say that, but –'

'Even before we were going out I told you to stay away from him, didn't I? He is a devious, manipulative, arrogant shit who will sleep with you for a while and then dump you because that's what he's like. I don't want to burst the bubble of your self-esteem, but he's just using you to get at me.'

'Thanks! Anyway, he told me you would say that!'

Jake leaned back in the chair, eyes narrowed. He was so angry he was almost detached from the whole thing. Which was good, but he knew the pain would come later.

'Let me see, I suppose he took you for a drink and it just sort of escalated from there. You can spare me the details.'

She had intended to do that anyway. It would be impossibly hurtful to Jake to explain how much fun she had had that first afternoon. They hadn't done anything wrong either, just listened to some music, which neither of them had liked, and talked, a lot. It turned out that they had plenty in common, so much that it seemed imperative and entirely natural to arrange to meet again. OK, this time it was in the sort of cocktail bar she'd always longed to be taken to (what woman didn't?) and yes, they had drunk Bollinger, which she'd only ever heard about on *Ab Fab*, but it was really to do with their personalities seeming to mesh together. That and the fact that when his hot blue gaze looked down at her (he was so tall!), being with him was like basking in a Mediterranean sun. And it was certainly unthinkable to describe how Harry's huge bed was made for the sort of inventive sex that would result in serious injury if they tried it on Jake's lumpy single mattress.

Jill concentrated instead on saying how sorry she was. She said it in so many ways Jake half wondered if she'd consulted a thesaurus before coming out. Eventually he could listen no longer.

'Enough! Is that the gist of what you have to say?'

She nodded miserably.

'Then you might as well just fuck off.'

When she'd gone, Jake lay down on his bed, watching the thirty-two candles dripping wax on the carpet and trying not to think about the fact that she had probably gone to see Harry, who was most likely even now enjoying the sex that he had planned for his own evening. Jake was awake for most of the night, thinking about little else.

Jill certainly had gone round to see Harry, but was shocked when his door was opened by a very beautiful girl wearing one of the bath towels she herself had enjoyed using. As she stood there in horror, Harry himself appeared, flagrantly, insultingly, wearing nothing at all and not giving a shit about it either.

'Oops,' was all he said, but it was enough.

Jill stared at him silently for a minute, while it slowly dawned on her what a fool she had been. 'You are such a loser, Harry. For some reason your personality is permanently in negative equity. I don't know why you feel the need to steal from Jake to make up the shortfall, but it will never be enough.'

For a second, Harry's mask dropped to show a face twisted in anger, then he smirked. 'Loser? With all this? I don't think so, babe!'

The swirling cauldron of emotions in the kitchen the next day was about as appealing as one of Mrs Goldman's casseroles – a dish she inflicted on her family from time to time and which was based on the simple premise that if you bunged roughly equal measures of the pantry and the fridge into the oven, something edible would emerge. It almost never did.

Jake was sad and furious at the same time, which made his head feel quite curdled. He tried very hard to leave all this personal stuff at the kitchen door, so to speak, and stay professional, but he wore a permanent scowl and spoke only in monosyllables. An equally unappetising combination of shame and despair made Jill clumsier than ever, while Harry's glee made him simply insufferable. He waited until the kitchen was full of people before holding out his hand and saying in a loud voice: 'I hope there are no hard feelings, mate? Please don't take this personally.'

'Why not? We both know it is,' said Jake acidly and stalked off, giving Harry all the time in the world to tell everyone how it wasn't really Jake's fault he was such a bad loser.

To all this was added the chef's hangover, which, even by his standards, was of monumental proportions.

It was a morning of curdled sauces, dropped crockery and knives sliding smoothly into fingers instead of vegetables. The third plate that Jill dropped echoed round the chef's throbbing head and sent him staggering to the first-aid box.

'Fucking hell! There isn't even one aspirin left in here!' He glared at everyone, holding his head and his bloodshot gaze came to rest on Jill, whose eyes were so swollen with crying she couldn't see she was putting all the knives in the forks tray.

'Stop messing up my kitchen, you stupid woman, and go and get me some aspirin, the extra strong sort,' he roared, and threw his wallet at her.

She scuttled off. On her way to get her coat she saw Harry laughing with one of the other waitresses and trying to pinch her bum. When she got to the shop she couldn't remember why she was there and had to wander up and down the aisles for ages. The supermarket had a help desk and she was very tempted to lay her head on the counter and ask for some but she didn't think they would be up to dealing with emotional fuck-ups. When she got back she was so late the chef had got tired of waiting and had sloped off home.

With difficulty she staggered through to the end of the shift, giving everyone the wrong orders and looking totally blank when they complained. No one left a tip that lunchtime. She was bringing the last plate back to the kitchen when Jake looked up briefly. His eyes were dark and sad, and she suddenly remembered all the fun they'd had. She couldn't possibly go on working with him. She was crap at her job anyway. She would go home to her mum. She would do it right now. There was no point in waiting for her wages because she probably owed more than that in broken crockery anyway.

Putting her hand into her pocket for her phone she found she still had the chef's wallet. She groaned. Jake was the only one left, wiping surfaces with a furious energy.

'Look, I'm going home for a while, could you give this back?'

'Whatever,' he said with studied indifference. She tossed it over to him and it landed in his tool box.

He forgot about the wallet almost instantly. It was his evening off, which he spent with two bottles of appalling red wine no one else in the supermarket had wanted. The only CDs he hadn't sold were Coldplay and Leonard Cohen, but they suited his mood perfectly.

After listening to three and half hours of angst-ridden musings on the bleakness of life, perversely he decided that things weren't that bad. He had lost a woman – well, so had plenty of others before him. More importantly, he still had cooking. To lose that would be the real tragedy.

Meanwhile, back at work, the chef was having a small temper tantrum at being one waitress down. Taking into account the fact that she was the worst waitress they'd ever had, it was probably no bad thing, but she seemed to have gone off with his wallet.

'I'm sure she put it in your office, Chef,' said Harry, always helpful.

'Well, it's not there now.'

Harry knew where the wallet was because he had seen it and covered it up with a tea towel, but was taking his time, waiting for the right moment.

It was a busy night. When the chef's knife snapped under the pressure, Harry offered him one of his. 'Mind you, I think Jake's left his.'

'Silly bastard. He knows he shouldn't do that. I'll have one of his; it serves him right for not taking them home.'

Harry bent down and schooled his face into a careful controlled look of surprise and confusion. He was practically salivating at the thought of revenge. The chef glanced over impatiently, then stopped.

'Fuck – what's he doing with my wallet?' he exploded.

'Well, I'm sure there's some sort of explanation,' Harry said, pretending to sound placating.

'You bet there is – he's a bloody thief!' The chef was a man of simple emotions and massive grudges. He always gave in to them.

When Jake walked into work on Monday he was sacked on the spot. What could he do, sue? Yeah, like he had plenty of spare cash for a court case. To make things worse, he then found himself the object of press attention, all of it unwelcome. 'College Star's Theft from Top Eatery' was the worst headline, from hacks seizing a double opportunity to sully both Jake's college and the restaurant. By the time he finally managed to get hold of Jill to try to clear his name, two weeks had passed and the chef had moved on, with his wallet, to a new job somewhere in the Med. This gave the press another field day when they blamed Jake for his departure. Things got so bad, he had to invest in a pair of dark glasses. During his enforced and poverty-stricken time off, Jake had ample time to sit around and fantasise. These dreams were:

1. That the Mediterranean was full of sharks.
2. That the chef got drunk one night and fell overboard, where his fat white bottom would provide a tasty snack.
3. That Jill fell into a decline and became a nun, because she had lost the one true love of her life.
4. That all journalists would spend the afterlife being spit-roasted in some sort of hell dimension.

While he was waiting for these things to happen and applying for hundreds of jobs, he spent his days stacking shelves for Mr Patel, who didn't really need anyone to do this and could only afford to pay Jake in the various goods that had reached their sell-by date. But no one else wanted to give him a job. Despite references from his lecturers at college saying he was superbly talented and totally honest, the Capital had given him a bad reputation. Which stuck, like grease round a fryer. In the frantic world he wanted to work in, no one had time to listen to the full story.

Almost the worst thing about this experience was the boredom. Because he didn't have any money, he couldn't even cook for himself at home, and after a while he had to stop going into bookshops because the assistants at Waterstone's were starting to give him nasty looks for riffling through the cooking section and then wearing out the cushions on the sofas, but never buying anything. He couldn't even become a busker on the London Underground because he couldn't sing.

He spent so much time hanging around places, people watching, he half thought of setting up his own food stall, which would also offer culinary counselling. For twenty quid he could tell people what a terrible diet they had and then offer them some decent grub instead. It was astonishing how much crap people bought: garishly coloured sweets; chocolate-flavoured things; health bars full of sugar and sandwiches containing what the manufacturer called cheese, but Jake reckoned was possibly only one molecule away from plastic.

There were far too many people in this world shoving food into their mouths without thinking. None of it seemed to make them any happier, even for a minute. They rushed from one place to another, barely even aware that they were eating. Jake knew that when he was allowed to be a chef he was often too busy to sit down for a proper meal, but when he did put food in his mouth he was always intensely aware of its flavour and texture. He couldn't imagine living without such sublime experiences.

Maybe he should become a food bandit, a culinary pirate. He would kidnap people, force them to give him money so he could cook for them and show them what they were missing. He would rob those starved of real food and make them rich in eating experiences. They would start to insist, like the French, that they had a decent breakfast in the morning and a two-hour lunch break so they could enjoy a proper meal served on a plate, not in a piece of cardboard. The country would grind to a halt but he would be a national hero. Oh crap, if he didn't get a job soon, he would go completely bonkers. He seemed to be halfway there already.

Eventually, when he was beginning to think he would have to give up and apply his new-found shelf-stacking experience at Sainsbury's, where at least they paid in money, he found work at a seedy hotel near Waterloo. After a couple of days it was quite obvious some people used it, not as an eating place, but to close mysterious and deeply illegal deals. The only reason he didn't get mugged on the way home was that he was cooking the muggers' dinners.

One day Jill came to see him. She wasn't wearing a habit, but he was shamefully pleased to see she was looking pale and unhappy.

'This is so unfair and it's all Harry's fault. You can't let him get away with it!' she cried.

'Right. I'll take him to a tribunal then. No problem, except that I've got no money, and it could take years and there's no guarantee the truth will come out anyway.'

'Well, what are you going to do?'

Jake shrugged. 'Nothing. Keep trying to find decent work, I suppose.'

She hung around for a while, looking like she was waiting for him to ask her out for a drink, but he didn't. She had screwed him over and he was as stubborn as hell. You only got one chance with him and she had blown it.

And so it continued for about two years.

Jake's family had been through more ups and downs than a yo-yo. When you were down, you picked yourself up, and started again. So that's what he did, but in a more wary, less innocent way. But there was no denying he seemed to camp out permanently at Rock Bottom.

He went on to do some really terrible jobs, which made the hotel at Waterloo look like the Ritz. But he had to: if there wasn't cooking, there was nothing. When things got really bad he would clench his teeth, until he remembered he didn't have enough money to go to the dentist. Still, looking back, he might not have made it in the end if Louis hadn't come to his rescue.

Louis Challon had learned his trade in the bistros of Paris that are now just a distant memory in the minds of those lucky enough to have eaten there – where the floors were covered with sawdust, the chef wore a beret and rows of enormous salamis hung from the ceiling. Sometimes the only food on offer was a *plat du jour*, but of such sublime quality people would queue halfway down the street to get in.

He moved to London with his French wife, Maria, and set up Brie, which swiftly became one of the best restaurants in town. He named it not after the cheese, but because it was the old name for an ancient province of France, somewhere east of Paris, where he had grown up. Although everything he touched turned to manna he became famous for his *oreiller de la belle Aurore* – a dish containing pheasant, woodcock, hare, pork, veal, foie gras, truffles and chicken livers, named after Brillat-Savarin's mother, and shaped like a sublime but terribly fattening pillow. Louis spent eighteen hours a day in his kitchen, tasted everything, but burned off more calories than an Olympic sprinter, and shouted, cajoled and praised his staff until they became the best team in town.

Any commis who wanted to work there was put through a grilling ordeal that started something like this.

'I don't give a fig how old you are, what your middle name is or how many cooking qualifications you have!' Louis roared. 'Get in that kitchen and show me what you can actually do!' It was the day-long trial in his kitchen that counted, and whether you were still on your feet at the end of it. Some enormously talented chefs weren't and were shown the door, which they reached on their knees.

The only job on offer was for a kitchen porter. Jake had decided it was better to expire quickly in a good kitchen than this slow death of the spirit in an awful one. He washed up like a maniac, uncomplainingly, for three weeks, until one day, in the afternoon shift break, Louis came in to the staffroom to find him asleep, using a cookbook as a pillow.

'Sorry,' he mumbled, getting up, ready to leave the great man in his domain, but Louis ignored him.

'I am going to make the mousse of fishes. Seeing as you are here you can help.'

Jake went to get his washing-up apron.

'No, no,' said Louis irritably, 'did I ask you to wash up?'

'Well, no, Chef.'

'So, show me what you can do with this,' and he passed Jake a tray of fish and a filleting knife.

It turned into a brilliant afternoon, even though Louis shouted, scolded and shook his head in despair at least every five minutes. When Jake proved more than proficient at simple tasks, Louis gave him more complicated things to do and even thanked him when they were finished.

'No, thank you, Chef – it was like being in a master class.' Jake went off to wash up, leaving Louis looking after him thoughtfully. He knew talent when he saw it and didn't intend to waste it.

Jake found he was being asked to do more cooking than washing-up, sometimes with Louis's nephew and second in command. Pierre was a huge and taciturn man of about thirty, with a luxuriant red beard that made him look piratical and which hid the fact that he was really quite shy. Then, more and more often, it seemed, Jake was working under the eagle eyes of the great man himself.

One night, at the end of service, he was getting ready to go home when Maria appeared. 'Come upstairs. I have cooked far too much casserole and you must help us finish it. You know how Louis hates waste.'

Bemused, he followed her upstairs to their flat. Louis was in his shirtsleeves, uncorking a bottle of red wine. 'First we eat. Then we discuss which rabbit dish we put on the menu next week.'

During the meal Louis listened attentively to Jake's suggestions and then disagreed with them all. But Jake didn't mind – he was having a wonderful time. When, at the end of the evening, he was hustled into the spare room on the grounds that the tube wasn't safe at that time of night, he didn't even try to argue. After a couple of weeks of this, he gave up resisting and moved in completely. This never stopped Louis from dishing out tons of criticism at work if he thought Jake needed it. Jake did protest, though, when Maria took his whites away for washing.

'I can do it myself.'

'Yes, but I have far more knowledge than you of the best ways of getting blood out of one's clothes.'

'Do me a favour and don't ever say that in public,' said Jake with a grin.

'I hope you don't mind that my wife fusses over you,' said Louis rather gruffly one day.

'Of course I don't – I love her,' said Jake simply. 'It's hard to explain, but before I met you I thought I had lost something very precious to me. But you gave it back. I owe you everything.'

'You certainly owe me the story of how a gifted young man like you came here to wash pots. But for now, that Jerusalem artichoke risotto will not make itself, so what are you waiting for?'

Chapter Seven

Nothing went right for Jake in the week before opening Cuisine. The hotel room cost a fortune; he had finally fallen asleep in the jacuzzi and woke up in cold water from a nightmare in which he was trying to cross the Channel in a pizza oven. Staggering into the bedroom, he found Georgia fast asleep on the bed with her mouth open, a position only she could make look adorable.

The new cooker he'd ordered arrived three days late and the maniacal youth they'd sent to install it somehow managed to cause a power failure down the whole street, a fiasco for which Jake was continuing to apologise every time he dared set foot outside.

The first commis chef, who at interview claimed he was so reliable and keen he would rather cook than eat, sleep or even have sex, ran away three hours into his first shift and one of the waitresses sent by the agency seemed to have a vocabulary of only three words – one of which was 'fuck'. Luckily, Kirsty, the other one, was hard-working, willing and only swore *in extremis*, which was quite understandable. Her only drawback was a tendency to tell long, complicated stories about people no one had ever heard of. By the time Jake had worked out who was who, he found he had missed the point, if there was one.

His supplier, who had promised the earth in edible form, delivered a case of broccoli so old it was practically mummified.

'What am I supposed to do with this, cook it or display it in a museum? Fresh from the fields? You have got to be joking! It looks like it has come straight from Tutankhamen's bloody tomb,' Jake snarled.

The one bright spot was the replacement commis.

Tess had spiky blonde hair, six piercings in one ear and a stud through her nose. She was small, thin and tougher than the broccoli.

She gave the worst interview Jake had ever experienced, being practically monosyllabic and radiating waves of such angry energy Jake had to turn the heating down. She had left school without any qualifications but with a baby. Despite this, she had never been out of work.

Jake didn't care that she was about as chatty as a Trappist monk. The real issue was, could she cook?

She bloody could. Not only that, she was organised, efficient and meticulously neat when she was working. She might look like her only hobby was biting people in the neck, but that was fine by him. It was as good a way as any for dealing with incompetent suppliers.

The only slight problem was Angelica, her daughter. Now six years old, Angel, as she was called, was a plump and gorgeous blonde who combined devastating charm with a will of iron.

Tess worked like a Trojan getting set up and even volunteered to come in on her day off.

'Trouble is, there's no one to look after Angel.'

Jake considered this. He knew by now that Tess burned with a zeal almost as strong as his own. She was a real kitchen junkie.

'Well, bring her in, if you want. What trouble can one small child cause?'

Tess snorted with derision at the stupidity of men.

Angel arrived with a pink plastic suitcase, containing Barbie, Barbie's entire wardrobe and Barbie's pony. The doll had more clothes than Georgia.

Angel was quite happy to sit in the office, showing Barbie how to type on Jake's computer and setting up an obstacle course for the pony with all his cookery books. But she also adopted Jake as her uncle, which made Tess blush, and she followed him everywhere, giving a running commentary on the work in progress.

'Kim's made a big puddle, Uncle Jake.'

He went to investigate. Kim, the vocabulary-challenged waitress, was standing by the dishwasher, which was spewing its contents over the floor.

Kim moved her chewing gum to her cheek, in order to tackle the fine art of communication. 'It's broken. There's watter all over t'floor.'

Jake considered this. She reeked of smoke and had obviously just been out for another fag, her third that morning – he had been counting. If she had any more breaks she would forget how to work all together, if indeed she had ever known. Instead of doing something remotely intelligent and useful, like getting a mop, she just stood there, chewing. She was the sort of person who could make a cow look clever.

Jake mulled over several approaches, but as usual, went for his favourite: the unvarnished truth. 'You are idle and inept and you smell like an old ashtray. You're sacked, so fuck off.'

There was an audible intake of breath, but not from the witless waitress.

'Uncle Jake, you used that word again. You said you would give me fifty pence if you said it again.'

Jake was outraged. 'I said twenty pence, actually.'

Angelica started to laugh and a lemon sherbet exploded out of her mouth and landed on Kim's jumper.

'I will sue you for unfair dismissal and damage to my clothes. This place is a dump anyway.'

'The only thing that was unfair was the fact that you were employed in the first place,' Jake yelled.

'If Uncle Jake tells you to fuck off, I really think you should,' advised Angel.

Jake escaped to the relative sanity of his office and Barbie's pony, but he only had peace for ten minutes before Angel, who was turning into a messenger of doom, reappeared. 'God's here.'

'Well, I hope He's come to take me away from all this,' muttered Jake.

God was actually Godfrey, who arrived for interview straight from his father's sheep farm, in a pair of wellingtons that were so disgustingly dirty Jake made him leave them ten yards outside the back door. Godfrey was at least six and half foot tall and extremely red in the face, having run down a fell to get to the interview on time.

'I'm sick of animals crapping on me and having to stick

my hand up their bums. I do all the cooking at home and I want to learn how to be a chef. I'll do anything you ask, if you give me a chance.'

'If I do, you will, believe me. You may find your farming experience comes in handy when I ask you to stuff twenty chickens. Seeing as you are the only applicant the agency sent who can speak English, you've got the job. Still,' Jake continued, 'cooking is quite like farming in many ways. The pay is abysmal, the hours are appalling and the customers can be full of shit, so you'll feel quite at home.'

'Er, what exactly will my job title be?'

'Slave,' said Jake briskly. 'Basically you will do whatever I ask you to. This will include some hideous jobs that you probably didn't even know existed. But every so often, as a special treat, you'll have a sort of holiday, when all I ask you to do is peel tons and tons of vegetables until your fingers are raw. Basically, you will have only one ambition – to say with utter conviction "Yes, Chef". It is all I want to hear. If I don't hear it, I may get slightly upset and feel the need to express myself loudly and in a politically incorrect way.'

Godfrey was so tall he lived in constant danger of knocking himself out on the extractor fan. He was immensely cheerful and willing, and didn't seem to have a temper to lose, which, in a kitchen, put his price above rubies.

Angel fell instantly in love and basely transferred most of her affections from Jake to Godfrey. She lent him her pony and wound her arms so tightly round his legs she had to be bribed with an ice lolly so he could do some work.

The final member of Jake's team was Hans, the barman, a skinny youth from Munich, who had started off his travelling gap year in Scotland and was supposed to be making his way south. But he had got pleasantly stuck in the Lake District at Easter and showed no signs of wanting to budge.

Georgia was away on a fashion shoot, for which large mercy Jake thanked whichever god happened to be listening. He had to focus on opening night. The paying public gave a restaurant only one chance, and every penny he owned, plus a huge loan, was riding on this.

Before anyone could even start cooking, they had to find things to cook with, which at the moment were still in their boxes and covering every available surface in the kitchen. Also, none of the boxes was labelled correctly so it was a bit like Christmas. Every so often someone would shout triumphantly: 'I've found the cutlery. It was in the box marked "frying pans". Oh blast, where are the frying pans then?' and so on.

As Jake couldn't afford a restaurant manager, he went to help Kirsty arrange the tables and chairs, confident that Tess could be left in charge.

'I don't think we should put this table here, 'cos there'll be a draught from the door. My gran went out for dinner once with her best friend, Mary. They've been friends ever since their prams collided when they were two months old. Anyway, Mary's married to the guy that has the garden centre – the one in Easedale, of course, not the one on the way to Ambleside – you must know him – he's got a withered arm. Well, this was just before the wedding. Or was it just after? Oh, silly me – of course it was before – that's the whole point of the story –'

'Kirsty, I feel as if I am going to take root here, which could be awkward for our customers.'

As they pieced the restaurant together, like a giant 3D puzzle, Jake listened with one ear to Kirsty's pointless anecdotes and with the other to the dialogue in the kitchen.

'Godfrey, why have you put the pans over there?'

'Er, dunno.'

'Exactly. Every time we want a pan we're gonna have to trek halfway across the flaming kitchen. Ooh, look, there's a shelf here, just next to the grill. I don't know, shall we put the wine bottles there, perhaps?'

'You don't want to do that. They'll get all warm.'

Then there was the sound of Tess slapping him with one of the towels she kept tied round her waist.

'. . . and that's why you should never sit in a draught!' said Kirsty, surprising him. This was the first of her stories that actually had an ending and now he'd missed it.

'Absolutely. I do take your point.' Well, I would if I knew what it was.

Godfrey was horrified to discover that everything had to be washed first. 'But it's just come out of the box. It can't be dirty!'

'You are an environmental health nightmare, you big oaf!'

Although it hadn't seemed possible at the start, everything found a home.

Jake came into the kitchen to find Godfrey lying on a pile of boxes, having found this was the best way to squash them flat. Also, he needed the rest.

'Come on, my lad, the real work is about to begin!'

Outside in the stores were even more boxes, full of the raw ingredients needed to serve sixty hungry customers every night for the next few days, until it had all been eaten and the next lot would come in.

'It should have been one of the Labours of Hercules. We get to the end of it and everyone has gone home happy, hopefully, and then we start all over again. And so it will go on, until we are all dead or mad, or both. Then, if you are very lucky, I will let you have a day off.'

Just when Godfrey got to the end of one pile of vegetables, he would be ordered off to find another. All the gleaming pans were pulled off the shelves, thrown onto the hobs, flung on the table to be washed, put back on the shelves for a nanosecond, it seemed, and then pulled off again.

The kitchen was filled with a huge crescendo of orders, advice and intense discussion between Jake and Tess, and over this wafted a heavenly series of smells – frying garlic, roasting vegetables, sautéed chicken, fillet steak and pastry, sponges and mousses.

The most wonderful thing of all, though, was that Godfrey was allowed – ordered, even – to try everything, including a lot of things he had never tasted before in his life. He didn't even mind that one minute he was tasting a fruit-filled pastry and the next, fresh mussels, which had been briefly simmered in an exquisite sauce.

His life as a farmer hadn't been particularly full of conversation – in fact he reckoned his dad would quite happily go for a whole day without talking to anyone. So it came as a surprise to him that Jake didn't seem to mind that he had to keep asking questions and he never took the piss out of him for doing so. So, because he was intensely curious and always hungry, he felt that he had walked into the perfect job.

Jake and Tess prepped the menu until their fingers were raw, and Godfrey's shoulders felt permanently hunched in an old man's stoop.

'Nervous, Boss?' asked Tess, who was dicing a pile of carrots so quickly her hands were a blur.

'Terrified,' agreed Jake.

It wasn't so much the food – well, of course it was; it was always about the food – but what the papers were bound to dredge up about him. It didn't matter what he did, how many awards he got, someone always resurrected the story of how he had been sacked for stealing at the Capital.

Tess must have been in mind-reading mode.

'The reviews will be great and what if they do rake up that old crap again – everyone knows you didn't really do it.'

Jake shot her a glance. 'You *know* about that?'

'I did my research.'

'Bloody journalists,' said Jake, chopping a cabbage in half with venom. 'Why do they call themselves that anyway? They are just a bunch of storytellers who cannot tell – no – who don't care that there is a difference between fact and fiction!'

'What did you do, Chef, stab someone with a carving knife?' asked Godfrey with interest.

'Ha! I wish I had. It was just a small incident a long time ago involving someone whose name I never want to hear again, much less see. And thank you, Godfrey, but I am not homicidal. It's true that I might, very occasionally, when slightly pissed off, chuck the odd, small utensil across the room, but –' He looked at Godfrey. 'You can get your mop and bucket out now and leave my chequered past where it belongs.'

Jake had briefly considered having an opening night party because his bank manager told him he should. Then he realised Mr Biggins couldn't run a restaurant if his life depended on it and he should go with his gut feelings on this. He wanted the food to speak for itself. So he looked sternly at Godfrey.

'I don't want to see a balloon or streamer anywhere near this place and I am prepared to strip-search you if necessary.'

'Don't worry, none of us wants to see him naked either,' said Kirsty, pretending to shudder.

'But why not?' asked Godfrey, who was always in search of a party and free beer.

'Restaurants – good ones – are about having a sublime eating experience and that is what we are going to concentrate on. They are not about gimmicks.'

So Cuisine opened quietly, without any fanfare, one Friday night. The only thing Jake did was make sure that the menu went up well in advance. People were seen licking their lips as they scanned it and because Jake hadn't put anything in the local paper, they were intrigued by the slight air of mystery that surrounded the place.

The first night they were practically full, but Jake wasn't entirely happy.

'I know everyone loved it, but as far as I could tell they were all tourists. We might never see them again.'

'There are plenty more where they came from, Boss,' said Tess.

'Yeah, but this place will have no heart if we can't get regulars in, and that means tempting the locals.'

'They are a cautious lot when it comes to food. Give them time. I'll get my dad to spread the word,' said Godfrey.

'What? On the fells! You said he was once up there for a week without seeing a soul,' scoffed Kirsty.

'That's enough, you lot. We've made a sound start, so well done, everyone!' Then Jake jumped out of his skin and swore, because Godfrey had just let off a party popper.

The owner of the London restaurant where Harry was head chef was a businessman, not a cook, which meant he was always having ideas about making more money, usually at the expense of the food.

He had popped in to see Harry in his office that morning to discuss taking the menu in a new direction.

'New?' echoed Harry in derision, his lip curling with barely concealed contempt. 'Fusion cooking is about as stale as turkey in January.'

'Some of our female customers have commented that the food, though absolutely top notch, of course,' he was rather frightened of Harry, 'is a trifle rich. I was wondering about some lighter alternatives, a menu that would evoke the sunshine and healthy lifestyle of the Southern Hemisphere.'

He was hoping it would also be lighter on the bills.

'Our female customers don't come here to eat, and when

they do they chuck it up half an hour later,' hissed Harry.

Mr Thomas shifted awkwardly in the extremely hard chair Harry had found for him. There was no doubt Harry was a brilliant chef, but it was always touch and go whether he actually remembered he wasn't the boss. The restaurant was successful – there was a two-month waiting list for a table, for a start – but as his accountant had reminded him only that morning, profits were still slim. Mr Thomas didn't care if his customers chose to vomit their dinner up, as long as they kept coming in and paying.

Harry stared at him while his head seethed with insults. This was what happened when you worked for someone. You were prey to every stupid idea they had, and some of this creep's were positively cretinous.

He couldn't just leave Harry to get on with it, could he? At least once a week he would shuffle into Harry's orbit with another 'bright idea' about generating more cash. This of course was always disguised as 'not getting stale' or 'trend-setting' or some other piece of crap culled from ten minutes of watching Jamie Oliver on the television, in between shagging his mistress. Shit, she probably lay there wishing he was Jamie Oliver.

Harry didn't give a crap about people, but he cared passionately about his food. He was tender, understanding and respectful towards ingredients – it was the animals that talked that he had a problem with.

Harry smiled, displaying all his perfectly capped teeth, which made Mr Thomas even more nervous. He should be. Harry was having a delightful fantasy about shoving this prick head first into the kitchen's biggest stockpot. If the wanker wanted to talk food with him, let him experience it close up first.

He was still smiling later as he walked through the double doors into his kitchen, but that was in expectation of finding someone he could pick on. Like Caligula searching the senate for a victim to chuck into the arena, his eyes roved thoughtfully over the rows of bent heads. Everyone's white chef's hats were bobbing like snowdrops in a breeze. The thing about working for Harry was, even though you were utterly convinced you were doing everything right, there was still a good chance of a bollocking so fierce your teeth would rattle.

Harry had mentally rewritten the Ten Commandments to keep him on track in his career. He had found he only needed two:

1. Use only the best ingredients.
2. Rule through terror.

He walked behind his staff, silent as a peckish panther. They quaked in their clogs.

Now his gaze came to rest on the pastry chef, who was trying to make exquisitely tiny lemon tarts, but his hand was shaking so much it slipped and the mixture blobbed onto the work surface. Harry slammed his fist on the counter so hard everyone thought their fillings would fall out. 'What's the matter – got Parkinson's disease?' he enquired nastily.

'Yes, Chef. I mean, no, Chef,' stuttered the poor man.

A commis was making a sauce to go with that night's fillet steak. The recipe had been scalded into his brain the week before. In this kitchen you followed the boss's orders down to the last peppercorn. There was no room here for hesitation, deviation or imagination.

Infuriatingly, he was getting it right. Harry's eyes snapped like an angry bull. He knew he would only feel better when he had head-butted someone.

He picked up a bread roll fresh from the oven and bit into it. He chewed in silence, then grabbed the baker by the scruff of his neck and spat it out, hitting him on the nose. 'This tastes like a dog turd, you tosser – start again.' He tossed the rest of the bread, including the tray, into the bin and stalked out.

Behind him, everyone stroked their knives lovingly, thinking about where they would like to put them.

Feeling marginally better, Harry rang for coffee and settled down to the latest edition of *Hotel and Caterer*. He scanned the jobs column first but no one was prepared to match the extortionate sum he had managed to screw out of Mr Thomas. Then he flicked back to 'Table Talk', the gossip column. There was often something about him there.

Blah, blah, blah, stuff about yet another chef who was making a television series. His lips curled in scorn at people who were prepared to prostitute their talent like that. What was even more annoying was that no one had approached him with a similar offer. He was far more photogenic than this guy, and a better cook. Harry came to the conclusion that it was just because the man was married to some B-list celebrity who was in that idiotic soap *Country Matters*. When she got written out, she'd probably never find another job in television.

His eyes flicked restlessly down the page.

> Word at the stove has it that gastronomes are pulling on their wellies and hiking to the country. The Pied Piper responsible for this exodus is Jake Goldman, who until recently was wowing palates at Brie. Unfortunately, the Jubilee Line doesn't go as far as his new restaurant, Cuisine, which is way up north in a little town called Easedale. Now you've probably not heard of it yet, but we reckon it will soon become as well known as Bray. We ate there last week and have only one thing to say – sublime. Jake has had a very mixed career but . . .

but Harry couldn't bear to read on.

There was a bellow of rage so loud the pastry chef quit on the spot.

Harry flung his cup against the wall, his heart as black and bitter as the tepid coffee dripping down next month's staff rota.

'The bastard! The slimy piece of shit! The . . .' Expletives failed him. He was so incandescent with fury he could practically feel his hair sizzling.

Harry only had to hear Jake's name and he was right back at the time of his greatest (well, only) humiliation. So much time had passed, yet he could still remember what it had felt like to come second. It was like a chronic disease – it was never going to get any better. Whatever he did to Jake, the bastard was going to bounce back, like some indestructible jack-in-the-box. Now, to add insult to injury, he had had the bloody nerve to bounce right into Harry's home territory! Harry sucked air deep into his lungs to get over the shock.

Then another thought struck him, even more teeth-grindingly infuriating than the first. Jake was now his own boss. No more kowtowing to someone else's half-baked ideas about fusion bloody cooking for him! He was bound to be stony broke and on the edge of a nervous breakdown, but he was master of his own fate, king of the kitchen. Harry could feel his veins flooding with corrosive envy. He might be able to make his staff pee in their pants with terror, but he was still at the mercy of his boss's curdled ideas about cooking.

He sat quietly, forcing himself to let the rage seep away so he could think more clearly. He thought affectionately of his aunt Agnes, not because he loved her, but because the old boot had died last month and left him a wad of money. This had been earmarked for a Porsche, but maybe there were more imaginative uses for it?

He smiled to himself. What Jake could do, he could certainly do better.

Chapter Eight

Kate, lying in bubbles, thought about her story. She had been mulling over it for several weeks, but now, with Jonathan backing her that she was on to something, she could feel the excitement welling up inside her. The first thing to do was get a job as a waitress. Well, that wouldn't be difficult. This town was full of restaurants and it wasn't exactly something you would need a qualification for.

Eventually hunger forced her out of the bath. Padding into the kitchen of her light airy flat, she peered hopefully into her fridge. Oh dear. A lot of research would be necessary to convince someone that she knew anything about food. Inside there was a mushroom that had been there so long it had welded itself for ever to the back panel. Next to that was a pack of bacon. Was it the fridge light or was it really giving off a greenish glow? And how long had those eggs been there? Kate was sure there was a method for determining whether eggs were fresh, but she was vague on the details. If they floated in water, were they rotten, or was it the other way round? Really, the only culinary knowledge she possessed was a nodding acquaintance with salmonella.

Kate toyed with the idea of ordering a pizza, but judging

by the stack of takeaway boxes piled up by the bin, she'd had a few too many of those recently. Basically, they were just bread and cheese, weren't they? Surely one needed to supplement one's diet with other food groups occasionally? While flinging on a T-shirt and a skirt, she realised she wanted company as well as dinner, so she rang Lydia.

Lydia was the editor's secretary and her best friend. Five foot ten inches tall, sometimes blonde and sometimes not, as the mood took her, she drank mostly by the pint and smoked Marlboro Lights by the carton. Lydia often claimed that the only thing she was ever prepared to give up was the belief that men could act like decent human beings. Kate called it tough love, as men tended to swarm to Lydia like lustful lemmings, regardless of how she treated them.

They had been friends ever since one excruciatingly awful office party, when they got blindingly drunk and discovered a mutual contempt for people who photocopied their own bottoms because they thought it was funny.

Lydia was also the newspaper's agony aunt, a job no one else in the office was prepared to take on, on the grounds that it wasn't proper journalism and therefore beneath them. Lydia said this wasn't a problem: 'If being a proper journalist means I have to look like you, you scruffy lot, then I'm delighted to be counted out.' She wrote extremely well, with great imagination and verve, which was because she made up most of the queries.

'Honestly, darling, what would you rather read over your morning cuppa – boring crap about how to get a stain out of a tea towel or the really thrilling life history of a transvestite farmer who insists on feeding the cows while wearing his wife's knickers?'

'Put like that . . .' giggled Kate, then became serious. 'Honestly, I know you think us hacks are a scruffy bunch, but with your talent you should really think about giving up being a secretary and taking up writing for a living.'

'What, and have to go to work at weekends? You must be joking,' retorted Lydia, who maintained she needed regular days off to have her nails done and indulge in some abuse of men.

Now Lydia picked up the phone on the third ring.

'I'm not disturbing you doing anything important, like housework, for instance?' asked Kate, and they both snorted with laughter. Lydia was always stunningly turned out, while her flat looked like the scene of a burglary. Kate maintained that if someone ever did break in, it would take them so long to find anything, there would be ample time to call the police.

'How the hell do you live like this?' she asked, the first time she had gone back there.

'Well, if it gets too bad I just take out my contact lenses.'

Half an hour later Lydia knocked at Kate's door. She went to answer it with a grin – Lydia's dress sense was always something else.

Today she was six-inch heels, black footless tights and a top from Topshop that was meant to be knee length but on Lydia skimmed her thighs in a jaw-dropping manner. It was also shocking pink.

'You are going to clash horribly with my hair,'

complained Kate as Lydia followed her through to the sitting room.

'Oh, for goodness' sake, I keep telling you, life is not about being co-ordinated,' said Lydia, marching in and looking round with great disapproval.

To anyone else, the flat would seem perfectly pleasant. It had cheerful light blue walls, warm wooden floors and was completely uncluttered, apart from the shelves full of books. Lydia thought it was monastic and that it showed Kate was repressing something vital in her emotional life. 'I see things haven't changed round here. You should really see someone about that. I think you've got issues.'

'Do you mean that pile of old copies of the *Guardian*? Seriously, I think you are talking rubbish. I cannot bear mess around me and I certainly can't work in it.'

'Yes, but life shouldn't be like that, not at our age. There should always be something slightly out of control and dangerous about it,' said Lydia, her eyes gleaming.

Kate sat down to pull on a pair of boots. Then she checked her freckled nose in the mirror, decided it wasn't too shiny and that she was ready to go out.

'You know your tights are laddered, don't you?'

Kate craned her neck to look round and nearly fell over. 'Oh, bother! Well, I can't see it so I'm going to pretend it isn't there. I need a large drink and some food more urgently than a change of clothes.'

Lydia sighed. 'What really annoys me is the fact that this "I couldn't care less" attitude really suits you. You are far too low-maintenance.'

'I prefer to maintain myself, actually,' said Kate.

They walked down the street and into the first bar they found.

Kate took a huge slug of her wine and said: 'So, whose lives are you interfering with now?'

Lydia took an envelope and a pair of glasses from her bag.

'Since when did you opt for glasses over contact lenses?'

'I haven't. I just like the way these make me look sometimes.'

'You look like you're getting ready to spank someone.'

'I know,' said Lydia smugly. 'Anyway, to business. I am thinking about inventing a woman who is having affairs simultaneously with three men. There are so many problems associated with this that I think it could run and run.'

'How will it end?'

'Oh, the poor woman will be so drained by what I am going to put her through, she will probably decide she's gay.'

'And does any reality ever filter through to your problem page?'

'Funny you should ask. I am just about to reply to a woman who's been having an affair with a married colleague.'

'Save your ink – it's completely over,' said Kate.

'I'm thrilled for you, honestly I am. It's not that I don't like Jonathan – actually, I don't really like him, but that's irrelevant – I just think you weren't doing each other any good. How do you feel?'

Cautiously, Kate prodded her feelings. 'Actually, I feel free,' she said slowly. 'A bit lonely, but not in a bad way. And

I think I've got a new project to take my mind off things so that will help.' She told Lydia about the idea for the 'Chefs Uncovered' story, as she was now thinking of it.

'Brilliant. Chefs are supposed to be very good with their hands, aren't they?' Lydia winked knowingly.

'Going to bed with a chef is the last thing on my mind at the moment, Lydia,' Kate sighed.

'Well, it shouldn't be the last thing. Obviously for a career woman and a feminist it shouldn't be the first thing either, but it should always be there, a sort of permanent memo to self – you know, number four on a to-do list: must have a shag.'

'I'll bear that in mind.'

'Aim higher this time. Jonathan is a clever man, but you are brighter.'

'It *was* a bit of a turn-off to discover that the sole topic of his post-coital conversation was the endlessly fascinating subject of himself,' said Kate ruefully. 'The thing was, I think I was drawn to him because we are both obsessed by our careers. But maybe that was the only thing we had in common.'

Lydia ordered tequila shots. 'A toast – to a new start!'

'Toast! That reminds me, I'm starving!'

'Shut up and drink up. We can eat later.'

'Come on – let's find somewhere with a menu.'

Unfortunately the next bar didn't serve food. While Kate was finding this out, Lydia had spotted a karaoke machine and insisted they waited for her turn.

'But no more shots. I shall stick to wine, so much more sensible,' said Kate.

They ran into some friends and spent a pleasant hour chatting. Then Lydia got up, put on her glasses, peered down at the microphone and gave the bar her unique interpretation of two Shirley Bassey numbers.

'That was word perfect!' said Kate when she had sat down to huge applause. 'Not really note perfect, but with your legs, I don't think anyone cared.' For some reason she found this very funny and laughed so hard she started choking.

'That wasn't your glass of water you've just downed in one, that was wine,' said Lydia.

'I know!' said Kate, now very drunk. 'Come on, time for a change of scene.'

They said goodbye to the girls and, as Kate weaved her way between the tables, it occurred to her that she hadn't actually managed to eat anything yet. As an eating companion Lydia was a useless choice. Her idea of a healthy diet was coming home to three gin and tonics and a packet of Twiglets. When she went out for a meal she spent most of her time smoking and eyeing up the waiters. Really, for her, a good restaurant was an ashtray and a man who wore an apron well.

'I'm in charge of this evening now,' said Kate, staggering as the fresh air collided with her large intake of wine and tequila. 'Now we really have to find a mule . . . I mean, a meal.' Bloody hell! How much had she drunk? She began counting on her fingers, but kept forgetting which drink she was up to. Rather blurrily she began scanning the street. 'Restaurant at ten o'clock – look!' and she grabbed Lydia, who was trying to reapply her lipstick.

'Oops, sorry. Don't think it's meant to go down your chin.'

Lydia looked at her sternly. 'Honestly, you are such a lightweight.'

'I've drunk about half a barrel of grapes on a empty stomach, that's why. Do you think that counts for my five fruit and veg a day? she said, tripping over the kerb. Her boots suddenly felt too big and she started to giggle again.

The menu outside the restaurant, which was called Cuisine, seemed to be written in a language she wasn't familiar with and the letters just wouldn't stay put on the page.

'Yum. Dover shole baked with spinach. No, that can't be right, I mean – spole – no . . . oh hell, let's just go in.'

They sat down at the bar, or, in Kate's case, tried to. Eventually Lydia managed to hoist her up.

'Where's the manager? I'd like to make a complaint – his stools are too slippery!'

The young guy behind the bar said his name was Hans and could he help, but Kate had lost interest and was trying to focus on the menu.

'My God, it's expensive here!'

'That's because you are seeing everything, including the prices, in triplicate,' explained Lydia patiently. Her diet of gin and Twiglets had made her fairly resistant to getting drunk.

Completely cross-eyed now, Kate was trying to read a notice pinned up behind the bar.

'Giraffe wanted,' she read out laboriously. 'What do they

want a giraffe for? They'd have a hell of a job fitting it in the oven, y'know.'

'Staff. Not giraffe.' Lydia was becoming aware that Kate, like all drunks, was talking far too loudly and people were glancing their way.

Kate nodded solemnly. Leaning over the bar, she said in what she clearly thought was a quiet tone: 'Hello, Hansel . . . Gretel . . . oh, whatever. Do you know that your eyes are tiny little pinpricks in your face? I think you had a whopping great joint before coming to work. But why? Is your boss a beast? Does he maintain discipline through the use of a rolling pin? Does he make your life hell?' Automatically, she felt in her pocket for her notebook.

'No. I save all that for idiotic customers,' said an icy voice behind her.

Kate swivelled round, a bad move. A glass skittered onto the floor and she lost her balance. But just before the ground rushed up to make contact with her nose, the man grabbed her and hoisted her upright. For a minute, their faces were so close she could have kissed him. Wanted to, she decided. OK, his eyes were looking absolutely furious at this moment, but they were very nice eyes, even though they were shadowed with tiredness. Furious, but gorgeous – a dazzling combination. Oh God, she hadn't said that out loud, had she?

'Are you going to go quietly, or do I have to shove you?' said the man, looking as if he would much prefer to do the latter.

Kate grabbed Lydia's arm and said, 'Please.'

'Absolutely,' said Lydia, who completely understood this

to mean, roughly: I am as drunk as a skunk – get me out of here, now!

'Thank you so much . . . delightful menu . . . wonderful ambience . . . will certainly be back. Or not, whichever you prefer . . . I mean, it's absolutely up to you,' she mumbled as she was dragged out.

Lydia's arm wasn't enough, so she clasped the nearest lamppost with fervour. 'I feel sick. Too much drink and lusht – sorry, mean lust. He was stern but sexy. I like men like that. Don't you agree? Why is that, then?'

'Tell you what, I'll come round and tell you tomorrow. It will take your mind off the fact that you've got your head down the loo.'

Chapter Nine

Godfrey's face was almost as red as the beetroot soup he was learning to make. He and every surface within a three-foot radius were covered in debris. Jake didn't mind about the floor or the fact that Godfrey looked very silly with parsley in his hair, but he minded a lot about his worktops.

'That garlic is far too close to the dough, which should have gone in the fridge an hour ago, and those carrot peelings should be in the bin by now. You've finished prepping up the stock so TIDY UP!'

It was always the same. They always wanted to cook when what they should be doing was learning how to organise themselves first.

'Look at the state of you! You don't know where you're at because everything is in such an awful mess! What did I say to you when we began? You wipe your board down after every job and you wipe your knives clean after you've used them, just like you wipe your arse after every crap!' He grinned.

Everyone laughed. Poor Godfrey, who had been feeling that everything was spiralling out of control, watched with gratitude as Jake swiftly reduced chaos to order with a few deft gestures.

'But you are always on my back shouting at me to hurry up. It makes me so confused,' protested Godfrey. Cooking at home was never like this.

Jake smiled, but sympathetically. 'Of course you're confused – you're a novice. But that shouldn't stop you trying. Work at it and it will come right, which I admit in your case will take so long I'll probably have given up the will to live, but miracles may happen. I was in your shoes once.'

The kitchen chorused gleefully: 'Never, Chef! You were born perfect, Chef!'

Godfrey sighed happily. He loved it here, the heat, the terror, the frantic pace, even the insults. This was a good thing because they rained down on him so regularly he should really take an umbrella to work. But he knew he had already learned more than he ever had in the back of the class at school, where he had spectacularly failed every exam he turned up for. His head was now so full of information he thought he might burst. In fact, last night he had, but that was only because he was tasting every dish on the go, as well as eating three large meals a day.

It was ironic, given that he was a cook, that Jake couldn't actually recall the last time he had sat down to a proper meal. He tasted all the time as well, of course, and still carried three tasting spoons in his pocket as he had been taught at college, but a whole meal – like normal people?

Chance would be a very fine thing indeed, he mused, pouring himself a cup of coffee, which was destined to follow the fate of all the others and go cold before he got time to drink it. He went through to his office. The staff were clearing up and pushing off for a kip before evening shift but he had a pile of paperwork to catch up on, a job he hated and always put off as long as possible. This was the tedious side of running a business.

He made a mental note to order more wine glasses to replace the ones that had gone the way of all glassware. Hans should have done this, as bar manager, but he had been totally useless today, getting orders wrong and losing bills.

'What you smoke when you are off duty is entirely up to you. But if you turn up for work again off your head, you will be sacked on the spot. Is that clear?'

'Absolutely,' said Hans unhappily. He was enjoying working for Jake and didn't want to blow it. Hans was a wannabe hippy and Jake was forever having to tear down posters that he had put up advertising protest marches.

'But, why, Boss? The plight of the coffee farmers in Brazil is *schrecklich*, I mean terrible!' he had protested a few days earlier.

'I agree, but the march took place last Saturday. In London. When we were slightly busy. None of us could have got there. Why don't you spend your afternoon off sourcing some decent fairly traded coffee for the restaurant to use?'

Also, fighting with Hans's hippy spirit was a Teutonic drive towards neatness and order. Generally, all the restaurant glasses stood to sparkling attention behind the bar like a crack troop in the army, and customers' bills were lined up as if they were on parade. But now Hans was so upset at the thought of losing his job that he had a disastrous lunchtime shift and got so many things wrong he was convinced Jake was going to sack him anyway, especially when he called Hans into his office.

'I bollocked you this morning and you deserved it, but I don't bear grudges, so chill out, man.'

Hans grinned and went off much happier.

What else was there to do? Oh, yes, the toilet in the men's loo was only flushing when it felt like it, which wasn't often enough. He could call a plumber, but it would be cheaper to fix it himself. Jake yawned and stretched – the life of a chef was such a glamorous one.

Also he had to write a prep list for Godfrey. It was imperative to give beginners at least ten things to do all at once at the beginning of their shift. It focused their little minds and taught them to move swiftly and with grace. At the moment Godfrey was blundering around like a small hippo on steroids. It was going to be a long haul.

Tess put her head round the door. 'Someone to see you, Boss.'

It was the drunken redhead from the night before, ghostly pale under an enormous pair of dark glasses. Jake hadn't ever realised before how attractive red hair was. This made him even crosser. He groaned, and then snapped: 'I suppose – well, I hope – you've come to apologise. I'm not sure I need this now.'

'You're right, I have. I am sorry to bother you, but you must let me grovel.'

'It will be my pleasure.' He waved her in impatiently.

Oh dear. He wasn't at all pleased to see her. Shame. She'd thought this had been an excellent plan. 'Staff needed.' So here she was. And despite her throbbing head

Kate was enjoying seeing him. He looked as tired as she did, though, but why? I bet he didn't spend the night throwing up, she thought.

'I am interested in just how many ways you can say sorry for last night. But don't throw up on this expensive carpet or I will have to hurt you.'

The carpet was actually threadbare and barely worth small change, but it gave her a faint glimmer of hope. He obviously had a sense of humour, so this might just work.

'There's nothing else to express but my shame. My deep shame. I am abject. I behaved appallingly.'

'You certainly did. You were a complete idiot and you looked like you got plenty of practice at it.' He shuffled some papers around on his very untidy desk in order to cover up a picture of the kitchen at work, as depicted by Angelica.

'It's no excuse, but I had too much wine on too little food. It won't happen again, I promise. I'm not really like that.'

'No, it won't. People have been booted out of restaurants before now for asking for some salt. I think I am quite within my rights to hope never to see you again.' He hoped he looked as if he really meant it.

'No chance of a job, then?'

Jake's jaw dropped.

'Yes, I know it's a huge cheek but you don't get anywhere without chutzpah, do you?' She took off her glasses and fixed him with what she hoped was an honest, open gaze.

'You want an answer right away? How about: I would sooner cut off my right foot?'

'Of course you would and who would blame you?'

Think, Kate. Except that today this was a bit like asking Steve Redgrave to row through treacle. Food – what did she know about it? Oh. Nothing. But she had flicked through the biography of a chef this morning, in between waiting to throw up.

'You are tired,' she said, trying to sound soothing. 'Your headache is probably worse than mine. You won't have slept properly in weeks and when you do, you have terrible nightmares. You just know your supplier will forget to deliver the mushrooms and no one will tell you until tonight, when you need them. Your punters will complain the steak tartare is undercooked and your commis will think it's really funny to lock a waitress in the walk-in freezer. All you want to do is cook and shout at your staff, but someone has lost the corkscrew and your waitress keeps getting *concasse* and *consommé* mixed up.

'Now, you might not be ready to believe this, but I am your salvation. I speak fluent English when I'm sober, which I will be for the rest of my life, I can assure you. I am intelligent, hard-working and dependable. In time you will forget last night ever happened.'

Despite himself, Jake was intrigued. That description was nothing like his own kitchen, of course, but . . . Then he looked pointedly at her Gucci sunglasses. 'If you can afford those why do you want to work here, where your pay packet will be so small you may need prescription glasses even to see it?'

Excellent. She had got her foot firmly wedged in the door. The rest should be a piece of cake. Oops, don't think about food.

'It's a good point. For the last five years I've been working in advertising, where to be frank, I probably earned more than all your staff put together. I was made redundant. Sure, I had some job offers lined up, but it seemed the right time to start working on the novel I've been planning since I left university. I've given myself a year to get it into print but my savings won't last that long without some extra income.' Well, she was going to write a story of sorts, wasn't she?

'What's it about?'

'What's what about?'

'Your book,' he said patiently.

'Oh.' Blast. She really hadn't thought this one through properly. 'It's, er, an historical novel about smugglers in the Lake District.'

'I think it's been done before,' he said kindly.

Bloody hell! He should be too busy to know about literature.

'Well, there's always room for another,' she said firmly.

Jake had a suspicion there was a hidden agenda here, though he couldn't work out what it was. But then waitressing was a job plenty of people did while they were trying to do something else. He had employed budding ballerinas, actresses, even a guy who was considering going into the priesthood. Most of them were still there, toiling away and dreaming, apart from the priest, who had gone off to become an accountant. He thought, I do need another waitress pretty damn quick. She seems quite bright and she can walk in a straight line when she's sober. She's very nice to look at. What the hell has that got to do with anything?

'You look like you can serve food without spilling it, I suppose,' he said, aiming to sounded grudging and barely interested. 'If you work for me you will be smartly dressed and sober at all times. Your shifts will finish when the customers leave – it's their call, not yours. I will not tolerate any whining about your workload, your wages or any pathetic excuses for turning up for work late. Ditto excuses for not turning up at all. Sickness, death, plague – I've heard them all before and none of them moves me in the slightest. So, to sum up, you will adopt an unfailing courtesy to the punters and an unfailing commitment to the work I will pile on you. Oh, and anything you break will be taken out of your wages. Is that clear?'

She wondered if he knew how sexy he was when he glowered. Anyone who worked for him probably spent their holidays chilling out on a labour camp in Siberia, just for light relief.

'The only reason I am offering you a job is because I want to punish you for last night. You can start tonight at five thirty on a week's trial. You won't get paid until the end of the week, just in case you do turn out to be a moron, after all.'

'Thank you so much!'

'Oh, I don't think you are going to be grateful,' he said grimly.

She stood up to escape and promptly dropped her bag. Its contents, included a slightly battered tampon, spilled out across the floor. Jake picked up her diary, which was the sort that had a supposedly uplifting but actually nauseating message at the start of each day. Lydia had bought it for her as a joke.

'Apparently today you will feel the spirit of change flowing through your body,' he read out mockingly.

Outside Kate decided that the only things flowing through *her* body were blood vessels soaked in alcohol. Never mind, a kip and some invalid food and she would be as right as rain. She felt very pleased with herself. This guy had fascinated her – in a purely professional capacity, of course – from the moment she had first clapped eyes on him. It was shame that when all this was over and Jake found out his kitchen had been harbouring a traitor, he would want her blood in a mixing bowl, but that was the price she would have to pay for being a spy.

Kate spent the afternoon snoozing and dipping into Antony Bourdain's cooking memoirs. In growing disbelief. The chefs seemed to spend their time taking vast quantities of drugs, playing nasty jokes on their colleagues and shagging everyone in sight. She giggled. They sounded a bit like journalists, actually.

In between small bites of dry toast, she logged onto the Internet, where waiters had their own website. The ways they took revenge on awkward customers would put you off eating out ever again. They broke every health and safety rule in the book, and the things they did to people's meals before they served them made her want to gag. Some of it wouldn't go down in a family newspaper. Well, she could get round it with innuendo and, anyway, stuff like this could easily be sent to the national tabloids.

It was time to get ready for work. She cast a longing eye at her bed then focused on the contents of her wardrobe. It was important to get this right. She didn't want to be too smart and therefore too conspicuous, but she was determined to make an impression. She wanted to make Jake respect her and take her into his confidence. Her long-sleeved woollen top was flattering and drew people's eyes to her breasts (never a bad thing), and she had a tight black skirt, which skimmed her figure nicely but wasn't obviously tarty. Now for shoes. Fuck-me stilettos were obviously out, but the pointy, kitten heels she wore to work would do.

The last thing she did was tuck a small notebook into her bag. There was bound to be the odd quiet moment when she could nip to the loo and jot down some notes.

When she arrived, feeling surprisingly nervous, the kitchen was already full of people. Jake looked up from where he was chopping furiously.

'Everyone, this is Kate. Kate, this is Tess on starters, Sally on puddings, Godfrey, our trainee, Tom washing up and Kirsty, head waitress, because until you arrived, she was our only waitress. She'll show you the ropes. Godfrey, explain to me why you have just put that knife into the dishwasher pointed end up. Are you planning to throw yourself on it now or later? I would prefer it if you waited until you've filled the salad tray.'

Godfrey said no, I mean yes, and then looked confused.

'Follow me,' said Kirsty. Mystified, Kate watched her dextrously pinch a bread roll on her way out.

'Here you are.' Kirsty tossed the roll across to Hans, who was washing glasses.

'Thanks, *Liebchen*. Didn't get any tea,' he explained. Then he saw Kate.

Before he could say anything she rushed in, 'I am sorry

about last night. I was way out of order. I am really sorry if I got you into trouble.'

He shrugged, then he smiled. 'You did, but I deserved it and everything is OK now.'

'Cool. I like your earring, by the way,' she said.

'Ooh – where did you get that done? Never mind, better tell me later,' said Kirsty. 'OK, we have this system here: that bit is Main – tables one to eight; then there is Annexe – tables nine to twelve, and Back – twelve A, I'm superstitious, to eighteen. The table in the middle is just called Middle.'

Kate looked at Kirsty blankly. What in God's name was she talking about?

Her confusion must have showed in her face because Kirsty explained patiently: 'It's how we make a note of the checks, so we know who we are serving. Oh hell, you really haven't done this before, have you? The checks are the food orders. Get them wrong and you are dead. We write a table number on the checks so we know where to take the food to. You think you are going to remember but, believe me, when it gets busy you won't.

'Always make sure the light over the porch is switched on. Jake gets really mad if we forget. Watch out for that table – it sticks out a bit.' Kate rubbed her thigh. She was going to have a massive bruise there later.

Back in the kitchen, Kirsty continued, 'This is called the pass, where Jake passes the food to you and bollocks you for not taking it quickly enough. Checks go here. Shout them out before putting them down, otherwise Jake goes –'

'Ballistic. Yes, I get the picture,' said Kate. How did he

find time to cook if he was so busy having tantrums she wondered.

'Jake is a bit like my mate Amy's dad,' confided Kirsty. 'His real name is Bernard, but we call him Yogi because he's got this really deep voice and it reminds you of –'

'Why is he like Jake?' Kate was a professional at cutting through drivel to get to facts. Kirsty didn't stand a chance with her.

'What? Oh, yes, he likes to act tougher than he really is. He's good at looking fierce but he's really a big softie underneath.'

Kate's first job was to slice bread, one loaf with walnuts, another with onions and rosemary. They smelled heavenly and her mouth watered.

The atmosphere seemed quite calm and controlled, even relaxed. People were slicing and stirring, and Sally was doing something quite complicated with vanilla pods and raspberries. Everything looked and smelled delicious. Jake and Tess were bantering in a friendly manner. She looked like a tough piece who could take care of herself.

Kate studied Jake covertly. He moved with a fluid grace, utterly sure of himself and, despite the jokes, completely focused on what he was doing.

She was setting up the coffee machine when the first guests arrived. Kirsty greeted them, took their coats and a drinks order and gave them menus with the ease borne of long practice. The first check came down to the kitchen swiftly followed by another. Kate tried to match Kirsty's apparently unhurried glide and thought she was doing quite well.

'We've got another booking for eight at eight and two more casuals,' said Kirsty.

Kate sashayed out with another basket of bread. God, people guzzled the stuff, she thought crossly, forgetting that was exactly what she did when she went out.

Oh. Where had all these people come from? She had to push past them to deliver the bread and once there she stopped to chat for a minute. It seemed that waitresses had to do Jake's PR as well as serve. We should be paid more, she thought crossly.

'Where the hell have you been?' snarled Jake when she got back. Kate blinked. She had only been gone a minute. She was yet to realise that a lot could happen in a kitchen during that time. She had left calm and order but now all hell had broken out. There were loads of plates waiting for her and a bear in a bad mood tapping his foot impatiently.

'Two soups – Main three; four mains – Annexe nine, and where are the starters from table two? You took them out ages ago. Get a move on, these plates have been here far too long. And you are writing a check, not *War and Peace*. You don't have to regurgitate the entire menu. I know what's on it – I bloody wrote it! Godfrey – sauté pan, please . . . Godfrey, where's that fucking pan? Sally, that cake has to come out of the oven, NOW! Tess, how's the Parma ham lasting?'

'Fine, Chef, slicing nicely. This rocket's shit, though.'

'Too late, can't do anything about it now. Give them lamb's lettuce instead and tell me sooner next time, will you?'

'Yes, Chef.'

'Right, two lamb – table seven, away now!'

'Ow, shit!'

'Oh, yes, remember to tell them the plates are hot and what the fuck do you think the serving cloths are for?'

Kate couldn't remember where any of the tables were now, or what she was serving or which way round the bloody plate was supposed to go.

'Godfrey, stop gasping and drink some water before you completely dehydrate. Sally, there won't be any raspberries left by nine o'clock at the rate you are using them up – sauté pan, please – what was wrong with that meal – there was nothing wrong with that meal!'

Everyone held their breath.

'Nothing, Boss. The punters are ancient – couldn't manage it all. Said it was wonderful, though,' said Kirsty calmly.

'OK,' said Jake, mollified, chucking a huge slug of brandy into a pan so that the flames shot up to the ceiling. The first time he'd done it, Kate had nearly called the fire brigade.

After that everything became a bit of a blur for her. Sneakily taking notes – ha! That would have been funny if she'd had time to laugh. She didn't have time to blow her nose. She barely had time to breathe. The kitchen had gone into some sort of manic overdrive and not only was she expected to go with it, but apparently she had to develop psychic powers as well and anticipate what everyone was going to say or want. Except that she couldn't. She just wasn't fast enough. It was like trying to ice-skate while wearing wellingtons. She had always felt quite smug about her ability to deal with the stress of a reporters' room and keep her cool, but now she knew there just weren't enough compartments in her head for all the little scenarios in which she was a small, but important, player. Everyone's meals were at different stages and she had to keep up with all of them, like Kirsty was doing, serving coffee to one table, explaining the wine list to another. Kirsty even seemed to know the name of the bloomin' sheep who had donated a leg to the party in the corner!

Kate began to hate the customers. She already loathed Jake and anyone else who gave her another plate to take out, God knows where.

For heaven's sake, salmon or steak, just bloody choose. It's not brain surgery! Don't you idiots realise I have three tables to clear while you are faffing around? Six coffees to get and, oh God, I forgot to ask how table eight wanted their steaks – where is table eight?

She was boiling hot in that stupid jumper, and when she asked Kirsty why the windows weren't open, Kirsty just laughed.

'You might be hot, but the customers aren't. Wear a sensible top next time.'

Bloody customers. They had to have everything their own way!

The kitchen was now a tornado of movement – pans slammed onto hobs, oven doors opened and slammed shut, and knives and spoons flashing. It was like some bizarre off-the-wall ballet, with everyone ducking and diving and, amazingly, not bumping into each other. They were all doing ten different things at once. She felt that she couldn't do anything.

Kirsty was brilliant. Nothing fazed her and her nose wasn't even shiny, whereas Kate could feel the sweat on her forehead and running down her shoulder blades. She quite expected to hear herself dripping every time she took a step.

It was all very upsetting. She hadn't felt this out of control and, well, scared, since her first day at big school.

She was just starting to think that it would be nice to die quietly, if only there was a corner free to do so, when it all seemed to be over and the kitchen, which had turned into a tape on fast forward, now turned back into real time.

'Not a bad night, everyone. A bit quiet, but we will really get into gear at the weekend,' said Jake, wiping down surfaces with great speed. He seemed quite relaxed.

Kate stopped for a minute, but then wished she hadn't, because she now discovered her feet were on fire and there were pains shooting up and down her legs, which she had been too busy to notice before. Her kitten heels, which had been fine for walking round an office, now felt like something the Spanish Inquisition could have used when they required a little information. Her feet had grown to at least a size ten. Any minute now they would burst out of her shoes and explode all over the kitchen floor.

'You did . . . er . . . how can I describe it? Oh, yes – you were crap, but I expect you'll be better tomorrow,' said Kirsty hopefully.

'Why, are we closed?'

Kirsty laughed.

The grim truth dawned on Kate. Oh God, she had to go through all this again tomorrow! This wasn't a job, it was

Jake's version of Dante's Hell. They were doomed perpetually to try to fill hordes of gaping mouths for ever and ever, amen. There was no respite. Even now, when all those demanding, picky people had gone, they had to make everything ready for the next lot. She was so tired she could barely remember which way round the knives and forks were supposed to go. Even when she had finally worked it out, she got a bollocking from Kirsty, who seemed to think that hiding the stains on the tablecloths by covering them with wine glasses and salt cellars instead of going to find new ones wasn't environmentally friendly and labour saving – it was idle and slipshod and NOT how they did things at this restaurant.

'Would you want to spend a small fortune eating at a place that did things like that?'

Well, no, she wouldn't, but that was in the days when she hadn't had the slightest consideration for the people who had to work in restaurants.

Finally, the kitchen was back to its sparkling, immaculate, original condition. But Kate watched in amazement and horror. Jake was starting to get pans out again.

'What the hell are you doing? Surely we don't do a midnight shift? Please, God – no!'

'I'm cooking supper for you all,' said Jake in surprise. 'I usually do, you know. Everyone has worked hard and now they are hungry.'

Kate stood and watched him chopping onions and garlic and tossing them deftly in a pan with some tomatoes and black olives. She wasn't hungry, but her legs had gone on strike. Also, it was fascinating how Jake had metamorphosed from a snarling tyrant into a nice human being again.

'My dad says if you promise to leave the garlic at home, he'll come for supper one night,' said Kirsty, getting out bowls and cutlery. 'He said you look a lot like a man he once knew but I don't know how he knows that, 'cos he never wears his specs and we all know he's as blind as a bat without them. Why, only the other day –'

'I don't think I've ever met your dad, have I? How does he know me?'

Kirsty stared at him. 'You've lived here for ages now – well, weeks – of course he knows you. He knows how old you are and that you haven't got any brothers or sisters –'

'Well, that must be weird,' interrupted Godfrey, who had four sisters and never knew a moment's peace at home. 'This is the country, Jake; everyone knows everything about you already,' he explained.

'I can't get the hang of this,' grumbled Jake. 'In London, I could walk the streets all day and never see anyone I knew.'

'Me auntie Mary, you know – the one who was married first to the man whose brother used to help Godfrey's dad with his dry-stone walling? Well, after they split up – which wasn't a day too soon as far as we were concerned – she took up with that John who she's married to now – anyway, the woman who lived in the cottage they bought after they had baby John, my cousin –'

Jake had started to laugh. 'Sorry, do go on, it's just a bit confusing. It's my fault, I'm a bit tired.'

She gave him a long look, then carried on, talking slowly,

as if to an idiot: 'Anyway, she used to say she knew the names of everyone in her village.'

'That's hardly difficult! There's only twenty people live in Hawsgill. It's really just a small street in the middle of nowt!' scoffed Tess.

'Well, I didn't know who it was lived two doors down from us when I was a kid, but that was because the police took them away in the middle of the night,' put in Jake, to stop the argument.

'Ah, so you're a city boy – that's why you work at a manic pace,' said Kate.

'No, that's because I'm a chef,' grinned Jake. 'OK, everyone – eat!'

After the meal, when Kate stood up to go, her legs felt so brittle she thought they might snap. She was going for her coat with the tottering gait of a very old woman, when Jake said: 'See you bright and early tomorrow – oh, sorry – I mean later on today!' There was an unpleasant glint in his eye. The bastard, he had enjoyed seeing her suffer! It was only the thought of a very long, hot bath that got her home.

'Soothing relief for tired muscles' read the label on the box of bubble bath. Hmm, it was going to have to work harder than that. What she really needed was another, better pair of legs.

Easing herself into the bath – yes, there was a huge bruise on her thigh from that bloody table at the start of the evening – she made some essential mental notes. Not for her story – sod that. This was survival stuff.

1. Run away. I wish.
2. Buy a very thin cotton blouse so don't have to spend entire evening feeling like a large, melting ice lolly.
3. Buy some very sensible shoes, no matter how hideous they look. The important thing here is comfort, not style. Also, no one ever seems to look at a waitress anyway, so it won't matter.
4. Source a supply of industrial-strength anti-perspirant.
5. Source a supply of industrial-strength painkillers . . .

Then she was asleep.

Chapter Ten

The next day Kate couldn't believe how sore her feet still were. She had blisters the size of shallots on both heels and she had washed her hair three times to try to get the food smells out of it. After the third go she had given up. She would have to resign herself to smelling like a frying pan for ever.

Her legs ached. She was in far too much pain to switch her laptop on.

Bollocks. That was a terrible excuse, even for her. You wrote with your hands, not with your feet, and anyway, you did it sitting down.

Take some bloody aspirin and get to work, she told herself fiercely.

She had to jot down some impressions of last night before she forgot them. She wished, actually, that she could forget them.

She had meant to do some work the night before, but when she woke up in the cooling bath she knew she was being way over-ambitious. 'Tomorrow and tomorrow and tomorrow . . .' she had muttered to herself, before falling into bed.

But when you are a writer tomorrow really does come.

Deadlines, editor's threats or simple poverty – one of these will eventually force you to put pen to paper.

But she hated this moment, staring at a blank screen that should be filled with words.

What was the time? Damn, only ten minutes since she had last looked. Was there a delaying tactic she could use? The windows of her flat could certainly do with being cleaned because, to Kate's knowledge, they never had been. Her plants, which had long ago learned, as does a camel, that water was something they wouldn't see much of, were in their perpetual state of nearly dead. But watering them would mean getting up and she wasn't going to do that until she absolutely had to. Besides, if she started watering them, they were going to expect this sort of treatment all the time.

What could she write anyway? Something along the lines of how crap a waitress she had been, probably.

She hadn't been in any way prepared for the urgency, stress and aggression you need just to feed a few people. Everyone got caught up in it apart from Kate, a pathetic and incompetent straggler. But Jake was at the centre, the eye of the storm, as it were, an all-seeing eye that could spot faults, cook and bark orders all at the same time. It made her tired just thinking about it, though it was also quite compelling, like getting hooked by a film or a book you never thought you would enjoy.

Jake himself was quite compelling, though undoubtedly a masochist. You had to be to work under such hideous conditions. But she liked the gleam of humour that ran under the surface of his tantrums and she liked the fact that he was so obviously driven. If he looked at his women the way he had looked at that piece of steak last night, it could be quite exciting. This, despite being an absorbing train of thought, would cut no ice with the readers of the *Easedale Gazette*, though one of the tabloids might take a short piece on 'Shagging the Chef'.

She sighed, wriggled her toes, just to confirm that they still hurt like hell, and proceeded to fill her screen with what she later decided was the biggest load of drivel she had ever written.

Steak was also on Jake's mind that afternoon. He cradled the phone against his ear so he could examine a new blister on his left hand and insult his supplier at the same time.

'Mr Bleasdon, I really don't care if you removed that fillet off the cow with your own bare hands, I don't care if it was hand-reared from grass in your own garden. The meat you sent me was tougher than a rugby player's jockstrap. You would need teeth made of steel to get through it and the sort of digestive tract that my customers, being human, simply don't possess . . . Yes, there is every need to talk like that. Frankly, I'm surprised you've not heard it before. . . . Well, there's always a first time, isn't there? . . . But I know exactly what can be done about it if you –' He waited patiently for a few minutes until the blustering had died down. 'No, Mr Bleasdon, this is what you are going to do. You are going to send me another fillet. It will arrive in my kitchen in half an hour. It will be free, as a sincere apology for trying to fob me off with inedible crap the first time. Then it might be possible for us to continue to do business together.'

Jake then quietly put the phone down on Mr Bleasdon

(family butchers since 1886 and never a customer as picky as this) and winced. The blister was now a small wound and about to drip blood onto next week's menu plan. He went into the kitchen to find a plaster and someone else to shout at.

Godfrey was usually a safe bet, though he was coming on in leaps and bounds. There was no way Jake was even considering telling him that yet. This was partly because his enthusiasm was bounding way ahead of his knowledge. He had discovered a recipe for squid that he was dead keen to try out, so Jake let him. Godfrey had interpreted flash-frying it (to keep it tender) as leaving it in the pan for twenty-five minutes while he chopped vegetables. The result was so tough that everyone said the next time they wanted to eat their own shoes they would let him know, thank you.

Now Godfrey was busy telling Sally how oysters screamed in agony when you poured lemon juice on them. 'If they don't squeal you know they're not fresh,' he blundered on, while poor Sally looked on in horror. She was as tender and delicate as the delicious confections she made for dessert and always had to look the other way when the lobsters came in.

Luckily Jake's attention was diverted by the sight of Tess, who looked as though she had been in a fight. Her mouth was very swollen and she was obviously in pain.

'What happened to you?'

'Toothache. It wasn't that bad this morning,' she said with difficulty, out of the corner of her mouth.

'Well, go to the dentist then, woman. You're no use to me like this.'

'Can't.'

'If it's the cost, I can lend you some money,' said Jake, who couldn't, really, but he would find it from somewhere.

''S not that – it's Angel. No one else to look after her. Can't take her with me. She bit the dentist the last time we went, and he had to go to hospital.'

Jake thought about all the work he had to do, trying to juggle his meagre finances so they would cover next week's wages and last week's bills.

'Tell you what, drop her off here. I'll look after her. She won't be any trouble.'

'You still haven't learned anything about kids, have you, Boss?'

Angel was very pleased to be with Jake. After Tess had gone he found out why. She had Barbie and Ken tucked under each arm.

'Barbie's hungry, Uncle Jake.'

'I'm not surprised. With a figure like that, she looks like she's never had a decent meal in her life.'

'We have to cook her a meal then, Uncle Jake. I want to do what Mummy does.'

Jake looked round his immaculate kitchen and sighed. 'I suppose we could do something simple.'

'What?'

'Er . . . we could make surprise lemon pudding.'

'What's the surprise?' asked Angel suspiciously.

'Well, the lemon, actually,' he admitted.

'I'm not surprised by that at all. I want to make doughnuts. With jam. With lots of jam.'

He could see that this was a plan that had been

fermenting for a long time. 'OK. But on one condition . . . no, a condition is . . . oh, never mind. You are NOT to go anywhere near the fryer.'

'But I want to plop them in. Mummy lets me,' she added craftily.

'Mummy is not here. I am. This is my kitchen. There will be no plopping. Take it or leave it.'

He waited while Angel debated with herself whether to give in or fling herself to the floor in a paroxysm of rage and grief. Greed won.

'Yes, then. But I am the stirrer.'

Given the size of the cook it would be better to do this on the floor, which was where most of the flour was going to end up anyway. He would just have to hope the Health Department didn't pick today to pay him a surprise visit. They were due one.

He was quite right about the flour. Angel's shiny red sandals were soon submerged in a sea of white and a fair amount went up her nose. She sneezed enormously into the mixing bowl.

'It doesn't matter, does it, Uncle Jake?'

'Well, God forbid anyone should hear me say this, but just this once, it doesn't.'

Angel stirred with vigour, shouting 'God forbid' at the top of her voice until he had to beg her to stop.

'Now sit on this stool and don't move. I've got to do the sizzling bit. Then you can do the jam. . . . Angelica, what part of "do not move" do you not understand?'

'All of it?'

'Don't be silly.'

'Are they ready yet?'

'No, they have to sizzle a bit longer.'

'Can Barbie watch?'

'Yes, but not there, she might fall in.'

'She could go for a swim.'

'Not in boiling hot fat, she couldn't. Angel, why has Ken done that?'

'He's died of hunger.'

'Blooming customers – they just can't wait. No, don't bury him, pick him up out of the flour. . . . Yes, it does look a bit like a snowstorm when you shake him so please don't do it . . . attishoo!'

When Jake had stopped sneezing he wiped his streaming eyes to see Angel trying to eat a half-cooked doughnut off the floor and Tess walking in at the same time. Tess's eyes were wide open in shock and horror and she seemed beyond speech, though her arms were waving frantically.

He could see how it must look to her. She had left her daughter in his care, her precious offspring, who was now busily ingesting a number of interesting germs from the floor, just inches away from a vat of boiling fat. He was a tough man, but he quailed. She would probably kill him, after she had handed in her notice.

It was obviously difficult still for her to speak, but she managed an anguished, 'Oh my God!'

'I know, I know, I'm not fit to be left alone with your offspring –'

'No, it's not that!'

Then he realised.

Walking in behind her, clad in a very natty Armani suit

(probably not from a charity shop, Jake thought wryly) and making no effort to hide the fact that he considered he was slumming it, was Harry.

Jake stared at him, his mouth suddenly dry. This was the person who had done his best to ruin Jake's career. A number of fantasies whipped through his head. They all involved ritual torture and humiliation. They all involved Harry screaming for mercy. Jake abandoned these with some regret. He had to deal with reality. He wasn't a young student any more and he didn't really want to torture anyone, even Harry. Anyway, he was a successful businessman now and Harry couldn't hurt him.

'Have you taken up child-minding to supplement your paltry income from the restaurant?' asked Harry, and he laughed.

'We're closed, so get out,' Jake said coldly. Not that that ever stopped anyone in this bloody county.

'Now is that any way to treat an old friend? I met your lovely commis chef just now . . .'

'No, you didn't! You stalked me all the way from the dentist's!' said a furious Tess.

'I've never stalked a woman in my life. Never had to, actually,' snapped Harry, his big smile slipping just a little. 'I've been meaning to call on you for the last few days, but what with one thing or another . . .' All the time he talked, his eyes were scanning the kitchen, taking in information, judging and finding fault.

There was plenty to find fault with. The kitchen, which only a short time before had been polished to an immaculate post-shift gloss, was now mostly covered in flour, and the bits which weren't had blobs of jam sticking to them. The doughnuts were frying to a deep shade of burned and Jake was aware that he didn't look his best. But then, compared to Harry, he never did.

Angel advanced, holding something sticky and revolting in her hand.

'Would you like a doughnut?'

Harry retreated in horror, his hands clasped protectively over his suit.

From the safety of the doorway he looked with completely unconcealed pleasure at his rival. As well as a slight dusting of flour, Jake was wearing jeans with holes in them that hadn't been put there by the manufacturer, and his hair had been very inexpertly cut by himself the week before. He looked a bit like Edward Scissorhands. Harry would see all this as a sign of weakness. Maybe it was, thought Jake. Harry was like a leech, sapping away all your self-confidence.

'I just thought I would call in, now that we are going to be neighbours, but I can see you are busy.'

'Bollocks – you've never made a purely friendly gesture in your life!' What did he mean, neighbours?

Harry sighed, saddened but not surprised at the appalling manners of the lower classes.

'I'll leave you to it. Oh, by the way, please pass on my regards to your lovely girlfriend. We got on so well when we met recently. What must she make of all this? Here, I've brought you something to read – it might interest you.' He flung a magazine down on the table as if it were a gauntlet, and left.

Tess covered Angel's ears for a minute while Jake gave free rein to his feelings.

When he had finished she read out the article in the magazine before he could chuck it into the hot oil.

Do London's chefs know something about the capital that we don't? Hot on the heels of Jake Goldman's defection comes the news that his one-time colleague Harry Hunter is 'going home'.

He has just bought a very swish little place in the Lake District. It's in a fabulous location on the edge of the lake and very near the station so you will be able to hop on a train at Euston and join him for dinner.

'I spent a very happy boyhood in what has to be one of the most beautiful parts of the world and now I want to give something back,' explained Mr Hunter. 'At the moment it has everything going for it but good cuisine.' (Ouch, Jake – what is it with you two guys?) 'My ambitions are simple: I intend to put Easedale on the food map.'

Jake knew the place he was referring to. It was so out of his price range he hadn't even considered looking at it, let alone buying it. He banged his fist so hard on the table Ken fell off it into the flour again.

'What's wrong with this guy? Why can't he just leave me alone? What have I ever done to him?'

'I think he hates the fact that you exist, Boss.'

'Well, surely this bloody country is big enough for the both of us! If I emigrated to Alaska, he'd follow me. I didn't know that he had grown up round here. I was never part of the pack that followed him round at college, lapping up his every word! Tell me, what the hell were the odds of me deciding to open a restaurant here, when it could have been anywhere – the Highlands of Scotland –'

'Too cold, for you. You're a lily-livered Londoner!'

'Well then, some peat bog in Ireland –'

'You know you loathe Guinness!'

'OK, Alaska! Now there's a place big enough –'

'Er, see Scotland – ditto too cold. Also, it's full of sex-starved fur trappers, I think. You are too good-looking – you'd be eaten alive.'

'Anyway, it wouldn't matter which country I picked, he'd find some excuse to follow me there too,' said Jake morosely.

'Look, it's just competition. You can handle that. You thrive on it!'

'Yeah, if that was all it was. But this is different. Nastier. It's a vendetta. You don't know this guy. I don't think he can let a grudge go, ever. He's got his teeth into me and he's going to carry on chewing until I'm just little bits!'

'I don't want anyone to eat you up!' wailed Angel.

'Great, that'll be the theme for this month's batch of nightmares, then,' muttered Tess.

'Sorry.' He picked Angel up. 'No one is going to eat me. I was just being silly.'

'If they tried, I would stomp on their toes and kick them –'

'Well, I don't think –'

'And then, I think I would hit them in their tummy, like this!'

'Ow!'

'Sorry about that, Boss. Angelica, come here. Now look what you've done!'

'No, I'm all right really – nothing a bit of surgery won't fix. Anyway, maybe I need to toughen up.' He thought about Alaska. 'It would almost be worth going there if it meant that I didn't have to see Harry again. But it wouldn't make any difference. He'd follow me – I know he would – and we end up slugging it out on some frozen tundra.'

'Er, I think you are over-reacting.'

'No. I'm not. I seriously think if there was only one other person left in the world apart from me and him, we'd have a fight over who would give him his last bloody meal!'

Chapter Eleven

The people employed to transform the establishment formerly known as Lakeside into a top-notch, swanky restaurant soon discovered there were a number of words that simply weren't part of Harry's vocabulary. Words like tea break, accident and – the builder's favourite – delay. Mention these words to Harry and he just stared with all the comprehension of an extremely large iceberg, but without its patience.

Since they constituted the major part of a workman's language, this might have posed a problem, so Harry cleared things up.

'Basically, my family is one of the most influential in this county. If you fuck up, you'll be lucky to find work even changing a tap washer,' he said, wishing he still lived in the days when the lower classes called people like himself 'sir', and touched their forelocks.

Once this simple message got through, the conversion proceeded with unprecedented efficiency. He was called Mr Stalin behind his back but everyone soon realised that the quicker they got the job done, the quicker they could return to normal life.

Kitchen equipment was delivered, installed and

thoroughly tested by a team who arrived at the crack of dawn and left after the streetlights were on. Painters and decorators wielded brushes until their fingers were blue, and not just with paint, because Harry refused to put any heating on until there were customers to pay for it.

When the van delivering the glassware crashed into a ditch to avoid a sheep, Harry rushed to the hospital, not to enquire after the driver's broken leg, but to find out how much crystal had smashed.

He went through job applications like a scythe through corn, weeding out idiots, liars and incompetents with brutal thoroughness. He fully intended to poach such members of Jake's kitchen as were deemed worthy of his own, but not just yet.

His waitresses, Tara and Annabelle, were friends of the family. Fresh from a season chalet-maiding in Val d'Isère, they were toned, tanned, fluent in French and stony-broke. Having been respectively Head Girl and Captain of Games at school, they were used to dealing with people. They both agreed Harry was a complete bastard, but as sexy as hell and planned to sleep with him to pass the time until they could get back to the Alps. Harry knew all this, but didn't care. There were plenty more fish from that particular pool.

Ronnie, his second in command in the kitchen, was a young man with superb cooking skills and zero social skills. Short and fat, with a complexion like mud, insults bounced off him like they were ping-pong balls. Ronnie wouldn't cultivate ideas above his station, because he didn't have any. But that was fine, because Harry had plenty of his own. His restaurant was going to be so good it would blow Jake's crappy place right out of the water.

Having assured himself that all his minions were working at back-breaking speed, Harry settled himself in his freshly painted and carpeted office, in front of his state-of-the-art computer, and began to plan. He had pinched a copy of Jake's menu and now he scanned it, snorting with derision. *Tournedos Choron* – fillet of beef garnished with artichoke hearts and filled with asparagus tips – how many times had that been done, he wondered, but ground his teeth because it was one of his favourite dishes.

He would sauté his fillets and arrange them in little tartlet shells filled with a purée of fresh peas.

His chicken dish would be stuffed with a mixture of lambs' sweetbreads, truffles and mushrooms, bound with a velouté sauce.

His puddings would include fruit-based soufflés with hazelnut praline or fresh apricot purée. They were a fucking pain to make and left staff sweating with terror in case they didn't rise, but they were very impressive when served.

Looking at a menu wasn't a very good way of sussing out competition, though. The real test was to eat there yourself. Jake probably couldn't afford to turn any customers away, even ones he hated. What could he do if Harry turned up as a customer? Rush out and start slashing away at him with a bread knife? No, he would have to grin and bear it, but his blood pressure would rise to boiling point. And what a marvellous opportunity for Harry to do a little PR for his own place at the same time.

He then spent a pleasurable hour walking round with a face like granite, checking on the progress of the work.

Everyone held their breath and wished they were somewhere else. This was what Judgment Day would feel like. Finally, his face cracked into a smile; he opened a bottle of very cheap wine, passed it round, and they all decided he was a great guy really.

Another day, another group of bloody customers to be nice to, thought Kate as she walked into the restaurant. Another ton of bread to slice and serve, another round of insults to grin and bear and a fresh set of blisters on her feet. She had already set up a standing order for plasters at her local chemist. The life of an undercover waitress was not an easy one. She should have applied for that reporting job in Baghdad. She bloody would, when this was over.

Jake looked even grumpier than she felt. He was busy slicing an onion like he wished it was someone's head and his happy mood had filtered over to everyone else. Tess was stirring a sauce and frowning so hard her eyebrows had met in the middle. Sally was muttering what sounded like a prayer under her breath as she made raspberry coulis.

Jake had got up early that morning so he could spend some precious, solitary time thinking about salmon. Would it be better to serve it impaled on skewers, coated in breadcrumbs or à la Florentine – with spinach leaves and grated parmesan? In the middle of this Georgia had rung from Milan.

She was having a terrible time. She'd had to model a dress covered with ostrich feathers, which had made her sneeze on the runway and brought her out in a rash; her period was late (oh, please God, no, thought Jake) and she couldn't find a tuna and sweetcorn sandwich anywhere and Jake knew it was the only thing she could eat to calm her nerves before a show.

'I hope you remembered to tape *Nip/Tuck* for me?' *Blast! I knew there was something I had to do to the telly!* 'You don't sound very cheerful – are you missing me?' *I know I should be – but actually I haven't given you a thought for days.* 'I want us to have a weekend away when I get back.' *Are you mad, woman? I'm like a mother with a new baby at the moment – I don't want to take my eyes off this place for a minute.*

Then he felt guilty for always putting his work before his relationship, though he couldn't think of a single successful chef who didn't.

He was so tired he'd put on his boxer shorts back to front that morning and hadn't even noticed until after lunch. He'd knocked a cup of cold coffee over the keyboard of his computer, which then developed a demented clicking noise. He was just debating whether to give in to temper and throw it out of the window, when he noticed a smell of burning. This was traced to a batch of bread that Godfrey had left in the oven. When he took the loaves out they were still perfectly formed but completely carbonised, like a relic from the ruins of Pompeii.

When he discovered that Harry had booked a table, he felt that he would quite like to erupt himself. In theory, all customers were good and it would be a pleasure to take money from this one, but Harry was just a slug. Wherever he went, he left a trail of something sticky and unpleasant.

Godfrey was used to being shouted it – for him it was just another working day. Tess knew it wasn't personal, but

Jake was aware that Sally trod a fine line between creativity and collapse. He didn't want to be the one who tipped her over the edge. His bad mood wasn't her fault. It was his problem and he should keep it to himself. This was a nice thought, but his heavy silence was making her more nervous than a tantrum would.

Kate was pretending she wasn't enjoying watching him prowl round the kitchen like a hunting panther. He was far too arrogant to deserve admiration, she decided, when he looked up and caught her eye.

'For God's sake, tie your hair back. My customers aren't paying to find it in their dinner,' he snarled.

'What's up with him tonight?' she whispered to Kirsty.

'A man by the name of Harry Hunter. He's reserved a table for this evening. He's opening a restaurant down by the lake. Jake hates him.'

'Why?'

'Well, apparently . . .' and Kirsty filled her in.

Kate's eyes widened in shock and, it has to be said, pleasure. Poor Jake, obviously, but what a great story, and now here they both were, in the same town, still slugging it out like a couple of Wild West cowboys, though with cooking knives instead of guns. With a bit of luck Harry would be as photogenic as Jake. Good pictures did round off a story nicely.

Two hours later Harry swaggered into Cuisine like a prizefighter before a big bout. Of course he was late, a nicely judged fifteen minutes, just to give Jake a bit more time to work himself up into a stew.

Jake was wound up like a demented spinning top, and

Kate and Kirsty found it was catching. They also had to pretend to listen quietly to advice Jake should have been giving himself.

'No matter how much this guy winds you up – and he will – do not rise to the bait. You will be courteous and helpful, however much he provokes you. He is going to have the best eating experience in his unpleasant and undeserving little life – whether he likes it or not.'

'So, we're not going to spit in his dinner then?' asked Godfrey, smirking, and was given a look so black he retreated to the safety of the dishwasher.

'Listen to me very carefully,' said Jake, through gritted teeth. 'We are professionals, not half-wits, and this is a restaurant, not a football terrace. We NEVER, whatever the provocation, stoop to the level of third-rate canteens. It is exactly what this idiot is looking for and it is exactly what he will not get. He is going to be hideously surprised by the total brilliance of his eating experience here – do you all get that?'

'Yes, Chef,' they all chorused, though as soon as they were out of earshot, Kate hissed: 'Blimey, I thought this was just a restaurant, not a bloody scene out of *Gladiator*.'

But Kirsty had been working in catering since she was fourteen. 'Chefs are all mad. They're all as competitive as crazy. There's always loads of bitching and back-stabbing in this business. Actually, Jake is one of the good guys and if he says this guy is a bastard, then I believe him.'

But Kate, well aware of her other life as a journalist, was determined to be objective and impartial, and she was bound to need some quotes from him in the future.

Harry had a very pretty girl with him, whom he almost

completely ignored. He was far too busy scanning the room for imperfections, like a heat-seeking missile homing in on its target. Kirsty, as the more experienced, was supposed to serve him, but she was delayed by a couple at another table who needed taking through the menu very slowly.

Kate walked over cautiously, annoyed with herself for being nervous. He wasn't a gangster, for heaven's sake. She was also incensed that he looked at her like he wanted to leap on her and gobble her up.

Oh God, she thought, another unreconstructed male.

But then he smiled and his blue eyes crinkled attractively, and instead of being a bastard, he was terribly polite. It made a nice change to go through the menu and wine list with someone who knew what they were talking about. Actually, he knew more than she did, but he was very nice about it.

'Well, what does he want?' growled Jake as she came in with the order.

Your head, on a plate, apparently, thought Kate, but she said: 'Calves' liver salad followed by two bloody fillets.'

She didn't think it was a good time to say that Harry had pressed her arm with anxious concern and asked: 'They can do a properly rare fillet here, can't they?' as if Jake were some callow youth just out of catering college.

Jake had every confidence in himself, but he felt as nervous as if he were cooking for food critics Michael Winner and A. A. Gill, and a pack of Michelin inspectors in one sitting. He knew Harry had deliberately picked a plain steak because there was nowhere to hide behind it. Jake also knew his crew were good but that didn't stop him hovering anxiously over their every move like a midwife presiding over a difficult birth.

Every leaf of the watercress salad was inspected, and the calves' liver, which had been briefly introduced to the pan, was laid on top as tenderly as if it were a baby. He quashed the fantasy of adding ground-up glass to it and asked Kirsty to serve it, which really annoyed Kate, who felt she was quite capable of carrying two small plates to a table without bringing his restaurant into disrepute.

But there were plenty of other customers to think about and the time slid by. That was the good thing – the only good thing – about this job, she thought. There simply wasn't enough time to dwell on the awfulness of it until it was all over.

Harry insisted on saying thank you to Jake in person after his meal. 'Don't bother him – I'll just pop down to the kitchen.'

'No bloody way,' growled Jake, already shrugging on a clean chef's jacket. The kitchen was his lair and Harry would only set foot here again over his dead body. He would meet him in the arena, sorry, restaurant where Harry would have to curb his tongue.

The other customers were gratifyingly pleased to see him. Jake was generally too reserved to do the sort of walkabout some chefs revelled in, but it was nice to hear so many compliments. Chefs soaked up praise like a sponge; there could never be enough of it. He gritted his teeth, took his hands out of his pockets and then put them back in again because they looked more relaxed there, and tried to saunter over to Harry's table, repeating silently to himself: 'Remember we are in public.'

'Hello, how are you?' *As if I care.*

'This is a nice little place you've got here.' *Christ! The colour on these walls went out of fashion years ago. What was the look you were aiming for? Oh yes, doctor's surgery, circa 1972.*

'I hope you enjoyed your meal, both of you.' *You know it was fantastic and I bet every mouthful stuck in your throat.*

'Oh, excellent grub, wasn't it, darling?' *A bit better than the chippy down the road, I suppose.*

Grub! You condescending little prick! 'It's good to see you can take some time off.' *Bloody part-timer – that's no way to run a restaurant.*

Harry shrugged easily. 'It's been a piece of cake really. I couldn't have asked for an easier ride.' *You look like shit. Been up all night worrying about the cashflow, eh?*

'Of course the real work starts when you're open, doesn't it?' *You won't be smiling then – you won't keep any staff longer than a day.*

'Oh, I'm ready for it. I've got plenty of stamina.' *You won't know what's hit you.*

I'll see you drop dead before I give you a single customer, you bastard.

Kate was eavesdropping shamelessly. She could pick up all the innuendoes as clearly as if they were being shouted across the room. It was like watching two lions fight it out over territory on a David Attenborough programme. She could almost hear his fluid tones on the voice-over. 'These two magnificent animals are circling each other looking for the right moment to strike. When they do, it will be a fight to the death . . .' Oh, no, there was no way she was going to spend the rest of the night on her knees, trying to get blood out of the carpet. She nipped out, waited a few seconds, and then nipped back.

'Excuse me, sorry for interrupting – there's a phone call for you, Jake.' She followed him back to the office. He stared at the phone, which was still on its cradle.

'Sorry. I made that up, but I thought I should help you beat a retreat.'

For a second, he looked furious at her interference. Then he grinned. 'Yeah, you did the right thing. Cool move.' He looked closer. 'You've got shadows under your eyes.' He ran his finger lightly across her cheek. 'No, they won't budge – it's tiredness, not streaky mascara this time. I know, let's get cleared up while everyone's clearing off and then we'll make Godfrey cook us supper and Hans open a few bottles of wine.' He didn't want to be alone, even though he was dog-tired. He knew he would just think obsessively about Harry and how much he hated him, and torture himself about what Harry's next move might be. There was bound to be one. I wish it was just the two of us, sharing the wine, he thought, then shook himself. He had no right to be having thoughts like that.

Kate followed him slowly back to the kitchen, and not just because her legs were tired. Her cheeks were tingling from where he had touched her. Oh dear, I don't need this, she thought.

Later, when they were all sprawled at the bar, she glanced round and said: 'I like this place better now it's all tidy and there are no customers.'

Jake hooted with laughter. 'It's a good time of day – the calm after the storm and cash in pocket,' he agreed.

Godfrey was practising his chat-up technique because he fancied a girl down the road. It turned out he didn't have a technique to speak of. 'How does this look?' he asked, arranging his features in what he hoped was a seductive look.

'Like you've got your dick caught in your zip,' said Jake promptly.

'So, do you have any hobbies, apart from cooking?' asked Kate. She wanted to get to know him better.

'Yeah, breathing. There's no time for anything else,' he said.

He was leaning against the wall, cradling a whisky, slitty-eyed from fatigue and other people's cigarette smoke. He was looking pretty seductive himself, even though he wasn't trying, thought Kate, comparing his style with Jonathan's at the *Gazette*. The journalist enjoyed wearing the trappings of his success. He had his hair cut regularly and always wore expensive aftershave. Jake, on the other hand, looked like he hadn't tried, because he really hadn't. There were dark circles under his eyes as well, and his hands had two new burn marks to add to the old ones. But Kate had seen how tenderly they coaxed life into ingredients.

The conversation turned to food. Did these people ever think about anything else?

'The best way to seduce a woman is with a meal. Tender spring lamb, very pink and delicate and, to start with, fresh asparagus because you have to eat with your fingers,' said Jake dreamily.

'Is that what you cook for your girlfriend?' said Godfrey, searching for a pen so he could take notes.

'Hell, no. Georgia thinks rare meat is still alive,' said Jake gloomily. Where was she again? He remembered her rash, but he couldn't remember the city. Shit, he'd forgotten to set the video for her again! If he didn't pull his socks up, this relationship would go the way of others, sacrificed to the incessant demands of his job. If he wasn't careful, he would end up old, alone and tetchy, with only a tattered copy of *Larousse Gastronomique* for company.

'So why are you and Harry such enemies?' asked Kate, who, though she had heard most of the story from Kirsty, wanted it from the horse's mouth.

But Jake clammed up like an oyster shell. 'He's a bastard – that's all you need to know.'

'He seemed very nice to me,' she said innocently, knowing that riling people was sometimes a good way to get them to open up.

'So do tigers when they are sitting snoozing in the sun. His charm is his greatest weapon. He should come with a sign on his forehead: "Believe nothing I say." There's no side to him – whichever way you look at him, he's horrible.'

'You're not always that nice yourself when you're cooking,' retorted Kate, still smarting from several, in her opinion, unjustified rebukes that evening.

Jake's eyes narrowed. 'Why are you so interested? Looking for a villain for your novel? I suppose he would make a good swashbuckling pirate or smuggler. What exactly is it you're writing again?'

This wasn't fair. He was turning the tables on her. She was too tired to invent plot lines for spurious books at this time of night.

'You make it sound like I'm writing some sort of bodice-and-bloomers crap,' she began weakly, but was rescued by Tess, who had been on the phone to her mother, who was Angelica-sitting.

'She woke up and won't go back to bed until she's said hello.'

Jake obligingly took the phone. 'Hello, Angel. Why aren't you asleep?'

'Because my dollies have been naughty and I have to tell them off, of course!'

'Oh, I see. Why have they been naughty?'

There was a pause, during which Angelica sucked the phone noisily and considered.

'They wet their knitters instead of going to the loo,' she said eventually. Jake was baffled by this until he remembered she still had difficulty with her ks.

'I think that's the first time I've seen you at a loss,' teased Kate.

'Children are quite scary; I would much rather cook for several hundred bad-tempered punters, to be honest.'

He watched Godfrey trying to chat Sally up. As Sally was pathologically shy, he was happily doing all the talking and singularly failing to notice that her eyes were glazing over with boredom. Jake butted in shamelessly. Sally was brilliant at what she did, but her self-confidence was dreadfully low and it was affecting her work.

'I might shout a bit when it gets busy, but I've never bitten anyone yet,' he teased, but she didn't laugh. The trouble was, she took everything very seriously and brooded on things too much.

'Your work is great, but you should know by now there's no time to nursemaid anyone who is having a crisis of confidence. Maybe if you said to yourself at the beginning of the shift: "I am good and that's why I am here", it might help.'

Kate was quite scathing about women who were too feeble to look after themselves in the workplace but, despite herself, she was touched by Jake's evident concern for all his staff. She knew that, in most professions, a lot of bosses would have said 'Sink or swim' and not really cared.

'I am aware that women can still have a rough time in this profession. The trade attracts some real low-lives. If you're a paranoid little shit with the hide of a rhino and the sensitivity of Attila the Hun, you'll feel right at home. Or if you are a complete idiot,' he added, watching Godfrey who was trying to drink a flaming sambuca and had just burned his nose. 'You've got to be tough to survive the heat and the criticism. Did Tess collapse in a heap when I didn't like her hollandaise sauce yesterday?'

'Didn't like! What you said, Boss, and I quote, was, "This stuff looks like it belongs in a hospital lab. It's what people excrete, not eat."'

'Oh dear, did I?'

'Yeah, but you were nicer when I got it right.'

Jake grinned and yawned.

'Maybe I should smoke dope, like Hans. Would it make me wittier?' said Godfrey. They all looked over. Hans was asleep, his mouth open, snoring gently.

'I knew this guy once –' began Kirsty.

'Oh, no, here we go again,' muttered Tess under her

breath. 'You know if you ever write your memoirs you're gonna require half the remaining rain forest.'

'Well, that's OK, 'cos the back of a stamp would do for yours,' said Kirsty, and smirked when everyone laughed. 'Anyway, as I was saying, this guy, he was having an affair with my sister's brother-in-law's second cousin, but we don't talk about him. Well, he used to work at the Go-Rite garage out along the Windermere road, though my dad says that most cars don't after they've been there – go right, I mean – so –'

'What? Yes! Who!' Hans's snores had got so loud he had woken himself up.

'Be quiet! I am in the middle of a story!' Kirsty took a deep breath. 'Oh bugger. I've forgotten.'

'We all need some sleep. Now Kate is dropping off.'

'My eyes are closed but I am still firing on all cylinders. I was thinking.'

'Napping, more like,' teased Jake. 'Well, what were you thinking about?'

She opened her eyes. Jake's dark eyes were on hers. He had a trick of looking at you as if you were the only person in the room, she thought. You, she wanted to say. I was thinking about you. 'Oh nothing, just about what we've got to do tomorrow,' she lied.

'Yeah, there's a hell of a lot of prep to do. Off you all go. I need my beauty sleep.'

'You'll need a hell of a lot of it then,' said Tess.

Kate dragged Godfrey out by the simple method of grabbing the seat of his pants and pulling. 'I'll give you a lift home but only if you leave the bloody matches behind!'

Chapter Twelve

Kate was not in a good mood. First, there was the email from Jonathan.

'Hi, babe.' Who did he think he was – Austin Powers? 'Why have we heard nothing from you? As far as I know, you are only a few miles away, not halfway down a cave in Afghanistan. Can I see some copy, and you, for a drink this evening?'

Kate typed 'No and no', added 'Fuck off, you sarcastic prick' and then deleted it. Jonathan was, after all, as he was fond of reminding her, her superior. Then she pressed 'Send', switched off her computer and then had to switch it on again to check she really had deleted the rude bits.

The previous night Jake had spent what she considered a ridiculous amount of time showing Godfrey how to make an omelette.

'For goodness' sake, it's just a few eggs in a pan,' she muttered now, getting some out of her fridge. She would show him. Any competent person could make an omelette. She beat eggs furiously, threw them into a non-stick pan and went off to put some mascara on.

When she came back, the inside of her pan seemed to have become stuck to the bottom of her omelette, which looked and tasted like something that might be better used wiping a car windscreen. It so wasn't going to be eggs for breakfast then.

Bloody Jonathan! Did he know just how hard waitresses had to work? It wasn't just the long hours. She was so tired when she got home she was practically nodding off in the shower. There was a whole reel of taped episodes of her favourite television thriller to catch up on, but she just couldn't seem to stay awake long enough to find out which particular life-threatening catastrophe was facing America at the moment.

She calmed down and admitted Jonathan did have a point. She was letting the job get in the way of her real work, and there was plenty to make a start on. She had downloaded some pretty juicy gossip on Jake and Harry. But one of her ideas – how chefs cut corners so they could rake in more profits – didn't apply to the kitchen she was working in. She knew Jake was short of money, but he was passionate about buying only the best-quality ingredients. He was one of the most critical and explosive people she had met, but she was starting to respect him for that. He was also very kind to Sally, who was a really pathetic drip, even if she could make cakes. Kate had no patience with her. Life was a tough deal and you just had to grit your teeth and get on with it.

Jake might blow a fuse if there was a drop of sauce in the wrong place on a plate but he worked like a dog without complaining, even the other night when he'd just about sliced the end of his finger off. His language was choice, but he'd calmly bandaged himself up, managing a pale grin at

Sally, who was having hysterics and threatening to phone an ambulance.

Then he'd gone quietly back to work until it started bleeding again, when he had apologised for not being able to help them clear up at the end of the shift.

He was bad-tempered, he was brave, he was good-looking . . . oh dear, concentrate, Kate told herself. But it was no good. She couldn't work here. She would break into the between-shifts calm and quiet of the kitchen and hope that the atmosphere would spark some inspiration.

A pale sun was filtering through the clouds and there were plenty of people about, mainly couples with children too young to be dragged up the fells. Kate had never walked up a hill by choice in her life before and until recently had considered that shoes made specifically for walking in were not worth buying.

To take away the hideous taste of the omelette she bought a couple of doughnuts and ate them while she walked.

Sitting outside the kitchen door was a box of lobsters. She had no idea why, but Jake would go ballistic if he found them. It would be kinder on everyone's nerves later on if she shoved them in the cold room and pretended she had been there when they were delivered.

Kicking the door open with her foot she staggered inside, knees buckling under the weight of the heavy box. She put them down and stood looking at them doubtfully. The last time she had seen a lobster it was ready to eat. These weren't. In fact she was sure they were still alive.

What was she supposed to do now? Fill the stockpot with

water so they could frolic away happily until they were murdered? Would they die anyway if it wasn't salty water? It would be really good if she could do something knowledgeable with them to impress Jake, but what? And was it her imagination or was the biggest one trying to edge its way out of the box?

She was about to creep stealthily towards it, rolling pin in hand and quite prepared to batter it senseless if she had to, when the door opened and a ridiculously beautiful woman walked in.

She had impossibly long legs, sheathed in leather so soft it gleamed like silk and was so tight it looked like it had been sprayed on. She was wearing a tiny pink top that screamed 'I may only be four square inches of material but I am designer-made and way out of your spending league, honey!' Her face was the sort you usually only ever see in a heavily airbrushed photograph. Kate just knew her rich golden hair didn't have a single split end, and it was obvious that the curved, pouting mouth owed everything to nature and not injections. But what the hell was she doing here?

'Er . . . who are you?' This seemed a fairly safe way to start.

'I'm Georgia,' said the vision simply, as if that was enough. 'Where's Jake? Why have you got jam on your nose?'

Kate remembered the doughnuts and instantly felt two stones overweight, although she generally thought of herself as skinny. So this was Jake's girlfriend! Somehow this information seemed to be making her feel very bad-tempered, which was absurd: it was no business of hers who he went out with.

She looked at her watch. 'He'll be upstairs in the flat, asleep probably. You have to bang on the door very hard or he won't hear.'

'I did,' said Georgia, examining her fingernails, which looked as if they never did anything more strenuous than tap open the lid of a Chanel compact.

'Well, I'm not sure what I can do,' said Kate. She certainly wasn't going to bang on the door herself, thus incurring a tired man's wrath and then have to watch while he flung himself into this gorgeous woman's arms. Honestly, if it wasn't seafood it was sex bombs. Couldn't they all just leave her in peace?

'I suppose I could try again,' said Georgia rather doubtfully.

'Yes, you do that,' said Kate briskly, and turned away in case she was expected to carry luggage upstairs like a lackey. She chucked the lobsters in the fridge and stomped off to the nearest café.

Sipping her cup of sludge, which was what passed for coffee, she took out her notebook, sucked the end of her pen and gazed into the middle distance. But it was no good. The only thing she could concentrate on was how beautiful Jake's girlfriend was. It really wasn't fair that God had given Georgia a slender body and large boobs, though with a bit of luck He hadn't given her a brain. She looked down at her thighs. Was it her imagination or were they spreading?

Pull yourself together, she told herself severely. The next boyfriend she had would be someone who fell in love with her mind, not her body. The trouble was, this meant she was in for a long spell of celibacy. If she met six men tomorrow, at least five of them would try and have a conversation with her breasts. This was so depressing she was quite pleased when it was time to go back to work.

Kirsty grabbed her the minute she walked back in. 'Guess what? Jake's girlfriend has turned up and they've just had a massive row upstairs. I could hear it all. She was screaming and slamming doors and when he tried to calm her down she yelled all he wanted her for now was sex and he said, well no, he didn't actually, because he was so bloody knackered he'd prefer an extra hour's kip any day. Then she burst into tears and threatened to stick her head in the oven because he didn't love her any more and he said she'd be waiting a long time for death then because that was an electric oven and it wasn't even plugged in and could she stop being such a silly tart, and did you know we've got an extra twenty booked in tonight and Godfrey can't find a clean apron and ohmigod, who is that?'

A man in a white overall had just walked in. He was carrying a clipboard and looked frighteningly official.

'Where is Jake Goldman, the owner of this establishment?'

'Who's asking?' said Jake, appearing before them and brandishing the knife he was about to use on the lobsters.

'Geoff Brown, Environmental Health. We have heard a report that there are rats in this kitchen. I have to inform you, sir, that we must close you down immediately while it is being investigated. I must warn you that the process could take at least two weeks,' he continued.

There was a stunned, horrified silence.

Nightmares filled Jake's head. He was crippled; no, he was ruined. By the time this was sorted out he would be a dead chef walking. Rats? The only rat that had ever been in his kitchen was –

'Ha ha! Got you. I *am* from Environmental Health, by the way, but we're the party booked in tonight. My friend Harry Hunter said you'd be up for a laugh. Hope I didn't scare you too much to cook a decent meal for us!'

'Gosh, no! Absolutely not! Yeah, very funny! My sides are nearly splitting – I do like a good joke. But that one –' But Kate clapped her hand over Jake's mouth just in case he was going to say something he would regret later.

When the man had gone Jake leaned against a wall for support. His knees were shaking.

'Water! Water! I think he's fainted!' shouted Godfrey.

'Don't be silly,' said Jake irritably. He was furious with himself for having been so easily taken in. But it was the thought of being shut down . . . Only a complete bastard like Harry would make a joke like that. As for the Environmental Health people . . .

'No, I don't think you should go out and tell them what you think of them. Remember – they – are – customers,' explained Kirsty, very slowly and clearly, as if to an idiot, flapping a clean tea towel in front of his face.

'Just think of all the money we'll make from them tonight,' said Godfrey encouragingly.

'They will love it here and recommend it to loads of people,' said Kate, hoping none of them would recognise her. She would walk with a stoop and cover her face with her hair. No, that would make her look like Quasimodo.

'I know how you feel,' soothed Godfrey. 'My dad hates officials as well. He once locked a man from DEFRA in the cowshed and left him there for an hour. He was so overcome by the pong he didn't realise he'd counted all the sheep twice and we got an enormous subsidy.'

'But your dad doesn't keep cows,' said Jake, trying to keep track of this conversation.

'You're right. There was nothing in there but two enormous cheeses my mum had brought back from France and had forgotten about.'

'Camembert?'

'Pont l'Évêque. They absolutely reeked. She wasn't allowed to keep them in the kitchen.'

'Well, what are you all doing standing around and gawping? Don't you realise there is work to do?' said Jake, getting up and waving the towel away crossly.

He then went into overdrive, reducing everyone to exasperation and heightened nerves.

He dealt with the lobsters by the simple method of chopping them in half and told Sally curtly that if she didn't like it she could take herself and her strawberry mousses to another kitchen.

He hated Tess's sauce for the pork, commenting that if he had wanted Polyfilla he would have asked for it.

When Kate returned to the kitchen after a furtive recce to see if there was anyone out there who might shop her, she found him icily congratulating Godfrey for making a salad that looked as if a blind man in boxing gloves had put it together.

'Honestly, Jake, calm down. They are really very nice people out there, and judging by the amount of wine they've ordered, it's going to be a massive bill. You are making us all so wound up, we're bound to do something wrong.' She stared him straight in the eyes, daring him to bawl her out.

Everyone cringed, waiting for the fallout. Jake opened his mouth, thought about it and shut it again. He gave her an apologetic grin. 'OK, you're right. Enjoy this moment – it won't happen very often.'

No one had ever smiled at her like that before. Well, maybe they had, but she hadn't cared about them.

When he left the room, everyone breathed out and relaxed, apart from Kate, who was suddenly so keyed up she needed a moment on her own. In the loo, she splashed cold water on her face. When Jake had smiled at her she had felt a jolt of connection between them, like an electrical spark. 'Control yourself, woman,' she said to her reflection in the mirror. 'You so don't need this complication.'

Back in the kitchen, Godfrey loosened his collar. 'Phew, I was getting a bit wound up myself.'

'Oh, come on – what's the worst he could do to you?'

'Quite a lot, actually. I've even come out in a funny rash since I started here.'

'Have you been shagging someone you shouldn't?' chortled Tess.

'Chance would be a fine thing,' said Godfrey gloomily. 'The doctor says it's nervous tension.'

'Well, I wouldn't start worrying until something falls off.'

Godfrey did looked worried and said: 'But I'm so knackered by the time I get home I don't even have the energy to flick through the channels to find *Baywatch*.'

'Well, in that case, you're bottling it all up – that's even worse,' said Tess wisely.

'Lucky Jake, that's all I can say. He's a brilliant chef and he's got a gorgeous girlfriend, even if she does shout a lot,' said Godfrey.

Yeah, thanks for reminding me, thought Kate.

Kate was right about the Environmental Health people. They were celebrating someone's birthday and, after fourteen bottles of wine, wouldn't have cared if they'd found a small mammal in their salad. They finished off with an alarming number of liqueur coffees and produced their own birthday cake, the shape of an enormous pair of breasts.

The men kept asking if Kate was a strippergram and she had great difficulty swallowing the pithy putdowns she would normally have responded with. What was perfectly acceptable language in a reporters' room would not go down well from a waitress. She was coming to have more and more admiration for Kirsty, who, as well as being efficient and organised, could put up with all sorts of stupid comments from punters without it denting her coolness or her self-confidence. Kate was starting to feel that this job required her to be metaphorically gagged and she wasn't used to it.

It was also her turn to be on late. She and Kirsty had a private agreement that they would take it turns to finish off if only one of them was needed. Jake came down just as she was relaying the last table. 'Do you want a nightcap?' he asked, pouring himself a whisky. Kate hesitated, but he didn't seem in any great hurry to go back upstairs.

'Georgia's asleep. Jet lag.'

'But she was only in Italy, wasn't she?'

'Yeah, but she's got this idea you get jet lag every time you set foot on a jet,' he grinned.

What was he doing with someone so dim, she wondered. No. Silly Kate. He was a man and Georgia's attractions were obvious.

Her back ached and she was acutely aware that her clothes and hair smelled of all the food she had served that night, which was delicious on a plate but no substitute for a shower and a splash of something by Chanel. Still, she was a journalist, one of a breed who had never been known to refuse a drink.

Jake gave an enormous yawn and tried to find a position that didn't remind him of his numerous aches and pains. People who had desk jobs and complained of repetitive strain injuries didn't know how lucky they were.

'Well, here's to your two-week anniversary.' He raised his glass.

'Have I been here that long? It feels like a year,' she said wryly.

'I didn't think you'd last this long, to be honest.'

Kate was slightly affronted. She never gave up on a job, especially if there was a story at the end of it. 'It's been harder than I thought it would be,' she admitted.

'It's certainly hard on your feet,' he agreed.

'Well, yes, but it isn't just that. To be honest, it's been a real pain being nice to people all the time, especially when – sorry, Jake, I know they are customers and we need them but – some of them are really stupid.'

'That's why you need the sanity of the kitchen to escape to. OK, I know it doesn't seem a very sane place in the middle of service, but you are part of a team, you know.'

She was touched by his thoughtfulness, but wished he hadn't said it. It made her feel guilty.

'So, are you getting enough free time for your novel?'

She was getting heartily sick of this mythical work of fiction she was supposed to be toiling away at. 'Oh, you know, late at night, early mornings, a notebook in the bath – that sort of thing. Isn't it part of the tradition that writers are supposed to struggle?'

'I wouldn't know. The only things I ever write are shopping lists. Even my job applications were terse. Any good chef would know that it's what you do, not what you say that counts.'

'So, has it lived up to expectations? I mean, people change careers quite regularly these days.'

He looked at her in surprise. 'It's the only thing I want to do. It's the only thing I've ever wanted to do.'

'But surely you must get bored, doing the same thing day after day?'

'Never. There are always new dishes to try and old ones to perfect. There are some things I feel I've never got quite right, but I know I can.'

'So you are happy then?'

He considered this. 'We are always chasing after it, aren't we? Well, we're always chasing something we think will make us happy, or imagining a future with things in it that we haven't got now. I don't think about the future much – I haven't got a pension plan worked out. Financially, I'm lucky if I can see the way into the next few weeks. But when I'm cooking, when my hands and my head and the ingredients are all working together to create a moment of perfection, well, I don't want anything else.'

'I know what you mean,' she said, picking her words carefully. 'I feel the same way when I've captured the essence of someone's personality on paper – when I've got someone right.'

She had a feeling he would completely understand her driving need to get a story before anyone else had because, like cooking, there was always the thought that, next time, the words would be even better. It was a very great pity she couldn't tell him any of this. He most certainly wouldn't want to speak to her ever again when he found out her story was about him.

Chapter Thirteen

The launch of the Café Anglais was an example of what you can do when money is no object, when you have no scruples, and when your rivals lack the financial resources to sue you.

The words 'first', 'best' and 'only' were bandied about with great freedom, much to the consternation of the girl from the posh PR firm Harry had employed.

'You can't use words like that. They imply that . . . well, you are the best, and of course you are,' she added hurriedly, not liking the look on Harry's face. 'It's just that it is potentially litigious,' she wailed.

Lisa had been so enthusiastic about this project at the beginning. A weekend in the country with a glamorous chef was the perfect excuse to escape London and a minor heat-wave. She was pleased with her resemblance to Gwyneth Paltrow in the film *Sliding Doors*, though five-inch heels turned out to be a definite mistake. She had had no idea she would be expected to trot around after Harry all day and most of the night while he barked out confusing and sometimes contradictory orders.

He looked at her coldly now. 'But I *am* the best. What on earth is the point of spending thousands of pounds with your firm if all you can come up with is "very nice"?'

This was unkind. She had worked hard to produce a guest list that included a respectable number of celebrities. She had got him publicity in several national newspapers and a number of glossy magazines. She had diligently researched a fifty-mile radius for local people with influence and money, and had spent nearly a week looking for exactly the right shade of balloons for the launch party. Until now she didn't know so many different sorts of balloons existed or how many shops sold balloons and nothing else. Or how far apart they were. Or that she had to personally go into every one. Or how much she now actually hated balloons. She was sick of the whole thing and couldn't wait to get home and book a session with her therapist. Harry had seemed such a charmer at first – until she actually had to work for him.

'I hope you are going to change your clothes before people arrive,' he added, eyeing her Donna Karan dress as if it were something Matalan had failed to shift in their January sale.

It was perfectly acceptable this morning, before I had to do twelve hours' hard labour, she wanted to scream at him; but she had learned it was not a good idea to answer back.

'Also . . .' he looked at the list in his hand, 'who is this Billy Martin you have foisted on me? I specifically said that only real celebs were to be invited to stay with my parents. The rest can stay in hotels.'

'He has just won that *Make Me a Star* programme on television. He is hot,' protested Lisa, who had been chuffed to get him.

'Here today, gone tomorrow. Probably thinks he knows about good food because he uses mayonnaise instead of salad cream,' sneered Harry, and went down to the kitchen to check on the progress of his canapés.

The menu at the Café Anglais was French, with an English twist – the black pudding in a cream and apple sauce was made with the best English apples and the venison steaks had been gambolling about on the local fells only a short while ago.

The local mayor and his wife were coming, both happily under the entirely false impression that they were the guests of honour, as indeed was everyone else. There was going to be so much jockeying for position, Lisa would need crampons just to stay upright.

Having bollocked his staff, who were also under the impression that they were working as hard as they could and doing everything exactly the way he wanted, Harry fired off a quick email to Jake. Gordon Ramsay was doing a television series in which he tried to help restaurants that were in trouble. Maybe Jake should apply to go on it, he suggested. He chuckled. This would make Jake absolutely livid and possibly cause him to become terminally careless with a carving knife. That he should have grown out of this sort of schoolboy jape long ago didn't occur to Harry. Even if it had, he wouldn't have cared.

Jake tried very hard not to get annoyed by this puerile missive, but eventually gave up and shouted 'Fuck you' so many times he was glad Angelica wasn't there or he would have owed a small fortune in fines.

He wasn't in a terribly good mood anyway, because Georgia, home for the weekend, had been nagging him all morning to take her shopping. Why she wanted to do this when she had been in Milan, Paris and then London over the last few weeks was completely beyond him.

The only shopping he was prepared to do was in cook shops, but he had no spare cash.

'I'm really far too busy,' he said, which was a complete lie, because they had hardly any lunchtime bookings at all, everyone having deserted him (only temporarily, please, God) for the Café Anglais.

He had the sort of headache that would inevitably turn into a migraine if it found itself in Harvey Nicks in Leeds, which was where she wanted to go. Plus, he was desperate to spend some training time with Sally and some choux pastry, which she was trying to fill with a rum and chocolate cream but which didn't seem to want to stay there.

Not for the first time, he said: 'How I wish you would learn to drive.'

She glared at him. 'Have you forgotten, my last instructor said some people were just too sensitive to cope with cars?'

'Yeah, but your problem is that you are too stupid,' said Kate, but very quietly, her head in a box of vegetables.

'You can get there by bus. You take the number twenty-four to Windermere, oh, except there isn't another one until after lunch. No, take the six up to Carlisle – they go every ten minutes past the hour. Then if you knew your way round Carlisle you'd be able to get a train, except I'm not precisely sure if there is one that goes direct, so you would have to change. Really you would be better to –'

'Is this person serious?' said Georgia.

'What would Georgia be better doing, Kirsty?' asked Jake gently.

'Going to Manchester instead.'

'Thank you for your help. Godfrey?'

'Sorry, Boss, but I had to drive the tractor to work this morning.'

'No, that wouldn't do,' said Jake gravely, trying not to laugh at the picture this induced.

'Well, why can't she take me?'

Kate emerged from the vegetable box, furious. Who the hell was she calling 'she'?

'It's true that I won't need two waitresses for the miserably small amount of meals we will probably do today.'

'So, are you saying you will actually pay me to go shopping?' said Kate.

'Ah, but you've never had the shopping experience with Georgia, have you? You'll need stout shoes, oxygen tanks and a bar of Kendal Mint Cake to stand a chance of returning in one piece.'

'Jake, *I* am not laughing,' reminded Georgia, in a voice that would have frozen hot tamales.

Georgia's perfect brow furrowed when she saw Kate's car and she would only get in after Jake had lined the passenger seat with kitchen towel. 'I know you think I'm being fussy but this coat was rather expensive.'

Kate grinned. 'It probably cost more than the car did,' she agreed, without rancour. She didn't think there was any need to add that in her line of work, something shabby but fast was essential. She had had to leave places in a bit of a hurry sometimes. Also, being tatty, it didn't matter if it got pelted with things, as it had been once when she was doing a story about a councillor who was bonking his daughter's under-age school friends.

As they sped off towards the motorway, Kate giving absolutely no quarter to tourists who wanted to amble along in the middle of the road at twenty miles an hour, she shamelessly asked questions about Georgia's life as a model.

'My parents would have had a fit if I'd said I wanted to take up modelling as a career. Not that they would have had me,' she laughed.

'No,' agreed Georgia. 'Luckily, of course, I have the looks and Mummy was behind me all the way.'

'It's a tough job, though,' said Kate, thinking of young girls, predatory men and drugs.

'It is. People are so bitchy, which is so unfair. I mean it's not my fault I look the way I do. Mummy had to take me to a counsellor after one of the girls told me I was a pound overweight.'

'How shocking!'

'So, what size are you? You're a size twelve, aren't you?' She said this accusingly, as if she was expecting Kate to lie.

'Yeah, pretty much, most of the time.'

'Doesn't it bother you?'

'Not as much as it should, apparently,' said Kate drily. 'Really, I don't think about it much, as long as I can fit into my clothes.'

'Of course, some of the girls I know are completely obsessive about their weight. Luckily I've never been like that. I only have to weigh myself twice a day.'

God, I'd hate to see what you're like with an obsession! 'Anyway, I had to throw my scales away.'

'Why?'

'Well, my friend and I got drunk one night and we were trying to cook rice, only I'd misplaced the kitchen scales, so Lydia got the other ones from the bathroom and for some reason we decided it would be a good idea to stand on them together, but I think I must have jumped on them too hard and . . . anyway, they broke,' she finished lamely. It was quite hard trying to tell a silly story to someone whose face was about as expressive as a security fence. 'Anyway, I refuse to starve myself just to conform to standards set by anorexic American actresses,' she finished firmly.

'Yes, but what other sort of standards are there?'

'Well, it must be hard watching what you eat when you live with such a fabulous chef.'

'Is he? I can't stand the stuff he cooks, myself, and anyway I hardly ever think about food.' She went on to explain how thoughtless Jake was, always wanting to watch cookery programmes on television.

'I could really identify with poor Princess Diana. There are three of us in our relationship, except that one of them isn't even a person – it's that awful job of his. He just doesn't understand how stressful my work is, and do you know' – she lowered her voice as if imparting some deep secret – 'I am a very sensitive person. Mummy always says I need a lot of attention.'

'Oh, how awful for you,' said Kate, well aware that sarcasm was a signal way out of Georgia's orbit.

'Yes, Mummy says I've got less layers of skin than

ordinary people. It's really hurtful that Jake is being so selfish at the moment.'

'Well, he's certainly work-obsessed and ambitious.'

'But I wish he was. I mean, who is going to notice him up here in the middle of nowhere? And of course he's lucky that he's so insensitive to his surroundings, not like me; all these horrible fields and puddles really fray my nerves.' She gazed blankly out at a scene so lovely that John Ruskin had described it in awe as the gateway to paradise.

Georgia went on to explain at length her extraordinary sensitivity. 'If I have to spend much longer in that awful flat of Jake's, I may get my depression back. It's really unlucky, but I am one of those people who needs to be surrounded with beautiful things before they can be happy. My doctor, Win Ko Lon – oh, you must have heard of him – he was extensively featured in the style section of the *Mail on Sunday* recently – anyway, he says I have a very fragile psyche. It is very rare, apparently. He's only ever treated one other person with a psyche more fragile than mine. He says that it is simply not strong enough,' her voice lowered, 'to deal with Jake's weirdness.'

Kate's mind whirled. Cross-dressing? Occult rituals? Surely not?

'He gave me such a fright the other night, thrashing about in this bizarre nightmare. He said it was about a food critic who was laying into him because there was salt in the butter! I mean, he knows I am the sort of person who shouldn't have to hear weird things like that. I simply daren't tell Mummy – she will be so worried about me.'

It was on the tip of Kate's tongue to offer to drive this

pathetic creature to Mummy's right now but they were already in Leeds, and she was desperate to get out of the car.

Georgia zoned in on Harvey Nicks like a heat-seeking missile. Inside, she sighed, like a pilgrim who has reached Mecca. Her shopping creed was simple: go straight to credit card – do not stop at price.

Kate waited until she had gone. Then she got out her phone.

'Lydia, hi, are you busy?'

'Weeell . . . that depends, doesn't it, on your definition of busy.'

'OK . . . are you actually engaged in an activity that qualifies you for a wage?'

'Don't be silly, of course not. It's lunchtime, but I've only just got back from having my nails done and I really must get through *Heat* magazine before the boss gets back. Why?'

''Cos I've completely screwed up. Somehow I have ended up on the shopping trip from Hell with an insane woman who eats half a Rice Krispie for breakfast. If she's treating herself.'

She held the phone away from her ear so Lydia could get the laughing over with. Kate's idea of a good shopping trip was a tour of all the bookshops, followed by lunch.

'So where are you now?' said Lydia eventually.

'Outside Harvey Nicks.'

'I am surprised you've even heard of it.'

'Ha ha.'

'Well, you did your entire season's shopping at Primark last year, didn't you?'

'And your point is? I think I looked rather good!'

'You did, but probably only you could carry it off.'

'That's because I've got chutzpah,' said Kate smugly.

'Pardon? Who told you that?'

'My new friend.'

'Hmm. At a guess – male, bit keen on cooking?'

'Yes, and, sadly, also the boyfriend of the shopaholic bimbo. Why do clever men end up with stupid women?'

'Because even if they are clever, they are still simple. They are completely incapable of thinking round corners.'

'Lydia, I'm not going to be able to prise brain-dead Barbie away from this place for hours. I may go mad with boredom and stab her with a coat hanger.'

'OK, I can hear the desperation in your voice. Your mission – and you've bloody got to accept it, so stop bleating – your mission is to learn and use the following codes. This season's colour – blue; this season's length – so short we are practically talking porn; this season's style – straight. So last season – frills, purple, swish. Anything that swishes is so out, you'd need a telescope to find it. Key words – angular, mannish – think Marlene Dietrich – think Marlene Dietrich strangling Doris Day with a black silk tie, but it must be black. Not blue.'

'What a load of –'

'Hush your mouth! How dare you think of uttering profanities near the holy temple of the great religion that is fashion retail?'

'OK. I'll give it a go, I suppose.'

'Well, for goodness' sake! It cannot be any worse than pretending to be a waitress!'

'Actually, I am rather enjoying it. Jake says –'

'Funny how he keeps cropping up in your conversation. Listen, missy, no passing the time with fantasies about you and your new best friend cavorting in the kitchen department!'

'Now, why would I do that?'

'That is up to you to figure out. Gotta go, sweetie – bye!'

Because she was currently getting two wages, one from the paper and one from Jake, Kate could indulge in some retail therapy of her own. If she could only get the hang of it. How on earth could anyone get so excited about the choice of a skirt with embroidery on the pocket or embroidery on the hem?

'Get a grip, woman – embroidery is so last year,' she muttered, and went to find Georgia. If anyone could give a master class in shopping, it would be her.

It was amazing how, for such a very thin woman, Georgia could take up so much space. She had already commandeered two of the changing rooms and three of the assistants.

Thank God for their sakes that they had recognised her, thought Kate.

'Even darling David knows that my aura is allergic to green and he's absolutely promised he won't ever make me wear it,' she was saying to one of them, who nodded, rapt. They were all drinking in every word while the goddess was with them.

'Purple, no – blue is so now, isn't it?' offered Kate, hoping she had got it right. They all stopped what they were doing to stare at her, so she stroked her jeans, rather self-consciously.

'Baggy,' said one of them in awe, and Kate was about to protest when she realised that this was a compliment. They were actually Jonathan's jeans, comfortable, but yes, so baggy she had only put them on because she thought she was on kitchen cleaning duty that day.

'They are going to be so big next season,' said one of the girls.

'Yeah, I can already fit both hands down them – oh, I see what you mean.'

'Of course that look is great for women who can't really do the skinny fit,' sniffed Georgia, who so could.

She carried on trying on clothes with the ease of someone who was used to walking around naked in front of other people. In a detached way, putting aside her dislike of Georgia, Kate could admire the way her angular, bony body made the dresses hang so beautifully, because the material wasn't impeded by any bumps at all. I could use this opportunity to pump her for information about what it is like to be an icon for thousands of anorexic teenagers, she thought.

But really, the woman was so bloody annoying! After two hours of Georgia dressing up, Kate's vision had become blurred. There was so much stuff about, it looked a bit like when Angel had gone mad with the poster paints.

'Please, I am starving. Can't we have a coffee break?

'Honestly,' Kate said, dragging an unwilling Georgia up to the restaurant, 'you must have tried on dozens of dresses. When are you going to buy any?'

'Never. Well, not today, here. I get loads of stuff free from the designers. I just like trying things on. I don't know why you've brought me here,' she grumbled, looking round. 'I never eat during the day.'

Kate ordered a large latte and a scone with jam and cream, and watched in horrified fascination as Georgia, after an agony of indecision, ordered tea. Carefully, almost to the drop, she measured out half a teaspoon of skimmed milk and added it reverently.

'How can you stand to live your life like that?' Kate burst out.

'Like what?'

'Tinkering around with food in that obsessive way.'

'Huh! Well, Jake is just as bad!'

'Yes, but . . . that's because he wants to make it taste perfect.'

'Well, I have to keep my body looking perfect.'

'Oh, fair enough, I suppose.'

'You have no idea,' continued Georgia, sipping tea delicately. 'I am under almost unbearable pressure to look good all the time. Obviously I wish I was ordinary, like the rest of you, but I'm not. I never know when someone will try to take a photo of me, so I always have to be prepared. People even hang around airports at five in the morning, hoping to catch you out looking scruffy.'

Oh dear. As a trainee Kate had been sent off to Heathrow with a photographer to do just that. She remembered it now as endless hours hanging around in ugly departure lounges drinking vile coffee, being told off by the staff for smoking, followed by mad sprints down corridors when a plane landed. If it was someone really famous, then there was a mad scrum of hacks all behaving badly, kicking each other in the shins and poking their mikes up your nose just when you were about to ask a question.

It was very off-putting to eat in front of someone who so obviously didn't and she was glad when they split up for a while so she could browse round a bookshop. She bought two books of journalists' memoirs, which she made the assistant double wrap, as if they were bottles of meths, so paranoid was she about being outed as a reporter, and spent the journey home nodding absently every so often at Georgia, while looking forward to starting one of the books with a bubble bath and a bottle of wine.

Jake eyed Georgia's modest collection of bags with some relief when they got back. 'You've been very abstemious,' he teased. He had had a very pleasant afternoon and was trying not to dwell on the fact that this was because he hadn't spent it with Georgia.

'What does that mean? Is it a real word or is it one of those foreign ones you are always using? This is all we could get in the car. The rest is being delivered. I found this fabulous furniture shop. It's time the flat was smartened up.'

Jake went paler than the rarest truffle. 'How much did you spend, exactly?'

'Not a lot, considering I got a new settee, a coffee table and a darling hand-woven rug from India – or was it China? Anyway, you should be pleased. Your flat is a tip and I am sure that sofa has got fleas. Look, I bought you two lovely silk ties.'

He couldn't remember the last time he'd worn a tie. At school probably. He couldn't think when he would ever need to wear one, let alone two. For the love of God, why had she bought a new sofa? He never had time to sit on one anyway.

He was tired and he could feel his temper rising, but he tried to hold on to it. 'I simply haven't got spare cash for things like that,' he began, but she interrupted.

'But you said you were doing really well!'

He took a deep breath. How could Georgia, who once got paid £20,000 for an afternoon's work, understand that in his world, doing well meant being able simply to pay the bills?

'You think that because a couple of punters pay a hundred quid for a meal, it all goes into my pocket, don't you? No – don't interrupt – I'll tell you where it goes.

'Firstly I have to pay the mortgage. And the rates. And gas and electricity, because we can't cook by candlelight. I can't run a restaurant without staff and they all need to be paid. If I want to cook food and serve wine, I have to buy it first. This isn't a charity shop, you know – it doesn't get donated.'

'I know that. I'm not stupid!'

'Do you know something, Georgy, if I'm really really lucky, that hundred pounds, and all the others I sweat blood to earn, might just cover all those bills, and if that means I have to sit on a lumpy sofa for ten minutes a week – if means I don't have a fucking sofa to sit on at all – I don't care!

'Maybe I could use these ties to truss the chicken tomorrow night! Or maybe I could give them to my bank manager instead of repaying the loan. Do you think he'll be happy with that?' He was furious now and he couldn't stop. He had only just been keeping a lid on his fear of not being able to pay the bills, before Georgia had sucked more money from their now threadbare joint account.

'I know you can pay for your half of all this stuff, but I've only got enough spare cash for one of the sofa cushions. It isn't going to work, is it?'

Her eyes filled with tears. 'Stop being horrible. I hate it when you get all cold and sarcastic! You know, since you moved up here you've become really nasty and boring.'

'I'm trying to run a business. It's actually rather tiring!'

'Oh, yes, and you'd much rather do that than spend some time with me.'

He was silent. She was right. Georgia wasn't too good with long words but, like any woman, she could read a silence. She gave a loud sob and ran out of the room.

'Where are you going?' he asked in exasperation.

'Anywhere! Away from you! You know I'm not supposed to have anyone shout at me – it's so bad for my nerves!'

This wasn't the first argument that had ended in her running out before they'd really got going, but suddenly he decided it was the last one when he would go after her. It was about time he stopped trying to help her see that people sometimes had differences of opinion and survived it.

Outside, Georgia was finding that it wasn't very easy to run in high heels and, anyway, no one was watching her, so she might as well walk and be comfortable. How dare Jake not follow her? How did he know she wasn't about to stumble into the path of an oncoming car? Her bosom heaved with the injustice of it all, though she had to admit she would certainly make an exceptionally good-looking corpse – lying down would really accentuate her long legs. She pictured herself, totally still, ghostly pale and Jake kneeling beside her, prone, a quivering heap of remorse and guilt.

She walked on, enjoying the thought of him suffering. He definitely would have to pay for making her feel so bad. Their relationship needed to get back on track – with him adoring and her in control. She walked on, hoping his anger had already dissolved into anxiety. That was good, but frantic anxiety would be better. But how could she make that happen? She stopped, because there was nowhere else to go but into the lake, and looked round.

There was nothing but trees, water and, a little further away, what looked like another restaurant, covered in fairy lights. The lights were tiny and white and very pretty but they only made her mood worse. She had wanted Jake to buy them for his restaurant, but he'd laughed and said he couldn't afford to switch them on, let alone pay for them. They were terribly expensive but very eye-catching. A taxi had pulled up outside to pick up some people who were spilling out onto the pavement. There was lots of laughter and air-kissing going on. Georgia sighed; it all looked like the most tremendous fun. Who was that man? Surely she had seen him before? She leaned forward, but remembered in time not to screw up her eyes in case of wrinkles. He had spotted her too and was turning round boldly to get a better look. There was something about the confident way he moved – of course! The man at the station – the one Jake didn't like! Huh! Well, that meant precisely nothing. Jake had already proved himself to be a man of very poor judgement.

Harry approached, a wide smile spread across his face. There was no way she could be rude to someone who was so well turned out and so gratifyingly pleased to see her.

'The beautiful stranger at the station! Let me say what an absolute pleasure it is simply to look at you, especially at the end of what has been rather a trying day.'

Now why couldn't Jake say things like that?

'I thought I would be doomed to only ever seeing you again on the cover of a magazine.'

Now this was rubbish because Harry only read the trade papers, and magazines with dead pheasants or deer on them, but she wouldn't know that. It always really annoyed him that Jake had ended up with someone so gorgeous. It was like seeing a scruffy tom cat with half an ear pairing up with a sleek pedigree Persian.

'Hello again. I've just been for a walk,' said Georgia, lamely.

If Harry thought it odd that someone was pounding the pavements of a little country town in four-inch heel Manolo Blahniks with little diamanté flowers round the toes, he didn't say so. But he instantly clocked the signs of a woman who had just had a row.

'I'd simply love to offer you a drink, but you know that Jake and I don't exactly get on. I'd hate to get you into trouble.'

'I'm in trouble already,' said Georgia gloomily.

'Well, you know what they say about champagne, don't you?'

'That it's expensive?'

'Well, yes, but what I meant was, it's good for you whatever mood you are in – happy or sad. I like to think of it as a delicious sort of medicine and I am prescribing some for you straight away.' Without looking to see if she was following, he turned and walked off.

Georgia did hesitate. Wasn't this flirting with the enemy? Then she recalled how vile and insensitive Jake had been. And hadn't Dr Ko Lon said she had to bask like a frolicking dolphin in other people's love and admiration? Or something like that, anyway. Certainly she didn't want to bask anywhere near Jake at the moment.

What perfect timing, Harry thought. All his important guests had gone, Lisa could deal with the others, and there was always a chilled bottle or two in his fridge. He didn't quite know where this was leading, but he was sure it was somewhere to his advantage.

'What a gorgeous flat,' said Georgia when she saw the light airy rooms and deceptively simple furniture.

'It's pretty basic, but comfortable, I think,' said Harry, who thought nothing of the sort. 'How odd – I've had these walls painted exactly the same colour as your eyes,' he continued.

'These are tinted contact lenses,' said Georgia. He laughed as if she had made a good joke, and produced the most gorgeous bottle of bubbly, covered in little hand-painted flowers.

She sat down and instantly sank back into the soft cushions of a sofa expressly designed to make one unwind, uncurl and chill out. This was more like how she should be treated. She took a delicate sip of champagne.

'There, I can tell by your face you've cheered up already. I won't ask why you've been crying – I wouldn't dream of prying.' There was no need: he was more than capable of softening a woman up and making her talk. 'I know it's tough living with a chef.' And Harry sighed, as if he was the innocent victim of many failed relationships.

'It's not that Jake is a chef; it's that he doesn't understand me,' wailed Georgia, who had never heard of holding back. Her eyes filled with tears, which only made her look more beautiful. 'I have tried and tried – you have absolutely no idea what he has put me through in the last few months. And do you know what? He just throws it all back at me!'

The next moment she found a crisp white handkerchief pressed into her hand, which Harry was now holding in a totally unthreatening, but sympathetic way. He said nothing, but his gentle smile simply begged for confidences.

'I shouldn't be sitting here,' said Georgia. 'Jake absolutely hates you.'

'I know, and I have tried on many occasions to rectify this situation. How ridiculous our petty quarrel seems now! I told him the last time we met that we were both now old enough and wise enough to put it behind us. But – and I am sorry to say this – he does find it rather hard to let go of a grudge.'

'Oh, you are so right! He just goes on and on!' said Georgia, thinking about their argument.

'That sort of attitude is very unhealthy,' said Harry sanctimoniously. 'I bet he told you I was a bit of a bastard, didn't he?' Harry shrugged, a picture of sincerity. 'Well, to be honest I am when I am working, but I am also a firm believer in not taking your job home with you.'

'Jake takes his to bed,' said Georgia bitterly. It was such a relief to talk to someone with such a high degree of empathy.

'Maybe he's bitten off more than he can chew.' With a bit of luck. 'There's a high burn-out rate in this business.'

'There is in mine too. Often I spend whole days under immense stress and anxiety, while all he does is potter round his little kitchen. Honestly, he's got such a simple, easy life. Gosh! Listen to me! I shouldn't be saying any of this and especially to you.'

'But you obviously need to get things off your chest,' said Harry, admiring it. He leaned forward, oozing empathy. 'That is a very profound thing you have just said.'

'Have I?'

'I think – and I say this as a purely disinterested observer of human nature – I think at heart Jake is quite simple – no, sorry – uncomplicated in his outlook. Whereas you, well, I think you have a very deep, multi-layered personality.'

'But that's exactly what Dr Ko Lon said!'

After three glasses of champagne on an empty stomach this made perfect sense. She carried on talking because Harry was really so nice and such a good listener. Honestly, she couldn't see why Jake disliked him so much. Then she realised she was having exactly the sort of evening she should have been having with Jake.

Always solicitous, Harry offered to drive her home, promising to park out of sight of Jake. He was so considerate.

The lovely warm feeling induced by the champagne and Harry himself wafted away as she walked up the stairs to

Jake's flat. They had a distinct smell of damp about them. She felt like she had been evicted from heaven.

He was sitting on the sofa, gazing at the television screen, which wasn't even on, and jumped up when she came in.

'I was thinking about calling out mountain rescue,' he said, trying to smile.

'I needed time to think,' she said with dignity, hoping he wouldn't ask where she had been doing the thinking.

He walked over to her. 'I'm sorry I've been such a bear,' he said, wondering why she smelled of alcohol.

He looked terribly tired and there were huge shadows under his eyes. She wondered if Harry was right and he really was burning out. 'I accept your apology. Let's go to bed – I'll give you a massage, that will make you feel better.'

Jake tried not to wince. Georgia's massages were not for the faint-hearted.

In the bedroom she fussed over him, picking up the shirt he had dropped on the floor. A piece of paper fell out of the pocket as she was putting it away. It was a receipt for an order for some awesomely expensive chef's knives. Even by her standards, this was a lot of money. She stood staring at it.

'Leave that and come to bed,' yawned Jake.

'You spent all this money just on knives,' she said slowly.

Jake sighed. His head was throbbing violently, probably because, apart from tasting, he couldn't remember having eaten all day.

'When were you going to tell me?'

'I wasn't. I didn't think you'd understand why I needed them.'

'I don't!' Georgia's voice rose to a shriek, which went through his head like a knife.

'I cannot work without decent knives and Godfrey mangled my best one in the dishwasher last week. It won't cut through a banana now, let alone fillet a steak,' he said, trying to make a joke of it.

But Georgia wasn't laughing. 'All you do is work and when you aren't working you think it's all right for us to spend time in this . . . dump! But I'm not allowed to spend a few pounds on trying to make it look just a bit better! But when you want to buy something? What does this knife look like, Jake? Is it gold-plated and diamond-encrusted?'

'Don't be silly! Look, you don't understand –'

'Oh, I understand you perfectly well! It's one rule for you and another for me, obviously!'

'I'm sorry,' he said tiredly. Why did it feel as if someone was playing a set of drums inside his head? 'I know you think that I'm being hypocritical, but I'm not. Come here, Georgy, and stop glaring at me. I will make this up to you.'

'I don't see how.' She left the bedroom but came back a minute later. 'When you buy stuff for your horrible restaurant – it's like it's your mistress!'

She was right. He was more concerned about what the restaurant needed than he was about her. He would nurture it with every ounce of energy that he had. With a surge of shame he realised he couldn't be bothered about nurturing Georgia. He just wanted her to exist on her own, without any help from him, and that was never going to happen because she was very high-maintenance.

'What are you doing?' he asked, as she opened the wardrobe door and pulled a bag out.

'Packing. I'm going back to London.'

'Don't be silly. How will you get there at this time of night?'

'By taxi. I've just rung up for one. I can't bear to stay a minute longer with someone who can't put me first.' She was sobbing now and couldn't see that she was stuffing his boxer shorts instead of her knickers in the bag.

'Er, you're in the wrong drawer, Georgy.'

'Oh! I hate you!' She picked up the bedside lamp and threw it at him. It missed and went straight through the window. Christ, all the neighbours would be awake now.

'There! You can stay in the bloody dark from now on. It will be cheaper for you!' she added viciously, and clattered downstairs.

Chapter Fourteen

Godfrey came out to greet Kate the next morning, waving his arms as if there was danger ahead. 'There's a lunatic in the kitchen – very scary – wish I was on holiday, in gaol or anywhere else but here,' he hissed, and scuttled off to hide in the fridge.

She poked her head warily round the door and stepped nervously inside.

Silence, apart from the sound of Jake, chopping. He looked deathly pale and was blasting peppers into shreds.

What was Godfrey on about? It was all quite normal so far. She ventured further in for a closer look and saw that Jake was shaking so hard it was a miracle he hadn't chopped a hand off. He wasn't prone to Sally-like bouts of nerves so he must be ill, she thought.

Jake had eventually fallen into an uneasy sleep last night, but when he woke up, his head and throat were on fire. It had taken him fifteen minutes just to get dressed. Now he felt as if he was floating about six inches off the kitchen floor. It was strange, but not unpleasant. He carried on working, deliriously unaware of the effect he was having on the rest of the kitchen.

'Um, would you like a cup of coffee?' asked Kate, thinking he might be better off sitting down.

Jake shook his head and winced. 'Water, please, with lots of ice,' he said hoarsely.

After she'd brought him some she said: 'Are you sure you're feeling all right? You look, well, you look bloody terrible.' She reached across and put her hand on his forehead. He was burning up and had the glassy-eyed look of someone with a high fever.

Jake wished people wouldn't keep asking him questions and making him shake his head because it hurt. His throat now felt like someone was attacking it with a rusty knife. 'I'll be fine,' he said irritably, then admitted: 'Could do with a couple of aspirin, though.'

The next few hours were hell. He absolutely refused to give up and go to bed, which meant they all had to spend the morning making sure he didn't hurt himself. Kirsty supplied glasses of water to cool him down, and Godfrey pretended total incompetence, so that Jake had to keep stopping his own work to tell him what to do, which he did in a husky, cracked voice. The incompetence bit was never difficult and it kept Jake away from sharp knives, which you should never use when your hands are shaking.

At first Kate was touched by his evident suffering. The last time Jonathan had flu, he seemed to expect her to instantly metamorphose into a qualified staff nurse in order to provide an endless supply of tissues, sympathy and disgusting paracetamol drinks flavoured with artificial lemon. Jake was different – he suffered in silence, adopting a stoical air – but he was still a complete pain in the arse.

An hour later, when he suddenly stopped what he was doing to rest his burning forehead on the cool surface of the work bench, Kate decided to cease pussyfooting around. 'Jake, you are behaving like a complete prick. You are absolutely no use here. In fact you are a liability. For goodness' sake, fuck off to bed before you do any real damage.'

Then, when he didn't move, because he didn't think he could, she took him firmly by the arm and steered him upstairs to the flat. He sank like a stone onto the unmade bed and only protested weakly as she undid the buttons of his chef's jacket.

'But I'm so cold.'

'That's because you've got a temperature of about 110 degrees. You'll feel better when you cool down,' she said briskly.

He tried to pull the duvet over his head but she whipped it off smartly. He curled up into the foetal position and groaned quietly. Kate covered him with a sheet, opened the windows, closed the curtains and brought him a glass of water. Beyond that, unfortunately, her medical knowledge ran dry.

The place looked like a shabby bedroom in a seedy hotel, from which the occupants had departed in a hurry. The wardrobe door was hanging open and looked empty; there were dirty tissues on the floor and nothing on the dressing table, apart from a dried-up bottle of nail varnish. The mirror was old and cracked and crooked.

Jake opened one eye and squinted at her. 'Georgia and I had a bit of a row.'

Kate sat down and mopped his brow with a damp cloth. 'I'm sorry,' she said awkwardly. Maybe he was sick with heartbreak, not the flu.

'I've got more fences to mend than after the Grand National. I'll manage somehow, I expect. Can't think properly, though. Must concentrate on work.'

'You're delirious. Shut up and get some sleep.' She stood up to go, but he grabbed her hand.

'Talk to me.'

'Well, I'm not going to talk about work. It will only make you want to get up and go back there.'

'Tell me about the novel you are writing. It will be like listening to *Book at Bedtime* on Radio Four.'

Shit. Oh well, he probably wouldn't remember anything anyway so she could say what she liked. 'It's about a man who comes home from a long voyage to find his younger brother has taken over the estate and married his fiancée.' Wasn't that the plot of *Poldark*? She hoped Jake didn't read a lot.

'He murders his brother, his fiancé goes mad and has to be locked up' – seem to have strayed into *Jane Eyre* here, oh well – 'the house burns down and he becomes a smuggler.' She hoped she would never have to make a living writing fiction.

'You might be waitressing for me for quite a long time,' croaked Jake, with just a suspicion of a laugh in his voice.

'It's a first draft and it's going to be very poetic,' she said crossly.

'What's the hero like?'

'He's called Edward and he's tall and dark. His face is

brown and rugged from weeks spent at sea. His younger brother was always the favourite so he has grown up bitter and tormented. His fiancée was always a bit of a flighty piece and never really loved him but the sea captain's daughter is a feisty woman who understands him and helps him rebuild his life.'

Jake seemed to have fallen asleep, which was a good thing and probably what any literary agent worth their salt would do if they had to read this imitative and slightly Freudian rubbish. She stood up and tiptoed out.

They managed perfectly well without Jake during lunch because there were hardly any customers. Kate prayed this was just a temporary blip. She thought of Jake upstairs. She had been around long enough to know that he had put everything he had in this venture, and felt slightly sick at the thought that it might fail.

Everyone had cleared up and was sloping off home. Kate was reluctant to go. What would happen to Jake if he was left on his own and had a terrible relapse? She went back up, but he seemed fast asleep, though he was still shivering violently, like a thoroughbred horse after a gruelling race. Maybe he would sleep it off.

It was warm enough to sit outside so she took a cup of coffee and a notebook out with her. But the story she had wanted to write just wasn't there any more. It had been blown away by the scorching heat and stress of a real kitchen and by a group of people who weren't a bunch of lazy, good-for-nothings. She liked them, for God's sake! Tess was admirable at juggling motherhood and a demanding job; Godfrey was funny and had real talent; and

Kirsty was better at the job than Kate herself would ever be.

And then there was Jake. He wasn't ruthless and money-grabbing, cooking crap and making a vast profit on the backs of unsuspecting customers. He was committed and passionate and driven. He was just like herself. He had also turned into the hero of her imaginary novel, which was very worrying. He would be furious when he found out what she was really doing. He would probably be more cutting than one of his own knives and most certainly would never want to see her again. She didn't want that.

The coffee went cold while she was trying to work out how she could do her real job without jeopardising the second one. Somehow, she had to write the sort of story Jonathan was expecting but without losing Jake's respect, which had become important to her, very important. It was tricky. No – it was downright impossible. She was screwed.

It was almost a relief to shut the notebook and go back to check on Jake. If anything, he was worse. He was so hoarse he could barely speak, but managed a ferocious scowl when she insisted on ringing the doctor.

'There's nothing wrong with me,' he said in a whisper, trying to sit up and failing. 'It's just a cold – no need to waste the doctor's time.'

'The doctor will probably point out that I am a waitress, not bloody Florence Nightingale, and will want to know why I didn't ring earlier.'

'You should have rung me earlier,' said the doctor, later, after telling Jake that he had a nasty bacterial infection with a very long Latin name. 'Another couple of hours and he would have collapsed. He's exhausted, dehydrated and probably hasn't been eating properly. Brought it on himself, of course – typical man. He should take at least a week off work, but he won't. Luckily it's not infectious. To be honest, if he were on his own, I would have thought about admitting him to hospital, but I am sure you can carry on looking after him.'

She wrote out a prescription that covered most of the page. 'He's to take these right away, and keep an eye on that temperature. Don't hesitate to ring me back if you are worried. Feel free to knock him out with a rolling pin if he even tries to get up. Men, eh! They are either the sort who go to bed for a week with a bunion, or they just don't know when to give in.' She smiled at Kate and left.

This was tricky. The doctor seemed under the impression they lived together and Kate hadn't managed to disabuse her. She didn't want to.

Jake was beyond speech when she came back with the prescription. He managed a weak but grateful smile, swallowed the pills with difficulty and sank into what she hoped was a restorative sleep and not a coma. He must be very bad – he hadn't even asked about the evening shift.

As second in command, Tess took charge. Luckily it was a quiet night and although she got rather sweaty and flustered, and there was even more bad language than usual, they all managed. After it was all over, Kate realised she had even quite enjoyed parts of it.

Even so, Godfrey had to sit down after the last order had gone out because his knees were shaking so hard he kept banging them against the oven.

'You did great and that guy really didn't mind that his

steak was rare instead of medium. He even said he was always going to have it like that from now on,' Kirsty reassured him. 'Of course I am going to tell on you when Jake's better, unless you buy me a lager on the way home.'

'What are we going to do about him? Do you think he'll be all right on his own?'

'I told the doctor I would sleep on the sofa,' said Kate.

Tess gave her a cool, appraising look, but said that was probably the right thing to do.

The room was in darkness when she got upstairs and she fell over one of Jake's shoes as she fumbled for the light switch. He woke up and looked round with dark, glittering, confused eyes.

'Why did you sleep with him, Jill? He might have a bigger dick than me but his ego is so huge there isn't room for two in his bed.'

'I'm not Jill, whoever she is – I'm Kate, and have some more of these pills.' She decided it was perfectly legitimate to stroke his forehead to check how hot he was. When she got up to fetch some more water, he pulled her back down.

'I'm so cold. If you won't let me have the duvet, you'll have to keep me warm.'

She tried to tell herself that lying down with a sick man was not a turn-on. He was delirious – he didn't even know who she was and this was definitely not part of her remit.

'I think you are a liar, Kate, but I like you. Isn't that odd?'

Her mouth went dry but before she could reply he pushed her away and sat up. 'My God! I must be demented! What happened to my restaurant?'

'Nothing. They all managed perfectly well without you. Everything's fine.'

He lay back down again and she stayed there, knowing she should get up, but not wanting to.

Jake started rambling on about food. Did he ever think of anything else? 'I read about this guy – he had three Michelin stars. Bastards took one away from him and he topped himself. This is a terrible business to be in; you can't let up for a minute or they'll have you. Are you on the same wavelength as me? Georgy and I aren't. It's like we are on different sections of the motorway, speeding off in opposite directions. All my relationships have been like that.

'There's this restaurant in France, you know. Georgia would hate it. It's the only place the *Gault Millau Guide* gave full marks to. It's in a converted farmhouse and it has glass floors, so you can look down on the sheep and pigs in the stable underneath you. The chef – can't remember his name – anyway, he does a *menu symphonie*. He doesn't care if people aren't smartly dressed. Food is food, even if you are naked, he says. I'd like to eat a meal with you naked.'

So would I, thought Kate. But if you were naked, I'd seriously consider skipping the meal.

He sighed and drifted off. She disengaged herself gently and crept across the room to sit by the window where the breeze might cool her down and blow some sense into her. She would spend the night on this very uncomfortable and prickly chair. She would not dwell on any of the things he'd said to her while drugged and feverish. She would certainly not think about the two of them in bed, feeding each other fresh strawberries and drinking champagne from each other's – she pinched herself very hard to stop this train of thought before it got more X-rated and dangerous.

To distract herself and because she didn't feel sleepy at all, she got up and crept into the living room. She could read a book or watch television to pass the time.

Or you could have a good snoop, a voice in her head suggested. After all, snoops often lead to scoops, it continued. Ah, yes, but some people would consider that poking your nose into someone else's business was more in the nature of trespass than research, pointed out another voice. Shut up, she said to this second 'holier than thou' voice.

She was struck forcibly by the fact that the flat seemed to bear witness to a huge clash between two very different personalities. There seemed to be no common ground here at all. The glossy magazines in an untidy heap on a very rickety sofa were Georgia's. The cookbooks were obviously Jake's. They were neatly stacked, but their spines were bent and the covers missing. When she picked one up it was faintly scented with garlic and rosemary.

The television must be Georgia's since it was tuned in to a channel that seemed to show nothing but soap operas. One side of the bathroom cabinet had some bath oils and expensive soap in it – the other side nothing but heavy-duty painkillers and blue plasters.

Who had bought the book on managing stress, she wondered. It was impossible to tell because it hadn't been opened.

The kitchen contained Illy espresso coffee beans and some instant stuff. A brown loaf and white sliced. In the fridge, two bags of Maltesers and a circle of Camembert in a wooden box.

Jake was sprawled right across the bed now, dreaming. He had made loads of money but the bank manager wanted it all and it still wasn't enough. However many notes he threw at him, the man kept shouting for more. Then the bank manager turned into Harry, who said: 'This place is mine now,' and put an apron on over his Armani suit.

'No, wait!' cried Kate in the dream. 'My novel will save us!' But she seemed to have two faces, each blurring into the other.

Kate woke up with a start and a stiff neck. It was light now and Jake was standing in front of her, still pale, but sane. He must be still shaky, because he sat down abruptly and put his head in his hands.

'My head feels like it's returned to my body, just. Thank you for looking after me.' He looked at her through his hands. He seemed embarrassed. 'What I can remember of last night doesn't seem to make much sense. I feel sure I was talking complete nonsense.'

'Well, maybe a bit. You went on about some mysterious but fascinating restaurant in France and then fell asleep. The doctor said someone should stay with you, so I did,' she said, trying to sound casual.

Was that all? He must have had some intensely vivid dreams then, because he could have sworn they had been lying in bed together, which had seemed very nice. He must have imagined it, but even that shouldn't have happened in the room he shared with Georgia. Or did he? Had she fucked off and left him for good?

Chapter Fifteen

A couple of days later Kate arrived early for work. She was doing that more often these days. It was as if she couldn't bear to stay away. Also, a germ of an idea for a story had sprouted in her head and it needed careful tending if it were to sprout into a healthy young shoot. Though she had to admit, it probably needed a greenhouse as well. The paper was on her back and they were getting nasty.

'What the hell's going on?' Jonathan had demanded irritably that morning. 'You're not usually so shy about sending copy.'

'This is going to take more time than I thought. What is it, do you not trust me any more? When have I not delivered?

'OK, OK,' he said grudgingly.

She had never had such a conflict between what she knew she should be writing and what she wanted to say. This was going to be a bit of a tightrope walk.

She hadn't been in the kitchen for more than two minutes when Jake walked in. He moved slowly, almost painfully, and she realised with a jolt how much the infection had wasted him. He had to tie his apron strings twice round his waist before it would stay up.

'You're keen,' he said in surprise.

'Oh, I was going to copy out a few recipes for my mum – she likes cooking,' Kate lied.

'Well, don't give her my signature dish. It's licensed only to me.'

'What is it?'

'Can't remember,' he grinned. 'My brain is still a bit woolly. I need sustenance.'

'You could do with fattening up a bit. There's some steak in the fridge.'

'When isn't there? No, I think I need some Jewish penicillin.' He laughed at the puzzled look on her face. 'Never had any? Then you haven't lived. It's brilliant but you won't find it at a chemist. Its real name is matzo ball soup – chicken soup with dumplings to a shiksa bird like you.'

'Like your mother used to make.'

'Oh, no, my mother is a terrible cook. Oma, my grandmother, would make this, gallons of it, to keep us going while Mum was at work.'

'Were you brought up in an Orthodox household?' she asked, thinking how cute he must have looked as a little boy if he'd had to wear one of those skullcaps.

Jake laughed. 'Hardly. We celebrated every religious festival going – Hanukkah, Christmas and – one January – even Chinese New Year, because the weather was lousy and Oma said we all needed cheering up. She used to say that the best revenge on the Nazis for the Holocaust was for those who survived to have as much fun as possible. She reckoned that every time Hitler heard a Jew laughing, Hell would get a bit hotter and she was sure God would understand and approve of this. She always spoke about God as if He was one of her favourite neighbours.'

'She sounds like a great woman. Here, I'll take that – I don't think you've got the strength to carry it. What is it?'

'She was the best woman I've ever known. It's called matzo meal – it sort of absorbs all the other ingredients. You shape it into little dumplings, like so, and then you put it in this soup I am making, which should really be made with a boiled chicken, but I can't wait so we'll have to use some of Godfrey's stock, which is actually not bad.'

Kate put an apron on and helped, enjoying watching him work. He did everything with such grace and confidence.

Because she seemed so interested, he carried on talking. 'It also used to be called "golden broth" because it was like amber, with golden globules of fat floating on top. Of course, many people skim the fat off now – we're all so health-conscious. But I was brought up on the stuff.' Now he was slicing some of Sally's bread. 'Are you going to have some?'

'Oh, yes, please. It smells delicious.' Who cared if she had to buy a bigger skirt?

Jake spooned soup into two bowls and they ate in an oddly companionable silence. He was so effortlessly generous, she thought. There was no way she could betray him, not after they had broken bread together. Oh dear, it was all starting to sound a bit biblical. She swallowed a large chunk of bread and choked. Jake patted her on the back and when this didn't work fetched a glass of water.

'Maybe this soup doesn't work on gentiles.'

This made her laugh and cough even more. She was still

spluttering, with tears streaming down her face when Godfrey arrived. 'What have you done to her?' he demanded of Jake sternly.

'Don't be silly. Let's get straight to the point. What have *you* been doing to my kitchen while I've been absent?'

Godfrey's disastrous school career wasn't long gone, and he still looked guilty when anyone asked him a question. He cast his mind back feverishly over the last couple of days and glanced round the kitchen in case there was a heinous crime he had committed. All was clean and tidy; he hadn't left the oven on and nothing looked like it was falling apart. 'Er, I did undercook a steak.'

'Well, it's better than overcooking it, I suppose,' said Jake grudgingly. Secretly, he was delighted that everything seemed to be in perfect order, though of course slightly miffed that they'd done so well without him.

'How many times have I told you that you're to test it by touching it?'

'About a million, I suppose. I did remember, but I was stressed.'

'So? It's like that all the time in a kitchen – get used to it.' He was feeling better by the minute. 'You should know by now that a kitchen is no place to indulge in a hissy fit. It's not backstage at the opera, for God's sake.'

Godfrey stuck his bottom lip out mutinously. He seemed to recall Jake taking time off to hurl a wooden spoon out of the window the other week. He also entertained a brief but delightful fantasy of Jake bound and gagged somewhere, leaving him in sole charge of the kitchen. Then he remembered he needed Jake's advice on béchamel sauce.

I should just tell him the truth, thought Kate. It's obvious we like each other. It's clear where we both want this to lead. It's real and it's good – or it will be when I've stopped lying to him. I have to sort this out now, before it gets any worse.

She followed him through to the office.

'Er . . . can I have a word?'

'Sure.'

They stood looking at each other. They were about the same height so she could look straight into his eyes. Good. Then he would know she was now telling the truth. How beautiful the bones of his face were, lying just under the too pale skin . . . Get to the point, you coward! No, I can't hit him with this just now. It might give him a relapse. I know I've got to come clean, but I've got to pick the right moment!

'I . . . I just wanted to say thank you for telling me about your family. I found it really interesting. It means a lot to me.'

'I don't tell everyone – I don't want it to sound like a sob story. But I knew you would understand. Um . . . is that it?'

'Yeah. Thanks. Great.' She fled. Well, that wasn't very well played, you silly woman!

'You're awfully red in the face, you know. What have you done?' asked Godfrey.

Slowly the staff filtered in to work, some pleased to see their boss back on his feet, some less so, particularly Tom, the part-time washer-upper, who had spent the previous shift reading the *Sun* and desultorily swishing water around pans. He had hidden a whole stash of dirty cutlery in a cupboard and now wondered how he was going to get it out and in the dishwasher, where it should have gone last night, without Jake spotting it.

At ten past six, Jake looked up from his chopping board and frowned. Sally was late. This was unheard of. She was genetically programmed to arrive early for everything. She would probably be the only bride hanging around outside the church and tapping her watch, waiting for the groom to arrive.

At twenty past six Jake was worried. Even if she was dying of the bubonic plague she would have got a message to him to let him know, surely? He went into the office and rang her. She still lived with her mum.

'Hello, Mrs Smith. Can I speak to Sally?'

'She's not here,' said Sally's mum.

'Well, where is she?' asked Jake briskly.

'I'm afraid I can't tell you that.' She sounded cagey.

'Why ever not? I'm her boss and I have a right to know why she hasn't turned up for work,' said Jake coldly. There was a click. He looked at the phone in disbelief. She had hung up on him! He dialled again and was asked to leave a message. He stomped back to the kitchen in a furious temper. 'OK, one of you must know where Sally is. Spill – now!'

But everyone looked at him in genuine puzzlement.

'Honestly, Chef, she was here yesterday just like usual – worked away – never said anything – well, she never does, much, does she?' Tess looked around and they all nodded in confirmation.

'Was she sick at all? Upset?'

'Hard to tell. I mean, she seemed perfectly fit and she

always looks like a neurotic mouse.'

'Right.' He thought for a minute. 'Kirsty, does your sister still want some waitressing work?'

She nodded.

'Well, ring her. Kate, stop drying all that cutlery – why wasn't it done yesterday? – and put this apron on.'

'Oh, no. Definitely no. I am a waitress, not a cook.'

'I'm not asking you to cook,' said Jake irritably. 'Most of the stuff for dessert is already made. All I need is someone to put it together. Perfectly simple. An idiot could do it, but Godfrey is busy.'

Kate backed away nervously. She had got used to being on the serving side of the pass; beyond it was foreign and hideous territory. It would be like stepping into no-man's-land.

Jake's tone softened. 'Honestly, Kate, it will be fine and it will only be for tonight. It will be a doddle, I promise you. We'll all look after you, won't we, guys?'

It was liked being lured by a snake-charmer. Entirely against her will she walked forward and took the apron he was holding out. He had a gentle, friendly smile.

'Good. Now the chocolate and tiramisu parfaits are already made and just need to come out of the moulds; the pan-roasted, cold plum soup just needs to be served with a swirl of yoghurt on the top; the passion fruit and orange tart just needs cutting into wedges; the ravioli of pineapple just has to be sandwiched together with strawberry cream; ditto the puff pastry slice, and we'll forget about the crêpes Suzette tonight.'

Kate noticed he was using the word 'just' a lot. He made

it sound so simple and reasonable a blind man with the tremors could do it. So why was Godfrey rolling his eyes in horror and sympathy as she crossed the great divide? Tess had her lips clamped together and refused to meet her gaze. It was going to be a long night.

Kate knew the constituents of the puddings by heart, having given lyrical descriptions of them to customers all week. A quick survey of the fridge showed her that Jake was right. Everything was there in all its different parts, beautifully made up. All it required was a steady hand and a steel nerve. Surely it couldn't be more difficult than laboriously uncovering a Roman artefact with a toothbrush, which she had been allowed to do on the dig, to her enormous pride? It was now behind glass in the museum at Keswick, with her name next to it. It was probably a good thing cooks were an uncultured lot and never visited museums.

Jake couldn't have been nicer at the start. With infinite patience and good humour he went through a trial run with her, showing her how to pipe cream onto a layer of puff pastry so delicate she hardly dared breathe in case it floated away.

'You have to arrange the fruit so it hangs down as if it's still on the bush – no, don't pull the stems of the blueberries and take care not to crush the raspberries. If you run a hot cloth round the moulds, the parfaits will slide out as easily as – well, I'll leave that to your imagination. Excellent – you're doing brilliantly!

'I'm really grateful you're doing this and I know you are probably a bit nervous,' he continued, in an encouraging manner.

A bit? She couldn't remember the last time she had heard such a ridiculous understatement.

'I do know how you feel. I felt the same way at the start of every shift when I was training. I felt even worse the night the restaurant opened. I know you can do it. Tomorrow we'll look back at this and laugh.'

'Yes, but we'll probably be in strait-jackets by then,' put in Godfrey, and received such a scowl from Jake he said no more.

Between them, they got everything as ready as it could be. Being orderly and meticulous herself, Kate enjoyed this and started to relax. Surely it wouldn't be that difficult to put it all together when someone actually ordered something?

This is easy – I can do this! Don't know what they all make such a fuss about. People get so anal about their jobs – think they are the only ones who can do it. All that running around and shouting is just for show . . .

'Shit, first order. Only for two, no problem.' She picked up a mould and promptly dropped it.

'Not to worry,' said Jake, rather too heartily, she thought.

He hovered over her like an anxious father in a delivery room. 'Don't poke at it, woman. It's not something nasty you've just found on the bottom of your shoe. Don't shake it about like that either! And people generally like the sauce in the middle of the plate, not dripping off the edge. There, that's better. What's the point of it tasting nice if it looks like shit? OK, take it away, Kirsty. What the hell are you waiting for – the Second Coming?

'You see, that went quite well, didn't it?'

Overcome by such praise she turned and tripped over Godfrey's enormous feet.

If only the orders would come in like the animals on Noah's Ark, neatly in pairs. But they didn't. How could people be so inconsiderate as to go out and eat in groups of eight? She only had one pair of hands, didn't she? Kate felt as if her face had frozen in a rictus of fear and her nose was so shiny they could probably use it as an emergency light should the power fail. Her thoughts began to flutter around crazily in her head like a flock of startled birds.

Another one – well you'll have to wait, mate. Get out of my way – can't you see I'm in a hurry – now look what's happened – wonder if I can pick the ice cream up with my fingers – crap, no I can't – Jake's looking. Hasn't he got anything else to do?

Fuck! This fucking parfait won't come out of the fucking mould! What did Sally do to it, weld it on? Yes I know there are another two orders – I am not blind, thank you – where's the piping bag, why isn't it clean? Because I didn't have time to clean it, that's why. God, it's coming out like a nasty case of diarrhoea – why is it not piping properly? Where's the fruit? WHERE'S THE FUCKING FRUIT? Oh – it's here. I never put it there – who moved it? Bastards! Oh, yes, I put it there. Christ, I'm hot; feel like I'm working in the oven, not next to it. Why won't the yoghurt swirl like it did when Jake did it? Yes, I know it looks like shit. There was no need to do that with it, Jake, and now I'll have to make up another and, look, the orders are piling up – I've only got one pair of hands and someone has STOLEN those ravioli thingies . . .

Shit – shit – shit – shit!

She was so hot the sweat was dripping down her nose and in danger of falling into the plum soup. Her swirls looked like bird droppings, the puff pastry crumbled into a thousand pieces. Jake was on her back constantly, criticising, complaining, chucking stuff away so she had to start all over again, which meant she was always behind. She developed a passionate hatred of him, of the stupid moulds, of the piping bag, which squirted cream out of the wrong end and into her eyes and on her fingers, which seemed to have turned into overcooked sausages and wouldn't bend properly any more. She was completely oblivious of everyone else and what they were doing except when she bumped into them and they both cursed, fiercely, automatically. She could feel herself turning into a stiff, sweaty pillar of terror. If she stopped for a second, she would simply snap in half.

'Come on! Come on!' yelled Jake, who seemed to be doing about fourteen things all at once, but still had time to notice there were smears of chocolate on the edge of the plate.

When this was over, she would hit him, very hard; she would knock him to the ground and stamp all over him and squirt that fucking strawberry sauce up his nose, having boiled it up first. What? Someone wanted two puddings? Greedy fucking bastards – she hoped their arteries exploded at the table.

Oh God! Oh God! Oh God!

When the last pudding had gone out, with its usual quota of criticisms, complaints and modifications, she looked at the clock and realised time hadn't stopped – it was after midnight. It was over. She threw her towel in the air and without thinking, grabbed Jake and kissed him. For a split second she could feel him pulling her closer, then he backed off.

'For heaven's sake, woman! Don't put ideas into Godfrey's head. Who knows where this would lead the next time he gets something right!' He bent down to retrieve a spoon from the floor, so no one could see his face.

Staggering outside, light-headed, as if she hadn't eaten for three days, she smoked three of Kirsty's cigarettes in succession, though she had given up years ago.

'Did you enjoy that?' asked Jake.

Kate ground the cigarette beneath her heel and took a few sweet seconds to collect everything she had to say.

'I hated it. I hate you. I hate puddings. I never want to see a strawberry ever again. I am never setting foot in there again. I don't care if you have to get your desserts from the ice-cream van down by the lake. If you ever, ever ask me to help out again I will . . . I will . . .' She was a journalist, but words had failed her.

'You didn't do that bad for a beginner.'

'Jake, you shouted at me for the whole fucking evening!'

'Of course I did,' he said, genuinely surprised. 'But I was just keeping a friendly eye on you, giving you the odd tip now and again.'

It was dark outside but she could tell he was laughing at her.

'It's good to see things from a different perspective now

and again. I bet you thought we just messed around in there, didn't you?'

'No!'

Well, yes, maybe a bit. Shamefully she recalled her and Jonathan's patronising conversation all that time ago, when she had a different life. They were such a pair of goobies – they didn't know the half of it.

Kirsty joined them and took her fags from Kate's nerveless fingers. 'Is there a special name for people who say they've given up smoking and then proceed to smoke everyone else's?'

'Yes – shameless,' grinned Kate, and pinched another.

'By the way, Jake, I found this note outside your office. Someone must have crept in and left it there during service.'

> Dear Jake,
>
> I am sorry I couldn't tell you this in person. I am handing in my notice as from now. I have been offered another job. It is better pay, with less hours. It is a good career move. Please don't get angry, but it's at Café Anglais. Mr Hunter says he won't let you in if you try to come round and give me a hard time. I'm sorry if I've dropped you in it.

It was signed 'Sally'.

Jake let out such a bellow of rage that Godfrey dropped a tray of crockery. It was a good thing all the customers had gone or they would have run away in fright.

'I just can't believe she would do that to me! And after all

I've done for her. Why do people always say sorry about something they don't give a toss about? How dare she just leave without handing in her notice properly?' He was incandescent with rage because he was powerless to do anything. Sally didn't need a reference because she had already got another job. Harry would probably have bouncers on the door at Café Anglais to stop him from entering and, anyway, he would just love it if Jake went storming round there.

He kicked the wall to vent his feelings and then howled with pain as well as fury. He would have to find another pastry chef, and fast. They had only got through tonight because everything had been made up, and anyway it hadn't been busy. Kate had been great but she wasn't a cook. He would have to stay up all night and make a new batch of puddings, and everyone would have to work twice as hard as they already were working. It could take weeks to find someone new.

It was a waste of time to brood on it, but he felt bitterly let down by Sally. He thought she had been happy here. He had been endlessly kind and patient with her because she had real talent. But she would be squashed to a pulp by Harry. Fewer hours – hah! She wasn't going to know what hit her! He would screw her, then dump her and dock her pay every time she fucked up. It was like sending a tiny kitten into a lion's den and expecting it to come out alive.

Kate wasn't feeling too good, either. In fact she was gibbering with panic, a state she had never before experienced. 'Listen, if you're expecting me to –'

'It's OK – don't worry.' Jake wasn't sure if he had broken

a toe when he slammed his foot into the wall, but the pain had cleared his head. 'I meant what I said: you did great, but I'm not expecting you to make a career change.'

Thank God for that. She'd had so many of those recently, she wasn't sure who she was any more.

Chapter Sixteen

Kate sniffed, stirred and tasted. She thought about it for a minute, then steeled herself for a second go. No. She was right the first time. It was impossible to say anything nice about Godfrey's soup. It was just terrible. It had all the flavour you would expect to find at the bottom of a very old sock. The surface of this revolting concoction was speckled with small black spots, which didn't improve the soup's desirability.

'Jake said to use white pepper but I thought it needed a bit of oomph. I also thought I would try to improve on the original,' he floundered on, aware that with his limited experience, this now sounded frankly ludicrous.

'And what do you call this creation?' Kate asked, genuinely curious.

'Er, cream of pea,' he said, desperately trying to remember what he had chucked into it.

'Hmm,' said Kate, wondering if she should try to be kind, but knowing this was impossible. 'The trouble is, I would call it a lot of things, but none of them would actually include the word edible.'

'Oh dear, you sound just like Jake.'

They both thought about Jake. Emma, the new pastry

chef, had been recruited after turning up at the back door, bearing a lemon mousse that Jake said was the best he had ever tasted.

'I am going to train to become a teacher, but I want to take some time out before going back to class – you know, to clear my head.'

'Hmm. I'm not sure that working here will actually do that, but start anyway,' said Jake.

She was talented but inexperienced, which meant that Jake was spending extra time training her. He didn't mind, but it was tiring. Now he was out, having a meeting with his bank manager. He had left Godfrey to make soup. He would expect soup when he got back. A good soup would restore his frayed nerves after a trying afternoon. This was so not a good soup.

Kate and Godfrey were alone in the kitchen. Everyone else had long gone and Godfrey was itching to do the same. 'The thing is, I've absolutely promised my dad to go and find some sheep this afternoon. About a hundred and forty of them. He'll be a bit peeved if I don't turn up.' This was a massive understatement. On a good day, when Godfrey's dad was shouting at his animals he could be heard in three counties.

Godfrey could either stay behind and make a soup someone would like to eat, but be bollocked by his dad, or he could race up and down the fell for a few hours, while looking forward to being bollocked by Jake when he got back. 'Either way, I'm screwed.'

Kate was secretly very proud of her stint in the kitchen, especially now that the horror had receded. Like a new mother, she had forgotten about the agonising birth pangs and could only remember the bliss of delivery.

A couple of hours on her own in the kitchen, and she could make a perfectly acceptable soup. All the ingredients were there for the soup Jake had wanted Godfrey to make, before he had got ideas above his station. She also wanted to impress Jake, for reasons she wasn't prepared to admit to herself.

'Go on, get up that fell. I'll make some more soup,' she said, trying to make it sound like a massive favour, reluctantly granted.

'Can you?' asked Godfrey, doubtfully.

'Could it be any worse than this?'

'Well . . .'

'Go on, then, I dare you to eat a bowl of that . . . that stuff.'

'I'll be back before six.'

Left on her own, Kate sauntered off to the fridge, humming. *Soupe aux moules*. Albert Roux had described it as a dish that would tempt even non-soup-eaters. Kate reckoned it would also be dead easy to make as it contained only a few ingredients and the instructions only covered a few lines. Any recipe method that had you turning over several pages of tightly written script was not worth doing, in her opinion. Also, she had to admit, that sort of stuff was probably best left to the professionals. Superbly talented and versatile she might be, but she was not a pro.

She was also well on her way to a winning soup, because Jake had thoughtfully provided the stock. It had taken hours to make but as she heated it up and its delicate fragrance hit her nose, she realised it was going to be a lot better than chucking a ready-made stock cube into some hot water.

She got out a chopping board and sliced onions, leaks, carrots and celery. How on earth did you sweat vegetables? Tell them they had to do a week's work with Jake? That could send anything into a lather of fear. Trial and error gave her the answer. She cooked the first batch on a high heat for about ten minutes, after which they were shrivelled to a very unappetising shade of burned. OK, maybe 'sweat' meant cook gently, in which case why didn't they bloody say so? It was as if cooking were some sort of arcane club into which only a select few were admitted.

'Debeard the mussels.'

This was a kitchen, not a barber's shop. Did they mean that funny bit hanging off the end that probably no one would want to eat? After a few false goes she eventually got into her stride. Crushing the garlic and chopping the tomatoes was easy and then all you had to do was leave it to simmer. She went out and sat in the sun for a few minutes, enjoying the fact that she was not sitting in a stuffy, noisy reporters' room.

The soup then had to be blended and cream and saffron added. Bloody hell, that actually tasted good! OK, the kitchen did look a bit of a mess because she had committed the cardinal sin of not tidying up as she went along, but at least she had produced something edible. One taste of Godfrey's soup and you lost the will to eat again.

She tried some more, shutting her eyes and enjoying the feeling of it moving silkily down her throat.

'If men could only make women look as happy as that.'

She jumped and dropped the spoon.

'Is this part of some cunning plot to take over my kitchen? Do your ambitions know no limits?' asked Jake, grinning.

She told him about the cream of pea débâcle, the urgent question of dozens of missing sheep and her own incredible good nature.

'Try this and tell me you don't like it.'

She couldn't understand why his lips were twitching but he took a taste and agreed, with some surprise, that it was a very good soup indeed. Then he looked round the kitchen.

'How long did it take you to do this?'

'Well, all afternoon, really. Reading the instructions was a bit like deciphering the Rosetta Stone. And I know I haven't been very neat, but I am only a novice and I can tell by the look on your face that it's a good soup, which is not what you would have said about Godfrey's. So why are you laughing? You should be bloody grateful,' she added, rather nettled.

Jake stopped pretending not to laugh and gave in. He leaned against a wall and laughed until his eyes watered. It was extremely annoying. She tapped her foot and advised him to let her in on the joke before she threw something at him. He wiped his eyes.

'OK, OK. Now, you are quite right. This is a perfectly lovely soup. I am full of admiration at the effort you have gone to, the evidence of which I can see all round my lovely kitchen. It is a magnificent soup and one which I would be proud to serve to my customers. The only question is, which one of them am I going to honour with this dish?'

He started laughing again at the puzzled look on her face. 'You have made enough soup for, well, about four people, if they are not very hungry. When we make soup we usually make enough to serve to a restaurant full of people, to avoid nasty quarrels between customers and – oh, yes – to avoid the small problem of us running out after five minutes.'

'You mean I have slaved away all afternoon just to provide soup for one small table? Oh fuck.' She was mortified.

Jake got out a pan big enough to bath a baby in and starting chopping potatoes and leeks with great speed. 'I shall make *potage bonne femme* in honour of you,' he said.

'And I shall wash up,' said Kate rather dolefully. There was an awful lot of it to do considering the very small snack she had prepared.

'I have to go and see some people tomorrow. They could be useful to me. I think, seeing as you are a writer and also keen on food, you will find them interesting. We needn't hurry back as we're closed tomorrow evening. Would you like to come?'

Kate was flattered.

'Of course, you've probably got something better to do,' he said hastily.

Well, she probably had, but the question was, did she want to do it? It was rather disturbing that the thought of spending the afternoon with Jake was what she wanted to do more than anything. No man had ever made her feel like that before.

'I would like to come, unless of course we have to trek for miles through bogs and up precipices to get there.'

'There is a road, of sorts,' he said, grinning.

Jake's car was even older and scruffier than Kate's, but immaculately tidy, apart from a king-size bag of jelly babies in the glove compartment.

'Georgia's. She swears they are a cure for car sickness.'

Kate bit the head off a red one thoughtfully. Here was a great opportunity. They were alone in the car; Jake was in a good mood – there would probably never be a better time for a confession. He could hardly take his hands off the wheel to throttle her, well, not without driving them both into a ditch. There would be plenty of time for him to shout and swear and get it all out of his system. This was it, then – this was the moment.

Oh, no, it so wasn't, she thought, a short while later.

'You know, Jake, you are not a bad driver.'

'Oh? Good.'

'No. You are an absolutely bloody AWFUL one. Please, watch out for that cyclist!'

'But I have. He's still on his bike, isn't he?'

'Yeah, but we were so close I could smell his aftershave!'

'Nonsense. You are just like all other drivers – you always think you can do it better!'

'All? By that I expect you mean every other poor sod who has had the bloody bad luck to sit in this passenger seat, don't you? I know you can slice the thinnest cucumbers in the land, but really, there's no need to shave so close to the bloody verge!'

'Look, it's much safer to hug the left-hand side of the road. You know what tourists are like, always wanting to drive in the middle.'

'Yes, but . . .' she began weakly, but then got flung round another bend. She was having an unexpected spurt of sympathy for Georgia. No wonder she had been driven to extreme cures for car sickness.

'Actually, it's quite endearing, in an "ohmigod I'm going to die" sort of way.'

'You are babbling now, you know.'

'No, what I mean is, you are so perfectly balanced in the kitchen, you never put a foot wrong; even though every shift it's like a dance with different steps. It's kind of good to know you are a bit of a klutz behind the wheel. Oh, no! Please tell me we're not going over Hard Knot Pass.'

'Relax, it's a perfectly easy road and the only way to get to the Roman fort. I like your description of me, by the way. You really do have a way with words. I'd like to read that book of yours when it's finished.'

'Oh God, please give me a break!'

'Sorry – what?'

'Nothing.' Listen God, I can't tell him now, I think I am going to be sick and I have to concentrate on the road otherwise we will go over the edge of this precipice.

'I don't think there is a brake on your side of the car, Kate.'

'Ha ha – very funny.'

Hard Knot Pass lived up to its name. It was the sort of road that should really have belonged in a cartoon, with its hairpin bends and steep drops. It should also have been called Burned Clutch Pass, because that was what happened to a lot of the cars. Locals tended to avoid it like the plague during the tourist season, but for once Kate was grateful for their cautious driving. It might force Jake to drive more slowly.

They did, but not before she had to point out: 'If you are entertaining even a fleeting thought of overtaking that Range Rover I will force-feed you jelly babies until you overdose on sugar.'

The Roman fort was perched on the side of the fell in lonely, broken splendour. The sun was shining, a soft breeze was blowing and the only sign of life was a lone buzzard circling above them. It was the perfect place for telling secrets.

The trouble was, Jake couldn't have had enough school trips when he was young, because he insisted on taking her hand and leading her through each of the ruined buildings.

'I'd have had this for the kitchen,' he said eventually. 'What must it have been like standing here, cooking stew for a hundred hungry soldiers and looking down on that magnificent view? Imagine being sent here, so far from the heat and bustle of Rome. They must have been very homesick. And I bet those pubs down there in the valley weren't open for business two thousand years ago.'

'They weren't Romans, they were foreign mercenaries, and I think it was a punishment posting,' said Kate absently.

'I didn't know local history was another of your talents,' said Jake in surprise.

'I went out with an archaeologist for a while.' Well, it was sort of true. Was there a saying about getting in so deep you drowned? Quick, change the subject. 'Are you really having problems with the bank?'

Jake shrugged. 'Teetering on a knife edge, would just about cover it. You wouldn't believe how easy it is for a restaurant to fail and not just because the food is bad either. It is quite possible in this business to be superbly talented, work like a dog and still go under.'

'My archaeologist friend had the same problem with funding. He used to wait until everyone had gone home and shout his frustrations to the hills and the sheep.'

Jake stood up and put his arms in the air. 'Bloody bank managers! I'd like to stick your heads down the waste-disposal unit – except, damn, Godfrey managed to block it this morning; I must remember to fix it when I get back. Anyway, I hate the lot of you! But you will not grind me down! And neither will that bastard Harry Hunter,' he added for good measure. He looked down. A carload of Japanese tourists was gazing up at them with astonishment and trepidation.

'It's all right, we'll tell them you were declaiming a Latin poem for the souls of dead centurions,' giggled Kate. 'We'll say it's a local custom and they might even pay you to do it again. You could supplement your income by becoming an aid to tourism.'

'Get back in the car, idiot. We have to see a woman about a cheese.'

Beck Farm was down a long, winding, rutted lane. It was the sort of road four-wheel drives were really made for, not half-mile school runs in the middle of Hackney.

As they pulled up, a pack of collies with slavering fangs

came bouncing up, looking for some soft flesh to sink their teeth into. They were followed by a woman with a truly dreadful perm, wearing a flowery dress, a red and white striped apron and ancient gumboots. She looked at them with deep suspicion and called the dogs off grudgingly, obviously quite prepared to unleash them again if she didn't like what they had to say.

Jake advanced bravely, hand outstretched. 'Hello, my name is Jake Goldman; I spoke to you on the phone last week.'

'Aye, you did. You wanted to see my cheese.' She said this with disbelief and disapproval, as if Jake was a man with a strange fetish. 'You'd better come in, I suppose. Don't mind the dogs; they'll do as they are told.'

She led the way into a large kitchen where a small wiry man in shirtsleeves, and with a heavily weather-beaten face, was eating his dinner.

'Geoff, this is the man about the cheese.'

Geoff shook his head as if he could never come to terms with the peculiarity of foreigners, which probably included anyone who lived further away than the lane end. Both of them completely ignored Kate, as if she didn't exist.

Jake and Kate followed the woman outside to the dairy, passing a huge Alsatian busily chewing what looked a bit like someone's thigh bone.

'This is our cheese – it's nowt special.'

Jake tried a sliver. 'Oh, no, Mrs Tomlinson, you are so wrong. It is very special.' He broke off a bit and gave some to Kate. It was cool and creamy and intense in flavour.

'This is fantastic. I haven't tasted English cheese like this since . . .' It wasn't the right time to mention she bought all her cheese, if she bought any, ready packed from a supermarket. That might be a bad word round here.

'If you can provide me with one of these a week to start off with I would be delighted,' said Jake. 'I've been searching for a good local product like this for some time now and I'm certain this is going to prove very popular.'

Mrs Tomlinson unbent a little in the face of this praise. 'We do our own hams as well,' she said.

'Please, lead the way.'

'This is as good as Parma ham, in its own way,' Jake said later, with his mouth full. After that, there was no stopping Mrs Tomlinson. They returned to the kitchen, followed by the Alsatian, which seemed to be taking too much interest in Kate's legs and were urged to try Mrs T's eggs, home-made chutney, Cumberland sauce, damson jam and rum butter, though – thankfully – not all at once.

'If you opened a shop selling this in a town, there would be queues outside the door,' said Kate, a long time later, wiping cream off her nose.

'Why would anyone want to do that?' asked Geoff. 'A town is no place for sensible people.'

It was early evening now and the Tomlinsons' two sons came in after a hard day chasing sheep. More food appeared; what had gone before was evidently just a snack and Kate and Jake were obviously expected to stay. Although the Tomlinson sons were about six and a half feet tall and built like steel girders, they were too shy to say much in front of visitors.

'We don't get many people calling in round here, apart from the wife's sister, and she's daft,' said Geoff.

'You look like you need a good meal. You're not much of an advert for your own restaurant,' said Mrs Tomlinson, producing an enormous casserole that had been simmering in the Aga and what looked like a field full of potatoes, smothered in butter. They all guffawed with laughter at her wit and helped themselves to an appalling quantity of cholesterol, which, despite what the doctors would say, didn't seem to be doing them any harm.

As the entire family had scant respect for Jake's career – 'A man cooking?' said one of the sons in disbelief – the conversation turned naturally to sheep.

'Let me get this right – you spend all day taking the sheep to one bit of hill; then get up at a ridiculously early hour to take them to another?'

'Aye, that's about it. I went to the city once,' said Geoff, leaning back and lighting a disgustingly smelly old pipe. 'It seemed to me all anyone ever did was scurry around them underground tunnels like lunatic ants.'

'Well, you've got a point,' admitted Jake.

'This is a great life. You can spend all day on the fell and never see another living soul,' said one of the brothers, pausing to consider whether he could manage another morsel of ham, deciding that he probably could and cutting himself a slice about three inches thick.

Jake managed to regain some lost ground by declaring a passion for Herdwick mutton stew, but no one seemed to want to say much to Kate – though they all enjoyed looking at her legs. She wished she had worn her baggy jeans.

Regretfully, she refused a second helping of apple pie. Another mouthful and buttons would start pinging.

By the time she stood up to go, a sliver of a moon was hanging in an inky blue sky. They were urged to take home presents of food, which Jake refused. 'You've been kind enough already and your produce is so good it deserves to be bought, not given away.'

They drove off to a chorus of barking, which Mrs T assured them was just the dogs' way of saying goodbye.

'Any time you need a decent meal, you're welcome to pop in,' said Geoff.

'That was totally brilliant,' said Kate. She was full of admiration for Jake, for finding this cornucopia of gluttony in the middle of nowhere. He had a journalist's ability when it came to ferreting out anything worth knowing about.

'I think restaurateurs have an absolute duty to support local suppliers. We still don't do anything like enough of it in this country, though I suppose things are slowly improving.'

They drove back over Burned Clutch Pass, which was free of traffic but full of sheep. 'The road is warmer than the grass – they like to sleep there,' said Jake.

When they were at the top, Kate said: 'Stop the car for a minute.'

'Why? Have you left something behind? Because if you have, it will have to stay there. It's nine o'clock and the Tomlinsons will be tucked up in bed by now.'

'It's my turn to show you something,' said Kate.

'What? Where?' There's nothing to see – it's too dark.'

'Look up,' she said simply.

Jake looked. The night sky was empty of clouds, but jam-packed full of stars, more than he had ever seen in his life. There were no other lights for miles around to hinder their brilliance. 'I didn't know there were that many stars!'

'You don't, when you live in a built-up area. Look, there's the Plough.'

'Where?'

'That group over there, shaped like, well, a plough. The Americans call it the Big Dipper.'

'Oh, yes, I can see it!'

'And over there is Orion the Hunter – that's his tunic and his sword hanging from his belt. And over there is Cassiopeia – she was a fabulously beautiful queen, oh, thousands of years ago.'

'Now that's what I call having your name in lights.' He looked down at her. 'Thank you,' he said softly. 'I think that is the nicest thing anyone has ever shown me.'

Although it was dark, she could see his eyes, glittering with a light reflected off the stars. His face was very close to hers. She wanted it to be closer. Then they both moved together as if they were a pair of magnets. The touch of his mouth on hers made a fire rise deep in her spine. Things must have started happening in slow motion because she could distinctly feel herself thinking – we shouldn't be doing this because we will start something we can't stop and there will be very complicated consequences, but, oh hell, I really don't care; I just want this to go on and on. I want to touch his mouth, his hair; I want to feel his heart juddering against mine and I want to do things to him that will make his eyes close in ecstasy.

For one wild moment she thought he would pull her down with him into the bracken and she would get her wish, but then they were both blinded by the lights of, unbelievably, a motorbike, which pulled up with a roar behind them.

'Broken down, have you?' said the rider, looking at them with interest.

The moment had gone. Maybe it was better that way.

'Er, no . . . we were just looking at the stars,' said Jake feebly.

The rider grinned at them. 'I'll leave you to it, then. They are up there, by the way.' He pointed upwards again, winked at Jake and roared off. The darkness swallowed him up and they were alone, but the moment had passed, for Jake, anyway.

'It's late – we'd better get back,' he said curtly, getting back into the car.

Damn, damn, damn, thought Kate, following him reluctantly.

Chapter Seventeen

Kate felt so rigid with sexual tension she thought she would snap. In her head she had replayed their kiss under the starlight so many times and with much more satisfactory endings that she could probably give up journalism and take up writing Mills and Boon novels instead. To get her mind out of this loop, she went out and bought herself a frighteningly large amount of chocolate to give her strength while she worked.

She unwrapped her third chocolate bar of the morning and was thinking so hard she didn't hear the doorbell ring. It was Lydia.

'My God, it looks like you've raided the Cadbury factory!'

'Don't be silly,' mumbled Kate, trying to unclamp her teeth from caramel and nougat.

'So, why the descent into sugar hell? What part of your life do you hate at the moment?'

'Pretty much all of it,' sighed Kate, and went off to brush her teeth and make tea.

Lydia followed her into the kitchen. 'Tell me everything, you know it helps.'

'Well, actually it usually doesn't. You have been the provider of some truly appalling advice in the past, you know.'

'You've either cocked up a story or you want to sleep with someone and can't.'

'How do you know?'

'These are the only two things that make you bad-tempered and drive you to chocolate. So who is it? I am assuming it can't be Jonathan.'

'My God, did I really sleep with him? What a terrible mistake. No, you're right – that's all firmly in the past.'

'Well, it must be the chef, then.'

'Oh, Lydia, I've gone and caught him. Like measles.'

'How very inconvenient. Shall I prescribe a darkened room and a cold compress?'

'A large dose of "come to your senses" pills, if you have any,' said Kate glumly.

'I think I'm being a bit stupid here, but what exactly is the problem?'

'Hmm . . . let me see. Oh, yes. I've woven such a tissue of lies about myself to Jake that when I tell him the truth I'm scared he will see a stranger. That is, if I can ever summon the nerve to come clean. And you know, I don't think I can now. I am a serial liar.'

'Tell me about the dreams.'

'Trust you! Well, if you really want to know, last night I dreamed that he and I were swimming naked in a sea of raspberry coulis.'

'That just sounds sticky, not sexy.'

'Lydia, if you used your fridge for anything other than keeping your gin cold, you would know that food can be very sexy indeed.'

'Well, as Freud would say –'

'Oh, does he write a column for *Heat* magazine? No, I thought not. You have absolutely no idea what Freud would say about anything. Ever.'

'OK, Ms Cleverer than Me Clogs, tell me just why is it you always fall for men who put work before any serious commitment to their private lives?'

'Oh, that's easy,' sighed Kate. 'It's because my work is important to me and they are likely to understand. The good thing about Jonathan was that he would even interruptus coitus for a story. The awful thing is that Jake would definitely understand, except that he doesn't know exactly what sort of career I've got.'

'So tell him.'

'I have tried, honestly. But fate keeps stepping in and stopping me. I don't know why. Oh, yes, it's because I'm a complete coward. He is so full of integrity. And whenever I think I've plucked up enough courage, he has to rush off because the carrots are curdling, or something. Or because my tongue had suddenly become superglued to the roof of my mouth.'

'Ouch.'

'Exactly.'

'Maybe you just need to sleep with him to get him out of your system, like you did with Jonathan.'

'But I don't think I can. I don't think I want to. Really, it's quite simple. All I've got to do is write a totally brilliant story with Jake as the hero, not the villain. It has got to be gripping enough for Jonathan not to notice that it's completely different from my original brief. Then I hypnotise Jake into forgetting I ever lied to him about . . . oh dear, so many things. Then I tackle the supermodel. Don't know quite how yet, but if I survive all the above it should be easy.'

'What are you waiting for?'

'Oh hell! I have started lying to you now. I said I had caught Jake like measles. But really it is much more serious than that,' said Kate sadly.

She was worried that things would be awkward between her and Jake so she dawdled getting ready. Then her tights developed a ladder and it took her another five minutes to find an unholey pair, so she ended up being late for work and barely had time to apologise before rushing into the restaurant.

Then she stopped short so suddenly, Kirsty cannoned into the back of her.

'Blimey! You could have given me some warning! You can't have run out of energy yet – we've only just started.'

'Sorry,' Kate said absently. A sweat of fear started to trickle down her back. Sitting at the bar was a familiar, lanky figure: her archaeologist, Jim.

'Well! Look what I've uncovered! What on earth are you doing here?' he said, beaming.

Kate opened her mouth to explain, but nothing came out except an anguished squawk. This was really too much. She cast around in her mind for something to say, given that Hans was standing nearby, polishing a glass and trying not to look nosy. 'This is a friend of mine from college,' she said, practically manhandling Jim off his bar stool and over to the most distant table.

'Why aren't you in the States counting all the bones you dug up? Surely there were enough of them?'

Jim looked bemused. 'And it's nice to see you too!'

'Oh, look – I'm sorry, but everything is very complicated,' she hissed. 'I can't explain it all now, but' – she glanced about anxiously, but no one was listening – 'I'm not Kate the reporter; I am Kate an ex-PR person, who is working as a waitress while writing her first novel, OK?'

Jim took this in, then a huge grin spread over his handsome, open face. 'You mean, you're undercover?'

Oh crap. She'd forgotten he was absolutely addicted to the American series *24*. Give him half an inch and he would have cast himself in a Kiefer Sutherland role. The only problem with this was that he would make a complete hash of it. There was no side to Jim. Angelica would do a better job of working as a double agent.

Grabbing a menu he scanned it briefly, then, giving her a huge wink, he said: 'I'll take the steak, as bloody as you like – as long as I don't have to hack my way through it – know what I mean?'

Kate sighed. And this was just the start of the evening. What the hell could she possibly do that would take his mind off her? Alcohol might work on most people, but not Jim, given his capacity for prodigious consumption. Then she grinned. Yes, that might just work . . .

In the privacy of the loo she dialled quickly.

'Lydia, thank goodness you're in. Listen, I don't care what you are doing, I need you down here fast and in your best frock.'

'Hold on, just reaching for a pen, sweetie. Right, who am I seducing?'

'An archaeologist, an American – the best sort – very bright, energetic and good-tempered. He loves history, whisky and intelligent women. What on earth do you need a pen for?'

'I'm taking notes, of course, so I can dress appropriately for the occasion. Fortunately for you, my hair and nails are always immaculate. Honestly, you are lucky that I'm always primed for action, so to speak. See you soon.'

Kate glanced briefly in the mirror and shuddered. Her hair hadn't seen the attentions of a professional for months and, as usual, smelled of kitchen. The strains of living a double life had caused her to start biting her nails again. Probably the only way she could seduce someone would be during a blackout.

Fifteen minutes later Lydia made her entrance. She was as tall as Georgia, but wider, and tonight she had gone for the Valkyrie with a PhD look. She wore a very short skirt teamed with a smart black blouse demurely buttoned all the way up. Lydia was rigid about sticking to the 'boobs or legs – never both together' rule. She was wearing the glasses again. She was also carrying a copy of *National Geographic* and looked as if this was always what she read when she popped out for dinner. She did a very credible impression of looking surprised to see Kate and just the right amount of interest tinged with caution when Kate drew her over to Jim's table and introduced her.

'Please don't feel you have to compromise your evening,' said Jim, standing up and guiding her to a seat.

'Oh, this?' Lydia waved the *National Geographic* airily. 'I was going to catch up with the latest on the excavations at

Santorini, but it will keep.' She flashed him her warmest smile.

'So you're interested in archaeology then?'

'Yes, in my spare time. I must say, I'm thrilled to meet a professional. Kate says you've finished a major dig?'

'Well, it's not on the scale of Santorini, but I think it's quite important . . .' and Kate watched with admiration as Lydia began to reel him in.

'What are you up to?' asked Jake, back in the kitchen.

'Er, nothing. Why?'

'I don't know. You have a look about you. I –'

'What on earth is that, floating in the beans?' asked Kate wildly, but it worked. By the time he was satisfied there was nothing in the beans but what should be there, two more big checks came in and he had to concentrate on cooking.

The next time Kate went near Jim's table, Lydia was saying: 'And the role of women in the Minoan culture – now that's very interesting, isn't it?' and Kate knew she could have served steaks while wearing a balaclava and he wouldn't have noticed.

Another successful mission completed, she thought smugly, later. Jim and Lydia were still deep in conversation over their coffee. Lydia had taken the specs off and was leaning her chin on her hand so she could look intently at Jim as he spoke. It looked like the evening might not end with the meal. Kate went over to refill their cups, and looked up, startled, as Jake walked in. He glanced round casually and then headed towards them. Kate could see he had recognised Lydia from that awful drunken evening when they had first turned up at the restaurant.

'Hello,' he said to Lydia, 'I believe we've met before, haven't we?'

'Delighted to see you again,' said Lydia with a perfectly straight face. Kate was glad someone was enjoying themselves.

Of course Kate had to introduce everyone then. Jim congratulated Jake on the superb meal. 'Please, let me buy you a drink.'

'Well, that's very nice, thank you,' said Jake, sitting down, while Kate gaped at him in horror. She was sure she had heard him saying earlier how tired he was.

'I thought you wanted to get an early night?'

'I did, but I haven't met any of your friends before. Well, not properly,' he said, smiling at Lydia.

Oh, great. Well, it was, in a way: it was always a good sign when a guy wanted to meet your friends. But why these friends and why now? Her mission was being sabotaged and now Jake was asking: 'So, how did you and Jim get to know each other?'

'Oh, we've known each other since we were kids,' Kate burst out. 'I'll take those cups, shall I?' she continued.

'But I thought we were going to have more coffee?' said Jim in surprise.

'I'd quite like a brandy,' and Jake turned round to call Hans over.

'Good idea. Make mine a whisky. And perhaps even a cigar. It's not a vice I indulge in very often, but it's been a very special night,' said Jim.

'Excuse me,' said Lydia, and got up as if to go to the loo. Outside: 'What the hell? You've "known each other since we were kids"? Where did that come from? And why?'

'Oh, hang on, I know – I was fresh out of good lies. There is a limit to how many I can tell in a week. Oh, Lydia, I don't think I can do this any more! I've told so many stories, my nose should be about two feet long. I'm tired and my feet hurt even more than my brain does.'

'Whoa! Calm down, woman. We'll get through this somehow. Just, well, try not to talk. It's not your strong point at the moment.'

They went back and sat down. Jake was pouring some brandy from what looked to be a very old and precious bottle.

'It is,' he grinned, when asked. 'My former boss gave it to me. It's from somewhere deep in rural France – the guy only makes a few bottles a year and, no, I don't know his name, so I'll probably never get another one. But this is a special occasion.' He looked round happily and Kate had to conjure up a cough in order to disguise a groan. She knew what was happening here, and in other circumstances she would have welcomed it. Jake liked her, so much so that he wanted to get to know her friends. In other circumstances this would have been great. In these circumstances – well, now she felt that she could write a pretty damn good article on what it must be like to face a firing squad.

Oh, no – first bullet! 'So, where did you two grow up?' asked Jake, looking puzzled.

'God! That was so long ago!' said Kate brightly. The men looked at her in surprise, as if she had suddenly changed before their eyes into a very old woman. 'Well, you know what I mean,' she began, hastily.

'No,' said Jake.

'I just think that talking about our childhood is best left for the therapy sessions you lot are so fond of,' she said, looking at Jim.

'Well, it is supposed to be the one place where you have to be honest,' said Jim, meaningfully. 'You know, if you were living a double life –'

'Jim, tell us some more about the Romans,' suggested Lydia, and Kate looked at her gratefully. Why hadn't she thought of that? Jake was fascinated by them, she knew, and it was a subject that Jim could talk for hours on. Not that she was going to let him.

Gallic Wars – blah, blah, blah – Julius Caesar – blah, blah, blah – it was all interesting stuff, but she was so scared he would slip up and mention her and the dig, she couldn't enjoy it.

'I remember reading about Roman cuisine,' began Jake dreamily.

'Oh, yeah? That's quite a specialist subject – what do you know about it?'

'Well, they were very highly paid, for a start. Cleopatra's cook was given a house as a reward for having cooked a great meal.'

'Of course, they were literally slaves in those days. They'd be clapped in irons for the least little thing, but I guess it must have kept them on their toes.'

'Their national dish for a long time was a sort of gruel, like polenta. But then they became obsessed with meat. They would eat anything – camels, puppies –'

'Oh, that's gross!' said Lydia.

'– dormice, guinea pigs, elephants –'

'Man, that is seriously weird,' said Hans, coming over to clear away glasses. Kate pretended to look at his watch.

'Gosh, is that the time? I had no idea it was so late!' She stretched.

'But it's only half-past eleven!' said Jake.

'Well, you know – the early bird and all that.'

'No I don't. You actually said the other day that going to bed early was just for wimps.'

'Did I?' Obviously I'm flattered, but do you really have to remember everything I say?

'Yeah, that's exactly what you said when I wouldn't go out for a drink with you all after work the other night. You called me names, as I recall.'

Oh, bloody hell, so I did!

She yawned several times. Wasn't it supposed to be catching? Never had an hour passed so slowly. It was worse than waiting to have her wisdom teeth extracted. But finally, when she had almost given up hope, Jake started to yawn of his own accord.

'Well, I don't care if you do want to call me names, I need my bed. It's been nice, though. I don't seem to do this socialising thing very often. We'll have to do this again some time.'

'Absolutely!' agreed Kate, hustling him through the door and drawing a hand across her throat when she was sure he wasn't looking.

Jake came down to work the next day to find that Angelica was drawing pink ballerinas all over next week's rota.

'Sorry, Jake,' muttered Tess, who was looking extremely harassed. 'My mum is coming for her any minute now, I promise.'

'Why aren't you at school?'

'I've got chicken pox,' said Angelica importantly.

'No you haven't, you little liar,' said Tess, seeing Jake's look of alarm.

'Nits, then.'

'No, you haven't got those either.'

'I've got spots.'

'Yes, but only because you drew them on with felt tip while you were supposed to be having breakfast. The truth is, she locked herself in the bathroom until after the school bus had gone and then my car wouldn't start and then she threw a whole bowl of Rice Krispies down her dress and then – well, I just gave up, I suppose.'

'And why do you not want to go to school?' asked Jake sternly.

'I wanted to see God.'

'We all want to do that, but you won't find Him here.'

'You'll see the back of my hand if you don't watch out, young lady,' muttered Tess.

'I do find him here,' said Angelica indignantly. 'He's walking in right now. Why do you want me to see the back of your hand, Mummy. Have you drawn spots on it as well?'

Jake retreated to his office. Conversations with Angelica were sometimes like being in a particularly surreal episode of *Star Trek: Voyager*.

His bank manager had written to him, grudgingly offering half the overdraft that Jake had asked for and threatening dire consequences if he exceeded this paltry limit by a penny. Jake wished he was running a restaurant in Ancient Rome. Then if his backers got greedy he could just offer Angelica as a slave, in lieu of payment. Or send Godfrey off to moonlight as a gladiator.

If he lived in ancient times he also wouldn't have to wade through emails like this latest one from Georgia. He was pretty sure that somewhere in the last dozen they had made up, though it was difficult to be sure.

Georgia hadn't cottoned on to the fact that emails were supposed to be brief and to the point. She adopted a stream of consciousness technique, which often ran on for pages. It took Jake four goes to finally pinpoint where she was, how long she was staying and when she would be back. He found himself hoping this wouldn't be for a long time, which was not how you should think about your girlfriend, but if you had just spent most of the previous night having disturbing dreams about a girl with red hair . . .

As if he had conjured her up, Kate walked in.

'You didn't pick up all your post,' she said, dropping an envelope on the desk. Kate had decided to pretend the night of the star-gazing hadn't happened, which she was finding difficult to do. This made her voice sound cold and distant.

'Thanks.'

God, he had really blown it there. She was obviously disgusted with him for trying it on, and really he couldn't blame her. It was the sort of behaviour he despised Harry for, and here he was, doing it himself. He should be ashamed.

He went back to Georgia's missive while he was opening

the letter, giving himself a nasty paper cut in the process. He skimmed through it absent-mindedly, the odd word leaping up at him – 'lonely . . . hard work . . . weather awful . . . bad cold . . . nearly sneezed on catwalk . . . I love you lots and lots and can't wait to see you again, darling, darling Jake.'

Georgia was feeling terribly guilty, but of course Jake wasn't to know this. Harry had been down to London twice and on both occasions managed to bump into her by accident. He had insisted on buying her a drink and the second time, dinner. She had enjoyed herself more than she had for a long time. There was something curiously restful about Harry. He seemed to think she was great company whatever she said. He didn't fall asleep halfway through a conversation and when they talked he gave the impression he had all the time in the world to listen, instead of always glancing at his watch and muttering things about having to get back to work.

'Must go – a friend is taking me out to dinner,' and she signed off with lots of guilty kisses.

Jake vaguely wondered who this friend in Paris was then he forgot all about her.

The letter Kate had brought in was from the Restaurant Club of Great Britain, a small but élite group of food critics, whose main joy in life was to destroy the spirit of every fool who thought he could cook. Only last month one of them had done such a hatchet job on a place in Devon that the chef had run out of the kitchen in his clogs and straight to his therapist. He was currently at the Priory and rumour had it that he was flatly refusing to leave.

The Club also gave out awards, which were the cooking equivalent of the Oscars. As most of its members were journalists they were horribly articulate in their meanness and they were hated and feared throughout the length and breadth of Britain. Their top award was in the shape of a miniature knife crafted in silver. It was a running joke among chefs that they should give them out to the losers instead, so they could slit their own throats.

They liked to warn chefs in advance that they might be in line for an award, because it made them sweat and suffer more, and sorted out the men from the puking boys.

Jake put aside the letter and shivered. It was like spending years in training for an assault on Everest, trekking to Base Camp and then finding out that actually you were too scared to go to the top. Ever since he had read about them, he had coveted one of those little silver knives. Now he was being offered the chance to go for it, he wanted to run away and get a nice, easy, undemanding job in a sandwich bar.

A few minutes later Kate popped her head round the door to find Jake pacing up and down, muttering: 'Get a grip, you stupid man,' in a quite demented way.

'I was going to ask if you wanted a coffee, but now I'm thinking it should come with a sedative.'

Jake stopped pacing, grabbed her and kissed her on both cheeks like a mad Italian. 'I don't need coffee – I need champagne!' he said exultantly, and showed her the letter.

She took in its meaning instantly. 'That's brilliant! I bet you're torn between dying from terror or going on a three-day bender.'

He looked at her, surprised. 'That's exactly it! How do you know?'

Oh hell, why couldn't she tell him? It was so unfair. They were cut from the same cloth, she and Jake. They shared the same qualities of driving ambition, punctuated by dizzying self-doubt. They were both, in their way, artists. They should be able to confide in each other. The fact that she was keeping secrets from him was weighing her down, as if she was carrying a massive sack of potatoes on her back.

Jake resumed pacing up and down.

'Christ, there's so much to do! They will be looking for a completely new menu. I wonder if we should redecorate – no, damn, I can't afford it. I wonder how handy Godfrey is with a paintbrush?'

He went into the kitchen to tell everyone.

'Woo hoo! Let's all get drunk tonight to celebrate!' said Godfrey.

Jake looked at him as if he were crazy. 'Are you mad? We're not even halfway there yet. Have you read some of the things they write about people?' He riffled though a pile of papers and found a cutting from a very old copy of the *Observer*. He had read it so many times it was danger of crumbling away.

'This is what they wrote about a colleague of mine. Listen.

For Mr Hudson, grease is obviously the new black. My *pasta pomodoro* arrived swimming in so much oil, I thought I was eating in a garage rather than a restaurant. The mange tout were limper than a drunken

> penis after a fourteen-pints-of-lager night out and the roast potatoes looked like they had set sail in a sea of fat.
>
> The décor is described as minimalist. This evidently means you are expected to eat your dinner without the requisite cutlery. When I pointed this out to the waitress, she looked at me accusingly, as if I had hidden them up my sleeves. I half expected to find we had been charged for them at the end of the meal. To give him his due, the wine waiter had obviously been mugging up, but his method of imparting information was to spew it out like a parrot on speed. When I asked to see Mr Hudson at the end of this ordeal, there was some delay. Apparently he was sitting in the chest freezer, sobbing.

'I know John Hudson well. He is a really good chef. Apparently he's on so much Valium now, he just stares glassy-eyed at the checks when they come in.

'If they like what you do, people are falling over themselves to get a table at your restaurant. If they don't, you spend the rest of your career wondering if your restaurant has a "Keep away – we've got the plague" sign on the door and you are the only one who can't see it.'

'Oh my, what a nice treat we've got to look forward to,' said Godfrey faintly.

Jake and Tess put their heads together and for the next few days everyone went into cooking overdrive.

It took Jake three goes to make a *poulet sauté Marengo* he was happy with, and then he decided, at three thirty in the morning, that actually he wasn't.

'This is boring and predictable and we are scrapping it. You can have it for lunch,' he told Godfrey.

'That's the third time I've had to eat chicken this week and it's only Wednesday,' complained Godfrey.

'You'll be having it for the next ten meals unless I come up with something I like,' snapped Jake.

'I am now thinking of *poulet de Bresse aux morilles*,' he continued, getting out the ingredients.

'I wish he would move on to lamb or beef. I've eaten so much bloody chicken, I feel like I'm about to lay an egg,' muttered Godfrey.

He was in luck. The next day they put their minds to fish.

First they tried salmon with puy lentils; then moved on to salmon with watercress, toyed with a salmon en croûte, flirted with the notion of sweet and sour salmon, considered searing it with pancetta, pine nuts and balsamic vinegar, and then, just when everyone was losing the will to live, Jake decided to go with fricassee of turbot with spinach parcels.

No one wanted supper after work because they all felt as if they had ingested food through their pores.

Kate went to bed that night and dreamed that she was a small sardine being chased by a dolphin.

The evening service started off by pretending it was going to be a dream shift. The customers were coming at sensible intervals, in nice easy groups of four or six. Most of them had been before and were passionate fans of Jake's cooking. He hoped they would have a great meal, obviously, but then have to hurry home. He was longing for his bed. He was desperate for sleep – eight hours, unbroken, no dreams.

A party of ten tourists came in, unbooked, which meant there had to be a swift and polished moving together of tables, never easy in a crowded restaurant, but they managed. When Kirsty brought the order down to the kitchen, it was apparent they didn't know what a menu was actually for.

'They fancy salmon fishcakes,' repeated Jake slowly.

'I know they're not on the menu, but they bullied me into asking. They said you could probably do some anyway, if you are that good a chef.'

'I am a good chef,' he agreed, watching Godfrey sidle out of the kitchen, but not so far away that he couldn't enjoy the explosion. 'I am to food what Michelangelo was to art. But no one asked him to take a quick break from painting the Sistine Chapel so he could do a sketch of their pet poodle, did they?'

'Er, I don't know. I've never heard of a restaurant called the Sistine –'

'Quiet, woman! I have assembled a dazzling array of mouth-watering dishes on this menu. I am offering them some of the classics of *haute cuisine* and if that's not good enough for them –'

Here Jake described graphically where they could put the fishcakes, supposing he had any.

'I think you'll find that's against the law,' said Kirsty, quite unmoved. 'I'll tell them fishcakes are off, shall I?'

When she next came back to the kitchen, it was to hiss to Kate that there was a punter in the restaurant who fancied her.

'It's the one in the corner, sitting on his own. He was definitely looking at you when you took his starter away.'

'Are you sure he had finished?' asked Jake coldly. He had heard what Kirsty had said. Of course, it was no business of his if a customer wanted to take Kate out for a drink. Absent-mindedly, he began sharpening his most lethal knife.

'Forget it – I'm not interested,' Kate hissed back at Kirsty, with perfect truth.

'Well, I think he would be just right for you,' continued Kirsty, who had chosen that day to be oblivious to tact. 'He's reading a book while he's eating, so that means he is clever like you, and he could afford to take you somewhere nice 'cos he's wearing an expensive jacket.'

'Fascinating,' said Jake icily. 'Let's all discuss the private lives of our customers, shall we? Oh, hang on, we are in the middle of service! So sorry to interrupt, but would one of you mind just popping out and actually doing your job?' His voice had risen to the level that is known in catering as 'chef reaching boiling point'.

Kate stomped out, also in a bad mood. She was furious with Kirsty and furious with herself for wanting to reassure Jake she wasn't remotely interested in anyone but him.

Hans was on the phone. He was looking upset and beckoned her over. 'Can you do the bar for me for a sec? I need to speak to Jake.'

She took a quick glance round to check everyone was happy and nodded.

Jake looked up in surprise as Hans thrust his head round the door. He shouldn't have to come down to the kitchen during service.

'Boss, can I have a quick word?'

'What's happened?' It had to be some disaster in the restaurant. He could taste the sour flavour of dread rising in his throat.

'It's nothing to do with the restaurant,' said Hans quickly, seeing his face.

'Well, it had better be good then,' he snapped, then he shook himself. Hans was looking really upset. He shouldn't take his own fears out on his staff, and he had to stop behaving as if there was a crisis round ever corner.

Inside the office Jake sat down. 'I really must get some of those herbal stress remedies the next time I'm at the chemist,' he said to himself, but Hans heard.

'Yes, you are too sensible to try anything else. Unfortunately, a friend of mine is not.'

Jake sighed. He sort of knew what was coming next.

'A friend of mine is in big trouble.'

'Uh-huh. Go on.'

Hans sighed. 'He is a decent bloke, but under a lot of pressure at work. Sometimes we smoke a bit of dope together. But for him, it has got worse. He has started taking cocaine. He says it helps him to cope at work, you know – gives him confidence and energy. But then he smokes more dope to take him down, help him relax.'

'Yeah, I saw plenty of this in London. One place I worked at, briefly, the entire kitchen were taking drugs. I am sorry for your friend, but I can't do anything, you know. It's up to him to deal with it, or not.'

'Yes, I know that, but . . .'

'There's more, isn't there? Come on, spit it out.'

'It's Ronnie, over at the Café Anglais. I am really worried,

Jake. He has been left in charge for the last couple of days – Harry is away. Things were already really getting to him and he'd started smoking some really strong weed. It must have made him paranoid, because now he has locked himself in the larder room and no one can get him out and everything is in uproar. When Harry gets back and finds out, he will crucify him. It will be the end of his career and he is in a bad enough way already. I know it is probably the last place you wish to go to, to help someone out, but I have only been here a few months – I don't know who else to ask.'

Jake was silent for a minute.

'So, Harry's going to find himself in a spot of bother, is he? Well, that makes a change. God, I can't wait to send him a short note of sympathy when word gets out, and round here, it will! Well, this is sweet. The gods must have decided that it's my turn to have some fun.'

Then he slammed a fist onto the table. 'Bloody hell! What's come over me? I sounded just like Harry then, didn't I?'

'It's all right, boss, I understand,' Hans reassured him. 'This is not your problem. It is just . . . well I thought . . . Ronnie . . . he is one of us, isn't he? He just wants to cook, like you do.'

'I know. I'm sorry. Of course, you are right.' Jake groaned. 'How could I be such a shit?'

'You're not. Really, it is nothing to do with you –'

'But that's not the point! I can't just stand by and watch while a fellow chef is pushed to breaking point. Ronnie has been a complete idiot, but, believe me, I understand just how stressed he had to be to go there.' He stood up.

'Mind you – I am not exactly sure what I can do to help, but I'll give it a go.' He stood up and then hesitated. This was an excursion into enemy territory and there might well be reprisals. But Hans was looking at him, all hopeful and trusting. 'Come on, then.'

He popped his head round the kitchen door and, without even looking up, Tess said: 'Everyone is eating happily and there's no one else looking and Godfrey and me can help Emma with puddings.'

'How did you know I was going to ask that?'

'I'm psychic – didn't I tell you that at the interview? No, seriously, Boss, you have a one-track mind and it's easy to read.'

He had to check up on Godfrey and Emma, who were busy building a little tower of white, dark and milk chocolate mousses. They were doing fine, except that Godfrey had a very soppy look on his face as he handed Emma the garnishes.

'That's good, but stop there. Any more and it will look tacky. Listen – I have to pop out. Are you sure you will be OK without me?'

'Of course! Though we'll sulk like mad if you don't tell us what's going on,' said Kirsty.

'Fat chance I've got of keeping anything secret from you lot. I'll call you later. Listen, you're to ring me if there's any sort of problem at all. Kirsty, tell Kate she'll have to do the bar; Hans had better come with me.'

He wasn't too happy about this, but he didn't really have a choice. He didn't want to leave Kate on the bar, probably being chatted up by that guy. But then, what business was it of his? If she wanted to go out with a smart guy in a posh jacket, she could. She was single, after all. She could go out with anyone she fancied. But you can't, Jake, because you are not free, he told himself, firmly.

When they were in the car, he made a determined effort to put her out of his mind and said: 'OK, fill me in on whatever else you know.'

'Ronnie is a good bloke, you know. OK, he doesn't have a lot to say for himself, because, well, there's no point – Harry wouldn't listen. Ronnie loves – no – he *loved* cooking. He told me once it was all he ever wanted to do. He was so pleased at first when he got this job. But Harry – well, you know what he's like. He doesn't talk to people, he shouts – and he doesn't listen to any of their ideas. He tells them it's his way or they can fuck off. He is nothing like you.'

'So when did things start to slide downhill for Ronnie?' asked Jake, ignoring the compliment.

'Almost straight away,' said Hans, gloomily. 'He said he couldn't cope without a line of coke – it made him feel sharp and focused. But then he needed more and more, to get him through a shift. It gives you a high, but it doesn't last long. And then, of course, after a while, he needed something to bring him down, so he would have a few joints.'

'So he took stuff to speed him up, then stuff to slow him down and now of course, his head is all over the place,' said Jake.

'Yeah, that's pretty much it.'

When they walked in to the kitchen at Café Anglais, all he could see was a huddle of white jackets and hats and a babble of voices. There was a line of checks on the table but everyone seemed to be too occupied talking and arguing among themselves to do any actual cooking. It was clear no one was in charge and none of them knew what to do.

'Where's Ronnie?' asked Jake curtly.

They sprang apart and one of them pointed to a door. Jake went over and tapped on it.

'Fuck off and leave me alone!'

'Well, he's still alive, at any rate. Is there anything in there he could do himself harm with?'

'It's just dry goods – tins and packets.'

'OK. Well, I think we should just leave him in there, at least until you've got the punters out of the way. You need to make a start with those checks – oh, hello, Sally.'

She was staring at him like a rabbit caught in the headlights. He could tell, even from a distance that her nervous eczema had flared up again. It was creeping up her arms in a fiery red rash and it contrasted horribly with the pallor of her face. Come to think of it, everyone here looked washed out, as if they were never allowed out into the sunshine. They were also all staring at him in a bewildered but rather hopeful way and he realised they had all been so cowed by Harry that they didn't have the faintest idea what to do when there was no one there to shout orders at them. It was a good thing he still had his jacket and apron on. He grinned suddenly, because it was quite funny. This was probably the only chance he would ever get to watch Harry's boat sinking and here he was, busily chucking out lifebelts.

'OK, guys, who's on starters? You? Right. You've got two soups and two lobster salads, followed by three steaks and a duck. What the hell are you all looking at?'

'Er, what are you doing?' asked one of the commis chefs.

Jake sighed. Terror had turned this kitchen into idiots.

'I am helping you out, because you so obviously need it.'

'But what will Chef Hunter say?'

Chef who? Oh, Harry. What a prick that man was.

'I don't know. He's not here. But if you can carry on without me . . .?'

'We can't,' said Sally, her voice barely above a whisper.

'Yeah. Didn't think so. Go and get me a menu so I can see what goes with this duck.'

Then followed a mad hour during which he had to take charge of a strange kitchen and cook a completely unfamiliar menu with a crew who ran around more like startled deer than pros. This was what happened when you didn't train people to think for themselves. Some of the punters had been waiting to eat for over an hour now, and others had complained and sent food back. It was a nightmare. Also, ridiculously, he felt quite nervous, because he was half-expecting Harry to appear out of nowhere, like the Demon King in a panto, and stab him between the ribs.

'Where did you say your boss was?' he asked someone rather nervously.

'Paris, I think. He's definitely not back till tomorrow.'

Jake entertained a brief vision of sliding notes under the steaks, advising the customers they would have a much nicer experience at Cuisine next time they wanted to go out and eat, and then found himself bawling at one of the waitresses for not wiping the plates properly before taking them out. The waitresses were efficient, but snooty. God, this was an awful place to work.

He worked on, trying to restore order to chaos and hating the atmosphere in this kitchen. It was heavy with tension and stress. No wonder it had all got too much for Ronnie. Jake's own team certainly jumped when he barked at them, but they didn't get into a lather of fear over it, even when they cocked up. Then he was distracted into wondering where Harry got such fantastic pigeons.

'He shoots them,' said the kitchen porter, when asked.

'Oh, that figures,' said Jake.

Eventually, it all came to an end. Everyone had enjoyed their meals, apparently, though Jake had had to practically force this information out of the waitresses. They were going to report absolutely everything he had done back to Harry, he could tell. There was going to be no way he could stop any of this getting out.

'OK, everyone, you need to get cleared up and out of here as quickly as possible so I can try and persuade Ronnie out.'

'I don't think you should be left here on your own,' said one of the waitresses.

'Why? Are you worried I might steal the silver? Oh, all right, do what you like. Just stay out of here until I tell you otherwise.'

He yawned and took a slug of coffee to keep alert. His eyes felt gritty with tiredness and he found himself obsessively picturing Kate, sitting somewhere expensive, having a drink with that guy. He didn't want to be here, trying to talk someone out of a drug-fuelled breakdown. But he felt desperately sorry for Ronnie, who had been driven to such desperate measures.

He sat down with his back against the door, next to Hans, and said as much, in what he hoped was a calm and reassuring voice. He described one or two people he had known in similar situations and how they had got themselves sorted. He suggested tea and something to eat – a good meal was always the best way to help someone think more sensibly, he felt. He went on in this manner for about twenty minutes, when suddenly the door opened and he and Hans nearly fell backwards.

Ronnie's hair was standing on end, his eyes were bloodshot and his face looked haggard. He had lost over a stone since coming to work here.

'It all suddenly got out of hand,' he said later, after two cups of tea. 'I had a really strong joint in the afternoon to help me sleep before the shift, but then when I got to work everything went a bit weird. I couldn't seem to control the knives – it was a bit like they had a life of their own, you know. I was worried they might make me do something awful, so I decided to go somewhere dark and quiet and stay there until I felt better.'

'In the circumstances, that was probably a wise move. Do you feel better?' asked Jake.

'Yeah, sure. I'm fine now.'

'Don't be stupid,' said Jake. 'You've got over tonight's crisis, but unless you really sort your head out, there will be others.'

'What would you do if I was in your kitchen?' asked Ronnie.

'I would sack you,' said Jake brutally. But then he explained, more gently: 'Listen, man, you are no use to yourself or anyone else in this state. You keep taking drugs and there will be a major accident in the kitchen, and then you will never forgive yourself. Look upon tonight as a warning and an opportunity to get out now, in one piece. Get the drugs out of your system and find someone nicer to work for – there are plenty of them around, you know.'

'So, are you going to tell him what happened?'

'I won't have to. The waiting staff are going to spill the beans as soon as they can.'

'Oh shit, I'll get the sack!'

'Not if you resign first, then go to your doctor and be honest with him so he can help you.'

'I'm beyond help,' said Ronnie.

'Don't talk bollocks – of course you're not! Look, do you still want to cook?'

Ronnie was silent for a long time, thinking. Then: 'I remember what it was like when I was starting out. I wanted to learn to cook so I could have my own pub, somewhere in Yorkshire – I'm from there. I used to go to bed and plan what I was going to put on the menu.' He sighed.

'You've still got that fire somewhere, even though it's burned pretty low. For God's sake – Harry could douse anyone's ambitions! You just got in with the wrong crowd, as my grandmother would say. Listen to me. I believe in you, but you have to get clean first.'

Inwardly, Jake breathed a sigh of relief. Ronnie's eyes had brightened up, only very slightly, but it was enough. He even managed a faint grin.

'This has been the worst job of my life. Now I know I can walk away it even seems a bit funny, but it wasn't then. He was always bawling me out. It didn't seem to matter how hard I tried – nothing pleased him. The coke made it all feel like it didn't matter and I could manage, you know.'

'Well, if you find somewhere decent to work, all you will need in the future is commitment,' said Jake, and gave a huge yawn.

'You can sleep on my floor tonight, and tomorrow morning, early, I will hand in your resignation for you and you can go home,' said Hans.

'Fine. I'll just tell one of Harry's slaves next door that we are going,' said Jake.

'I heard that!' said Annabelle, bouncing into the kitchen so smartly Jake knew she had been eavesdropping the whole time. 'I shall be ringing Harry the moment I've locked the door on you.'

'Do what you like, I don't care.'

But as he was driving the guys home he had a moment's unease, which was stupid, wasn't it? Of course he had the upper hand here. Harry wouldn't want any of this being broadcast, because it wouldn't do his reputation any good at all, and reputation was important in a small town like this. The only thing Harry could do now was grind his teeth down to the gums and thank Jake nicely. Right?

Chapter Eighteen

It was early morning by the time Jake got to bed and his whole body protested when the alarm rang, a ridiculously short time later. He had spent the night in fitful dreams, none of them very pleasant, and for a minute he just lay there, thinking longingly of holidays (when was the last time he had actually had one?), or even jobs where you got the weekend off. Then with a groan, he got up.

With the Restaurant Club award looming, there was no time to lie in bed feeling faint-hearted. He was convinced, despite what his customers were saying, that there was a huge amount of work still to be done before his cooking skills were up to standard.

Coming to the conclusion he would go mad if he thought about it any more, he decided to cheer himself up by putting sautéed veal kidneys with a puree of potato on the menu.

Meanwhile, several thousand feet above him, a stewardess was jumping back in fright when she discovered that a croissant could be used as an offensive weapon. At least it could be in Harry's hands.

'There is no need to wave your breakfast at me in a threatening manner, sir,' she said.

'Well don't try and tell me this crap is edible!' he roared.

'Everyone else is eating it quite happily. Perhaps you just want coffee?'

Harry subsided with ill grace. He was in a stormingly bad temper and there was no one to vent it on. He sipped coffee and brooded.

Up until a few hours ago he had been having a wonderful time. It had been brilliant to see the look on Georgia's face when she strutted down the catwalk and realised he was sitting in the front row. A true professional, she didn't lose her stride, but her eyes had widened in surprise and unmistakable pleasure.

After the show he had somehow managed to blag his way backstage. He cut a swathe through the giggling, naked models without even casting a glance in their direction. He walked straight up to her and held out his hand. In it was a single long-stemmed rose. It was corny but Harry could pull it off.

'I have a table booked for two. I'd rather you came as you were,' he dropped his eyes to her bare breasts, 'but I guess people will stare.' He bent his head and lightly kissed one nipple. 'I'm saving the other for later.'

All the girls and some of the men sighed with envy. It was just like a scene out of a really cool film, thought Georgia.

They went to a little restaurant he knew that was discreet and served superb food and wine. He kept the conversation light and casual, though he insisted on serving her little morsels of his fillet steak to go with her salad. Then they walked back to her hotel, because it wasn't far and Paris at night was a lovers' dream. Outside the door to her room, they stopped, Georgia quivering with anticipation.

'I've got unfinished business with your body,' said Harry.

'Yes, yes,' breathed Georgia, who had completely forgotten that Jake even existed.

'But not tonight.'

'What?'

'You think you know yourself, but I know you better. You think you're ready for this, but you aren't. Yet. I am sad, but I can wait.' He kissed her hand and turned.

'Really – I am sooo ready,' wailed Georgia in frustration, but it was too late. He had gone. One of the secrets of Harry's success with women was that he always knew exactly the right moment to take them to bed, when they were panting with desire and would do anything he asked. He was grinning to himself at the thought of pleasure to come, when his mobile rang.

He was very calm to begin with. There was no point in having a tantrum until you were in possession of all the facts and had assessed the situation coolly. That done, he swore quietly to himself to begin with, which then built up to a crescendo of oaths that culminated in him flinging the phone onto the pavement, where it bounced twice and broke into four pieces. The cab driver he had summoned took one look at this and sped off. Some fares just weren't worth it.

'Pick up the pieces and put it back together,' he ordered the concierge, who was staring at him. And he went inside to book a flight home.

He wanted to kill two people. Ronnie, for having fucked

up in such a spectacular way and brought his restaurant into disrepute, and Jake, who had dared to play the white knight and would now be expecting Harry's gratitude. God! The thought of having to do that really hurt! Was it actually possible to say thank you to the man he hated more than anyone else? Sitting in the plane, he practised the smile he would have to give, which obviously needed some work, as it made a small child cry.

You can do this, he told himself. You can do this because what that stupid prick doesn't know is that you are in the middle of a very successful campaign to seduce his girlfriend. Jake may have won a minor and insignificant skirmish, but he has no idea how to win a war. You will have the last laugh, Harry my boy.

Everyone liked the kidneys, except Kirsty, who refused flatly even to try them, on the grounds that things like that were disgusting.

'Things like what?' demanded Jake.

'You know perfectly well what I mean.'

'No I don't! If you will eat an animal's legs, or its breasts, you might as well eat everything else. It's dead anyway so it's not going to complain, is it?'

'I don't care. I am quite capable of lying to the customers and telling them it's absolutely delicious, so it doesn't matter, does it?'

'I just want to broaden your eating horizons.'

'They don't need to be broadened. They are quite happy where they are, thank you,' she retorted and went off to answer the phone.

'It's whatsername, that posh tart from Café Anglais,' she hissed, coming back. Jake took the phone. Annabelle said Harry would be delighted if Jake could come over for a coffee that afternoon. 'He would like to thank you for the very great kindness you did for poor Ronnie,' she said, almost managing to sound like she believed it.

'It was nothing,' said Jake, and pretended to go off and look in his diary, which he knew was quite empty, apart from a blob of gravy.

'Yes, I think I can manage half an hour,' he said, enjoying all this tremendously.

Everyone was against him going, though.

'I know you think you have all the power here –' began Kate.

'I do. If I was a nasty sort, I could spread this story all round town. It wouldn't put him out of business, but it would do a lot of damage. Of course, I'm not going to do anything of the sort, though I must say, it is tempting. I just don't intend to use poor Ronnie to score a cheap trick. But Harry doesn't know that.'

Kate sighed. 'Jake, you are just a novice in deviousness compared to people like Harry. He'll beat you hands down every time,' she said.

'Well I don't see how he can, this time,' said Jake, and went off to get changed.

Harry's flat was also above the shop, as it were, but there any resemblance to Jake's flat ended. Like Georgia had, before him, he couldn't help but compare their horribly different lifestyles. The two flats looked like the before and after on a television makeover show, he thought, as Annabelle showed him in, saying Harry wouldn't be a minute.

Jake sank down onto a sofa so soft and comfortable it practically begged him to put his feet up and doze off. There was a huge, plasma-screen television in the corner, antique ornaments on the shelves and some rather nice watercolours on the walls. Jake wanted to hate it all, but he couldn't. It was the sort of flat he would love to have for himself.

Harry made him wait ten minutes and, despite his earlier comments, Jake started to get nervous. He now couldn't make up his mind whether Harry would be furious with him for interfering or grateful for his help. He got up and stood nearer the door. That way he could just walk out if he had to.

But when Harry entered, he was exuding friendliness and bonhomie.

'Sorry to keep you. I've been on the phone to the agency, getting another chef,' he said, smiling and looking over at Jake in what he hoped was a 'gosh, this is a bit of a pickle but we are all going to get through it like gentlemen' sort of a way.

Jake smiled back, but warily. 'Have you heard from Ronnie?' he asked carefully.

'Nothing, apart from the letter of resignation that was waiting for me when I got back. I don't expect to hear any more and I don't care, frankly.'

'Well, he has certainly got a lot of work to do before he can return to cooking,' said Jake.

Harry gritted his teeth and took a deep breath. 'Yes, he has. Thank you for coming in and helping out. I am extremely grateful.' There, it was over.

But Jake wasn't looking entirely convinced. 'I got involved only to help a fellow chef in trouble and I am sure you know I don't mean you. Nothing would give me more pleasure than to see you in deep shit but, unlike you, I have standards.'

How dare he look so contemptuously at me? thought Harry, furiously, and a plan that had been half-forming in his mind crystallised.

'Yes, I appreciate that. There is a lot of bad blood between us, isn't there?'

'Yeah, a whole river full, Harry. Do I look stupid enough to want to jump across?'

This was going to be harder than Harry had anticipated. 'Look, let's sit down, shall we?' He rested his chin on his hands and took his time before speaking. Jake had to believe this was coming from the heart. 'I can't go back and change the past but I can help to change how we behave in the future. Like it or not, we are both running businesses in a town so small we are bound to bump into each other. Now, I am a realist – we are not going to be friends. But maybe we need to learn how to behave in a civilised manner towards each other. I would really like to do that, Jake, because I can only benefit in the long run.' This was perfectly true. Harry was going to take Georgia from Jake and he was going to do it right under Jake's nose – not because it was better that way, but because he could. The only thing Harry liked better than winning was winning with style. He put on a slightly awkward, self-conscious grin. 'I know it's up to me to set the ball rolling and so I would like to invite you and your staff to a little party I'm throwing next week at the family home. And no, I don't envisage us ending up with our arms round each other's shoulders, but if we could drink a glass of wine together, it might be a start.' Harry sat back and looked down at his knees modestly. He was fairly sure his eyes had radiated sincerity, but it wouldn't do to be too cocky.

As Harry had hoped, Jake was completely taken aback by this. He had expected a number of things, but not this calm reasonableness. But after all, at some point everyone had to grow up, even Harry. Maybe the realities of running his own business had brought him maturity. No, they certainly wouldn't ever become friends, but how pleasant life would be if they could learn to deal with each other amicably. He took a deep breath. He had to respond properly to this overture because it might not happen again.

'OK, let's give it a go.'

Harry nodded soberly, the picture of a man who was ready for some serious fence-mending. God, he was good at this!

Later, back in his own kitchen, Jake said: 'I thought about it and I really can't come up with any reason why Harry would be saying these things if he wasn't genuine.'

Tess looked at him. She couldn't either, but she would bet next week's wages that there was one.

'Look, we are adults now – we've got more important things to do than fight!'

Yeah, you have, thought Tess. That's because you're a

decent guy. But Harry isn't and I would love to know what he's playing at. 'Well, OK, we'll go to this bloody party, if we have to.' That way, at least we can watch your back for you.

Harry's house stood in its own grounds. Like an A-list star at a party, it was far too important to mingle with anyone else. It simply flaunted money, like a celebrity on a shopping spree. Gleaming brilliant white in the sunshine, it was ringed by trees, which clustered round the building like a bunch of tough bodyguards.

An intercom on the gate buzzed Jake's party through.

'It's like going into a prison, though I can't imagine anyone wanting to visit Harry's family if they are all like him,' grumbled Jake.

As they drove slowly up the winding driveway they realised they were joining the cream of Lake District society – to judge by the other cars. He reckoned none of them had cost less than £30,000, which made his battered Ford Fiesta look just a mite conspicuous, for all the wrong reasons.

'Someone's bound to come out and tell us to park round the back with the other tradesmen.'

'Oh, for goodness' sake, stop being so touchy!' Georgia was trying to apply lipstick with a hand that was distinctly nervous. She was excited and scared at the thought of seeing Harry again, and guilty because she really shouldn't be looking forward to it and then angry with Jake for making her feel guilty. Jake could feel the waves of energy rising from her but was at a loss to know why, but he supposed that this sort of party mattered much more to her than him. She would, understandably, be keen to make a good impression, but he couldn't work out why this should be making her so cross.

'You look perfect, as always,' he reassured her, slightly puzzled as to why she hadn't ticked him off for dressing so casually.

Georgia hadn't commented on the jeans because she simply hadn't noticed them. She had been far too pre-occupied choosing her own outfit. Harry, unlike Jake, was very aware of clothes and she was determined to make a stunning impression. Her long floaty Chloé dress certainly did that. It tucked itself neatly round her pert breasts and sidled down her long legs in a coy but very suggestive manner. She barely acknowledged Jake's compliments because they had long since ceased to mean anything to her.

As they got out of the car, three figures popped out from behind a tree.

'We were too scared to go in without you,' giggled Kirsty, whose high heels kept getting stuck in the grass.

'Probably a good thing. If anyone sees Godfrey they'll think he's a bloody waiter. The only thing you are missing is a tray of canapés.'

'Ha ha. Mum said I had to wear this suit. It took me ages to find the tie – someone was using it as a dog lead.'

'If anyone asks you for a drink, just bark. I detect a faint whiff of dog about you anyway,' said Hans. He'd had an enormous spliff before setting out, so, unlike the others, was feeling chilled out and mellow.

'Well, let's get this over with,' said Jake. This was his first evening off for ages and he had to spend it here, of all places. How annoying was that?

They went up the wide steps, between two stone lions and into a hall.

'My mum was here ages ago, helping out at a party,' said Kirsty. 'They wanted her to wear a black dress, but she said, you'll have to pay me a lot more than four quid an hour to put that thing on when it's still got sweaty marks under the arms, and as for those shoes, why they'll be bloody lethal on this floor and –'

'Please shut up,' begged Jake, catching sight of Georgia's stony face.

They didn't know it but the butler had only been hired for the evening and was massively pissed off already after being bawled out for nipping off for a sneaky fag.

'As the weather is so fine, the party has assembled on the terrace by the pool,' he intoned automatically. Then he recognised Jake because his dad sometimes supplied the restaurant with veg. 'How you doing, mate? Didn't expect to see you at this sort of do.'

'Likewise,' grinned Jake. 'I thought you would be far too busy trying to offload those cauliflowers I told you I hadn't ordered.'

'They're paying me a hundred quid for tonight. Mind you, I'm earning every penny of it. They are all out the back – just head for the noise, you can't miss them,' he said, gloomily.

At the back of the house was an enormous terrace and beyond that, a pool. And loads of people, all dressed up, talking and laughing loudly. Harry's mother was in the middle of the largest group, holding court and taking fortifying sips from a very large gin. She was still very beautiful, though her skin was starting to look slightly too stretched over her face.

She came over to greet them. 'You must be Harry's new friend!'

Jake tried not to shudder. That was truly a horrible thought.

'He has told us all about your brave attempt to set up in the restaurant trade. Good for you! And please don't forget that Harry is always very generous with advice.'

Jake wanted to retort that the only thing Harry was usually generous with were insults and that he would know he was done for if he ever had to go to him for help, but luckily Georgia interrupted.

'What a gorgeous pool.'

'I'm afraid we haven't put the heating on,' said Mrs Hunter quickly. She had clocked Georgia's youth and beauty instantly and the fact that men's eyes were swivelling over from every corner of the garden. There was no way she was going to let her take off her clothes and cause even more of a stir.

'Glad you could make it!' Harry appeared, a picture of friendliness. 'There's someone from *Elle* magazine over there – he says he knows you. Let me get you a glass of champagne and take you over to him,' he continued, whisking Georgia away with his usual skill. Tess's eyes followed them suspiciously, but what trouble could they get into in a garden full of people?

'I can't see anyone I know,' Georgia said, leaning forward to peer short-sightedly round and causing one nipple to venture out from the inadequate folds of her dress.

Harry swallowed, seriously turned on. 'I lied. I just wanted to get you on your own.'

Georgia was hugely flattered but scared. 'How sweet, but you shouldn't have done that. I can't leave Jake on his own.'

'He has disappeared already,' said Harry with perfect truth. 'At least let me get you a drink.

Wrinkling her nose to try to see more clearly (she had forgotten her contact lenses again), Georgia couldn't see Jake anywhere.

As soon as her back was turned Jake had made off. His crew had made a beeline for the bar. He was on his own and feeling very out of place.

'What a bunch of superficial, shallow wankers,' he muttered out loud to make himself feel better.

'I couldn't agree more, sir,' said the butler, appearing out of nowhere. 'Personally, I would recommend vast quantities of alcohol, but avoid the whisky – it tends to make one want to biff someone.' Jake laughed so much, the bubbles from the champagne went up his nose. Coughing and spluttering, he retreated to the door so that he wouldn't embarrass Georgia.

As Jake stood on the steps Kate's equally shabby car shot up the drive with no regard for a very old and hugely overweight Jack Russell terrier which had just sat down to get its breath back after trying and failing miserably to catch a rabbit. Kate flew in between two Rollers, narrowly missing a wing mirror, and parked on a slant, as if she didn't give a damn, which she didn't.

Jake suddenly felt much more cheerful. There was a splendid air of self-confidence about her as she kicked the door shut, which was the only way of getting it to stay shut. She was wearing a very short, bright red skirt and flat shoes, which only served to draw attention to her long, slender legs, which were covered with fake tan. Waitresses, she had discovered, rarely saw daylight, let alone sunshine. There hadn't been time to blow dry her hair, so she had just tied it back and slapped on some blusher. Her sharply clever little face glowed. Unseen, he watched her look up at the house and assess it. Then she saw him and gave him a grin of complete complicity. She came over.

'What's it like? Loads of money, but no style?' she hissed hopefully.

Jake was forced to be honest. 'Actually, the house is lovely – it has real character. I wish it was mine.'

'Makes you want to spit, doesn't it?'

'I wouldn't dare do anything so working class here. They might set the dogs on me.'

'Well, that one wouldn't be able to give you a run for your money,' she said, pointing to the terrier, which was lying down and wheezing. 'He's obviously eating too many scraps from Harry's restaurant.'

'So does his dad. Harry's, I mean, not the dog's. I passed him just now. His stomach is practically down to his knees and he looked at me in total disbelief, as if he couldn't work out what the hell such a scruffy person was doing in his house.'

'You look fine – for someone who obviously doesn't want to spend money on clothes.'

They wandered over to the pool, where they were greeted with relief by their colleagues.

'Absolutely no one is talking to us,' complained Godfrey.

'Well, we are prepared to slum it, just this once,' said Jake, sitting down.

'Shouldn't you be schmoozing and making lots of useful contacts?' asked Kirsty.

'Probably, but I can't bring myself to, yet. I should find Georgy, though.'

'Oh, she went off with Harry, but she looked like she could take care of herself.'

'That's good.' Jake felt slightly uneasy at this, but was distracted by having to stop Hans from rolling a joint in front of the chief constable.

'That stuff makes you so bloody mellow, you lose all sense of reason!' he complained.

'That's why I smoke it – when I'm sober I'm just too strait-laced and sensible!' Hans grinned in reply.

In the end Jake didn't have to schmooze. A number of people found him and said such nice things about his cooking he perked up no end.

It was obvious to Kate that the men appreciated the food. The women were too busy appreciating the chef. It was also obvious that Jake was completely unaware of this. He chattered away happily about sauces and restaurants and other cooking-related subjects, while the women nodded and smiled and looked lustfully at him. She sighed. He probably thought they were just rather hungry.

Godfrey was pursuing an ambition to see how many champagne slammers he could get down before someone stopped him. Nature intervened when the third one went down the wrong way.

'By dose is going to explode!' he spluttered.

Jake and Kate leaned forward at the same time to slap him on the back. As she leaned forward he could see right down her top. She'd fake-tanned her breasts, but in rather a slapdash way and there were one or two pale streaks on her skin. Jake found himself wondering how far down she had gone. But someone had put the Beatles on a state-of-the-art sound system, and as the music drifted over, a woman asked him to dance. He got up with a certain amount of relief, even though he knew he was terrible dancer.

The woman didn't mind at all because it meant she kept having to put her arm on his to stop him falling in the pool. He kept glancing over at Kate to see what she was doing. Maybe it would be better if he just fell in and cooled down before he did something silly.

Harry had taken Georgia to the summerhouse, the scene of many nefarious activities in his youth. He had smoked his first joint here, screwed his first girl, dumped his first girl. Built like a tiny log cabin, it was hidden among the trees, cool and private. There were no chairs to sit on, just masses of cushions piled up on the floor. It gave an impression of rustic simplicity, but it was cleaned and polished by the housekeeper every week.

Harry had brought a bottle of Bollinger with him and was rummaging around in a little cupboard for the glasses he kept there.

Georgia sat down and waited in silence. She had a feeling she shouldn't be doing this, but not being an introspective person she was unable to take this thought much further. But taking things too far was Harry's forte. He gave Georgia two large glasses of bubbly in quick succession to weaken her defences and then pulled her towards him.

It was so long since she and Jake had kissed like this it was quite overwhelming, especially as Harry kept breaking off to look deep into her eyes and stroke her hair and neck as if he was examining a priceless piece of porcelain.

'You are far too thin,' he grumbled.

'I have to be – it's in my contract.'

'But I want to lick every inch of your body and I'd be finished far too soon. I suppose then I could start all over again,' he whispered into her neck and she shivered with pleasure.

'You're much bigger than Jake,' she said, stroking the powerful muscles in his neck and back.

'I'm big everywhere,' he grinned. 'If I wanted to, I could break you.' He put his hands on her breasts in a proprietary way.

'I haven't felt like this for such a long time,' she said dreamily, between kisses.

'Like what?' Harry always had to know in great detail how good he was. He could never get enough of himself.

'So helpless, I mean. I know we shouldn't be doing this, but I don't want to stop, and somehow it feels so right.'

'Then we won't stop. We should go where our . . . er, hearts, lead us.'

'Yes, of course. I hadn't thought of it like that, but now it all makes sense.'

He put his tongue very gently to her nipple, then pulled

away, just as she was squirming with excitement. He made sure she was watching him manfully regaining his composure, then he said: 'I can't do this and then just walk away.'

Georgia, who hadn't been thinking at all, beyond the next sensation of pleasure, tried to muster her senses, such as they were. 'But we can't just stop here!'

He took her hand and traced the lines on her palm. 'Maybe we should. I wish I could read our future here, but I can't. You have to help me. Where will the next days, weeks, months, take us? Will we be together?'

Georgia felt strong, in control. 'Of course! For the first time I feel . . . I feel that I have power!'

'You poor darling! Does he treat you so badly?'

Georgia settled down for a good griping session. 'Only in a way too subtle for most people to see. The only thing he ever looks at greedily is food. He's already got a family, though they are just staff, and the restaurant is like some monster baby that never sleeps and always needs feeding! The only attention I ever get is whatever little bit he has left over. I am just second or third best!' she wailed and started to cry. She looked at him with huge, doe eyes, as two tears rolled down her cheeks.

Harry was surprised to discover he was genuinely moved by this. Dimly he realised that she was the only thing belonging to Jake that he didn't want to smash up. But he *would* take her from him.

Back at the party, everyone else had gathered round a buffet of mammoth proportions. Harry's minions had been slaving away all week, as well as cooking for the restaurant.

Godfrey was making his way through the food with steady concentration, in the vague hope that if he ate something the world would stop spinning. Jake had never felt less hungry in his life but Kate kept insisting he try things from her plate. 'Too much salt,' he grumbled. She just looked at him.

'OK, it's all very nice really. I suppose you are right – I am at his party; I should at least be polite.'

'It's not that. I don't care how rude you are about him. It's just that dissing the opposition won't make it go away. You have to build on your strengths and their weaknesses.'

'Sounds like it's a cut-throat world in PR.'

What? She looked at him blankly for a minute. Oh bollocks, that was her imaginary previous job, wasn't it? She didn't want to be reminded of her double life just now, so she fed him another canapé to shut him up.

Out on the terrace they were playing soft music.

'I know this. Shall we dance?'

It was amazing, how, out of the kitchen, Jake seemed to lose all his grace, Kate thought. It was quite endearing really. It was funny how wonderful it felt even though he was treading on her toes and humming tunelessly in her ear.

He leaned closer so his lips were just brushing her ears. Right moves, wrong woman, he thought to himself wryly and then it hit him between the eyes and he could no longer deny it. This was most definitely the right woman for him. This was what really being in love felt like, and everything that he had felt before this was just practice. So this was what all the poets were always banging on about, he mused, in wonder. He had always thought them rather overrated until now. But this – this was something amazing, exhilarating and slightly scary, like diving into a deep pool.

But the sound of water wasn't just in his imagination. Godfrey had just fallen into the Hunters' swimming pool.

'It's all right, I can swim,' he shouted and promptly disappeared in a cloud of bubbles.

'Oh bugger,' said Jake, and jumped in after him.

Life-saving lessons at school were never like this, he thought. Godfrey was a dead weight in the water, and it was made worse by the fact that every time he surfaced for air he started laughing and sank again. Eventually Jake grabbed him by his collar and managed to drag him to the side of the pool. The noise had brought everyone running.

'What on earth are you doing?' said Georgia, appearing suddenly and looking down at the sodden pair of them with distaste.

'What does it look like?' snapped Jake, detaching himself from Godfrey, who was spread out by the side of the pool like a big starfish, giggling and hiccupping.

'I'm sorry, but I think we should take him home.' In a way he was grateful to Godfrey. He needed to be out of here, to try to make sense of what was happening to him. When he was with Kate all sense seemed to fly out of the window. Or maybe it flew in? Either way he had to do some sober thinking.

Between them the Cuisine crew managed to get Godfrey in the back of the car, but Jake had to stop twice on the way home to let him throw up.

Chapter Nineteen

It was well into the afternoon the following day before Georgia got up, and a lie-in hadn't improved her temper.

'Covering the floor with all those books isn't hiding the fact that this carpet is disgusting,' she said acidly. Everything about her life with Jake felt wrong, compared to the glorious promise of a future with Harry.

'I'm not trying to cover anything up. I'm looking for the best way to cook the venison I've ordered.'

He bent his head. Who am I kidding, he thought. I'm desperately trying to cover up my feelings for Kate.

Georgia turned and stubbed her toe on a disgustingly graphic description of how to dismember a deer.

'Ugh! What are those horrible pictures? And now my manicure is ruined. This is a really bad start to the day. My chakras must be completely out of balance!'

'My finances certainly are,' muttered Jake. What am I going to do? I don't want to spend the rest of this afternoon with her, let alone the rest of my life, he thought, bleakly.

'There is nothing to do here – I'm bored, and maybe,' she said darkly, 'maybe that is only the tip of the iceberg.

Who knows what other dark feelings are simmering away in my subconscious? Oh God! All this stress could be giving me lines!'

'What on earth are you talking about?' Jake snapped, throwing the book down so hard it raised a cloud of dust. He sneezed violently. 'You're right – this is a tip. Let's get out of here!'

'Oh, good!' Georgia was thinking of nice hotels and cocktails.

'Yes! Let's go for a walk!'

'A what? Why?'

'Fresh air, sunshine, glorious scenery, and all of it for free – what would be better?'

'Well, practically anything, Jake. I've never been on a walk. I haven't got the right sort of shoes!'

'Georgia, you have twenty-seven pairs clogging up the wardrobe. One of them must be a pair without six-inch heels and diamonds, surely?'

'Well, yes, but –'

'Well, go and put them on. I've heard that walking is terribly good for one's chakras.'

'Are you making fun of me?'

'Now, why would I do that?'

Georgia gave him a long look before disappearing into the bedroom. Jake's good intentions about lightening the mood started to fade as the minutes went by and she didn't return. Eventually he could take it no longer. 'For goodness' sake! Edmund Hillary didn't take this long to get ready for Everest!'

She emerged, with a sulky look on her face and a

beautiful pair of soft leather mules with soles about as thin as a carrot peeling. He looked at them in disbelief.

'Is that the best you can do?' he said, trying to sound polite.

Georgia had been fighting her own demons, the ones telling her how wonderfully charming and understanding Harry was in comparison to Jake. With a certain amount of relief she gave in to them.

'You're horrible when you're like this. Dr Ko Lon says my aura is particularly susceptible to damage when people around me are shouting.'

'Well, mine happens to be allergic to idiots like your Dr Colon! I'll go on this bloody walk on my own!' He stomped down the stairs and out of the house.

I'm susceptible too – to a certain redhead, he thought, walking fast, anywhere, to try and get his feelings under control. Kate had got right under his defences and he couldn't get her out. He didn't want to, either. He liked thinking about her when she wasn't there – so he could look forward to being with her again. He had even started having imaginary conversations with her. This was getting serious.

He tried to focus on something harmless, like tonight's prep list for the kitchen, but found himself wondering where he would take her if he was free – Italy or France? French food spoke for itself, of course, but there was something so seductive and romantic about a piazza in the moonlight, a table for two and feeding someone delicious morsels of lobster linguine . . .

Now, where the hell was he? He seemed to have climbed

a hill and walked across two . . . no, three fields. Oh well, the views were worth it. Surely a landscape this beautiful would put everything in perspective?

Then a gloriously red streak of fur flashed by him so quickly it took Jake a second or two to work out it was a fox. He was used to them, of course – they were more common in London than stray dogs now. But city foxes were pale, sluggish creatures compared to this vivid, taut and alert hunter. The fox turned for a second and he could feel its bright intelligent eyes assessing him before it jumped into a stream and out the other side into the bushes. He stood stock-still and realised he was holding his breath with the wonderfulness of it all.

'Wow!' and then – 'Shit!' as he was knocked to the ground by four baying hounds. They charged over to the water, sniffed, confused and then darted back to jump on his chest in a perfectly friendly way.

'Well, well, look what we have here!' said a familiar drawling voice and Jake realised that lying in the grass with a large dog on his stomach which was trying to lick his ear off wasn't how he would choose to meet Harry. It obviously suited Harry, though, because he made no attempt to call the dogs off. To complete Jake's mortification, he was then joined by four or five men, whom he guessed were all friends of Harry's.

'What the hell are you doing, lying in the mud, man?' asked one.

'Meditating, of course,' snapped Jake. He managed to push away the hound and scrambled awkwardly to his feet, brushing off what he hoped was just mud. Typical. He couldn't even go for a walk on his own without bumping into Harry. Worse still, he had been trying to woo the locals for weeks now, and for them to find him lying flat on his back like a prat was about the worst way they could meet. Harry, on the other had, looked completely at home here. I never will, Jake suddenly thought, despairingly. I'm always going to be on the outside, looking in. Oh bugger – once a townie, always a townie. I might as well be proud of it.

'Mislaid a fox, have you?' he said slyly, suddenly very much on the fox's side.

'I'll answer that when you tell me what you're doing on private land,' said one of the men, stepping forward and glaring at Jake.

'Oh. I'm sorry. I didn't know I was trespassing,' said Jake, wrong-footed.

'You're not very familiar with the country, are you? Hope you didn't leave any gates open?' continued the man.

'I'm not stupid,' said Jake hotly and decided that attack was the best form of defence. 'I'm a bit confused here, but isn't hunting foxes with a pack of hounds against the law now?'

'There's nowt in the law books about going for a walk with your dogs on your own land, though, is there? Or are you one of them people that move here from the city and think you've got the right to tell us simple folk how to live our lives?'

Oh crap. Well done, Jake, antagonising country folk, like a typical bratty city boy. 'No, of course I don't think that,' he began. 'I think we've –'

'You see, it's all very well giving us a lecture about the rights of wild animals, but have you ever tried talking to a henhouse full of murdered chickens?'

'No, of course not, but –'

'Or maybe you know what it is like to sit up all night hand-rearing a lamb, only to see it carried off squealing, for foxy's supper. Or maybe you don't,' said the man, coming a little too close for Jake's comfort. He clicked his fingers and the dogs clustered around him, so close he could feel their hot breath and their sandpaper tongues. Now he knew exactly how that fox had felt.

Not only was he in severe danger of being eaten by the dogs and then buried where no one would ever find him (Georgia wouldn't even try – but Kate, now she wouldn't ever give up looking) but these men were all local. He should be wooing them as potential customers, not pissing them off. He couldn't afford to irritate anyone at the moment, especially someone with a gun.

Harry was leaning on his rifle and trying not to smirk. This afternoon was turning out so much more entertaining than he expected. He practically had Georgia in the bag, so to speak, and now here was his rival being made to look a fool in front of a bunch of locals. He thought how amusing it would be to carry on duping Jake. It would make Jake doubly furious when he found out that the person who had stood up for him had also stolen his woman.

'Oh, come on, Briggsy,' he said to the man, 'Jake's new to the country and doesn't completely know his way around our customs yet. After all, you go down to London a couple of times a year and no one expects you to know the underground map off by heart.'

'Are you defending this fella? Is he a friend of yours?' said Mr Briggs suspiciously. Harry flashed an awkward grin at Jake. 'Well, to be perfectly honest with you, we are not really friends, but we're working on it – isn't that right, Jake?'

Jake nodded warily, and Mr Briggs laughed suddenly. 'You know, your expression reminds me a bit of that fox! Why? Are you worried he's going to shoot you?' He nodded over at Harry.

'That wouldn't have been out of the question in the past,' Jake began.

'Yeah, we've got a bit of history, Jake and I,' said Harry. 'But we've recently come to a bit of an agreement – to keep the past where it belongs.'

Jake flashed Harry a grateful glance, which was something he never thought he would find himself doing. He took a deep breath and prepared to stand up to Mr Briggs. 'You're right. I have no idea what it is like to be a farmer. But I know what it's like to spend time and money nurturing something fragile and precious. I'd do anything I had to, to protect it. But I wouldn't make a sport out of it. And no one's going to stop me standing up for what I believe in!'

'And, frankly, that fox deserved to outwit the hounds. They really are the most inept pack we've had for a long time,' said Harry helpfully. God, he was so good at this!

Mr Briggs sucked his teeth thoughtfully, while he made his mind up. 'I like to think that any pal of the Hunters is a pal of mine. I don't agree with what you're saying, but I respect the fact that you've got the bottle to say it.' He looked at Jake thoughtfully for a moment. 'A mate of mine was talking about you the other day – Geoff Tomlinson. He reckons he owes you a bit of a thank you. It's his wife, see – she's got depression. But she's so busy putting together all the stuff you're ordering from her, she says she hasn't got time to think about it any more. Well, I reckon you've done quite a bit of good there. I still think you're a fool over the foxes, mind, but what d'you say we all go back to Bill's for a spot of whisky to cement our differences?'

'I'd say that's a bloody good way to sign a peace treaty,' said Jake, grinning.

You are almost as easy to outwit as a fox, thought Harry.

The next day, nursing a rather bad head from more whisky than he was used to, Jake was on his own in the kitchen making *torte aux trois mousses* to put on the menu that evening. It was a slightly tricky dish to get absolutely right and he preferred to be on his own while he was doing it. For other reasons as well, solitude was good. He wanted to look at Kate all the time, but didn't want anyone else to notice this, so he found himself deliberately not looking at her, which was plainly impracticable during service.

Georgia had inexplicably taken herself off for a few days to visit her mother, she said. This was something she hardly ever did but Jake was too relieved to see her go to ask questions. This seemed to annoy her.

'Aren't you going to ask why?' she'd said, her tone heavy with meaning.

'Oh. OK – why?'

'I can't tell you – you wouldn't understand,' she'd replied and swept out, leaving Jake furious and baffled. He had spent some time trying to work out what was going on, but then a letter had arrived in the post from the Lake District's regional television station. They had just finished a very successful series on cooking and were keen to capitalise on it. The idea was for a sort of cook-off between the area's top chefs, with viewers ringing in during the programme to vote for their favourite.

Jake had no patience with the current mood for cooking on television. It distracted chefs from their true work and took the edge off their art. They allowed themselves to take part in unreal situations and either tried to charm the viewers or claim some dubious crown for being the most unpleasant. It was all too tacky for words, and he was so busy grumbling to himself about cooks who thought they were film stars that he didn't hear the door open.

'Surprise!'

Jake was so taken aback he dropped his spoon.

It was Louis Challon, his old boss at Brie. He burst in through the door, his ample arms full of wine and a huge, toe-curlingly smelly parcel of Camembert.

He dropped his presents onto a worktop and enveloped Jake in a crushing bear hug. '*Mon ami!* It's been too long!'

'My God, it's good to see you, old friend! But what on earth are you doing here and why didn't you let me know you were coming?'

'Because he pretends to forget you are no longer a member of his staff. You must remember how he used to like to creep up on you all to catch you out in some crime,' said Maria, following her husband in more quietly, kissing Jake on the cheek and looking him up and down critically.

'You have lost weight, my dear boy. Do you not eat your own food?' she demanded.

'Of course not! He has that much sense at least,' scoffed Louis, peering into saucepans with a professional eye.

'Ah! The mousse of little fishes – I have fond memories of that dish.'

'I remember that the language you used when you tried my first attempt nearly had me in tears,' said Jake.

'Well, you should have wept. It was an abomination. But the question is, what did you learn from that débâcle? Recite to me, please, the herbs you are planning to use.'

'Citronella, coriander, rosebuds, lavender seeds, fennel and juniper,' Jake reeled off meekly and grinned at Maria.

'White or black pepper?'

'White, of course.'

'That's good.' Then triumphantly: 'But you forget the lime flowers, do you not? What have you got against these inoffensive little leaves?'

Jake shrugged his shoulders in sorrow and looked at his feet. 'I couldn't get any, Chef,' he murmured.

'Couldn't get any? What sort of answer is that? Unacceptable, I say,' said Louis. 'Anyway, what do you expect, trying to run a restaurant in the middle of nowhere?' He ran a suspicious finger along the work benches looking for drips, tested the sharpness of Jake's knife against his finger and helped himself to a clean apron.

'So why are you here?' asked Jake, hoping to deflect his

former boss's attention from his work, which he was instantly sure would not bear scrutiny.

'We are supposed to be on a short break, but how funny – we find ourselves in a kitchen,' Maria said in the resigned tone of voice of a woman to whom this often happened.

'I will make you some tea.'

'Come here,' growled Louis. 'She can make her own. Now tell me what you are doing here.'

It was as if the past had melted away. Jake could even feel a familiar film of sweat beading his brow. He had forgotten what it was like to stand with sweaty palms waiting for the great god Chef to pass judgement on his work. He promised himself he would be very kind to Godfrey when he came in that evening, a resolve which was forgotten half a minute after he actually walked into the kitchen.

Louis tasted the salmon, hake and sole mousses, which Jake had already made, and pronounced them edible, which was high praise, but decided that the puff pastry that Jake had rolled out was far too thick.

'This you could use to line a loft with. Your diners will be dead of exhaustion by the time they have waded through all this,' he complained.

Jake looked pleadingly at Maria, a look that would have melted many a woman's heart, but Maria, as she had done quite a few times in the past, just patted his shoulder reassuringly and took herself off for an unguided tour of his restaurant.

By the time the pastry shells were chilling in the fridge, the mousses were baking in the oven and a sauce containing oysters and double cream was simmering on the hob, Jake felt quite exhausted. But this was why Louis had three Michelin stars and why every young chef in the business wanted to work with him.

Maria came back and put the kettle on just as Louis was saying: 'Not bad, I suppose, for an Englishman who dares to think he can cook.' Louis was of the old school that believed that cooking had started in France and had never really left. 'Now, if you had stayed with me,' he wiped an imaginary tear from his eye, 'I might have made something of you.'

'This is a very nice little restaurant and anyway you told him it was time he spread his wings,' retorted Maria. Louis might be one of the greatest chefs in the business, but he was still a contrary old boot who needed to be put in his place from time to time.

Louis reasserted himself by snatching the tea leaves from her. 'None of us wants tea, woman! Why do you think I removed this excellent Pouilly Fumé from my own cellar?'

'How are things down in London?' asked Jake, getting glasses.

Louis sniffed. 'New restaurants opening up everywhere and then closing down again because the cooks cannot cook or they think they can make a fortune by shoving out gimmicky food. They all think they are Harry Potter and can magic people in through the door. We see them come, we see them go.' He opened the wine with a flourish, poured it and gave Jake a nudge. 'She misses you, you know,' he said in a loud whisper, gesturing towards his wife.

Maria gave him a look.

'All right, all right. We both miss you, I suppose. You are inept, of course, but you have a touch others lack.'

Jake accepted this for what it was: an enormous compliment.

Because he had been in the business for forty-five years, Louis knew everything that was going on in the cooking world, sometimes before it happened. Framed on his kitchen wall was an interview he had given when the nouvelle cuisine fad was at its height, in which he said 'this will never last'. 'I said this was rubbish then and I was right. I know everything.' Now he leaned forward. 'I hear you are expecting an important visitor.'

Jake nodded and his throat went dry with fear. The Restaurant Club. Maria patted his arm comfortingly. Sometimes she dreamed he was the son she had never had. 'This club man was in for a meal a few weeks ago. They were talking about you. Inept indeed! Louis says you are one of the best young chefs in the country and this man will be delighted with your food.'

Louis glared at his wife. 'Stop talking nonsense. I just put in a kind word, that is all. This man will present himself as a Mr Blair. He is tall, with a beard and glasses. He looks more like he inspects the taxes than the food, but he is no fool and will be fair. You, of course, will sweat blood before he eats and be ready to kill yourself by the time he has finished, but you have been trained by me so things may turn out all right.'

Jake raised his glass. 'I'll drink to that.'

At that moment, Kate came in, her arms full of fresh

flowers for the tables. She stopped dead and sniffed the air with deep suspicion.

'Phwoar, what is that smell?'

'Cheese, but it went in the cold room hours ago.'

'Its presence lingers, believe me. But that's a relief. I was wondering how to tell you that you really need to wash your socks. Back in a minute, but I really must put these in water.'

Louis pretended to look hurt. 'Your girlfriend, the lovely model? It seems she no longer recognises me.'

'See! I keep telling you that you need glasses, you old fool! How long before you start mistaking frozen mushrooms for truffles. This is a completely different woman,' snapped Maria.

'Frozen mushrooms! I have never used one in my restaurant ever!' said Louis, who had spotted Georgia two days ago, coming out of a restaurant with a man who certainly wasn't Jake. Ever since, Louis had been wondering what the hell was going on.

'Kate is my mistress – I mean waitress,' said Jake, choking on his wine. He really wasn't up to par if he was coming out with Freudian slips like that. He looked up and met two curious, but kind, stares. 'You can guess how busy I've been here. Georgia hates it, and frankly I don't blame her. I feel a bit like a juggler who's developed a squint. I'm keeping some of the plates in the air, but others are crashing down behind me.'

They nodded understandingly. Chefs' partners were often casualties of ambition and obsession.

'Well, it has been obvious for a long time that men can

only use one part of their brain at a time and their women must supply the rest,' said Maria. From what she knew of Georgia, she doubted she could supply anyone with anything. It had also always seemed to her that Jake had taken her on as if she was a particularly difficult dish he was determined to master.

Louis must have been thinking along the same lines, because he asked now: 'Do you recall the first time you made *poulet fermier aux escargots*?'

Jake winced. 'You tasted it, pulled a horrible face, then threw it in the bin.'

Louis nodded. 'Sometimes you just have to ditch things and start again.'

'I can't dispose of Georgia like she's something nasty at the bottom of a saucepan,' said Jake, outraged.

'Of course not. You do not have it in you to be so ruthless. But you are not married and therefore you must ask yourself some difficult questions,' said Maria. 'A woman is not a dish you can keep trying to get right. If there is a good understanding between you it will work out anyway. A good relationship is not about two people being joined at the hip. But you must ask yourself, are you both travelling the same road together?'

Jake was silent. If he was honest with himself, he would have to say that he didn't even know which road Georgia was on.

'Maria is right, as usual,' said Louis. 'This is an important question. But Jake, I must ask others, possibly even more important. What in God's name are you going to serve this man from the Restaurant Club?' He looked round the kitchen, as if there might be spies hiding in the pan cupboard, and he lowered his voice. 'It is not a well-known fact, but I have it on very good authority that he is not partial to tuna.' He leaned back, satisfied, as if he had just passed on the meaning to Life, the Universe and Everything.

And maybe he had, thought Jake.

Chapter Twenty

Georgia wasn't at her mother's house. At this moment she was lying naked on Harry's king-size bed, admiring her reflection in the mirror he had put up on the ceiling.

'Naff, isn't it?' he said lazily. 'The thing is, we are both so astonishingly good-looking, the tackiness is redeemed, don't you think?'

'Yes, you're right,' she agreed. 'But how many women have you said that to?'

He leaned over on one elbow to look at her. There was still sweat on his brow. 'Plenty. But I only really meant it about you.'

She nodded, satisfied. He was right. Whenever she had glanced up during their very busy night, there they were, a tangle of limbs, muscular and soft skin perfectly complementing each other. It was like watching a living painting, thought Georgia. 'Jake would be in fits of laughter if he could see it,' she said. If there was a rule that you shouldn't talk about a previous love to your new love, Georgia certainly didn't know it. But Harry wasn't offended. He liked hearing about his rivals – it gave him more opportunity to put the boot in.

He lay on his back, legs splayed. Then he took her hand

almost casually and put it on his cock. 'He's got a weird sense of humour. I'm sure he wouldn't have been able to understand half the things we got up to last night.'

'No. He simply does not get why I cannot have carbs for dinner. Oh – I see what you mean.'

He reached over and pulled her on top of him so he could stroke her arse and look at it in the mirror at the same time. He was already more than satisfied and not at all put off by her dimness. Only one of them needed the brains, after all.

Jake was on the phone, trying to talk to Tess. He had asked for her three times already, in increasing desperation, but Angelica was determined to take him through a step-by-step account of her day at school.

'Mrs Parkinson wears big, round shiny earrings.'

'Does she? Is that the name of your teacher? Is she nice?'

'I tried to pull one off and she told me to sit in the Quiet Corner.'

'Well, anyway –'

'I had rice pudding for my lunch and Emily fell over and hurt her knee.'

'Oh dear. Is Emily your friend?'

'I don't know yet,' said Angelica, thoughtfully. 'Kevin Brady is my friend.'

'That's nice. Now –'

'I drew a picture of him in the kitchen with you. Do you know Kevin has a tiny willy all of his own?'

'Er, no. Well, yes, but –'

'I want one. Have you got one?'

'Please, Angelica, get your mummy!'

'Round and round the garden, like a teddy bear –'

'That's enough, Angel. Now give me the phone. Hi, Jake, what did you want?'

'I haven't the faintest idea now. I mean, I did, when I rang you, but then everything went a bit surreal. Is it normal for small girls to have a fixation with willies?'

'Yes. They usually grow out of it, though.'

'Oh hell – there's someone at the door. I'll get back to you.'

He was expecting three boxes of vegetables so he was a bit taken aback to find Georgia on the doorstep, looking distraught and pale, eyes hidden by enormous dark glasses even though the day was overcast. Although he didn't know it, she was wearing her full complement of make-up, but it was cunningly muted to give the impression she wasn't. A tiny touch of blusher round the eyes would make it look as if she had been crying.

'Goodness, I'm sorry, I didn't know you were due back today. Why didn't you ring me? I would have met you at the station.'

'You didn't answer any of my messages,' she said reproachfully. She hadn't actually sent any but she was correctly assuming he had been too busy to check his phone. She was right. Jake immediately looked guilt-stricken, which was how she had planned to set the tone of the ensuing conversation.

'Jake, we have to talk.'

He instantly felt a jolting moment of *déjà vu*.

'Oh hell, Georgy. I can't begin to tell you how much I hate that phrase.'

Having got him feeling slightly sick with apprehension, she then made it even worse by having him wait while they went upstairs, where she disappeared into the bathroom for what seemed like ages.

It was like waiting for his head to be lopped off while the executioner picked his nose and polished his sword. Jake wasn't very good at waiting for anything.

'For fuck's sake, what are you doing? Come out at once,' he shouted, banging on the door, driven beyond endurance.

When Georgia emerged, she was holding a tissue to her nose, delicately. 'I've just had the worst two days of my life,' she announced.

'What happened? Have you been binge-eating on half a chocolate biscuit again?'

She looked at him sadly. 'Let's sit down.'

'Only if you take those ridiculous glasses off and stop acting as if this is a scene out of a second-rate film noir.'

As soon as he sat down, she got up and began pacing up and down the room. Unfortunately, she automatically adopted the strutting and silly catwalk stride, which always made Jake want to laugh. He bit his lip and tried to focus.

'What happened to me in the last two days was a crisis. I really think I've had some sort of emotional breakdown.'

'Well, I'm sure your mother is used to coping.'

'I wasn't at home. I wasn't with mother.' She stared at him and he just looked back her, uncomprehending. 'Oh, for goodness' sake, don't be so dim, Jake! Our relationship would have worked so much better if you'd been a bit more jealous, like other men!'

'Would it?' he said quietly. 'I thought one of the reasons you loved me was because I trusted you.'

'Yes, well; there can be too much trust.' She was cross now and couldn't remember which bit came next. 'Anyway I suddenly realised how much you have changed. There are three of us in this relationship now and one of them is this stupid restaurant. I went to some very dark places, Jake –'

'I keep telling you not to wear your sunglasses indoors,' he muttered before he could stop himself. She glared at him.

'But I finally came to the conclusion, after a great deal of suffering, that our dreams are no longer the same. This is very painful for me, but I know I have to set you free.' As she said this, Georgia really believed it and started to cry in earnest.

'I don't think I've changed that much,' he said slowly, 'well, not in that way. Work is an important part of my life, but it always has been.'

'But it's taken you over, Jake! You think about food all day; you dream about it at night, and even when we make love you compare me to food. That is seriously weird and kinky, especially when you know how I feel about food, Jake!' Her voice rose hysterically.

Jake felt better at once. He had been sure she had realised he had fallen for Kate. But this was just Georgia having one of her episodes. She was needy and insecure, and he had probably been neglecting her. She lived in such a fragile little world. Something petty had sparked this off – an unflattering photo of her, perhaps, or a bitchy comment in the press, which he hadn't read because he never had time to read crap like that. But these things were important to her and who was he to judge? He too depended upon the kindness of others.

He looked at her tenderly with affection. Then his eyes narrowed. There was something different about her today. As he looked closer he saw that she radiated a sort of guilty energy. Having experienced it himself, he recognised it instantly for what it was and, belatedly, the penny dropped.

'You've been seeing someone else, haven't you?'

She was furious. How typical of Jake to describe thus her life-changing affair. Also, she wanted to be the one to drop the bombshell. This was her show and she had planned some really good stuff still to come, mostly variations on how much she had been suffering. Now she would have to fast-forward a whole range of feelings that were designed to illustrate how none of this was her fault.

'I have met someone else. We have known each other for a while now and our feelings for each other have deepened. For a long time we really fought this – it's been terrible, you can't imagine the stress I've been under. We had this instant connection from almost the first time we met. He really understands me,' she continued and although she tried to look sorrowful, she just ended up looking smug.

Jake wasn't listening. It was glaringly obvious to him that neither of them had been honest with the other. OK, Georgia had slept with this bloke, whoever he was – that wasn't important. How guilty was he for thinking the same things about Kate? OK, thinking wasn't the same thing as doing, but the principle was the same, he reasoned, being hard on himself, but somehow that felt better than blaming Georgia. He probably had been neglecting her a little.

'I'm sorry,' he said humbly. 'Maybe you need more from me than I can ever give. At the end of the day I'm always going to be a scruffy workaholic with no money and big dreams. We were happy together once and I take some of the responsibility for the fact that we aren't now. But I hope we can always be friends?'

Georgia stopped pacing in irritation. This wasn't what she wanted at all. OK, it looked like parting was going to be painless, but surely he should care a lot more? He really wasn't as broken up about this as he bloody should be. It was all rather galling. She was easily the most beautiful thing he had ever had in his life. Did he not know just what he was losing? Apparently not, because he just carried on sitting opposite her, smiling sadly but not even fraying slightly round the edges.

'I hope you will be happy,' he said.

'I'm sure we will. And we will take every care to stay out of your way.'

'Oh, I don't think that will be a problem,' said Jake easily. Whoever he was, he was probably based in London and part of her fashion world. He doubted their paths would ever cross. It was probably someone he had never heard of, a rival rendered insignificant by the fact that he was an unknown.

'Well, I am glad you can say that. We were both worried that you were going to find this very difficult,' said Georgia importantly. Actually, what Harry had said was: 'He is going to be mad with rage, hopefully. I shall probably have to hire bodyguards.'

'You don't know who I am talking about, do you?'

'Well, of course I don't. I'm not a mind-reader. I don't know half the people you hang around with at work, do I?' said Jake, tetchily.

God, he was stupid, she thought crossly. 'Jake, I know you are not going to want to hear this, but . . . the person I have fallen in love with is Harry Hunter.'

Chapter Twenty-one

'You stupid woman,' he said.

This didn't go down well at all. Georgia wouldn't have particularly minded being called a heartless bitch, or something dramatic like that, but no one likes to be called stupid, especially when they are.

Jake stood up and looked down at her coldly. 'I have never wanted to say this before but you really are a complete fool. Have you listened to nothing I have told you about this man? He is a complete bastard and he is just using you to get at me. He really is that pathetic. When he thinks he's scored enough points – because that's how sad he is – he'll dump you.'

'Why are you smiling? None of this is funny,' she cried.

'No, you are right – it's not,' he said, and thought wryly to himself: he nearly had me there. I was eighty per cent sure he wanted to bury the hatchet.

'This is not about you! This is about me and my needs. Anyway, you're wrong about Harry. He has told me the whole story and it sounds very different the way he says it.'

'I don't doubt that for a minute,' snarled Jake. 'He's made a career out of thinking of ways to twist the truth.

He's got so many faces he probably has to keep checking the mirror to see which one he has got on.'

'He said you would react like this. He knows you've always been insanely jealous of him –'

'I have not!'

'He says he seriously thinks there's something wrong with your personality because you've never been able to accept competition. He says it's not his fault that he's so talented and that things have happened more easily for him than for you. He says you might even do better when you stop blaming him for things that are really your own responsibility. You've got to face the facts, he –'

'Oh, spare me any more of the garbage thoughts of Chairman Harry!'

'And he's an absolutely brilliant lover, Jake. He could teach you a thing or two!'

'I really couldn't give a shit!'

'And his restaurant's so full he's had to turn people away, and he was kind enough to send them up to you, which I think is really nice of him, considering the way you always talk about him.'

Now that hurt. Jake had instantly dismissed the sex jibe because it wasn't about acrobatics; it was about communicating love, and he no longer had any for Georgia. But recently he had been feeling more and more confident that the Harry threat was fading. He thought they could talk to each other civilly. He thought he could just get on with his own life. But now he could feel Harry's malevolence coiling around him like one of those giant snakes that squashes you before eating you. Jake had a sudden hideous vision of

Harry squeezing tighter and tighter until he was just a pile of dust. He shook his head to clear it. That way, madness lay.

'Just go, Georgia. Take yourself and your stupid fantasies, but don't think you can come crawling back when he drops you.'

'Oh, he won't do that. I wasn't going to tell you this, but you'll have to know soon. We're engaged. I might as well wear this now.' Out of her bag she took a ring covered with enough diamonds to pay all of Jake's bills until he was an old, old man.

As she clattered down the stairs, he thought, well, this really is the last time I'll ever have to listen to that. He sat down and put his head in his hands, but when he looked up, the room was still dark. Outside, as well as in here, the clouds had been gathering, and just as he heard the door slam shut it started to rain. She'll get soaked, he thought with satisfaction and then chided himself for being mean. She hadn't broken his heart – to be truthful, it wasn't even dented – but once he'd cleared that up in his head he found he had to face the thing that was really gnawing away at him. It was pathetic to be so disturbed by the spiteful things she had said about him but he couldn't seem to shake them off, he thought, looking out of the window and watching the tourists clearing the street to find shelter from the rain, which was turning into one of those downpours that the Lake District in the summer so enjoyed.

He would find his own refuge in the kitchen, he decided. Work was the only way to stop his mind dwelling pointlessly on stupid things. Halfway down, he stopped. But what if they were true? Rubbish. Who cared how people found their way to his restaurant? Once they were there he made damn sure they had an unforgettable experience. And there was nothing wrong with his personality that a really nasty prep list for Godfrey wouldn't cure.

By stages, his staff arrived for work, all soaking wet, even if, like Kate, they just had to make a quick sprint from car to door.

'It's bloody wet out there,' remarked Godfrey, shaking himself like a dog.

Jake looked up. He hadn't been paying attention to the weather, but now he noticed that it wasn't just raining. Water was hammering against the windowpanes like a mob of angry creditors desperately trying to get in.

Kirsty came back from answering the phone. 'The Thomases, the table for six, have just cancelled. They got caught in this weather coming off a hill and they've decided to stay put in their hotel tonight.'

There were another three phone calls in quick succession, all with the same bad news. Great, thought Jake. Tonight of all nights he could have done with a really busy shift to keep his mind occupied. Also, his bank manager wasn't likely to be sympathetic to the fact that he couldn't make any money because the weather was bad. 'If it seems like it's too quiet out there, put some music on. Let's make sure that the people who do brave this weather have a great evening,' he told Kirsty.

He hoped there was enough rain to make the lake rise and flood Harry's restaurant. He was to regret this thought later on that evening.

Two or three couples did make their bookings, though Kirsty kept having to turn the music up to drown out the weather. As the evening wore on Jake noticed that Godfrey was getting increasingly twitchy.

'Ok, this check says two salads, so why have you made three?'

'Sorry, Chef. I'm just a bit worried. My dad will be out in this and he's all on his own because my brother's away.'

'I thought sheep liked the rain.'

'They might get waterlogged because they haven't been sheared yet.'

'Oh, for goodness' sake! Well, you are no use to me, and I suppose it's quiet enough – you'd better go home and make sure they are all wrung out.'

Godfrey must have been worried, because he didn't even stop to change out of his cooking gear. He had only been gone for a couple of minutes when all the lights went out. Jake swore freely but he had a good stock of candles and all his cookers were powered by gas. The hot water would run out but Godfrey could do all the washing up when he came in tomorrow. It would serve him right for opting to spend the night with a load of soggy sheep.

Candlelight worked very well in the restaurant, but it cast strange shadows in the kitchen. It made everyone clumsy, even Jake. Twice he dropped his knife and had to scrabble around the floor feeling for it and hoping he didn't put his hand round the sharp edge. Everyone was fed and happy, though Kate had a hard time explaining to an American couple why the espresso machine wasn't working.

'At home we have generators for this sort of eventuality.'

'Well, we don't. We have candles.'

'How quaint!'

Back in the kitchen Jake looked out of the window sombrely. 'I've never seen rain like this. In London it falls in a straight line and you just get very wet. But this stuff – it hits you in the face, like a fist. It's like the weather has a grudge against us.'

He was doing some desultory tidying up, trying and failing to summon his usual end of shift energy, when Hans rushed into the kitchen. One look at his face told Jake his barman was the bearer of some seriously shit tidings.

'Boss, there is water coming in through the door of the restaurant.'

Jake dropped his cloth and ran through, hoping Hans was having a drug-induced hallucination. But he wasn't. Water was indeed trickling slowly but steadily through the door. Peering through the wall of water that was still pouring down the windowpanes he could see that the drain outside was no longer taking the rain away. A small lake was forming in the road and it didn't look like it had anywhere to ebb away to except through his door.

'Fuck,' said Jake, forgetting his customers for the first time in his life, and shouted for somebody to get a brush.

'We need sandbags,' said Hans.

'Great idea, but who the hell do we get them from? I don't think the corner shop stocks them somehow! Kirsty, get Kate and start moving everything off the floor and then we'll try and pull the carpet back.'

Kate jumped guiltily when Kirsty came into the kitchen. She had been listening to the local news on the radio. There was severe flooding everywhere; a man had nearly drowned trying to cross a stream (she hoped it wasn't Godfrey or his dad) and the local theatre, which was in a basement in town, was being evacuated. There was mass panic going on there, with tales of people being trampled in the rush to get out, explained the reporter, who was standing outside. A river had also risen and had found a new route down the motorway, causing a mass pile-up. It was all very dreadful, but Kate's nose was twitching at the thought of several good stories going to waste while she was here. She was just wondering if she could escape when Kirsty came in, told her to come and help, and rushed out again. Kate was completely torn. She needed to find out what was happening out on the streets. This was a compulsion as strong as Jake's urge to cook. But she couldn't go, could she? He was down one member of staff already. Damn Godfrey! He was probably sitting at home now, drinking Horlicks and watching his bloody sheep dry out on the Aga.

Hans was standing by the door, frantically trying to sweep the water back faster than it was coming in, like a crazed Canute. The last few customers had already rushed off to higher ground. She and Kirsty scrambled to lift tables and chairs onto any surface more than three feet high. They were working like mad when they heard a cry from the kitchen.

'It's coming in through the back door now!' called Tess, despair in her voice.

Jake called a halt when he realised that water was now sloshing round his ankles. 'We've done all we can; go home now while you still can. Angelica is bound to be awake and she might be worried, and so might your parents,' he said to Tess.

'My room is on a ground floor. I need to inspect the damage,' said Hans mournfully.

'My flat is on the first floor, so I am fine,' said Kate. She was resigned to staying now. Jake would need help moving all the things that were piled up on his stairs. His eyes were like black holes in his white face. He looked done in. Having worked faster and more efficiently than anyone else, he looked like he might just lie down and let the water lap over him if he was left on his own.

Between them they grimly and silently unblocked the stairs, passing things to each other and occasionally grunting with the effort. As soon as their access was clear Jake made her go and wash her hands.

'We've no way of knowing what's in that water, but I doubt they will be bottling it for the tourists,' he said.

When Kate came back into the sitting room he was peering out of the window. 'It's still coming down. I hope we don't have to be rescued by boat. I get terribly seasick.' His tone was light, but Kate knew it was gallows humour.

'Remember, you are insured.'

'Oh, yes. But there's going to be a lot of claims. Who knows how long it will take them to get round to me? We certainly can't cook and serve food to customers who might have to paddle through sewage to get to it. What are you doing?'

Kate was groping around in cupboards. 'You must have some alcohol up here.'

'Only a horrible bottle of whisky a supplier gave me as a bribe. It didn't work.'

'It'll be fine. This is emergency drinking.'

'It might not be a good idea to get drunk, though I am tempted. We might need to keep our wits about us.'

'No, apparently that's just what we shouldn't do. The man on the *Titanic* didn't.'

'What?'

'Well, I can't remember all the details, but when he saw the boat was going down he got pissed, fell overboard and paddled about quite happily until he spotted a lifeboat. Or something like that. If we have to swim for it, I'd rather you were singing rugby songs than clutching me and looking green.'

'I'd clutch you *and* sing, though I admit it wouldn't be easy listening. Even when sober, I tend to sing off key. To tell the truth, I don't think my heart can go on much longer. It feels like it's been through the dishwasher several times today.'

'All the more need for alcohol-induced fortitude, then. Cheers, anyway. To the end of a really bad day.'

'You could say that. I've been dumped, had a character assassination and everything I own is soaking wet.'

'I'm sorry. Georgia has really bad timing.'

'She certainly has.'

'I wouldn't take anything to heart that she said during the dumping. People will say anything so they can go off and screw someone else,' she said awkwardly. She wanted to comfort him, but she wasn't really sorry at all.

'Especially when the someone else is Harry Hunter.'

'Ah.' She looked at him more closely. 'I don't know what was said, but you look as if she really stuck the knife in. I bet it was something to do with your cooking.'

Jake grinned slightly. 'I don't give a shit about the personal stuff,' he agreed.

Kate was silent and longed to tell him that she knew just how he felt. Her writing was the one area of her life where she could feel very vulnerable. Her stories were her children; she loved them dearly, would protect them fiercely and felt acute anxiety when they came under other people's scrutiny. Jake gave the same passion and dedication to his cooking. Then she thought, why not tell him? He wasn't likely to cast her out into tonight's storm. She would tell him, she decided. It would be good to get everything out in the open and she wanted a relationship with him that was based on honesty. It had to be; it would not work any other way.

She took a deep breath, leaned forward – and kissed him. Hang on! This wasn't supposed to happen. But she was glad it had, because it felt so good and he obviously thought the same way, because he was kissing her back.

'Jake – I've got something to tell you.'

'Mmm . . . OK, but first I've got things to do to you, like this . . . and this . . .'

'No, listen –'

'Are you telling me you want me to stop?'

'Oh, certainly not.'

'Was this what you had to say – that your bra fastens at the front instead of at the back?'

'Yeah . . . I guess so . . .'

Georgia was quite wrong about this sofa, Jake thought, hazily, some time later. It was a brilliant sofa. It was perfectly comfortable. It accommodated two people very well indeed and allowed them to do all sorts of things. To be sure, it may have creaked a little, but only in a gentle, friendly way. It shut out the wind and rain, the devastation to his business downstairs, and it blew away the bitterness which had permeated the room only a few hours before.

It was cold in this room, but their skin gleamed with sweat as they explored each other's bodies with great delight. Although Jake's touch was soft and sure, she could feel the muscles rippling under his skin. And he discovered once more, with pleased astonishment, how much more interesting a woman's body was when there were flesh and curves to sink into.

It was as if their bodies were having a most satisfying conversation. Like compatriots meeting in a foreign land, they shared the same language. It was a long time since his skin had talked like this to a woman, and there was so much else he wanted to say, when the phone rang.

They listened to it for a few minutes, wondering whether to push the world away and then realised in perfect accord that they couldn't, and shouldn't. Jake got up and answered it.

'Man, it's wild out there,' said Godfrey. 'One of our trees fell down and missed the house by inches half the roof of the barn blew off but luckily there are no animals in it I got soaked to the skin twice and then Tess rang and she told me what happened is everything in a real mess?'

Jake mentally added some punctuation to this breathless

speech, extracted the sense and replied happily that, yes, it was a complete disaster downstairs.

'Er, you sound a bit light-headed, Boss; are you sure you haven't had a bang on the head?'

'Never felt better.'

'It's been a hell of a night.'

'It certainly has,' said Jake happily, then pulled himself together and told Godfrey to get his butt into work early tomorrow. Reassured by this return to normality, Godfrey rang off.

Jake looked at Kate. It had been a long night but he was still buzzing with energy. The wind and rain had died down at last.

'Do you fancy a walk?'

'That's exactly what I want to do,' said Kate. How wonderful that they were in such perfect agreement about everything! Tonight was a time for kissing, not confession. But tomorrow, when they had sobered up slightly from each other – but not too much, she hoped – then she would talk.

They found their clothes, got dressed and went out by the back door because Jake couldn't face the chaos within just yet. Outside, in the now serene sky, it was as if the storm had never happened. Underfoot, it was a different matter. The rain was at last draining away but there were still huge puddles swamping the pavements and they had to negotiate an obstacle course of broken roof tiles and litter. In the end they gave up and decided it was safer to walk in the road. Kate was wearing an old coat of Jake's, which was extremely shabby but smelled deliciously of him. She tucked her arm into his, where it fitted perfectly. They walked down to the lake, which was now lapping peacefully across the road. It had come close to the row of buildings that housed Harry's restaurant, but not near enough to do any damage. It was typical; Harry had the luck of the devil, thought Jake, but he didn't care – he had his own luck tonight. One or two ducks were swimming about quite happily in the road. Kate pointed them out and they both laughed. The wind had finally blown all the clouds away and a huge moon was skirting the tops of the trees.

'What a perfect night,' she said.

'I feel exactly the same. Though you do realise that makes us both completely mad?'

'Well, in that case, insanity is a good place to be. It feels just right.'

'Get used to it. I seem to spend most of my time there.'

Kate hugged to herself the implied acceptance that they had a future together. Then she shivered. She needed to tell him now while they were still silly with love and sex.

But before she could open her mouth, Jake said: 'Are you cold? You mustn't get cold. I have a bed as well as a sofa, you know. The duvet, I admit, does have a very old cover, which will tell you that I used to have a slight obsession with *Star Wars*. But it is clean and warm and we can pretend we are hurtling through space under it.'

What was the matter with him? He was talking absolute drivel. He never talked like this. How wonderful that he had found someone who didn't seem to mind what nonsense came out of his mouth. Indeed, she seemed to encourage it.

'I don't mind at all if you want me to pretend I'm Princess Leia.'

'Actually, I would prefer it if you stayed yourself. Race you back!'

When they got to the door, he hesitated for a moment.

There! Now, just say it! urged Kate's conscience. But again he spoke first.

'I think, just for a few more hours, we will forget about the rest of the world.'

'Absolutely, Chef,' said Kate.

Chapter Twenty-two

'"If you can meet with triumph and disaster/And treat those two impostors just the same,"' said Kirsty, adding, when they all stared at her: 'I had to do Kipling for GCSE.'

'Oh, I'm on first-name terms with disaster,' said Jake.

The team were all standing in the restaurant, trying not to breathe in too deeply. The carpet was completely ruined; the whole place would need repainting and it stank of stagnant water.

Jake had been on the phone to the insurance people that morning. They would certainly pay up, but that wasn't the problem, as he explained to Godfrey, who was unable to see that there was any sort of problem at all.

'Even if the cheque arrives tomorrow it will be at least two weeks before we can open again. If there are no customers, there's no money coming in. No money at all.'

A few people went pale as they thought about overdrafts and no wages.

'Don't panic. The bank has agreed to loan me enough to pay you all.'

That was typical of Jake, thought Kate. He took care of his people before himself.

'I've got cash. You don't need to pay me,' she said,

feeling horribly guilty and making frantic calculations about how much she could lend him. Not enough, probably.

'My dad will bail me out for a couple of weeks,' Godfrey offered.

'And I have finally got a huge maintenance cheque, so I'm rich, rich!' said Tess.

Jake swallowed. They were all being so nice. He couldn't bring himself to tell them that their wages were but a drop in the ocean of debt that he was swimming in. 'Oh, well, let's go and clean the kitchen, again. Maybe one of us will come up with a cunning plan.'

They had already cleaned the kitchen twice but he still wasn't satisfied. If he was going down, it would be immaculately.

All the way down his street people were stopping their mopping-up operations to share similar tales of woe. The delicatessen two doors down had lost nearly all of its stock. 'We've only just clawed back what we lost during foot and mouth,' said the owner tearfully, when Jake met her on his way to buy coffee and doughnuts.

Jake had no appetite. The elation he had felt the previous night was being sucked away by the spectre of financial ruin. What would happen to him and Kate if he had to close? He knew he could always find work with Louis down in London, but she might not want to follow him there.

Back in front of his computer screen the figures danced in front of him, mockingly. He could swear they were talking to him. 'You arrogant fool,' they whispered. 'Better chefs than you have run aground on these very rocks. Why did you think you were any different?'

'Aargh!' he shouted, picked up all the bills, which had been carefully stacked in order of importance, and flung them across the room. It didn't matter if they were all messed up – he couldn't pay any of them.

When Jake was unhappy he conjured up an image of his grandmother. She had survived far worse than he had ever faced. 'You can mope all you like. You still have to get on with things. And tidy up that dreadful mess you've just made,' she would have added briskly.

'OK, Oma,' he said, and bent down to pick up the papers. 'I might as well burn them,' he grumbled, and then noticed the letter from the television company.

> We are calling the programme *Great Grub* because that is exactly what it is all about. Viewers are sick of people telling them how to make a good bacon butty. We want to show them that we have the best chefs in the county and that they can cook the most sublime food away from the comfort of their own kitchens. We know you can cook, but are you up to the challenge of doing it with the eyes of the county on you?
>
> We would of course pay you to take part, and the winner will walk away with a cheque for £20,000 and an increased profile, which can only be good for your business.

'Oh, no, I might as well jack it all in and become a burger chef.'

'Stop kvetching,' said his grandmother irritably. 'Your grandfather had to take a job as a street cleaner after the war, and him with a university education. If he hadn't, we wouldn't have survived. Of course, if you're too proud to pay the bills this way . . .'

'I haven't got much to be proud of at the moment.'

'Well, I wouldn't say that. For instance, you seem to have made a very nice new friend in that girl . . .'

'Oh God! I'd forgotten you were dead and in heaven and see everything,' groaned Jake.

'Please come out of there and stop talking to yourself – it's scaring us,' said Tess, appearing in the doorway.

He took the letter out and read it to them.

'Under normal circumstances, I wouldn't dream of doing anything like this. But I need to make some cash and, apparently, I can't afford to be picky.'

To his great annoyance, they all thought it was a brilliant idea.

'You'd go down a storm,' said Godfrey.

'You'd knock the spots off any competition,' said Tess.

'Move aside, Jamie Oliver. Anyway, you're far better-looking,' grinned Kirsty. 'Even when you're scowling, you have a certain charisma.'

'I certainly do not,' said Jake firmly. Harry had charisma, of a nasty, hypnotic sort, he considered, quite unaware that he had his own brand of charm.

'So, you think I should look into it, then?'

'Yes!' they all shouted.

Kate had been studying the letter. 'You might have left it a bit late. The competition starts next week.'

Tess handed him the phone and they all stood looking at him.

'You want me to do this now and you all want to listen in, right. Oh, OK.'

It was impossible to work out what was going on. The conversation was terse, at least from Jake's side, his contribution being, 'Uh-huh. . . . Oh, I see. . . . Well, never mind. . . . Oh, really? . . . Yes, I think so. . . . OK, thanks very much, I think.'

He put the phone down. 'Well, first of all, you were right, Kate.'

There was a chorus of groans at this.

'Everyone they asked, apart from me, accepted. There were also quite a few people who begged to take part, apparently, whom they put on a reserve list. But they've just found out that one of the chefs has done a bunk with his head waitress. His wife has said that if he still takes part she plans to be part of the audience, armed with a meat cleaver. Anyway, then I rang up and . . .' he paused, milking the moment, 'for some reason they put me at the top of the list anyway and – I'm in!'

When the cheering had died down, he said: 'You know, I can't help thinking this is all going to be a very big mistake.'

'Well, you won't know that until you've done it,' said Kirsty.

'The other thing is that I need to bring two assistants with me.'

'Tess for one,' said Godfrey, and everyone nodded. Then he looked at Kate.

She knew he had seen her come out of Jake's flat that

morning and had jumped to a bunch of entirely correct conclusions. They were a couple – of course she could go. But she couldn't. She knew at least half the people who worked at Lakes Television and there was no way she could get round them all and warn them to keep quiet. They wouldn't, anyway.

'There is no doubt that Kirsty is a much better waitress than I'll ever be. For one thing, she has learned not to swear in front of the public, which I, alas, have not.'

'That's true. But you did apologise very nicely after you dropped table four's wine and said, "Oh, fuck it",' grinned Jake, who was still in that 'my loved one can do no wrong' mood.

'Well, that's really nice of you, Kate,' said Kirsty. 'Are you sure? I'd love to do it – ooh, I'm excited already!'

Everyone agreed that it was really nice of Kate, so she had to slip out, pretending she wanted a fag. She actually felt slightly sick with shame. She wasn't being nice at all. She was being duplicitous. Oh God! Why hadn't she just told Jake yesterday? Every day she let pass without saying something made it more difficult. Now it was practically impossible. For a minute she entertained a wild notion of handing in her notice at the paper and becoming a bona fide waitress. Then she really could write a novel in her spare time. It couldn't be that difficult. Loads of people did it. But what she loved about journalism was having to pare things down to an absolute minimum so that every word counted. And anyway, if she wrote a real novel, it would have to be about Jake, and there, she was back at square one again.

'Are you all right?' Jake had followed her out.

'I'm fine, but are you?' He was looking slightly green.

'I just think this is such an unprofessional thing to do. And I am a hypocrite – the things I've said about TV chefs in the past! I daren't let my old boss hear of this. It's only local television, though, isn't it? Probably only a handful of people and their dogs will be watching.' He started pacing up and down. He even looked as though he were about to wring his hands.

'You're absolutely terrified, aren't you? Kate said slowly. 'Not about cooking, of course. You're scared of having to stand up in front of a bunch of strangers.'

'You're right – you're absolutely right. I'd rather cook a meal for Michael Winner than have to perform to some smirking guy behind a camera. I just know I'm going to be totally crap and I'm going to look a complete fool! If I don't manage it myself, Harry will certainly ensure that I do, in some underhand way. Yes, he's taking part, of course. He was the first to reply. Prat!'

'Which of you does that epithet refer to?'

'Both of us – him for being such a show-off and me for being pathetic.'

'Look, television hasn't done Gordon Ramsay or Jamie Oliver any real harm, has it?'

'I don't have their television-friendly qualities. Anyway, I have to say that for someone who used to be in PR, you're being a bit idealistic. The telly is such a distorting medium. They'll decide how they want me to come across and that's how it will be, whatever I say or do. The media are manipulative and dishonest, driven solely by ratings and completely lacking in any moral sense.'

Kate winced. And then Jake made it worse by kissing her, which she couldn't enjoy at all because she felt like Judas for kissing him back.

They were ten minutes late setting off for the studios because Jake decided just as they were leaving that he needed his lucky apron. Louis had lent it to him one night and never asked for it back. Jake had never thought of it as a talisman before, but now, with the irrationality borne out of sheer terror, he decided that he had cooked all his best meals while wearing it.

When he got back in the car, he put his hand on the gearstick and his mind went completely blank. He looked at it and for a split second, which actually felt like an hour – nothing. He didn't know what it was, or what you did with it, and he had been driving for years. Pulling away very, very slowly, in case he had also forgotten where the brake was, he thought: that's it, we're doomed. If this happens, and it probably will when Tess hands me a saucepan, the last thing I will see before I die of shame is Harry smirking at me.

Luckily, he had Kirsty sitting next to him and she had so much to say there was no space for anyone to think their own thoughts. Kirsty was positively fizzing with excitement and anticipation. Basically, she couldn't wait for her chance to show off.

'Of course, all waitresses are performers really. Maybe I'm in the wrong job; maybe I should move to Hollywood.'

'Are you trying to tell me that I give you a good wage to tell tales to my customers?'

'Well, they did hear you swearing once so I told them you were this mad creative genius like Van Gogh and they were absolutely thrilled – they were Americans, of course – and then I had to stop them coming down to the kitchen and taking a picture of you.'

The conversation moved on to Kirsty's current boyfriend, whom she was planning to ditch. 'He's really nice, but there's no spark, you know.'

'Oh, there have got to be sparks,' agreed Jake, thinking of Kate. He glanced in the mirror but Tess was listening to music on her headphones and obviously wasn't interested in talking.

Lakes Television was in Windermere and as they parked, all of Jake's butterflies came back. A young girl with a clipboard and a harassed expression met them in the foyer. Jake was the tenth chef she had met that morning. In her opinion they were all temperamental, egotistical bastards. Jake was feeling so sick by now he could only smile at her and she instantly revised her opinion. This one seemed really sweet.

Jake couldn't believe how many people were apparently needed to make one poxy programme. There were dozens of them, all milling around in what he hoped was organised chaos. Lakes Television didn't have the best reputation for slick, professional programming and were only hanging on to their franchise by a whisker. It was quite probable that he would go on set to find that they were expecting him to cook a three-course meal on one hob.

He was shaking so much by the time they arrived in make-up that the girl had to hold his face steady while she applied powder, to which he submitted meekly, being incapable of doing anything else by now.

They were allowed on to the set to have a look around and familiarise themselves, and Jake had a small argument with one of the organisers who didn't want him to use his own knives.

'They look much sharper than ours. We are worried about people cutting themselves.'

'Of course they are sharp – they are meant to be! And yes, it's highly likely someone will cut themselves – it's a kitchen hazard. You want to see some real cooking, you're going to get it – sweat, stress and blood, if necessary.'

And plenty of bad language too, thought the organiser, pleased, as Jake turned round and swore when he realised he was already being filmed.

The competition called for each chef to cook a meal, the nature of which was written on a piece of paper that they picked at random out of a velvet bag. This meant that no one could practise in advance or opt to cook their favourite meal. The audience was seated at mock restaurant tables and could watch the chef's as they cooked. The audience and the viewers had to vote on which meal they would want to eat in a real restaurant.

The show was hosted by Lakes TV's hottest star, Melina Marvin, who was hoping that *Great Grub* would launch her on to national television. She was wearing, most inappropriately, Jake considered, a sequinned gown cut very low on top and with a long slit up the side. 'You would be no use in a kitchen,' he muttered. He was very pleased he hadn't brought Godfrey, who would have gone into a trance at the sight of all this flesh and been no use to him at all.

They were setting out all his favourite knives when he suddenly realised that Tess might well be no use to him either. She was absolutely rigid with fear and was clenching the worktop like a climber stuck on a rock face.

Jake was horrified. His throat constricted. She was doing this for him, without a word of complaint, even though she quite obviously felt like dying from stage fright. He felt a sudden surge of love and admiration for her courage, and pulled himself together instantly. There simply wasn't time to give in to his own idiotic sense of inadequacy. It was up to him to get her out of this and, by God, he would.

In his imagination, the studio dimmed and faded away, as did all the scary people with cameras. He was just in a kitchen, showing a nervous young commis how to make the best of her talents, how to bring a gift out of her that she didn't know she had. He remembered what Louis had once told him – a great chef is in the middle of his team, not strutting ahead out of sight. Briefly, he touched his apron in acknowledgement to a great master and teacher and picked up his knife. His hands were steady.

Their menu started off with Gorgonzola risotto with peas, broad beans and asparagus; to follow, a fillet of halibut on a bed of spinach with Muscat grapes and a Noilly Prat sauce; and for pudding a mint *crème brûlée* with strawberries.

'This is going to be fantastic, though what will happen if we put too much liquid in the risotto?' Melina Marvin asked Tess.

Tess gaped at her blankly as if language was something she hadn't quite got to grips with, so Jake equably provided the answer himself. 'I have a small temper tantrum and that cameraman over there gets to wear the risotto. Putting too much liquid in is a common mistake when cooking rice, though we don't want to undercook it and make the customers choke.'

With this and other nonsense he was gently coaxing Tess out of her catatonic state and, though he was unaware of this, making good entertainment, because television hates silence.

The familiar routine of chopping, slicing and stirring was comforting, and Tess found that if she concentrated on that she could forget about the awful place they were in.

Jake forgot as well. He was in a kitchen, cooking, and all that mattered was the fact that the starter was ready to go and his bloody waitress wasn't there to serve it. 'I'm so sorry to interrupt your private life but this food is getting cold!' he bawled, to which Kirsty responded with her usual equanimity. The audience loved it. They were enthralled by the sight of him and Tess moving round like they were in some carefully choreographed dance. They loved the banter because they sensed correctly that none of it was forced and their eyes kept moving to Jake as if he was a magnet.

Jake talked like he always did in a kitchen. Whether there were two of you or twenty you couldn't put together a meal without communicating.

'Kirsty, stop flirting with the cameraman and get us all more water. You know how hot it gets in a kitchen and now we've got lights to contend with as well. I hope you haven't forgotten what I always say?'

'If the kitchen is hot, your kidneys are overheating – but as a catchphrase it really sucks,' muttered Tess without thinking.

'Well, I am agog with anticipation as to what you lot would come up with as an alternative.'

'Give over, Chef – we have a life,' said Tess, and blinked in surprise when people laughed. She had momentarily forgotten they were there.

Harry, however, was finding it difficult to be himself because he was quite rightly worried that the audience would hate him for it, so he was trying to play nice. But the staff he had brought with him were confused by the fact that they had arrived with Genghis Khan but now seemed to be working with the Easter Bunny. It threw them completely off track and they kept dropping things and forgetting to stir their sauces. Also, they were quite aware that Genghis would make a comeback as soon as the cameras were turned off, which wasn't something to look forward to.

The crew kept wanting to stop filming so the make-up girl could wipe the sweat off people's faces. Jake drew an imaginary line on the floor with his finger. 'Anyone crossing that line while I am working will go in the mincer. Do I make myself clear?'

'Yes, Chef,' said the make-up girl, giggling and retreating.

'Bloody interruptions,' muttered Jake.

'Absolutely, Chef,' said Tess, handing him a clean towel so he could mop his face.

The audience were loving it. It was like being a window on a whole new world, a slightly hellish one, to be sure, but that made it even more fun to watch.

When they had finished, the cooks had a short break while the tasters tested the meals and the votes were counted. Jake heaved a huge sigh of relief. He had done the best he could, which was all that mattered, whether he won or not. Tess was no longer looking like she was teetering on the edge of some enormous chasm. In fact, she was busy being chatted up by someone who went under the mysterious title of 'Chief Grip' and was called Griff. Jake reckoned he would need a very firm grip if he was going to make any headway with Tess, who regarded men in the same way some people regarded woodlice. Eavesdropping shamelessly, he could hear her saying that she worked all the hours God sent and when she wasn't, being a single mum meant that her daughter took priority.

'I work stupid hours too and I spend a lot of time babysitting my brother's three kids. I don't mind – I like kids.'

'You wouldn't like mine – she's a proper little madam.'

'So is my niece. She had a tantrum in Tesco's the other day and nearly threw herself out of the shopping trolley. When I grabbed hold of her she screamed even louder and everyone looked at me like they wanted to ring Childline.'

'Tantrums are tough but you've just got to be firm,' said Tess and then Jake had to go and do the short interview that would be shown at the beginning of the programme.

'You've proved quite a hit with the audience. Several of

the women said they were quite weak at the knees watching you cook. I think a few of them are planning to ring you up and ask for a job.'

'Well, they'll be no use to me if they can't stand upright,' snapped Jake.

'But do you think you could teach anyone to cook?'

'Yes, if they have passion, stamina and patience. What they are seeing here is the result of years of intensive learning. What is the point of trying to make carpaccio of beef if you can't even recognise a really good fillet? You can't begin to make a sauce to go with it if you haven't learned to make stock. It's like expecting one of these guys with the cameras to be able to point the thing in the right direction while wearing a blindfold!'

'Do you think chefs deserve their reputation for being bad-tempered bullies?'

'We only shout when people aren't listening. I haven't got time to go and check if people have heard me correctly and I need to know what people are doing all the time, otherwise the pudding would go out before the main course and some people wouldn't get fed at all, because the guy in the corner hadn't heard there was an order for two soups, for instance. He needs to shout back "Yes, Chef" so I know he's heard. Of course, he might still go on to screw things up, but that's another story. Oh, sorry, I shouldn't swear on telly.'

'I think our viewers would be very disappointed if they tuned in to a cooking programme that didn't contain beeps.'

Jake was furious when he found out they all had to line up to hear the result as if it was *Pop Idol*. He scowled, then winked at Tess in case she was feeling nervous again. It was torture making everyone wait for interminable minutes before the four finalists were announced.

'Oh, for goodness' sake, get on with it!' He said this out loud, without thinking, and everyone laughed.

The first finalist was Ali, who ran a hugely successful Indian restaurant in Carlisle, which was reputed to sell the best curry outside India, or at least north of Bradford. Despite refusing to cook chicken tikka masala ever, because it wasn't authentic Indian food, his restaurant was booked up for weeks on end.

When Harry's name was called he stepped into the spotlight as if he owned it. Jake could practically see the waves of arrogant self-confidence emanating off him.

Li Wang from the Lotus Garden in Keswick was picked next. His entire staff was made up of his family, including his eighty-year-old mother, who ran the place with ruthless efficiency, allowing Li to produce Chinese food of breathtaking quality.

Suddenly Jake felt Tess take his hand. He didn't know whether she was trying to give or receive comfort but he was glad, even though her hand was icy cold and shaking violently. Or was that his hand?

He was so certain he wasn't through that when they announced his name he didn't really believe it and Tess had to shove him forward into the lights and applause.

Everyone congratulated each other, though the programme editor leaned forward, alert, when Harry and Jake shook hands, 'I think there is a slight *frisson* of something there, Bob,' he told the sound man.

'Don't know what a *frisson* is, mate, but I have a feeling they don't really like each other.'

'Yes, that's about it,' said the editor thoughtfully.

'I'm sure it was fixed,' said Jake on the way home, having phoned through the good news and made sure there was champagne in the fridge.

'Who cares? You're a winner, you got cash and you've got a chance at the final,' said Tess. 'Oh shit, and bloody hell – that means I've got to go through it all again!'

'Yes, but that will be nice, you'll be able to catch up with your new friend,' said Jake slyly. 'By the way, I happened to overhear what they've got planned for the final. We've all got to cook each other's dishes. So Harry and I will do Indian or Chinese; the other two French or Italian. Don't you think it's very neat that it turned out like that?'

'Did anyone hear you overhearing?' asked Kirsty.

'Er, no.'

'So you are the only person who knows this?'

'Out of all the chefs, yes.'

'Woo-hoo! All you have to do between now and then is mug up on Eastern cookery like mad and you'll have a huge advantage over everyone else. I bet that Mr Wang has never made a béchamel sauce in his life.'

'I couldn't do that,' said Jake firmly. 'That would be cheating.'

'And what do think Harry would do in your position?' retorted Tess.

'Cheat, of course! But I am not Harry. No, you can both stop right now and please don't tell anyone else I told you this. I am not going to do anything underhand to win a stupid prize and that's that.'

'Do you know something, Jake? You are, without doubt, the most aggravating, infuriating, fucking mental, straight-up guy I have ever met.'

'Well, I think that's the nicest thing you've ever said to me, Tess!'

Chapter Twenty-three

Jake pulled all the carpets up and left them outside, where they rotted gently in the summer sunshine until, after many threats to the council, they were finally taken away.

'If you don't pick them up today I will personally deposit them inside your chief executive's office and wait until he comes down with some foul disease. I mean, what on earth do I pay my rates for?' he demanded, but everyone was too hot to answer. The weather, which had been so cruel to them, was now being just as unpleasant, but in a different way. Sunshine followed the storm; days of cloudless blue skies and Mediterranean-style temperatures. The Lake District was packed with people, but Jake couldn't feed any of them. His restaurant was a shell to which the faint smell of damp still clung, however many times they cleaned it.

It was Kate who pointed out that the backyard needed only a coat of whitewash and some potted plants, and then they could at least serve lunches and early suppers.

'More expense,' groaned Jake, but it was better than sitting around all day looking at his bank balance.

'Of course, we will do all this and then it will start raining,' he pointed out, but they all told him to shut up.

'We're bored with our enforced holiday and Godfrey will get into trouble if he's not kept occupied,' said Tess.

Godfrey had found himself a girlfriend and turned up each morning with a neck covered in love bites and a dazed expression on his face. She was called Anne and she must have been a saint because Godfrey spent half his time lecturing her on the poor quality of food served at the hotel where she worked. When Kirsty asked him if they were sleeping together yet he turned so red Jake took pity on him and sent him into the yard with a paint pot where he could be heard warbling in a tuneless imitation of Kylie that he should be so lucky.

Kate found some cheap red-checked tablecloths in a shop down the road, which Jake said would make the place look like a comedy French bistro and if anyone dared suggest candles in wine bottles they would be sacked on the spot. But secretly he was pleased to get the chance to do some real cooking again.

He also took the opportunity to change the menu, which Godfrey said was typical of the nasty way he behaved – he was only just starting to get the hang of the first one.

'We need to keep the theme simple, redolent of sunshine and summer. I'll explain what that means later, and don't bring that paint pot in my kitchen without a lid on, you silly boy!'

Jake wanted salads full of colour, lightly grilled fish, seared tuna, olives and lots of the herbs that were growing in pots outside. 'If you want them, you'll have to go out in front of the customers to get 'em. They'll love it – they will feel part of the cooking process. It will be casual, informal, but superlatively good. Only remember to watch your language.'

He put signs up in the window saying: 'Open for al fresco dining', which he thought was a bit naff, but he didn't want people to think they were just walking past a builder's yard. The restaurant doors were opened wide and he made sure that Mozart or Vivaldi was playing to help entice people in.

He was busy saying gloomily to anyone who would listen that this was bound not to work, when Frank Briggs turned up, with his wife. 'I thought you'd be out on the fells, sabotaging our pest control,' he said with a grin when he saw Jake.

'Nah, I only do that part-time,' said Jake. 'Come in – it's nice to see you again.'

'To be honest, lad, I'm more a pie-and-chips sort of a man, but the wife is on a health kick, so we thought we'd give the pub a miss for once.'

'You won't be disappointed,' said Jake. He knew he sounded confident, but he knew these were people with eating habits so ingrained they would be very hard to shift. But if they did . . . well, Frank knew a lot of people round here and his word had clout.

Later – 'I don't mind saying that I wasn't really expecting to like that broccoli and stilton soup, but it was bloody good,' said Frank.

'I think that's partly because all the ingredients are from round here.'

'Aye – that's the way to do business,' said Frank, nodding his approval.

There was only room to feed about twenty people at a

time, but soon, and to Jake's surprise, they were packed out every lunchtime. Jake got Tess and Godfrey and Emma baking like mad, and they served homemade, mouth-watering cakes and pastries and ice cream during the afternoon, and then simple, but delicious suppers in the early evening. It was keeping the financial wolf from the door, just.

'I'm telling everyone that you're the chef from the television – it really brings them in,' said Hans helpfully one day. Jake was trying to make cherry ice cream but Godfrey kept leaving the stones in. He frowned and took a deep breath. Everyone took a step back.

'They come because the food is fucking brilliant, not because we've been on some silly television programme – get it? Really, I don't know why I bother trying to run a restaurant in the first place. I would probably be better off buying some plastic tables and chairs, a portable barbecue and setting up stall on the beach by the lake. There would be no overheads, no washing up if we used disposable plates – I'd probably make a fortune,' he grumbled. In the winter he could do soup and home-made burgers and hot roasted chestnuts, and go home with Kate every night. It wouldn't matter if he was as poor as a church mouse, as long as they had a bed. It was a happy dream.

It was a brief, but golden time, if one could forget there was a business to run, or in Kate's case, secrets to keep. Jonathan was getting impatient and she knew she didn't have a lot of time left. The good weather would definitely break soon. When it did, she would sort it all out, she promised herself. Until then . . .

They tended to finish earlier in the evening because the nights could get quite chilly. It was fine for walking hand in hand down to the lake, though. They would take any left-over wine and some stale bread and sit on the jetty trying to wake the ducks up by lobbing bits of bread roll at them. They would take it in turns to swig from the bottle and try to guess what it was because it was too dark to see the label. Then they would go home and make love in the dark with the window open to blow a cooling breeze over their hot limbs. Later, Kate would look back on this time and think it was like the best holiday she'd ever had.

Even Jake felt a Monday-morning, back-to-school dread creep over him, when, glancing at the calendar, he realised that the final of *Great Grub* was upon him. Matters weren't helped when Kirsty rang up full of sorrow and sickness.

'It must have been something I ate,' she wailed.

'Well, it wasn't at my restaurant!'

'Of course it wasn't! I think it was some chicken I found in the fridge at home last night, but I feel so sick, I don't really care. I'm terribly sorry, but you really don't want to watch me serving food while trying not to puke in it.'

'I certainly don't – it sounds most revolting. Look, don't worry –'

'But I feel awful about letting you down!'

'You're not,' he said firmly. 'You've been an absolute tower of strength and we will manage without you. After all, Kate has come a long way as a waitress, though she'll never be as good as you. Just concentrate on getting better and if you feel up to it, you can watch us on the telly.'

'She must be really bad, poor girl,' he told the others.

'She didn't even try to tell a story about her second cousin twice removed whom none of us has ever met! It's an ill wind, I suppose, because it's now your turn to become a star, Kate!'

'It's just like those films where the understudy has to take over at the last minute,' said Godfrey, who was planning to watch the programme with Anne, from the depths of a large sofa. He was hoping to be so occupied he would miss most of it.

Kate pretended to look pleased and then spent most of the day furtively ringing everyone at the station that she knew and begging them to keep shtum. Of course, a lot of them thought it was a great joke and made various lewd suggestions about what it might take to keep them quiet. It was all very unfunny and she felt quite worn out when she came off the phone. She wasn't even sure she had got round all of them, and seriously considered going out and buying a wig. She could always tell Jake she would feel less nervous in a disguise. Oh dear, more lies. There was going to be a terrible reckoning soon. She had put it off for so long, it was bound to all come spilling out at the wrong moment. Right. That was it. Today, on the way back from the studio, it was going to be truth time. She felt better already, because she knew that this time she really would go through with it.

'What on earth is the matter with you? You look like you're auditioning for *The Hunchback of Notre Dame*.' demanded Jake.

They were walking into the studio and Kate was doing her best to be small and inconspicuous. She guessed she'd overdone it a bit.

Of course they walked slap-bang into Harry and Georgia, who was making no effort to fend off all the men who were swarming round her. It didn't seem to be annoying Harry, who was enjoying the attention. He lip was curling in a particularly aggravating way. It was obvious he was thinking: look, but don't touch, you sad bastards, because she's mine.

Georgia stopped preening and her mouth took on its famous pout when she saw Jake. She was wearing a fabulous frock, dark green and shiny.

I don't know why she's looking so cross – she dumped me, thought Jake as he walked past, giving her the stiff, entirely false smile that is customary when greeting a newly ex-partner.

Georgia was pouting because although she was obviously much happier with Harry, it would have been nice if Jake had looked a little more grief-stricken. There hadn't even been a slightly sorrowful phone call and now here he was, looking positively cheerful, bouncy even. It was really annoying.

Jake was right – they all had to cook each other's cuisine. He got Chinese and Harry got Indian, which, by the look on his face didn't please him at all. Harry would never set foot inside an Indian restaurant, deeming them to be full of lager louts demanding impossibly hot vindaloo. He had never visited India, considering it to be hot, smelly and noisy, but then the same could be said of London.

Jake explained to Tess: 'The secret here will be in the preparation. We get everything ready first and then spend about half a minute cooking like lunatics.' He looked sternly at the audience.

'Have your chopsticks at the ready – this meal will wait for no one!'

The audience grinned in greedy anticipation. Ali also got a laugh by producing from somewhere a beret and a rope of garlic but Harry's commis chef, Ken, was in an awful state. He was a regular at one of the local Indian restaurants because it was the only place that was still open after he finished work. The stress of working for Harry meant he usually drank four or five pints of lager before the meal arrived, by which time he was so drunk he couldn't taste it anyway. He gazed at the bowls of garam masala, cumin and chillies with a sort of dull despair and wished he was at home.

The audience continued to laugh when Tess dropped a bowl on Jake's foot and he hopped about in agony.

'Sorry, Chef, but you are wearing steel-toed boots. You could drop the Empire State Building on them and you probably wouldn't feel it.'

'That's hardly the point!'

'Oh, don't be such a wuss,' she muttered, pushing past him. She had found out that if she concentrated on her work it was fairly easy to pretend she was just doing her normal job in a normal kitchen, which was exactly what the show's producers were hoping for.

Everyone's meals were coming together quite nicely when Ken forgot what he was doing and wiped his sweating face with a hand that had just been in contact with red-hot chillies. He yelled in agony as some of the chilli went into his eye and they had to stop filming while he went off to first aid.

It couldn't have happened at a worse time for Jake because his meal was just ready to be served. Everyone else was glad of the unexpected break and raced off for coffees and fags.

'Will you be able to keep that hot?' asked the presenter.

Jake gave her a withering glance. 'Of course I can keep it hot,' he explained with laboured patience. 'I just can't keep it edible – it's not a bloody casserole!' He threw off his chef's hat and swore. 'We will have to do it again from scratch.'

'Oh, blimey! I hope we've got enough ingredients.'

'Well, you'd better find some,' said Jake, and went off to join the others.

Harry was loitering with intent near two of the crew who were discussing the state of play.

'It's neck and neck so far between the Indian guy and the Englishman.'

Harry smirked.

'They are both good but it would be good novelty value having a Jewish chef win. We could film him later on cooking some kosher food.'

'What exactly is that?'

'Dunno.'

They wandered off, leaving Harry quite rigid with shock and fury. He wasn't about to lose this, surely? Bile rose in his throat and he tasted the sour and almost unfamiliar flavour of possible failure. He even started to have flash-backs. No. This couldn't be happening again. Never mind that he had the girl and a much posher restaurant – there was no way he was going to come second to Jake again! His eyes slewed round, desperately searching for a way to sabotage this outcome to end in his favour, but even he had to concede that this might be difficult, given that the eyes of the whole county would be on him.

He went to his work station to reassure himself that his dishes were as good as they could be. They were good, if you liked that sort of thing and he didn't, and they would only get better in the waiting, unlike Jake's.

Two of the cameramen were jabbering away to each other and he looked up in irritation, wanting them to fuck off and leave him in peace.

'I didn't expect to see Kate here tonight.'

'That's why she's such a good journalist – she's always popping up in unexpected places. She's going to have to be quick to get her "Chefs Uncovered" story out before her cover's blown and she gets the sack. That Jake has got a hell of a temper. He's not going to be happy when he finds out he's been taken for a ride.'

At first Harry was furious. The little bitch! Pretending to be a waitress while all the time she was snooping around looking for shit to besmirch his profession! Of course, if she'd tried to get a job in his restaurant he would have smelled a rat instantly. Then he realised exactly what had happened and a wide and unpleasant smile spread across his face. She wasn't working for him – she was pretending to work for Jake and he'd already picked up a few signs that they were more pally than they should be. His nose twitched like a fox that had just caught the scent of a nearby henhouse. But there wasn't a moment to lose. He had to find Jake and impart this interesting information just before he had to go in front of the cameras and cook again.

He found Jake leaning against a wall, looking down at a plastic cup of canteen coffee with a sort of disgusted wonder: did people really believe they were refuelling themselves with this stuff? He didn't realise Harry was coming towards him until it was too late. Inwardly he groaned. Conversations with Harry always ended badly and just now he couldn't be bothered. All he wanted to do was get this over and go home.

'I just wanted to say that it is good we can both be so civilised over this business with Georgia.'

Jake shrugged. 'Water under the bridge,' he said, and turned to move off, but Harry seemed determined to continue the conversation. 'It looks like you've moved on as well. I'm glad. Kate seems like a nice person.'

'Uh-huh – oh good – it looks like we're getting going again,' he said with relief. If Harry was trying to be nice, it would be better to keep the conversation short.

But Harry continued to drone in his ear like a persistent wasp. 'I must say, I think you're very brave letting a journalist into your kitchen, especially one who's looking for a warts-and-all story.'

'A what? What on earth are you talking about?'

Harry almost purred with pleasure at the thought of inflicting pain. 'Oh, so you didn't know? Well, I don't know what she told you, but she's really a reporter. Apparently she's doing some piece called "Chefs Uncovered". It will be some crappy story that tries to bring our profession into disrepute – not that you've got anything to worry about, I'm sure.'

'Oh, there you are,' said Tess, giving Harry a basilisk stare and wondering what the hell he had said to make Jake go so pale.

When Jake didn't seem to be moving, she took him by the arm and gave it a little shake. 'Come on – we're on again.'

'Well, good luck,' said Harry and went off with a spring in his step. He knew he had just delivered a lethal blow and without even grazing his knuckles.

'What on earth's the matter?' demanded Tess.

'Nothing. Everything.' Jake had his hand over his mouth. He looked like he was going to be sick.

'He was only talking to you for about thirty seconds.'

'Yeah, that was all he needed.'

Jake was glad he was leaning against the wall because he needed its support. The enormity of what Harry had told him was still sinking in and it was getting worse with every second.

Tess was very worried. He looked like he was in serious shock but there wasn't time for warm blankets and a cup of tea. She took his face in her hands and forced him to look down at her. 'Focus, Jake. Whatever has just happened will have to wait until after this bloody programme is over. Shall I get Kate?'

This galvanised him. 'Oh God, no. I need time to think. Let me go – I've got to get out of here.'

'You can't,' she hissed. 'The only thing you can think about now is food. Think bamboo shoots, noodles, woks. You are going to have to cook, Jake, and I can't do this without you.' She was shaking him so hard now she thought she could hear his teeth rattling. If she could just get him over to the kitchen and put a knife in his hand he might come to. Oh fuck, it was like he had turned into a zombie. When this was over, if they got through it, she would . . . well, whatever it was, Harry wouldn't like it.

The next hour was hell. It knocked giving birth into a miserable second place and so far that particular event had been top of Tess's absolutely shitty, never-to-be-repeated events. Jake had gone into automatic pilot when she handed him the knife, but there was a white, set look about his face that didn't make for good television.

The camera crew were puzzled. The dynamics of these two seemed to have changed. Now it was the girl who was doing all the talking – the guy had lost it completely. He was moving round the kitchen like a man in a trance.

Tess was desperate. This was torture by television. Every second she was getting more keyed up for the moment when Jake just turned round and walked off the set, and if he did that she would be on her own in front of the cameras and she would just die. Quite deliberately, hoping it would be edited out, because if it wasn't she would probably be arrested for assault, she dripped some boiling hot oil on his hand.

'Christ, woman! How many more scars do you want me to have?'

'Sorry, Chef,' said Tess meekly and listened in relief to Jake's diatribe on the incompetence and clumsiness of kitchen staff. It seemed to have broken the spell and, thank God, they were nearly done.

She glanced up and saw Kate's face, white and scared and sort of guilty. When this is over, thought Tess, chopping chives with manic energy, I'm going to give them both hell, and the camera crew and anyone else that gets in my way. Well, maybe not Griff, she thought, as he smiled at her and gave her a thumbs-up sign.

When Jake put his knife down for the last time, a huge weariness came over him. The numbness that comes with shock was beginning to wear off and pain was setting in. He was the victim of some monstrous scam. The happiness of the last few weeks tasted like ashes in his mouth.

As soon as the cameras stopped rolling, Kate came over, but he just brushed past her.

Oh, no – he's found out! she thought, and could feel herself breaking out in a sweat of cold terror. Not only had he learned the truth, but it was in the worst possible time and place, and of course, not from her. Now she could recall with hideous clarity all the opportunities she had missed; all the times when she could have told him the truth. Sure, he would have been angry, but she could have explained the whole thing properly, how it had started off as just a story, but then he had become part of her life. Now, when it was far too late, she knew exactly what she should have said – that she was a fake waitress but not a fake lover. But one look at his blank, closed-off face told her that he was no longer prepared to listen.

'Just what the hell is going on?' demanded Tess.

Kate looked at her tiredly. 'You may as well know – I'm a reporter. I work for the *Easedale Gazette*. I got a job as a waitress to cover a story about what it's really like in a restaurant kitchen.' She thought back. It was hard to remember the crap she had spouted so glibly all those weeks ago when she had known nothing.

'Oh. My. God.'

'Yeah. But everything changed, Tess. I still want to do the story but it's going to be the real one, about the passion and sweat and dedication . . .'

'Well, your timing sucks, doesn't it? If you'd told Jake, instead of waiting until that creep let the cat out of the bag . . .'

'I've blown it, haven't I?'

'Well, you see, Jake has this little thing about being let down and lied to –'

'I know, I know. And he would be right, but that was only at the beginning. Everything changed, even before I fell in love with him. Ninety-five per cent of what I said and did has been honest and truthful . . .'

'Ah, but it's that other five per cent that's screwed you.'

'Oh God, what am I going to do?'

'I think you've done more than enough, haven't you?' Then she relented, because she really liked Kate. 'Look, if I were you, I'd lie low for a bit, let the storm settle. You know what Jake is like. Eventually he is bound to calm down a bit and maybe even see the funny side of it.'

'There's a funny side?'

'No, not really. I was just trying to cheer you up.'

Everyone was being called back on to the set to hear the results. Jake walked in and saw Kate. 'Judas,' he said and stalked off.

The next few minutes were designed purely to torture

the poor contestants, as if their cooking ordeals hadn't been enough. They were forced to stand sweating in the spotlight while the announcer jabbered on about how brilliant and entertaining they had been and then milked the breathless hush between her announcements until everyone's toes were curling with tension and suspense. Everyone apart from Jake. He found it quite calming to be in this limbo where he couldn't do a thing about any of his problems, his struggling business or his relationship with Kate, which seemed to have nose-dived into disaster, like all the others had. He didn't really care whether he had won or lost; he just wanted to stand there quietly, insulated from life. He knew he hadn't won, anyway. His first dish had been superb but while cooking the second, his hands had lost their customary grace and skill. His sorrow had seeped out and given an acrid flavour to the dish. It was shit and everyone knew it.

But the audience had taken to Jake in the first programme and his air of vulnerability in the second had only added to his appeal. The competition was as much about personality as about food, and the voters had decided Jake was a star and that was that.

Harry came third, and in other circumstances Jake would have enjoyed listening to him grinding his teeth before pasting on a hugely false smile.

Ali's astonishingly good noisettes of lamb came second. Idiots, thought Jake to himself, who had tasted them and thought that Ali could be serious competition if he ever wanted to open a French restaurant.

'And the winner is . . .' Another excruciating pause,

which he wanted to go on for ever so he didn't have to think about trying to pick up the pieces of his life.

It was such a shock when they called his name out he just stood there blinking in disbelief. His brief spell in limbo was broken and everything came rushing back, painfully. The presenter stepped forward with his award, which was a ridiculous, silver-plated chef's hat on a little stand. She leaned forward to give him a congratulatory kiss and whispered: 'Smile – you've won!'

'Bollocks!' said Jake, and realising by the shocked look on her face that he had actually said this aloud instead of just thinking it, decided he might as well carry on. He gestured towards the congealing remains of his squid and steamed prawn dumplings. 'This is probably the worst meal I have ever cooked in my life. The sauce tastes like wallpaper paste and the squid is so tough you could probably make tyres out of it. It belongs here . . .' And with a single gesture, he swept the lot into the bin, while they all gaped at him, open-mouthed and rooted to the spot.

'I am humbled by the contrast that this meal provided,' he continued, gesturing towards Ali's dish. 'The lamb is gloriously tender and flavoursome and the potatoes are so light and fluffy even an anorexic supermodel –' he gestured at Georgia '– even she scoffed two of them! You're wrong; you're all complete idiots for not seeing that Ali is the chef who deserves this award! Well, in my own way, I am an idiot too,' he glared at Kate, 'but I am not dishonest and I refuse to accept this award.' He grabbed the hat out of the presenter's shaking hands and gave it to a gobsmacked Ali, who nearly dropped it in surprise.

'There,' said Jake thoughtfully. 'That is justice, I think. Enjoy your prize – you have earned it.' He grinned briefly at everyone and stalked out.

This sort of thing had never happened before on television. Members of the public were supposed to be in awe of the whole process and jolly grateful to be on it at all. Plenty of people simpered that they didn't deserve to win a prize, but no one had ever gone so far as to hand one back. It was, though, thought the producer, rubbing his hands in glee, bloody amazing telly. It would be in all the papers tomorrow and everyone would clamour to see it repeated.

Behind him, Jake left Harry explaining to anyone who would listen that Jake just didn't know how to play by the rules. Kate rushed over to Tess. 'Go after him!'

'You go!'

But Kate had seen the look in his eyes when he had called her a Judas. 'He never wants to see me again,' she said miserably.

Jake had brushed past people like they were flies. Outside, he leaned against a wall. His hands were shaking so much they weren't fit to hold a butter knife, he thought ruefully. Speaking his mind back there had seemed so satisfying, but now he became dimly aware that all he had probably achieved was a scene where he had made a complete fool of himself. He should have just kept his big mouth shut and taken the prize and the cash, which he desperately needed. But, oh no, he had to play the hero. When would he learn that speaking the truth was not actually a wise move if you needed to make your way in the world he thought, bitterly. As if on cue, he looked up and saw Kate, a person who told lies with impunity and got along very nicely, thank you. He turned round and leaned his head against the wall because it was too hard to look into the face of someone you loved when you knew they were treacherous.

'Fuck off. I never want to see you or talk to you again.'

'I know, but you've got to let me explain –'

'Well, you should have done that right at the start and saved yourself all the bother because I still would have told you to fuck off!'

'If you would only let me tell you –'

'Save it! I know it all anyway! You were looking to write a nasty little piece about how restaurants are just a big con, charging customers a fortune for meals which cost a few pence to make! About how chefs are arrogant bastards who treat their staff like shit! No wonder you were always in the kitchen – you were probably hoping to catch me out scraping a bit of mould off a steak before serving it up to some unsuspecting punter. I hope you've got it all written down – all the tantrums, all the times I've made you work ridiculous hours without a break, and do you know the best thing of all? I'm so pathetic that even by doing all that I still can't make the bloody place pay! I've really got my comeuppance, haven't I?'

Kate was silent. This was all so close to what she had originally set out to do she didn't know where to begin to defend herself. But she had to try.

'You're right,' she said at last. 'That's how it started. But that's not what it turned into. Oh, for God's sake, please turn round and look at me. I can't talk to your back!'

'Why not? Is it too full of knives?'

'I deserve that. I was just looking out for a good story – it's what I do! But then I realised there was a better story in the passion and dedication you bring to your craft.' Kate had never told anyone she loved them before. She had had no practice for it, but even she knew it wasn't a good moment for it. 'I didn't mean things to turn out this way,' she finished off miserably.

Where had Jake heard that before? Oh yes, every time he had got himself involved with a woman. He was such a schmuck! He must have a big sign on his head asking women to treat him like shit. Well, it wasn't surprising really, given that he had just made such a spectacle of himself in front of half the county.

'Well, funnily enough, they have. All the wrong ingredients have gone into this dish and it really doesn't taste very nice. I won't be trying it again. But then you are a shabby little liar and I am a gullible fool. You seem to have lots of friends in there – get a lift home with one of your media pals. Goodbye.' He prised himself off the wall and hoped that Kate couldn't see how dejected he looked as he walked away.

He was going round a roundabout for the third time having no real idea where he was going and getting some funny looks from other drivers when his phone bleeped. Pulling into the nearest lay-by he saw there was a text message from Tess. Poor girl! He'd forgotten all about her!

'Cum bak. Al is not lost.'

'It is. Wil cum bak 4u tho. Sory.'

'Grif wil give me lift hom but cum bak aniwa. No muni lef on fone. Hav to explain.'

But Jake didn't reply and Tess was left staring at her phone with frustration. She didn't have enough call time left to explain how much everyone had loved his outburst. They were thrilled by the fact that he had spoken passionately, from his heart. Also, the fact that he was good-looking made for excellent television. In fact, the producer reckoned that Jake was such a treat people would be clamouring for more.

Chapter Twenty-four

It was late when Kate got back home, having endured a lift home with Tess and Griff. She liked them both but just now it was torture having to be around a couple who were obviously getting on so well.

She sat in the back of Griff's ramshackle Mini, a miserable gooseberry to two people who were doing things the right way. There was no lying or trickery going on here, just a guy and a girl who liked each other. She hated them for making it seem so easy. She hated herself. She was so arrogant, so sure of herself, except in the things that really mattered.

She ran up the four flights of stairs instead of taking the lift so she could pretend it was the exercise that was making her shaky and dizzy.

'What you need is a nice cup of tea and a sit-down,' she said out loud. Then she winced because that was what Godfrey always said at the end of a shift, and his words brought all the happiness of the last few weeks flooding back and she wasn't a part of that any more.

By nine o'clock the tea had gone cold. But, looking down at the cup, she realised she had made a pot of hot water. The teabags were still on the worktop. Kate had thought that if she sat down she might be able to see her way clearly out of this awful situation. She was good at getting out of trouble. She liked a challenge. But she wasn't able to think at all because going round and round in her head, loudly, were the words 'shabby little liar'.

At ten past nine she said to herself: 'You've been called things before. Get over it.' But she couldn't.

At nine thirty she felt so desperate she had to phone Lydia. What you needed in a time of crisis was a sympathetic female to mull things over with.

She got the answer phone.

'Lyd – I don't care if you are screwing Brad Pitt. Ring me back immediately.'

At nine forty-five: 'Ignore previous message. Sorry. But ring back anyway.'

The trouble was, she thought in what she hoped was a rational way, the trouble was . . . he had looked so . . . betrayed.

She could have coped with the anger. They both had hot tempers. And it had all started because she was doing her job, a job she loved and was proud of, thank you very much, Jake. She wasn't just a nasty little hack, she was a professional.

Rubbish! She had really hurt him and his anger was just a mask to keep the damage hidden.

At ten o'clock there was a clap of thunder and all the lights went out. It was a bit of a relief to find that the rest of the building was out too. She had half thought it might be Jake's God calling down some sort of retribution on her, though a power cut was a rather pathetic sort of punishment. Jake would have found the idea quite funny, except that of course he wasn't there to laugh about it with her.

Five minutes later she realised that scented candles were pretty and fragrant but bugger all use at providing any real light. It was possible, however, to feel her way in the dark to the vodka but hardly worth the fuss of trying to find a glass.

10.15 p.m. Betrayal? Ridiculous! This wasn't a cheesy episode of *EastEnders*.

10.20 p.m. This is all his fault. He's a stuck-up prig who thinks he's better than everyone else.

10.30 p.m. He is better than anyone else I've ever met. It's all my fault.

10.35 p.m. If he refuses to speak to me, I will write to him.

10.36 p.m. He'll probably tear it up and stamp on it.

10.40 p.m. I'll camp outside his bloody restaurant until he's just got to let me in.

10.45 p.m. He'll probably throw yesterday's old soup over me.

10.50 p.m. I'll die and then he'll be sorry.

Then she screamed because suddenly there was figure in the room next to her.

'What the hell are you doing in the dark with the front door wide open?' said Lydia.

'Power cut. Anyway there's enough light for me to drink myself to death by.' She squinted at the bottle. It looked depressingly empty.

'Hm, a crisis. Do you want to sober up or continue sliding towards a coma?'

'Coma, definitely.' And she told Lydia all about it.

'Look, calm down,' said Lydia briskly. 'You should have expected this. He's bound to be pissed off. He probably thinks he hates you right now, but he'll come round. He might even see the funny side.'

'And which side would that be, exactly?'

'I must say, I've never seen you in such a state over a man before.'

'That's because I've never met a man like him before. He turns my insides to jelly. I can't get enough of being with him. And do you know when I found this out? When he told me to fuck off! Oh, my God!' whimpered Kate, clutching the vodka bottle as though it was a comfort blanket, 'I'm turning into bloody Bridget Jones! I don't even know why I love him! He is unbearably picky when he's working. He makes an outrageous fuss about a tiny drop of sauce on the wrong side of the plate but he hasn't got a single item of clothing that hasn't got a hole in it. He seems incapable of shaving himself properly, or he just doesn't care, and surely no sane man would get so excited about a delivery of new saucepans? Saucepans, for God's sake!'

Lydia went into the kitchen to make coffee. Kate had to be restored to her usual sane and focused self. It was actually rather unnerving to see her like this. But when she came back Kate had fallen asleep. The lights came back on so Lydia blew the candles out. Kate would have a hell of a headache in the morning, but at least she wouldn't have set fire to her hair.

It was only when Jake was standing in his flat that he realised that he hadn't the faintest idea how he had got there. He must have done the usual things – changing gears, indicating, stopping at red lights (at least, he hoped he had) but he couldn't remember any of it. So he got into the shower, turned the cold tap on and stood there until his teeth were chattering with cold. But even that didn't seem to bring him round so he sat down on the bed, rolled himself in the duvet and gave himself up to self-pity. It wasn't an emotion he was used to, so it took him a while to work out what it was. When he did, it was quite comforting.

Just give in and give up, it seemed to be saying. You are a loser. Everyone fucks you up sooner or later. Your business is going down the pan and your love life? Well, don't get me started on that!

But it did, anyway.

Sooner or later all the women you love dump you or screw you up. Mostly, they find someone else first and you are too stupid to know what's going on. Georgia probably screwed Harry here, and you were too far up your own arse to know what was going on.

Jake opened one eye, which was enough to take in the appallingly scruffy and disreputable state of his bedroom, and was forced to admit that only a complete idiot would try to seduce a woman here. Of course Kate hadn't minded! She was busy with other agendas. And there he was thinking it was because she liked him!

Self-pity continued to whisper its poison in his ear.

You are so deluded you even thought you had a connection with this woman. Well, you did, but not in that way. She was using you. You were just a stepping stone. If you looked in a mirror you could see the marks of her footprints on your back.

Jake was just nodding agreement to all this when his grandmother elbowed her way into his consciousness. He could actually see her, not how she had looked just before she died, but how she was when he was a small boy and the centre of his life. She was in her kitchen, of course, and was wearing a ridiculous apron that he had bought her for her birthday when he was fourteen. It was designed to make her look like a can-can dancer, and his mother had told him off for it.

'That is a most unsuitable present for a woman of seventy-five,' she scolded but Oma had thought it was a hoot and insisted on wearing it.

She gave Jake's self-pity a withering glance. 'Bollocks,' she said. Actually it was something long and involved in Yiddish, but he knew it meant the same thing. 'So you've had a setback. What are you – a man or a mouse? I'll tell you what you are. You are a fighter, you are a survivor. Goldmans don't give in, they pick themselves up and get on with it.'

'But I loved her!' howled Jake. 'This was different; this was the real thing, except it wasn't because it was all built on lies.'

'Lies, schmise! No one is ever completely honest. It just means she isn't perfect but then she is a human being, not a doll.'

'She didn't bloody have to be perfect. I knew that anyway. She always slops the sauce over the plate when she serves food. She pretends to have given up smoking and then nicks everyone else's. She hasn't bought a new bra in two years because whenever she goes shopping she ends up in bookshops. Not that she needs a bra anyway – I should know, I – anyway . . . Her nose is always shiny at the end of a shift and one of her eyebrows is definitely crooked. I didn't care, but then I didn't know she had a crooked heart as well.'

'And of course you know that, even though you didn't give her a chance to explain –'

'Yeah, and I don't intend to. She's blown it and I never want to see her again. Go away – you're not really here anyway.' And he pulled the duvet over his head in case he had any more hallucinations.

Great Grub had become the most popular programme Lakes Television had ever made and an incredibly boring conference was arranged so they could work out why and how to capitalise on it.

A young lad on work experience in the studio's canteen could have told them. 'It was because he was honest. He spoke it like it was. Respect, man!' But he was talking to himself and an enormous pile of dirty saucepans at the time so nobody heard him.

Jake couldn't have cared less anyway. He was far too busy taking phone calls from people who had seen the programme and wanted to eat at his restaurant in the simple belief that, if the man could cook as well as he spoke his mind, the restaurant was worth a visit.

When Jake explained that he had to lay his new carpet first, several people even offered to come and give him a hand if it meant they could get a table more quickly. He also found he was a minor celebrity now. At the bakery, as he stood in the queue for the now essential staff doughnut break, someone asked for his autograph and a few people in the street stopped him to offer their congratulations. Jake hated it because it kept reminding him of the time he had stopped being happy. He didn't want to think about it. He wanted to pretend it had never happened but that was impossible because Kate's absence in his kitchen was like a gaping hole. He missed everything about her: the way she always refused a doughnut because they were bad for you and then scoffed his when he wasn't looking; her enthusiasm for every dish he cooked – she would try anything once, she said, because she trusted him – and her intelligent questions about food. Well, that wasn't surprising, he thought bitterly. She was a journalist. It was probably second nature to her and something she did with everyone. And there was him thinking it was because she was interested in him! Well, he wouldn't make that mistake again. He was off women for good. They only brought trouble. Of course that meant he would end up a crabby, lonely and bitter old man and would die alone, slowly, atrophying among a pile of ancient *Hotel and Caterer* magazines and being eaten by rats, a fitting way for an old chef to go.

Tess had warned everyone not to say anything about the Situation (she thought it was so serious, it deserved a capital letter), but it didn't matter anyway, because Jake went round with such a black look on his face nobody wanted to say anything to him. What was worrying was that he had also lost his fire. They all looked back nostalgically to those happy days of explosions over imperfect béchamel sauces or pips in the pomegranate purée. He had turned into a haggard, monosyllabic wreck and Godfrey was shaken to his very core when Jake cooked a whole meal without tasting or commenting on any of it.

'We've got to do something,' he said to Tess one afternoon when they were clearing up after lunch. 'If he cooks like this for that Restaurant Club man he's going to fuck it up completely. Do you know he didn't even wince when I dripped hot oil on him this morning? It must have hurt like hell but I don't think he even noticed it.'

'Yeah, but we can't do anything because we're not the problem. Kate is.'

'But I can't stand it for much longer. It's like working in some hell dimension. I mean, it was hell before, of course, but I knew where I was but now it's like he just doesn't CARE!'

'You're right,' said Tess, slowly. Jake not caring about cooking was like waking up one morning to find that the sun had turned green. It just wasn't right. 'I just bloody hope that bloody Kate knows exactly how much bloody damage she's done,' she added, aiming a vicious kick at Godfrey's mop and bucket on her way out.

Kate was at her desk, wondering why this most familiar of places didn't feel like home to her any more. She could have worked on her story in her flat but she hadn't known how loud and mocking a silence can be when you have a guilty conscience. But the reporters' room of the *Easedale Gazette* wasn't bringing her any comfort either. Normally she loved the background of phones ringing, people talking, reporters and photographers rushing importantly in and out of the big room and sub-editors hassling her because they needed a quick, four-line story to fill a gap at the bottom of page five. She liked the fact that she could distance herself from all this and dip in and out of whatever she was working on without losing her thread. But today she didn't have a thread to lose. She had been staring at a blank screen for three-quarters of a hour and – nothing. She had played thirty-seven games of solitaire, read all her emails and even tried typing in a whole page of 'the quick brown fox jumps over the lazy dog' because that sometimes worked. But not today. She had lied to the most important person in her world and God had punished her for it by taking away her ability to write. She was like Samson after his haircut.

Her phone rang.

'Some people in the front office want to see a reporter,' said the secretary.

'Well, tell Paul,' Kate snapped.

Paul was the cub reporter and it was his job to deal with members of the public because it was usually people who had come in to complain that the paper had spelled their names wrong.

'They want to see you particularly.'

Kate slouched downstairs in a sulk, convinced, now that she had been interrupted, that she had been about to write something brilliant. She nearly turned round and ran away when she saw the motley crew clustered round the front desk. They were still dressed in their cooking gear and a tantalising aroma of garlic, oil and roasted lamb wafted from them. But were they friends or foes? Were there knives concealed under those chef's jackets? If there were, she could hardly blame them. She approached warily.

'So, this is where you really work,' said Kirsty brightly.

'Have you come to bury me or praise me?'

'Eh, what?' said Godfrey.

'We've come to talk,' said Tess firmly.

'OK, but not here.' Kate didn't want the events of the last few months rehashed in front of the counter staff, who were always up for gossip and scandal. Also, people were starting to cast strange looks at the various bloodstains that adorned Godfrey's white jacket.

They adjourned to a nearby park and sat down on the grass under the shade of a huge oak tree because it was so hot. Automatically, Kate leaned forward to pinch one of Kirsty's fags, then drew back. Maybe things weren't like that between them any more.

'Oh, go on, then. At least some things haven't changed,' grumbled Kirsty.

Kate took one, lit up and drew a deep breath. 'Guys, I am really sorry. You have to believe me, I never meant for you to find out like you did.' Oh, brilliant, she thought. That little speech would really set them at their ease. Even with the nicotine flooding through her system she felt too shy to say what she really felt – that she loved them and respected them. She felt so bad that she couldn't even look them in the eye. Miserably she stared at the ground, absent-mindedly pulling little bits of grass up.

'We are very cross with you.'

'I deserve it,' said Kate humbly. 'You must feel that you had a Trojan horse in the kitchen with you all this time, and maybe it was like that at the start but then everything changed. You changed me; you destroyed all my crappy preconceptions and –'

'I don't know what you mean about horses – it's about the only thing Jake hasn't made me cook yet. Anyway, it's him we have come to talk about. You've knocked the stuffing out of him – he's like a piece of wilted lettuce, he –'

Tess broke in on Godfrey as the conversation seemed to be going in ever decreasing culinary circles. 'We need to know the full story, Kate, because we only got a garbled version from Jake. When we've got the facts, all of them, then we can consider your apology and whether we are prepared to accept it.' She looked extremely fierce as she delivered this little speech.

This was fair, though. Kate took another deep breath, pulled up a dandelion and started at the beginning. Succinctly she filled them in, without sparing herself: her arrogance, her preconceived ideas, the exposé story she thought she was going to write and how she'd come to realise that she couldn't because it wasn't true.

'A lot of people don't think cooking is a proper job and in a sense it isn't because most people wouldn't be allowed to work under the conditions you do – sweaty, scared and permanently knackered.'

'That's true. My sister is always giving me a hard time about when I'm going to get a proper job. She thinks I spend all day flouncing around with a whisk,' said Godfrey.

'And people watching cookery programmes on television can't feel how hot it gets in a busy kitchen, and they never get to see the mountain of clearing up you have to do at the end of a shift.'

'They think any dimwit can be a waitress, but it's not that easy, is it?' said Kirsty.

'They watch Jamie Oliver and they think all chefs are rich,' said Tess, thinking about how Jake had to juggle any minuscule profit he made to cover all his bills.

'Exactly!' said Kate eagerly. 'I am a good journalist; I am certainly better at it than I am as a waitress –'

'We wouldn't know – we never have time to read a paper.'

'Well, I am. We are not all tabloid hacks. I have integrity, though I know I might have squandered the chances of you believing that. I don't write lies. I don't have to. The truth is much more interesting. But by the time I realised that, I was in a bit too deep and I thought that if I waited until you could see what I had written you might be more prepared to forgive me for telling one or two fibs.'

'Well, I think it was worse than a few fibs, but I believe you meant to do the right thing,' said Tess, and looked round at the others. They all nodded.

'But you've missed something out, haven't you? You've avoided mentioning Jake in all this. How does he fit in?'

Blimey, she was sharp, thought Kate admiringly. She had hoped they wouldn't notice she had kept Jake out of it. But they weren't going to let her off that easily.

Nervously she started making a daisy chain. She'd had no practice in telling people she was in love with someone because it hadn't happened before. Trust her to screw things up the one time it did.

'That's when it all got really complicated. I, er . . . oh God, this is difficult. I fell in love with him, hook, line and sinker, the whole caboodle, hearts, flowers – the whole lot. And I'm pretty sure he quite liked me too, when he thought I was a struggling writer. How is he really, by the way?'

'Well, we think he needs therapy but we can't afford to send him. You see, he can't sort the fact from the fiction and it's making him crazy, which is why we are here.'

'Oh God!' wailed Kate, and buried her head in the flowers.

'We were pretty sure you weren't the complete bitch he is making out you are,' said Kirsty kindly. 'None of you have ever probably met one, but I have. My sister was going out with this guy once – actually, that's quite funny 'cos he really was called Guy – anyway his best mate at school had a sister who you wouldn't believe –'

'Kirsty, you are a great girl, but if you don't shut up this second, I may have to sit on your head. Good. I knew you could do it. Right. Back to the Problem. The trouble is that he is hurt and he's stubborn, which is not a good combination. Life has been hell since you left,' said Tess frankly. 'And the question is: what are we going to do about it?'

'Tell me first: am I forgiven?'

'Oh, well, I suppose so, as long as you don't write about that time Jake told me to flower the tomatoes and I thought he meant put flour on them when what he wanted was me to cut them in the shape of a flower, which was a mistake anyone could have made and –'

'Shut up, Godfrey, but yes. He speaks for all of us, minus the verbal diarrhoea.'

'Thank you. You don't know what that means to me, guys.'

'Well, hopefully it means you can stop digging up the park before we get chucked out for vandalism. The park attendant has been past three times and he's starting to look nasty,' said Kirsty.

'I keep trying to ring Jake but he just tells me he doesn't want to talk and then he puts the phone down. I think I'm just making things worse.'

'You are. We always know when you've called because the atmosphere goes from frosty to glacial, which you'd think was impossible in a bloody kitchen,' said Tess.

'When does this story of yours come out?'

'Soon,' said Kate, getting anxious again but she had to be honest with them now. 'The story is going to be great – you will love it. But . . .'

'But?'

'But the paper wants a load of pictures of you all, and Jake especially, of course, to go with it.'

Hans started to laugh, a trifle hysterically. 'Oh *wunderbar*! I hope the cameraman can take a picture with a flash shoved up his . . . what do you call it?'

'And we'd probably be serving up deep-fried camera for dinner. Oh shit.'

'Look, I think you should write the story, while we all pray it's as nice as you say it is –'

'It is, it is! You are all heroes, even Godfrey –'

'Well, we're not expecting you to perform miracles, Kate.

Personally I think you are as daft as Jake if you think you can pull that off – no, shut up, everyone, we need to focus here. Right. This is what we will do. You, Kate, will write the story and I will smuggle it into the restaurant, tie Jake up, if necessary, but somehow make him read it,' said Tess. 'It is, I admit, a pretty weak plan but it's all we've got. Blimey, is that the time? We'd better get back – it's nearly time for service.'

They all stood up, wiping grass and daisies off their clothes.

Kirsty gave Kate a quick, shy hug. 'Don't worry, we'll get you two back together somehow. We've got to – you are so right for each other.'

Kate felt tears welling up in her eyes. She must really be losing it, but this was much more than she deserved.

'Oh, well, it's worth a try. I mean, things can't possibly get any worse, can they?' said Godfrey.

'I hate it when people say that. It means they always do,' said Kirsty.

Chapter Twenty-five

While Jake was suffering emotional turmoil in his debt-ridden restaurant, Georgia was having a little crisis of her own, but in the far more comfortable surroundings of a first-class flight from Rome. And on the surface, at least, she had nothing to complain about. She had just finished shooting the cover of *Marie Claire* magazine. Beside her being cosseted in a five-star hotel, her every need instantly gratified, this two-day job had netted her a cool twenty thousand quid. When she landed at Heathrow, Harry would be waiting for her, or, if he was still stuck in that meeting, a limousine, which would whisk her off to another posh hotel. If Harry was still late, she had no doubt that champagne and flowers and very expensive bath oils would smooth the interval until he arrived. She had nothing to complain about. But still dissatisfaction and confusion nagged away at her, like toothache. It was very upsetting and would do nothing for her looks.

It was this that was sending her slightly crazy. She remembered a time when Jake had promised to meet her at Gatwick and then forgot all about it. She'd ended up having to get a bus, for God's sake, and then when she got to his flat, in the middle of January the heating wasn't working;

hadn't been for days judging by the frost on the inside of the windows. His mobile was switched off and he hadn't come home until three in the morning, having had to cook dinner for three very drunk junior Cabinet ministers. He had been very, very sorry, but it really wasn't good enough.

She couldn't argue with a limousine, however. Or a bunch of red roses with a sexy note attached to them. She couldn't argue with Harry either, even if he was late, because he would storm in, throw her onto the bed and cover her with kisses before she even had time to open her mouth. This was everything she had ever wanted in a relationship, so why the turmoil? Georgia frowned, then remembered she didn't want wrinkles, or to be spotted by a photographer going for botox.

'Oh God, she's flicking her finger again,' said one of the three cabin crew. They were taking it in turns to serve her. It got very wearing after a while to wait on someone who apparently didn't know the words 'please' and 'thank you' and didn't even look at you when they talked and then claimed she didn't want the things she had asked for when they were brought to her.

Georgia called for – and got – paper and a pen, a bottle of Evian with ice and lemon and a Mars bar to snack on, while she worked. She was going to make a list of pros and cons.

Harry was obviously the pro. Underneath his name she wrote: 'Handsome, wealthy, charming, attentive, sexy, generous.'

Jake next. She sucked the end of the pen, then wrote firmly: 'Scruffy, poor, absent-minded, stingy, selfish, sexy.'

Then she realised she had also written 'sexy' under his name as well. Furiously she scribbled that last bit out so hard she wore a hole in the paper and got ink on her new dress. It was absurd to think she still found him attractive. She remembered the last time she had seen him at the studios for that stupid cookery programme that had sent Harry into such a temper. He had looked a complete mess, as usual, with dark shadows under his eyes, though his eyes had still crinkled attractively when he smiled at that Kate, who worked at the restaurant.

Irritably, Georgia waved away the attendant who had been summoned to provide a wet wipe to try to get rid of the ink stain. She was having a moment of deep psychological revelation and she needed to be left in peace to do it. It was that smile that had sparked off this gnawing dissatisfaction. Did this mean she was still hankering after him? She remembered his obsession with cooking and shuddered. No, she couldn't go back to that. But he should have been suffering after she had left him, not smiling like that at someone else. It was right and proper that she had left him but he shouldn't have looked so damn pleased about it.

Georgia had packed and left Jake's flat in rather a hurry. Now she remembered a very expensive scarf that had been left behind. There was nothing strange about wanting to pop back to retrieve it. Obviously she would be looking at her stunning best when she did this and, just as obviously, Jake would be extremely upset to see her and be reminded of everything he had lost. With this picture in her mind, Georgia became cheerful again. She decided she had plumbed the depths of psychological revelations for today, so she went off to the loo to vomit up the Mars bar instead.

'Hello, Jake,' said Georgia softly.

He looked up, stared blankly at her for a second, said: 'Oh God!' and dropped the carving knife. She was gratified by this response but would have been less pleased to know the reason for it.

It was mid-afternoon, two days later, and he had come down to the empty kitchen, having come to the conclusion that part of the reason why he was feeling like shit might be due to the fact that he hadn't eaten a decent meal for days. He didn't feel even the slightest bit inclined to eat, but it was something that everyone seemed to do so it was worth a go.

The reason he had looked blank on seeing Georgia was that for a second he didn't know who she was. He had simply forgotten about her. He felt quite bad about this. He bent down to pick up the knife and compose his face into something more friendly and realised how bad things had got. He must really be losing the plot. He had come down to cook in his stockinged feet, for God's sake! A real chef only enters a kitchen when properly attired. If Louis could see him now he would get a real bollocking, and he deserved it.

He waved the carving knife in what he thought was a friendly manner but Georgia flinched and stepped back. Jake put the knife down hastily and tried to pull himself together.

'Sorry. Hello. How are you?'

'I'm fine. You look terrible.'

'Thank you. It's good to know we haven't changed much, then,' he said wryly.

'I'm sorry to barge in like this, but I think I must have left a scarf behind and I really need it.'

'It could be anywhere. Go up and have a look.'

Excellent, she thought as she went up the stairs. He wasn't following her so she could snoop around to her heart's content.

It was a small shock to open the door onto the still shabby, but now tidy flat and her first thought was that he had a new woman and that she must have cleaned up. Jake was positively anal about a stray crumb in his kitchen but as far as she knew hadn't got the vacuum cleaner out of the cupboard since he'd moved in. But this was no longer true. He'd had a manic cleaning session the night before, but only because it was three o'clock in the morning, he couldn't sleep and anything was better than lying in bed thinking the same dreary thoughts over and over.

She investigated further. The bathroom was empty of anything female – tampons, tweezers or face creams – and there was only one toothbrush lying on the basin, obviously his.

She went into the bedroom. Only his clothes were in the wardrobe; there was nothing on the bedside table on her side of the bed, but on his – a pair of frilly knickers. Surely they didn't belong to anyone round here? Despite herself she had to pick them up and then she realised they were hers. There was no doubt. They were La Perla panties, made specially for her. They even had a tiny G embroidered on the crotch. He hadn't got over her or why were they by his bed? Oh my God! What had he been doing with them during the long, lonely hours of the night? It hardly bore thinking about, but Georgia did, with a certain amount of satisfaction.

She went back downstairs. Jake was still in the kitchen staring at the sandwich he'd just made like he had never seen one before.

'Did you find the scarf?'

Shit! She had completely forgotten to look for it and she was still clutching her knickers.

Jake saw them and looked embarrassed. As well he might, she thought.

Jake was embarrassed, but not for the reasons Georgia thought. During his desperate cleaning session last night they had got sucked up from somewhere underneath his bed and then snarled up in the vacuum cleaner. This put him in such a bad temper he had ripped them while pulling them out. Of course he had instantly forgotten about them and only realised now that Georgia would be furious to find them in bits.

'Oh, sorry, I should never have –'

'No you shouldn't, but it's all right. I understand.'

What was there to understand, and did he care? Jake was so tired and undernourished he didn't have the strength to work this out or try to put on a brave face. What was the point? It was probably all round town that he had been duped by a journalist. He probably had a big sign on his back saying 'Cook, Pauper, Laughing Stock'. But Georgia was looking friendly and sympathetic. He bore her no grudges. It would be nice if they could remain friends.

'I'm sorry you are taking this so badly,' she said, thinking about their break-up.

'Well, I thought it was the real thing,' he said, thinking about Kate.

Georgia sighed happily. 'Maybe it was, for a while, but it could never have lasted.'

'Sooner or later the shit was bound to hit the fan,' he agreed.

This was better than she had hoped for. He was obviously far more cut up than she thought.

'In the end I suppose it was just about two people with deep feelings who needed to walk different roads.'

'You can say that again.'

'I am sure that one day you will be able to look back and take comfort from your happy memories.'

His face cracked up. 'But that's the worst bit, looking back and knowing that I've lost it. And I can't get away from them; they're everywhere, where I work, where I sleep . . .'

Well, obviously, if you spent last night burying your head in my knickers, she thought. 'I should go. I'm probably only making things worse.'

'No, it was nice to see you,' he said politely.

Poor man! He was obviously desperate for every tiny crumb of comfort he could get. Would it be cruel to kiss him goodbye? Well, yes, but he would be able to live on the memory of it for weeks. She leaned over, brushed his cheek with her lips and looked at him tenderly. 'Let the memories heal you, work with them. One day you will be able to move on,' she said, and left.

Blimey, she didn't half talk crappy glossy magazine nonsense, he thought irritably when she'd gone.

When Tess came in for work later, she found him sitting on the steps outside, smoking. 'Er, Jake, you don't actually approve of cigarettes, or had you forgotten?'

'I know. I thought I would give them a try. Actually, they are quite revolting.' He couldn't tell her that they reminded him of Kate, outside, furtively smoking someone else's and swearing this was her last.

She had brought a plate out with her and now thrust it under his nose. 'This, on the other hand, is food, essential sustenance but you actually have to eat it for it to do you any good.'

They both looked at the sandwich. Two pieces of stale bread that Tess had actually left out for feeding the birds, surrounding a chunk of dry cheese. It was unadorned by mayo, relish or even butter.

'We'll chuck this, shall we? I'll get out some of that nice carrot and coriander soup,' said Tess kindly.

'I'm not an invalid,' said Jake crossly and got up, galvanised into action by the sight of the disgusting sandwich. 'Come on, let's get to work, there's loads to do; we haven't got time to stand around chatting.'

He burst into the kitchen, frightening the life out of Godfrey, who was leaning on a worktop and gazing vacantly into space.

The next morning, upstairs at Café Anglais, Georgia was being grilled by Harry, who had seen her coming out of Jake's restaurant.

'Have you been spying on me?' demanded Georgia. But she was secretly thrilled.

'No, but one of the staff has. Well, he wasn't spying, but he did see you. What the hell were you doing there?'

'Nothing,' said Georgia, securely innocent. She loved Harry for being so jealous and passionate. There was nothing more boring than someone who trusted you. 'I merely went to pick up a scarf I'd left behind and we had a quick chat.'

'Are you sure that's all you did?'

'There isn't anything else I want to do with him,' she lied.

'He's still a loser, even if he did win a crappy local telly show,' murmured Harry into her ear. He blew gently and she squealed with pleasure.

'Really we should feel sorry for him,' she continued virtuously. 'He's in a really bad way, completely lost the plot.'

'Excellent,' he said, nuzzling her neck.

'It was a bit kinky, actually.'

'What was? I thought you just went in for your scarf?'

'I did. But then I found something else –'

'And it was where –'

'And it looked like he had been –'

'Well, what else could he have been doing?'

Harry ceased nuzzling and started roaring. 'That fucking pervert! He's disgusting!'

'Well, it's quite sad really. Like I said, we should feel sorry for him.'

'Like hell we should!' Harry started to laugh. He had never felt sorry for anyone in his life and it was inconceivable that he would start by pitying Jake, of all men.

Later, after sex, he was downstairs tying on a crisp new apron, when there was a knock on the door. It was Hans.

'I am just delivering a message from my friend Ronnie.'

'I couldn't care less what that loser has to say!'

Hans shrugged. 'Suit yourself. Tear it up if you like,' he said and went off to work.

Harry wanted to chuck the letter in the bin, but curiosity won. Maybe it contained a desperate plea for his old job. It would give Harry a great deal of pleasure to ignore that.

But Ronnie had written:

> I am getting better, slowly. I think if I had had a good boss and friend like Jake to start with, it would never have got that bad. I am really pleased that the only place the Restaurant Club are visiting in Cumbria is his, not yours. With that sort of recognition, his restaurant will eclipse yours. Frankly that's only half of what you deserve.

Harry cursed, fluently and imaginatively. He didn't know how Ronnie had come by this information but he didn't doubt it was true and it made him feel quite sick with fury. He felt so bad he wanted to hurt someone so they felt bad too. Actually, only hurting Jake would do, but he couldn't go over there like a spoiled child having a tantrum because Jake had got something he wanted. He didn't want to see Jake's look of satisfaction. Then he remembered that ridiculous story about Georgia's knickers. It was the perfect excuse to go and beat the hell out of Jake.

*

When Harry stormed in, Jake looked up, wearily. This wasn't fair. First Georgia and now Harry. What had he done to deserve this?

'Fuck off, Harry, I don't want to see you in here,' he said automatically.

Harry just stood there, arms akimbo, exuding menace. But Jake just felt pissed off.

'You look like you've got a bad attack of constipation, but you've come to the wrong place – the chemist is round the corner, mate.' He knew he shouldn't be winding Harry up more than he obviously was already, but just now he didn't care.

'You really are a pathetic waste of oxygen, you bastard!'

'Well, never mind. I really couldn't even begin to care.'

The staff hovered uneasily. Someone had to be pulled away or things would get broken. They could all smell a fight brewing. It was then that a strange man in glasses popped his head round the door but no one noticed him.

Harry looked at Jake with contempt, but a small smile was playing round the corners of his mouth. His staff weren't going to look at their boss with the same respect in a minute. 'I'll go when you apologise for spending your spare time sniffing Georgia's old knickers, you sad pervert!'

There was a deathly silence as everyone tried to make sense of this and failed. The silence was broken by an embarrassed cough from the man in the glasses.

'Er, this seems to be a bad time. The name's Blair. I'll come back later,' and he backed hurriedly out of the restaurant.

Jake was finding it difficult to process all the information that had come his way in the last few seconds but basically it meant that the man for whom he was going to produce the most important meal of his career had witnessed a crazy scene and might not want to come back. Briefly, he pondered the wisdom of chasing Mr Blair at full pelt through the restaurant but the man was probably already a few yards' sprint ahead of him. He would have to wrestle him to the ground in the car park in order to explain that this was all a hideous misunderstanding and then the restaurant critic would think he was possibly psychotic as well as a pervert.

He turned on Harry. 'I always thought you were stupid, but now I know you are mad as well!'

'Fine words, but you're the sexual inadequate who can only get his kicks by jacking off into his ex-girlfriend's underwear!'

'For the last time! I don't know what you are talking about, you lunatic!' Jake clenched his fists. The anger was turning to a red rage, which was surging through his veins, telling him to stick one of those fists right through Harry's expensively capped teeth. But he knew if he started he might not be able to stop. His first priority was to find out where Mr Blair lived and then grovel to him, and he couldn't do that from a police cell on a murder charge. Visibly, he forced himself to calm down. But this only enraged Harry further. He leaped forward, grabbed Jake by the shoulders and drew his arm back, ready to plunge it into his nose.

But Jake was quicker and lighter on his feet. His fist connected with Harry's nose in a deeply satisfying way. As the blood spurted out Jake knew a moment of pure pleasure. Then he thought, shit, he's going to hit me back and he's heavier than me!

Everyone had been rooted to the spot. Everyone except Godfrey. You had to be quick on your feet when you were working with sheep. It was surprising how nasty those creatures could turn at shearing time. He grabbed hold of Harry's arm just as it was moving forward to knock Jake into unconsciousness. Harry slipped and lost his balance. Both men staggered and fell awkwardly to the ground, Harry on top of Jake.

Despite the scuffling and swearing, everyone could hear quite clearly the perfectly horrible noise of Jake's head meeting the steel side of a very hot oven.

Moving as one, Tess and Kirsty rushed forward to pull Harry away from Jake's scarily inert body. He lay half on his side, deathly pale, unmoving.

'Ohmigod! Ohmigod!' cried Tess, leaning over and, with a shaking hand, feeling for his pulse. Her heart was beating so loudly it seemed to be drowning out all her other senses and for one awful moment she thought he was dead. But when she put her face near his she could feel his breath, shallow and faint.

'Don't touch him!' shrieked Kirsty, who had seen far too many episodes of *Casualty* for her own comfort.

'Well, we can't just leave him there,' Godfrey pointed out, and raced out into the street, where they could dimly hear him shouting, 'Is there a doctor round here?'

'We must cover him up with something,' said Kirsty.

'Why? He's not dead – yet,' sobbed Tess.

'Yes, but he'll be in shock. His body temperature will be dropping.'

'Believe me it won't – it's about a hundred and ten degrees down here,' muttered Tess, her face inches away from the hot oven. 'Jake, Jake! Please wake up!' she sobbed.

Everyone had forgotten about Harry until he started moving. He had landed on top of Jake so he wasn't hurt but when he heard that sickening thud he knew things had gone too far. He would have been delighted to see Jake permanently out of action, but now the red mist was clearing and he suddenly didn't care for the pictures that were dancing his mind – pictures of him going to gaol for having murdered his rival.

'Stay where you are – you've done enough damage!' yelled Tess.

'I'm getting my mobile to phone an ambulance,' said Harry, trying to sound calm, though his hands were shaking.

Godfrey hadn't been able to find a doctor but a very old lady in the bun shop next door had done a first-aid certificate so he brought her instead. She was thrilled to be involved in such a drama. 'On no account must he be moved until the paramedics arrive but we have to keep talking to him so he doesn't fall into a coma.'

'But what do we say?'

'Anything.'

No one felt like chatting so Godfrey said: 'I'll read him the prep list.'

This was utterly surreal, thought Tess as she held a towel to Jake's forehead to stop the blood, which was gushing out at an alarming rate, while listening to Godfrey solemnly reciting: 'Peel and dice spuds, wash and dice carrots, make stock,' and on and on until she was itching to knock him out as well. She turned round and was about to shout: 'Where is that fucking ambulance?' when Jake stirred slightly, groaned and said to the old lady: 'Where am I and who the hell are you?'

Oh God, he had amnesia as well as concussion, thought Tess. Though, given the events of the last few minutes, this might be no bad thing.

'What is your name, dear? Tell us who you are.'

Jake blinked at her. He seemed to be lying down, wherever he was, and everything was shifting in and out of focus like a television on the blink. Who was he? It seemed a perfectly reasonable question, except he didn't know the answer. He felt he should know but his head hurt and it was warm and sticky. That wasn't right, surely? The old lady didn't look like his oma, but he didn't know any other old ladies. Maybe she had got a makeover in heaven, but hazily he decided it would be rude to say he preferred her old look.

'I am doing my best, you know,' he said weakly, but someone must have switched off all the lights because it was getting all dark . . .

Tess tried to stifle a sob and then thought, what the hell? This is as good a time to lose it as any. Her shoulders started shaking and she was about to throw herself across his prone body in a paroxysm of grief, when the paramedics arrived.

They were very professional and kind, but she found

their scientific talk more frightening than reassuring. She was determined to go in the ambulance with him but then the old lady tried to get up but couldn't because she had arthritis, so they had to cart her off as well and there was no room in the ambulance for anyone else.

'Follow on in your own cars,' advised the paramedic.

'He will be all right, won't he?'

'He'll get the best possible care.'

'That's not an answer!' yelled Kirsty after the departing ambulance.

'Oh God! I'm going to sick,' muttered Godfrey, and was. It was only a small comfort to know that he was throwing up all over Harry's two-hundred-pound Gucci loafers.

Tess stood on the pavement, trying to get her head together. What would Jake want her to do?

'Right. I'm going on to the hospital. You lot stay here and try to open up. Put on a simple menu and leave out anything you don't feel confident about tackling on your own, Godfrey.'

'That'll be everything then.'

'Pull yourself together. Jake is going to wake up soon with a very bad headache and we don't want to make it worse by telling him the restaurant is closed. Kirsty, you need to ring round every hotel in Cumbria to track down Mr Blair. Tell him – oh God, what do we tell him? Tell him there has been a misunderstanding and Jake will get in touch as soon as possible. Don't all look at me like that – he is going to be all right, do you hear?'

Kirsty ran after her. 'Do you think we should tell Kate what's happened?'

Tess tried to think about this. 'I don't know. Do whatever you think is best.'

Alone in the car, she gripped the steering wheel and shut her eyes for a moment. 'Dear God, if there is one – and I really don't care if You are Christian, Jewish or some New Age white magic Wicca woman – make things right, please!'

She drove off, still with the sound of the ambulance siren ringing in her ears. They probably have to do that for every minor emergency, she tried to tell herself. And please let him be in A & E and not in intensive care, she added.

He was in intensive care and they wouldn't let her see him. She endured two hours of terror and boredom during which she bought several cups of tea, but didn't drink any of them, paced up and down the corridor so many times she got a blister on her foot, read all the notices on the walls without taking in a word, and clamped her lips together so tightly so as not to scream that they went quite numb. It was a relief when she looked up and saw Kate striding down the corridor. It might help, a bit, to have someone to share this torture with.

Kate took the situation in at a glance. 'You haven't heard anything yet then?'

Tess shook her head, dumbly. Kate sank down next to her, took one of her hands and gripped it fiercely. Part of her was bursting with all the stock journalist questions of 'What, why, who, when and where?', but she couldn't bring herself to speak them. She had been profoundly shocked when Kirsty rang her with the news, tearful and incoherent. It all sounded complete gobbledegook, apart from the 'Jake is unconscious in hospital' bit. Some time in the future she would have to answer for all the red lights she had driven through, but only if he was all right and there was a future.

'Is either of you a relative of Mr Goldman?'

'I am his fiancée,' said Kate, and dared Tess with her eyes to contradict her.

'Well, he's suffered a nasty concussion and needed quite a few stitches. There's a bit of retrograde amnesia but we don't expect it to be permanent.' The nurse smiled kindly. 'You'll be able to take him home in a few days.'

Wordlessly Kate and Tess hugged each other.

'Can we see him?'

'Well, you can, seeing as you are his fiancée, but only for a few minutes – he is still very groggy.'

Kate panicked. 'He might not want to see me!' Then when the nurse looked puzzled, she said, feebly: 'We had a bit of a lovers' tiff.'

'If your name is Kate, then I think he does. He's been talking about you.'

'Give him my love,' said Tess. 'I'm going outside to phone the others.'

Kate tiptoed in. Jake was lying very still and pale. There was blood seeping through the bandage on his head and his eyes were closed. She sat down by him, took hold of his hand and looked at it closely because she didn't want him to wake up and see her crying. His hand was warm and covered with scars. She thought she had never seen such a beautiful hand in all her life.

He moved slightly and opened his eyes. 'Kate,' he whispered. 'I was dreaming about you. I – I can't remember what happened.'

'Don't worry. You are in hospital but you are going to be fine.'

'Oh. OK.' He frowned. 'But there was something I had to say to you.'

'Just rest now. You can tell me later.'

'No. It's important. Ah, yes, of course. I love you, Kate.'

'I love you too.'

He smiled faintly and closed his eyes again.

One of the nurses came over. 'We are going to take him up to a ward now but you can see him again when he's settled.'

In a way Kate was glad to go. Despite all the trauma, it had been a perfect moment and she wanted to hold on to it for as long as she could, which would probably be until he got his memory back.

She was very glad she had said she was his fiancée because when they put him in a little side room off one of the main wards he suddenly became a magnet for what seemed like half the female staff at the hospital. It seemed impossible that so many young and pretty nurses all thought it was their job to come in and take his temperature or check his pulse. Jake was in a lot of pain but all the attention seemed to cheer him up.

'Talk to him as much as he wants but don't tire him,' said the doctor, also female, who was stroking the hair out of his eyes, quite unnecessarily, Kate thought.

Tess popped in during a lull and they conferred in whispers because Jake seemed to be asleep. 'They are all very relieved, of course, but that means they've gone back to their usual habits of cocking things up,' she hissed.

She had just spent a fraught ten minutes on the phone with Kirsty. What no one knew was that Mr Blair had gone back to his hotel and rung his old friend Louis to ask plaintively why the great chef had sent him on a wild goose chase to a madhouse populated by sexual deviants. Louis had then had one of his famous Gallic tantrums and had to be pulled away from the phone by his wife.

'I do not understand a word of this. You start off this conversation about cooking and then we seem to be talking about underwear! Louis has gone quite purple – no, Louis, you cannot have the phone back – I will deal with this. Let us cut the crap, as young people would say. We recommended you eat with Jake because he is a chef of sublime ability and we think you will look complete fools if you do not recognise this. I also have to say that I have known this young chef for years and he is one of the most honest, decent and straightforward young men I have ever met. Louis is incensed that you would think he would send you on a wild goose chase and is threatening to stop stocking that 1965 claret you seem so fond of. *Au revoir!*'

Mr Blair picked up the phone again, rang Cuisine, booked a table for that night and went out for a walk to build up an appetite and burn off some calories in order to make room for the several thousand more he intended to ingest.

He had booked the table with Godfrey, and Kirsty went ballistic when she found out.

'But I thought you would be pleased!'

'One of the most influential people in the world of cookery is coming to eat here tonight and our chef is twenty miles away in bloody hospital, you oaf!'

'But he's OK, isn't he?'

'Oh, he's fine, apart from the fact that he doesn't know what day it is.'

At the hospital Tess related the gist of this conversation to Kate, adding: 'Obviously Kirsty tried to ring him and cancel the booking but he went out and no one at the hotel knows when he'll be back. I think we are going to have to go back to the restaurant and try and get through this evening without Jake.'

'Oh God! Could today get much worse?'

'If I don't get out of here, it surely will,' said a faint voice from the bed. Gingerly Jake tried to ease himself up into a sitting position. He had been dozing until he heard the hideous words: 'Get through this evening without Jake'. He wasn't sure what they were going to try to do without him but it sounded like a recipe for disaster.

Both women shrieked: 'Lie back down again at once!' And then realised they were making his head hurt. Kate ran out of the room. Where were those bloody nurses when you really needed them?

A harassed-looking male doctor came in and said: 'You cannot possibly leave.'

'I can. It's called discharging yourself without permission.'

'What on earth is so important that you have to leave hospital?'

'You wouldn't understand,' said Jake, who didn't really himself, but would go to hell in a handcart before he let the doctor know this. The doctor got out an instrument and looked into Jake's eyes. 'How many fingers am I holding up?'

'Three,' and then when the doctor looked triumphant, he added kindly, 'the other digit is your thumb.'

'What day is it today?'

The doctor had a copy of the *Guardian* folded up in his jacket pocket. Jake squinted carelessly. 'Thursday.'

'And who is this?' pointing at Kate.

'That is the woman I am going to marry.'

'Is that right?'

What could she say? It was another of those occasions when it wasn't the right time to tell the truth.

She looked at Jake. He was smiling at her and there was a look in his eyes that she wanted to keep there for ever. 'Yes,' she said. When he got his memory back it would all be over, so she might as well make the most of this moment.

'You are of course entitled to do what you like but you will have to sign a form taking all responsibility for this foolhardy action.'

'Absolutely,' said Jake cheerfully. Blimey, he hoped he could remember how to use a pen. Now a knife, well, that was a different matter. That was engrained into his subconscious like breathing.

'He will have a headache but if he starts talking nonsense or acting erratically, get him back here pronto.'

'The trouble is, Doctor, how am I possibly going to be able to tell the difference?' said Tess drily.

Several nurses were very eager to help Jake get dressed but Kate shooed them away. 'I am perfectly capable of helping my boyfriend put on a pair of trousers,' she snapped. But she was very tempted to go and snaffle some sedatives for him. It was quite obvious, watching him move so slowly and painfully, that he was in no state to go home, let alone cook.

'This is ridiculous,' she said eventually, when he'd had to lie down after managing to get one sock on, and he was looking so pale she thought he was going to pass out. 'The doctor was right. You are in no state to go anywhere except back to bed.'

Jake didn't say anything but his face took on that familiar look of stubbornness. 'I am going back to my restaurant, with or without your help.'

'Just for the record, I am doing this against all my better instincts,' she grumbled as he had to lean on her to walk out.

Tess took his other arm and the nurses watched them go with regret. They had been drawing straws as to who should be the ones to give him a bed bath.

Jake got in the car and shut his eyes but the world still felt as if it was spinning.

'Just how much do you remember of the last few weeks?' asked Tess.

He thought, but even doing that was painful. 'We had a flood and I am going to that stupid television competition, aren't I? And then there was shouting and fighting, wasn't there? What am I missing?'

Tess raised her eyebrows and looked at Kate. Over to you, she seemed to be saying, but before Kate could open her mouth, Jake said: 'Oh God! Sorry, guys – think I'm going to be sick,' stumbled out of the car and threw up down a drain.

Kate rooted around in her bag, found some tissues and a bottle of water, got out and hovered anxiously.

'Sorry,' he muttered.

She took him in her arms. He was shaking like a leaf.

'Oh, Jake, I love you so much. You have nothing to apologise to me for, ever.'

'Can I have that in writing?'

'Why?'

'Well, I admit I am pretty confused at the moment, but I feel absolutely certain I was going to propose to you in the near future and it would be kind of handy to know I could skip ever having to say sorry.'

Joy surged through her. 'I will let you know when you do propose then.'

'Well, I'm certainly not going to do it here. Those people across the road at the bus stop think I am a drunk who can't hold his liquor.'

'Let's go home,' said Kate happily, because that was exactly what his restaurant felt like to her.

They were met by Godfrey, who told them that he had cleaned all the blood off the kitchen floor.

'Have you disinfected?' asked Jake.

'Absolutely,' said Godfrey, resolving to do this as soon as Jake's back was turned.

Jake leaned on a work bench. His memory seemed to be returning in patches and he'd just had the fright of his life when he remembered Mr Blair. 'OK, this is my plan. I will go upstairs and rest as long as someone promises to keep trying to contact Mr Blair. If he is happy to postpone, fine. If not, I will have to come down and cook his meal.' He put up a hand to forestall any protests. There was a desperate look in his eyes. 'I know you think I am completely mad and it is not that important, but it is; it is. You might not be able to understand, but you have got to accept that I simply have to do this. You are all absolutely brilliant and I don't know quite what I would do without you, but only one person can cook this man's meal and that person is me.'

They all looked at each other. Eventually Tess spoke. 'OK. You are, of course, completely mad and so are we, but we will go along with this.'

Jake looked relieved, then suspicious.

'No, I give you my word – we won't try to pull any stunts. If it looks like this guy is coming we will come and get you,' said Tess.

'I wonder if I should quickly check the fridge –'

'NO!' they all shouted at him in unison.

'You won't be fit to heat up a baked bean if you don't lie down now. Honestly, what is it with men? You give in to them and then they always need to take that extra inch,' complained Tess.

Chapter Twenty-six

On his way to gaze at the top of a mountain, Mr Blair met a very old friend who was on his way down it and who insisted on taking him to meet the family. Because he hadn't exerted himself in any way, Mr Blair decided that a quick wash and brush-up at his friend's house would suffice before he left for the restaurant.

Of course, no one at Cuisine knew this and so they carried on ringing his hotel with dedicated but infuriating regularity until the receptionist lost her temper and told them to fuck off. After that, they rationed the calls to once every half-hour, but as the time ticked by, the tension mounted.

By six o'clock it also became apparent that, Blair or no Blair, they were in for a very busy night indeed.

'We've only got that little table for two in the corner left,' said Kirsty, coming off the phone and looking with horror at the bookings diary.

'Oh crap. Why tonight of all nights?'

'It's the thirteenth culinary commandment: "Thou shalt be hideously busy when thy chef's brains have been battered",' said Kate.

'How do you know?' asked Godfrey.

'Because all professions have one. For journalists it's: "Thou shalt only find out the tape recorder is broken after the most important interview of thy career." I'll go and wake Jake up, shall I?'

Jake had only pretended to swallow one of the monster painkillers the hospital had given him, because he was terrified it would knock him out for the whole evening. This meant, of course, that he didn't get any real rest at all, but just dozed fitfully, in between experiencing the most peculiar dreams in which he and Kate seemed to be having the most tremendous argument about a page out of a newspaper, for heaven's sake! It was all rather disturbing and he was quite glad to get up, even though his head hurt like hell and his vision kept going slightly blurry.

Kate tapped on the door and walked in. 'You are aware, of course, how tempted I am to find a strait-jacket and pin you to the bed?'

'Sounds slightly kinky, but fun. Maybe later, eh?'

'Ha, ha.'

'I assume that our special guest is proving elusive?'

'Godfrey even went out and searched the streets for him. No luck. He is coming here tonight, whether we want him or not.'

'Shit. Oh, well, could be worse, I suppose.'

'How, exactly?'

'Er . . . I could have had my right hand chopped off. Even I would have had to take a few weeks off to learn how to dice with my left hand.'

Kate moved towards him and kissed him tenderly on

the lips. She might as well make the most of his amnesia while it lasted. 'I'll be right there with you, babe,' she whispered.

'Don't tell anyone, but you are my favourite waitress.'

'Now, Blair isn't due for another hour, so –'

'I'm coming down anyway. It's got to be better than lying here having weird dreams.'

Jake could smell the fear even before he walked into the kitchen. It emanated from everyone's pores, although a casual observer would just have seen a group of people rushing around and being quite efficient. But he knew better. A quick glance at the table told him they had a huge amount of work on, and Kirsty brought another check in as he looked.

'Perfect, Godfrey – that's exactly the way I want that starter to look.'

'But why are you frowning then, boss?'

'It's the only way I can avoid seeing two of you,' he explained patiently, and moved round to his side of the kitchen. Instantly he felt a bit better. He took a deep breath. This was his place; this was familiar – he could do this.

'If you fall over halfway through this hell, I hope you realise we are just going to step over you and carry on cooking?' said Tess.

'I would expect no less.'

She grinned. She wasn't going to say so, but it was good to have him here. Tess was in no doubt about her own talents, but a good kitchen needed a leader and even though Jake was wounded, it was what he was brilliant at. Although her hands and most of her brain were busy with the task in front of her, part of her was watching him take control and feeling relieved because of it.

Godfrey had been skimming through the orders and now decided he couldn't do any of them. His brain felt like it was full of confetti, and when he looked down at the knives on his work bench he couldn't remember what each specifically was for, except that any of them would do if he felt driven to slitting his throat.

'Three *moules marinière* and a Caesar salad. Get the mussels on first and remember – don't rip the lettuce apart this time,' Jake told him.

OK, he could do that and then worry about the rest later.

Jake concentrated on radiating calm and control, even though it seemed as though the kitchen floor had turned into cotton wool. Having concussion felt a bit like being on a really bad trip, he thought, and then Kirsty came into the kitchen.

'He's here,' she said and rushed out again. Instantly, everyone felt any other career would have been better than this.

Please don't let him order the woodcock, thought Tess as she carried on cooking for a table of five, outwardly calm.

I bet he orders the woodcock. It's the most complicated dish on the menu. Why in God's name did I leave it on? wondered Jake. Because it's a fucking fantastic dish, that's why, you fool, he told himself.

'OK, here it is. He wants the *gratinée Normandie*, followed by the woodcock. What did I say?'

Jake took a deep breath, like a diver who is about to plunge into thirty feet of icy-cold water and doesn't know if there are rocks at the bottom. 'Focus – you can do this,' he said to himself, and then realised he was talking out loud.

''Course you can, Chef,' said Tess, but now she was starting to doubt it. Jake was now almost as pale as when he had been unconscious, and his right hand was definitely shaking. If he overcooked the bird it would be as tough as Godfrey's old boots, and if there was too much or too little of any one of the six components of the sauce it would taste like a buggered old boot.

Time seemed to stand still for Jake. If I get this wrong, he thought quite calmly, as if he had all the time in the world for thinking, if I fuck this up, I've had it. I don't have the money or the resources to wait for a second chance. This is it.

He looked up and realised they were all staring at him, with a mixture of hope and fear and absolute faith. He wondered if it was the concussion that had brought tears to his eyes.

'I am going to cook now,' he said, simply.

So he did.

Ditch all the crap that isn't relevant, he told himself. Ditch all those weird flashbacks that don't seem to make any sense; pretend that someone isn't trying to force a screw-driver into your skull; ignore the terror.

He picked up a knife and looked sternly at his hand until it stopped shaking. All around him he could vaguely hear the noises of several people catering for the sixty other hungry customers in the restaurant that night. He blotted the sounds out and tried to cocoon himself in a bubble of concentration.

Kate could see the sweat running down his face, which was twisted in pain, and she couldn't bear to watch, but then drove Kirsty crazy by asking her for constant updates.

'Go into the kitchen and see for yourself!'

'But what if the sight of me brings all his memory back at just the wrong moment?'

'For God's sake! He is still on his feet and that table over there are positively gagging for the wine they ordered from you about half an hour ago. Jake still thinks you are just a waitress, so try and be one!'

Poor Tess felt like she had lost about five and a half years of her life watching Jake cook this one meal. She was desperate to offer support but didn't dare do anything that might break his concentration. For one awful moment his hand faltered while he was adding the redcurrants to the sauce and she nearly screamed. Then he looked over, gave her a brief grin and carried on.

Kirsty was waiting to take the plate out but before she could reach over for it, Godfrey was there with a cloth, wiping away a tiny bit of sauce on the wrong side of the plate.

'Bloody hell – I missed that,' said Jake. 'Thanks.' Then, in an attempt to regain some authority, he snapped: 'Off you go. What the hell are you waiting for?'

'Well, stop staring, then,' retorted Kirsty. 'I am quite capable of walking in a straight line without dropping this plate – or I was until this evening.' She picked up the plate, straightened her back and carried it out reverently. The kitchen breathed out collectively.

'You did good there,' Jake said to Godfrey. He

shuddered at the consequences of nearly sending out a dish that wasn't one hundred per cent perfect.

When Kirsty brought Mr Blair's plate back to the kitchen, he pounced on it, if someone on the verge of collapse could be said to pounce.

'Well, he's eaten the lot – that's a good sign, isn't it? What did he say?'

'He said, "Thank you."'

'Hmm, now what does that mean?'

'Thank you very much, that was bloody brilliant,' offered Godfrey hopefully.

'Thank you very much – now I can get the hell out of here,' worried Jake.

'Thank you very much, and I wish all waitresses were as hot as you?'

They all looked at Kirsty.

'Well, I don't bloody know! What do you want me to do now – get Godfrey's bicycle lamp, shove it in his face and interrogate him?'

Mr Blair stayed and stayed.

He had pudding – hot raspberry soufflés – and then he ordered another one – peaches poached in champagne. Jake fretted aloud if this was because he was just greedy or hated the first one and was giving them another chance.

Mr Blair had coffee and petits fours. Then he had more coffee.

Was he ever going to leave?

'Maybe he's forgotten his wallet and doesn't dare say so,' suggested Godfrey, who was cleaning the floor in the only way he knew how, which was to get himself almost as wet as the mop.

Kate was seriously worried about Jake, who looked ready to drop and was staring at the kitchen in a glassy-eyed manner as if he had never seen it before. He was leaning against a work bench, being mopped around, and hadn't even noticed that the oven door had a huge greasy stain down it. She was dying to go on the Internet and find out what might happen to people who had concussion and refused to lie down, but she didn't want to leave him.

Jake felt as if his memory was doing some complicated dance, but the rest of him didn't know the steps. His brain kept hopping backwards and forwards, and then spinning round until he felt quite dizzy. Images whizzed before his eyes, but he couldn't put them into any sort of order. He wasn't even sure if they were real or just half-remembered dreams.

Why was he getting mixed messages of love and hate towards Kate, for instance? Had they quarrelled and, if so, what had it been about? It must have been a silly lovers' tiff, nothing that couldn't be mended. The one thing he knew for certain was that he and Kate were soul mates. Oh crap – he was starting to sound like he was in the pages of some romantic novel or tabloid newspaper article . . . Oh, that wasn't a nice thought at all . . .

'Mr Blair wants to know if you will join him for a drink. Jake, are you all right?'

He ignored Kirsty. He frowned, trying to shut everything else out, so he could focus on Kate. She could see what was happening and flinched from the implications, but stood her ground.

'Everything is starting to come back, isn't it?'

'Unfortunately, yes.'

'I don't think Mr Blair is going to wait for ever.' Kirsty sounded anxious.

'He will probably last longer than Kate's words. You think you know her and then you don't. What else is there to know about you that isn't real?'

'Nothing! You are being ridiculous! And I don't appreciate you talking about my personality as if it was a pair of fake breasts!'

'The more I hear about your private life, the less I wish to know. It all sounds most unsavoury and, frankly, if your food wasn't so sublime you wouldn't be seeing my heels for dust,' said Mr Blair crossly, peering round the kitchen door.

'Oh, for God's sake! You have a talent for appearing at the wrong moment and getting the wrong end of the stick. This is nothing like it sounds. Let's go into the restaurant.' Jake ushered the critic out, pausing only to turn round and say threateningly to Kate, 'Wait there. This is not over!'

Mr Blair sat down, took a deep breath and ordered a large brandy.

'Every time I come here I feel as if I've strayed on to the set of some tacky television show, except that you obviously think you are auditioning for an episode of *Casualty*. Mad, quite mad and yet, the food . . .' He gestured in despair as words failed him and took a huge slug of the restaurant's finest cognac. This gave him the strength to carry on. 'It feels as though I've come to a lunatic asylum and yet I have just been served one of the best meals of my life. How is this? And why?'

'Well, for starters, I don't think any decent chef is entirely sane,' said Jake, putting on what he hoped was a winning, but not certifiable, smile. He really wanted to hug the critic for saying such nice things about him, but didn't want to frighten him.

'Your waitress, the one with whom you seem to be enjoying a rather turbulent sex life, explained some of the circumstances of this completely bizarre gastronomic experience. Your concussion, I mean. I have absolutely no desire to probe further into the knicker episode, which I trust will always remain a mystery.'

'Frankly, it was a mystery to me to, even before I got knocked on the head.'

'Yes, you seem to enjoy a rather turbulent relationship with other chefs as well.'

'I don't know why. All I ever wanted to do was to be left alone to cook.'

'That is a wise plan. Good brandy, by the way. I take it your mentor, Louis, passed on the secret of where he gets it from?'

'He was kind enough to let me in on it.'

'He thinks highly of you.' Mr Blair sighed, rather plaintively. 'People who know nothing envy me this job. I don't know why. I have had to eat more revolting meals than anyone I know. Of course, they don't cost me anything, but believe me, I pay.' He patted his stomach sadly.

'All I wanted to do tonight was sit on some lonely crag with only the sunset and a cheese baguette for company. I still think you are completely crazy, but I am glad I came. There was no view, but the food more than made up for it. Generally, the restaurants I visit have to wait some time before hearing my opinion. I once ate what I considered a reasonably pleasant meal only to be rushed to hospital later that evening with food poisoning.

'Genius is unmistakable, however, and you are certainly in need of a good night's sleep. There is nothing to weigh up. I can tell you now that the award the Club will be giving you will be the first of many in what I hope will be, if your private life permits, a long and successful career.

'Wow,' said Jake faintly. It had been a long and hard road to this moment, and he knew exactly why people blubbed when they got Oscars. He wanted to pinch himself to check that this wasn't a concussion-induced hallucination.

Mr Blair downed the last of his brandy, looked at the bottle longingly, but shook his head and stood up. 'I should go. It has been a tiring and confusing day. It will be quite a relief to return to London, where chefs have normal tantrums, but I am sure I will return. Congratulations, young man.'

He shook Jake's hand and gave a thumbs-up salute. When Jake turned round he realised why. Everyone's noses were pressed up against the door to the restaurant.

'You have a very loyal crew. Goodbye.'

As soon as the critic had gone, they all burst in, cheering and patting Jake on the back, but carefully, in case he fell over.

'You've completely smudged the glass in the door. I expect someone to polish it tomorrow first thing,' he grumbled, but he was smiling so widely he thought his face would split.

'So, does this award thingy mean you are going to become rich and famous?' asked Kirsty.

'God, I hope not.'

Her face fell.

'The people who matter, people who are passionate about food, will hear about it and want to try the food for themselves, so, if we carry on working incredibly hard and try not to fuck up too often, this place should become quite successful.'

'So all your troubles are over,' Kirsty persisted. She did like a happy ending.

Jake looked at his crew. At Hans, who had slipped out for a spliff, which had been much stronger than he intended and was now imagining he could smell sherbet. At Kirsty, who was sulking slightly because she had appeared on telly and wanted more. At Tess, who was talking to Angelica on the phone, saying: 'I don't care if you do know the number for Childline, you are not coming down here in your jimjams to give Jake a kiss.' At Godfrey, who was picking his nose thoughtfully and trying to drum up support for opening several bottles of champagne.

'Hell, no. With you lot, I have a feeling they've only just started.'

But he said it absent-mindedly, because he was now looking over at Kate, who was standing on her own in the corner. She was looking at him with a mixture of love and terror. He loved his crew but he wanted them all to go home so he could talk to Kate in private, but before he could say this, the phone rang.

'I don't care who you are – go away. Oh, no – not you, Louis! I am really pleased you called. . . . Yes, tonight. . . . Well, one or two small problems. . . . No, well, some of it doesn't make any sense to me either. . . . Thank you, that means everything, coming from you. . . . Oh, you did – you had faith in me when no one else could give a damn.'

'Who is he talking to? It's about as difficult to make out as one of Kirsty's stories,' said Godfrey.

'Well, I think the whole world has gone crazy,' said Hans.

'Shut up, the lot of you,' said Tess, who was listening intently.

'What sort of an idea? . . . Oh, I see. . . . Blimey, I don't know what to say – I never expected that, and pretty much everything that could have happened has happened today. . . . Yes, of course I will sleep on it. . . . And, Louis, thank you; I am really honoured.' He put the phone down. 'Well, it never rains but it's a bloody great downpour.'

'Nice of him to ring up and congratulate you. What else did he say?' asked Tess.

'Do you ever take a rest from being so sharp?' said Jake wryly.

'No. Wish I could, but really, there's never a good time.'

Godfrey was looking from one to the other, bewildered. 'Well, I don't mind admitting I'm stupid, so will someone please tell me out loud what the hell is going on?'

Jake sighed. 'This is not a good time. That was Louis. I used to work for him in London. He rang to congratulate me. And . . . to offer me a partnership in his business.'

'In London?'

'Well, yes, Godfrey.'

'Oh. So that's why Tess is looking so . . . well, like that.'

No one dared look at Kate, not even Jake, she noticed.

Chapter Twenty-seven

After that, they all just seemed to melt away. No one really knew what to say. Obviously, congratulations were in order, but seeing as this might leave them without a job, no one even wanted to pretend.

'What do you think is going to happen?' asked Godfrey outside.

'What do you think I am – a bleeding oracle?'

'I think – sorry, Kate – but I think he will take that guy up on his offer,' said Kirsty.

They all looked at Kate. 'Yeah, I think so too, she said dully. 'That guy, as you call him, happens to own one of London's top restaurants. It's the place where top chefs go for a meal on their nights off. Gordon Ramsay had his birthday bash there. So, yeah, it's the chance of a lifetime and it would send his career into the stratosphere. There is no way he would turn that down for – what? – a woman who lied to him and a little place like this.'

'Bugger. Sorry, Kate. I'd better get me CV out when I get home,' said Godfrey and clumped off, head down. No one had ever seen him looking so low.

Kate drove off fast, without looking back. It was her first step towards severing her ties with the restaurant. With

Cuisine. Maybe Jake would forgive her in time. When they were both back to living their separate lives.

When she got back to her cold and empty flat, there was still so much adrenalin swilling round her system, she knew there wasn't even the faintest hope of sleep, so she picked up the phone.

'No, sweetie, it's fine. Jim doesn't mind waiting, do you, honey?'

'Oh God! I am so sorry! I forgot for a minute that you have a life too.' To Kate's horror Jim then came on the line.

'Carry on – take as long as you want – I could do with a break!'

'That's really more information than I need,' said Kate sternly. She was furious with herself, though, for feeling a sharp stab of jealousy. Lydia and Jim had got it right and sounded so happy. As she might have done if she'd played it straight.

Lydia came back on the line and Kate gave her a quick summary. 'Well, you have had a busy day. So he's got his award – and you've got a hell of a story.'

'Yes. And it feels like I've got nothing.'

'You do sound low.'

'Oh, I'll get over it!' said Kate, making a huge effort to sound more cheerful. She didn't want Lydia coming round – which she would, she was that sort of a friend – when she really ought be with Jim. 'Look, you're busy, and I've got a story to write. Have fun – I'll talk soon!' She put the phone down. What was her mantra? When all else failed, there was always work? It didn't feel like it was going to comfort her this time, but it was worth a try.

*

Back at the restaurant, Jake couldn't remember saying goodbye to anyone. One minute they were all there and the next time he looked up, he was on his own. He didn't blame them. That was a hell of a bombshell to land at his feet at the end of this ridiculous day. But then, hardly thinking about what he was doing, he reached over for the phone to call Kate. She was different. He needed to talk to her. How dare she just run off like that? He hesitated, then drew his hand back slowly. Exactly where would they start? Surely he needed to get a few things sorted in his head before he could have a sensible conversation with anyone? He pulled a handful of cushions off chairs and sat down on the carpet. There was no point in going upstairs to think. He needed to do it down here, in his restaurant. This was where he did his real living. He looked round, soothed by its familiarity. Thanks to the intensive cleaning sessions post-flood, he knew every inch of it, intimately, like it was a lover. And he did love it. This was his place and the people who had just left were his people.

But he had just been offered an opportunity that had him quite dazzled by its implications. Surely only a complete moron would turn down the chance to go into partnership with one of the country's leading chefs? It would be like cooking in Heaven but without having to go through all the bother of dying first. At a stroke all his worries would be over. *Heat* magazine would probably start taking his picture again. Hell, even Georgia would want him back and, more to the point, this would be the move that would ensure once and for all that he would never have to cross swords with Harry again. He closed his eyes so he could savour this blissful vision. He imagined his car, all packed up and ready to go, him at the wheel saying jubilantly: 'I'm off! This is it! I will never have to see you again!'

But then Harry bent down and was banging on the window. He was shouting something . . . 'Jake! Jake!'

Jake woke with a start. His first thought was: this is a hell of a headache. His second was: why is Harry shouting at me?

He blinked. It was early morning and, unfortunately, he wasn't dreaming. Harry was standing outside at the window, banging on it and shouting. He actually, for Harry, looked quite anxious. Jake got up slowly. It hadn't been the best place to spend the night, but he grinned. Harry must have looked in and panicked, thinking that he had collapsed, maybe even died. He hoped Harry had had a few visions himself, hideous ones of being carted off to gaol for manslaughter.

'It's all right – I'm still alive,' he grumbled, going to the door. 'What the hell do you want? Not to hit me again, I hope?'

'Don't be ridiculous! I came to see how you were. Things got rather out of control yesterday. It was all most unfortunate.'

'Is that your idea of an apology?' asked Jake icily. 'Because if it is, it's crap, frankly. You really need to do much better than that to have even a fighting chance of me believing you. Actually, scrap that. From now on, I am never going to believe a word you say – it will save a lot of time.'

'I certainly did not want to cause you lasting harm,' said Harry, mendaciously. For a nasty moment there he had thought Jake was dead and that was going to be a tricky one to get out of. 'I admit I lost my temper, but I felt it was with just cause. Georgia and I are together now and nothing you can do will change that.'

'Dear God – you are really stupid! Ow! OK, shouting hurts. Bad for head. Listen very carefully, you moron, because I am only going to say this once. Much as it might dent her ego to hear this, but since we split up I haven't given Georgia another thought. I have no bloody idea what your fevered brain imagined I was getting up to, but I can assure you I wasn't. I don't love her any more. You can have her. With pleasure. Because she is definitely the last girlfriend of mine you will ever nick.'

'Oh, I'm going to marry Georgia!' said Harry confidently. 'I've netted the big one this time. She was always way out of your league, you know.'

'Whatever. Oh dear, how am I going to get this through to you? – *I don't care*.'

'Just don't come sniffing round at the reception!'

Jake couldn't resist it. 'Harry, I've just been offered a partnership with Louis Challon down in London. I guess I'll have better things to do than boycott your wedding!'

Jake wasn't a vindictive man, but the next few seconds gave him intense pleasure. Harry's face, shorn of subterfuge, was a picture of shock and naked envy. He tried to cover his tracks, but it was too late. Jake watched as Harry mentally staggered back from this crippling blow. He was outraged. The god of good luck should serve only him! He tried to fight it, but his head filled with awful pictures of Jake driving off to the bright lights and leaving him behind. He would be forgotten. Their feud would fizzle out simply because Jake had better things to do. It was unthinkable!

He suddenly felt like he was floundering in a quicksand, and flailed around in search of solid ground. 'Well, you are very welcome to the noise and pollution.' He took a deep breath of the crisp morning air to prove his point, but he knew this was pathetically weak stuff. 'Let's face it, Jake,' he said kindly, 'you've tried to take the city out of the boy and put the country in, but it's never really worked, has it? Admit it – you've never really felt at home here. You don't understand our ways. You've tried to copy them, but they've never really sat comfortably on you. And your life here has always been a struggle, hasn't it? Big ideas but not quite enough wherewithal or talent to make them work.'

He glanced up and Jake followed his gaze – dammit, the bloody windowsills needed painting again. Oh. It probably wouldn't be his problem. Someone else would have this place. Probably paint them pukey green again. Why did he care?

Harry carried on more confidently, aware that he was hitting home. 'I know you have found it difficult to settle and make friends – it's so much easier in the city, where, let's face it, things are more superficial –'

'Let me know when you finally run out of this garbage you are spewing out!' said Jake furiously. 'You don't half talk a lot of crap when you get going. I am just as much a part of this place now as you are. My staff are all local and so are a great many of my customers, even the ones who don't share my views on fox-hunting. I've got a standing invitation to go for tea at the Tomlinson farm any time I want. I like it here and the people like me!'

Despite the fact that his head was now beating out a very strange tattoo, he had never felt more clear-headed and calm. In a way he was grateful to Harry. He'd made him see where his priorities were.

No, he'd done more than that. He had made him see where his heart was.

'Listen to me, dumb-arse!' Jake grinned. He was going to enjoy this. 'This is my home now, as well as yours, so you are just going to have to shove over and let me in. I'm not going anywhere. You are going to have to get up for work every morning and know that there is an award-winning restaurant just down the road from you, pulling in all the most discerning punters and thinking up the best menus.'

'Yah! Putting on some poncy dish that you'll have no hope of ever shifting! You have no idea of what I've got planned for the autumn, but I'm telling you, it'll blow this place out of the water!' blustered Harry. He hadn't got anything planned, but he was absolutely sure he'd be able to come up with something.

Jake faked a yawn.

'You really are too old to believe in fairy tales, you know! But, seeing as I am feeling in quite a good mood this morning, I'll give you a little warning – you won't ever have to watch your back from now on, because I won't be there. I'll be out front – so far ahead of you, I'll probably be out of sight!' And he slammed the door, leaving Harry outside, gibbering with rage.

Jake leaned against the door and smiled to himself. Despite his headache he suddenly felt strong and confident. He liked what he had said so much, he said it again, so he could get used to it. 'This is my home. I belong here now.' Then he added, because he was always a realist: 'If I have to, I will meet trouble head on. There will be trouble, no doubt about that, because Harry will be here. But that's tough. For him.'

So what was he doing just standing here? There were things to do, phone calls to make, windowsills to paint. But first he had to have it out with Kate. There were things that needed to be said. Things would probably change for ever as a result and he would have to take the consequences. He thought about those for a minute, then he squared his shoulders. This was a day for making tough decisions.

Kate was very nervous as she walked into the restaurant. Jake had sounded quite curt on the phone when he asked her to come over, which didn't bode well for what he was obviously going to say to her. She would let him get it all out of his system, but then she would say a few things too. There was no way he was going to walk out of her life before then.

He was sitting in the office just like he had on the day she had gone for her hangover interview. That seemed an awfully long time ago now. So much had happened since then. She absolutely had to tell him that, whatever happened next, being with him had changed her for ever and she wasn't going to regret this for a minute.

She took a deep breath and walked in.

'So – who are you this morning?'

'Jake, please listen –'

'No. I am going to talk first. I have to. I have to tell you how awful it felt to be lied to, by you of all people. You see, I fell in love with you. It's going to sound really trite, but I felt connected to you in a way I never have with anyone before, so the fact that you lied to me made it much, much worse.'

'I know. There isn't a name you could call me that I haven't already called myself. It wasn't meant to be like this. I've fallen in love with you too. Look at me, Jake. I can say I'm sorry in a thousand different ways – I am bloody good with words, after all. But can't you see the truth of it in my face?'

He looked. She did look terrible. Her hair was a mess; her nose was red and her cheeks were splotchy from too many salty tears, but it was her eyes that held him.

'At least,' she faltered, 'I know I've got no right to ask anything of you, but please, please, whatever else you need to say to me – please read this first.' She handed him a sheaf of papers. 'This is the article that's going in the *Easedale Gazette* next week.' She took a deep breath. 'It wasn't what I thought I was going to write. But real life is like that – it doesn't follow a neat plan. Sometimes you have to get things very messily wrong so you can see how to get them right. Oh, and I would have written this article even if I hadn't fallen, totally, catastrophically, irrevocably in love with you. Please. You have to read it. Give me that much at least.'

Chef Jake Goldman has twenty-one scars running

> down his right arm. I know because I've counted them. Some are already fading, but some are deep and will lie on his skin for ever, mute witnesses to his obsessive quest for culinary perfection.
>
> Forget what you know, or think you know about people who cook for a career. This is what it's really like.

She bit her lip as she watched him read. It was infuriating how well he could school his face into impassivity. But then his lips twitched slightly.

'Surely your first shift here wasn't that bad?'

'Worse, actually. Some of it the readers simply wouldn't have believed.'

> I thought I was going to a gourmet's paradise. That was certainly true for the customers, but there should have been a sign above the kitchen door: 'Staff – abandon all hope of a life, all ye who enter here.'

This was worse than her first day as a cub reporter, watching while her editor remorselessly sliced through her story with a red pen, as sharp as a knife. Oh, no, now he was frowning – why was he frowning? What had she got wrong?

'They just left the lobsters outside the back door? I'll have their guts for garters. How many times has that happened?'

'Just once,' she reassured him. He bent his head back to the article, only slightly mollified.

'God, yes, the flood was really bad. But so much has

happened since then.' He read on.

'You're looking cross again! Why? Which bit do you not like?'

'I'm looking cross because you've got it absolutely right about the teamwork involved and how it's not just the chef who should get the credit! It's about bloody time we stood up for the people who stand behind us, as you put it.'

He read on.

> Chefs are driven people, like athletes, or great artists. They have a vision, but they are also haunted by the fear of failure. Rising through the ranks isn't like being on *Pop Idol* – belting out a few songs that someone else has written. It's about blood and sweat and the black dog that sits on every chef's shoulder, whispering: 'You got it right today, but maybe you'll screw up tomorrow.'

She watched him and chewed on a fingernail until she was practically down to bone. Finally he finished. He put the article on the table and arranged it neatly so it lined up with the edge. He seemed unable to look her in the eye. He must have hated it.

'You are a very good writer.' He said this with a certain amount of surprise.

'This actually comes as quite a relief, because you are not,' he paused, trying to think of the right words, 'you are not a brilliant waitress.'

'No,' she agreed.

'I mean, you've never really got the hang of carrying more than two plates at a time, have you?'

'Well, no.'

'Sometimes you've had difficulty with just the two, to be honest.'

'Come on! That's not totally fair!'

'I meant being able to carry two plates without getting your thumb in the sauce?'

'OK. Well, if you put it like that –'

He surged on remorselessly. 'And you do have a habit of sharing too much, don't you?'

'Sharing what?'

'Your own personal thoughts for a start. Things like "Oh fuck, there goes another ladder in my tights." Generally not the sort of stuff one expects one's waitress to utter while delivering one's dinner.'

'Oh dear, I'd forgotten that.'

'And I think everyone on the street heard your comments after you picked up the *pommes dauphinoise*.'

'They were bloody hot!'

'They had just come out of the bloody oven, that's why! A fact that you would have cottoned on to if you'd actually been listening when I said, "This dish is hot. It has just come out of the oven." '

'Yeah, well, you see, Kirsty was telling me one of her coma-inducing stories and –'

'So, with all this in mind, it's good to know you've got another job lined up.'

Ah, yes. Of course. He *was* going to leave them.

'You see – oh, by the way, I'm not going anywhere, I'm

staying right here – but you see, I am going to have to sack you.'

'Yes. I do understand.' No she didn't.

'I don't think you do, seeing as you've spent this entire conversation looking at your feet instead of at me. The thing is, I've realised it's just not on, having a relationship with one of my waitresses. I really don't think it's very good for kitchen morale or yours, for that matter, when I have to bawl you out. But if I were to have a relationship with an exceptionally gifted journalist, who was allowed in my kitchen to make breakfast before going out to work –'

'You mean, start over?'

'No,' said Jake slowly, 'we can't do that and, anyway, I don't want to. A good relationship isn't about chucking stuff away and starting over, like you sometimes have to do in cooking. I think it's about surviving stuff. I am glad we survived this. We know each other better now and anyway, I never stopped loving you, even when I thought I hated you.'

She went over and sat in his lap, so that she was facing him. She was so full of emotion, she was, for the first time ever, completely at a loss for words, but she knew she was with the only man in the world who would ever make her feel like that. So she kissed him.

Some time later, when they really had to come up for air, she managed to say: 'Well, that's our first row over with, then.'

'Yeah. I expect there will be others,' said Jake, but he seemed perfectly happy with this notion. 'I should warn you now, I plan on asking you to marry me sometime before lunch one day. If we fit in the ceremony before dinner it won't need to get in the way of service. That all right with you?'

'Sounds lovely to me – just as long as I haven't got a good story on. Where are we honeymooning, by the way? Over by the sink while we're doing the washing-up? And, no, don't kiss me again – it's very distracting.'

'Who cares? Oh God – I've just had a horrible thought! Harry and Georgia are getting hitched too. They won't want a double ceremony, will they?'

Kate snorted with laughter. 'No, but I'm sure they'll drop by with the photos just to confirm how much more glamorous their do was.'

'Yes, they are perfectly suited,' said Jake happily. 'Er, don't look now, but we've got an audience.'

Kate swivelled round, just in time to see several heads disappear from the window.

'You lot are going to have to get a lot quicker on your feet now we are an award-winning restaurant,' he grumbled.

'Does that mean we get a pay rise?' asked Godfrey, popping his head up hopefully.

'Oh, that's so funny! I expect, as usual, we'll be lucky to get paid at all,' said Tess, but she was grinning.

'Ooh, you both look so romantic sitting there. It reminds me of a film I went to see with my boyfriend, once. Or was it my Nanna? No, it was –'

'Shut up, the lot of you – can't you see I'm in the middle of something!' yelled Jake.

'OK, we're going, but one quick question – what about Harry?' asked Tess.

Jake shrugged.

'What about him? He'll always be here and we'll always be fighting, probably. He was sent here to try me, as my gran would say. I'll tell you one thing, though – it'll be a cold day in Hell before we become friends. Now, bugger off, all of you. No, of course I don't mean you, you silly woman! I'll tell you what I want you to do.' He pulled her closer and whispered in her ear.

'Well, I've never done that with chocolate before, but as an investigative journalist, I'm certainly prepared to give it a try!'

ALSO AVAILABLE IN ARROW

The Accidental Wife

Rowan Coleman

How do you know if your life has taken a wrong turn?

Alison James thinks she might be living the wrong life. She loves her husband Marc and their three children but somehow in the process she seems to have lost herself. And sometimes she worries that she's being punished for how it all started – for the day she ran away with her best friend's boyfriend.

Catherine Ashley knows she's living the wrong life. She adores her two daughters, but she'd always thought that at thirty-one she'd be more than a near-divorcee with a dead-end job. In those dark middle-of-the-night moments, her mind still flicks back to the love of her life: Marc James. And she still wonders whether Alison stole her life as well as her boyfriend.

Alison and Catherine have been living separate lives, a hundred miles apart, for fifteen years – since Alison and Marc ran away. But now Alison's moving back to Farmington, the town in which they both grew up. And they're about to find out just how different both their lives could still be . . .

Praise for Rowan Coleman

'Brilliant . . . moving, funny – just the tonic every knackered woman needs' *New Woman*

'Touching and thought-provoking' *B*

arrow books

ALSO AVAILABLE IN ARROW

Acting Up

Melissa Nathan

It is a truth universally acknowledged that a single man in possession of a large ego must be in want of a woman to cut him down to size . . .

When journalist Jasmin Field lands the coveted role of Elizabeth Bennet in a one-off fundraising adaptation of *Pride and Prejudice*, she is not surprised to find that the play's director, Hollywood heart-throb Harry Noble, is every bit as obnoxious as she could have hoped. Which means a lot of material for her column. And a lot of fun in rehearsals.

And then disaster strikes. Jasmin's best friend abandons her for a man not worthy to buy her chocolate, her family starts to crumble before her eyes and her award-winning column hits the skids. Worse still, Harry Noble keeps staring at her.

As the lights dim, the audience hush and Jasmin awaits her cue, she realises two very important things, one: she can't remember her lines, and two: Harry Noble looks amazing in breeches . . .

'Tremendous fun' *Jilly Cooper*

'A modern-day Lizzy and Darcy tale you won't be able to put down' *Company*

arrow books